SIMPLE

ALSO BY KATHLEEN GEORGE

SIMPLE

KATHLEEN GEORGE

MINOTAUR BOOKS

A THOMAS DUNNE BOOK

NEW YORK

A THOMAS DUNNE BOOK FOR MINOTAUR BOOKS.
An imprint of St. Martin's Publishing Group.

www.thomasdunnebooks.com
www.minotaurbooks.com

Library of Congress Cataloging-in-Publication Data

George, Kathleen, 1943–
    Simple / Kathleen George.—1st ed.
      p. cm.
    "A Thomas Dunne book."
    ISBN 978-0-312-56914-3 (hardcover)
    ISBN 978-1-250-01129-9 (e-book)
    1. Women law students—Fiction.   2. Women—Violence against—Fiction.
3. Murder—Investigation—Fiction.   4. Police—Pennsylvania—Pittsburgh—
Fiction.   5. Pittsburgh (Pa.)—Fiction.   I. Title.
    PS3557.E487S56 2012
    813'.54—dc22

2012016579

First Edition: August 2012

10 9 8 7 6 5 4 3 2 1

For Hilary

ACKNOWLEDGMENTS

MY HEARTFELT THANKS go to Susan Yohe, a super attorney who escorted me around Pittsburgh law offices and answered many questions about law and politics; Captain Bradley Flood, who showed me the workings of the Allegheny County Jail; Cynthia McSwiggen, who talked to me about inmate lives; Paul Larkin, who consulted with me about bail proceedings; Lisa Middleman, Public Defender, who took time to talk about court hearings; and, not least, to retired Commander Ronald B. Freeman, who walked me through the facts of police procedure and forensic evidence and who gave me the gift of Bert. The research was fun and fascinating all along the way.

I have been fortunate to have many cheerleaders for my novels at the University of Pittsburgh, where I teach. I also have the support of writer friends; we call ourselves The Six and we lunch together eagerly. For any and all propping up, my friends, many thanks.

Books don't happen without book lovers working tirelessly on the publishing end of things. I would like to express my gratitude to Ann Rittenberg, the agent who took a chance on me, to my warm and fantastically enthusiastic editor, Marcia Markland, and to the whole staff at St. Martin's.

Thanks in no small measure to my wonderful family, whose love sustains me: Jan and Sam Taylor, Jenny and Robin Taylor, Richard, Cathy, and Tony George, and Vivian and John Preston.

Finally, I have the best of husbands, Hilary Masters, who is patient, loving, and wise. He's an inspiration in the way he does his own writing work—always thoughtful and full of integrity. He deserves my thanks every day.

SIMPLE

ONE

THEY ARE IN HIS OFFICE, the door locked. He has an eye on the clock because if she stays for a long time, people will talk.

She comes in farther, looking about again as if to memorize the furniture though this is not the first time he's summoned her. He has a sofa in there, comfortable chairs. He gestures her toward the sofa.

"It's been an exhausting day." He throws up a hand awkwardly. She smiles. "Sit for just a minute," he says. He rubs his hands over his eyes and sits on the sofa next to her. "I worry about too many things, and I'm not sure worry does any good at all."

"You remind me of a saint," she says.

"Well, no. Not at all. I'm not sure I'm flattered."

"You look kind of holy. I'm not sure what it is—long face, eyes a little moist." She laughed then.

"Well, you don't seem very taken with me."

"Oh . . . I am, though."

And that's what he was waiting to hear. But after she said it—and lightly, as if teasing—she slumped, defeated. Then he said, as if brushing it aside, he said, "I am, too. I mean there's a lot of something in the air between us. I don't want to act on it."

"I know." She glanced at the picture of his wife and two sons on the desk and then quickly averted her eyes. "I'm pretty mixed up. I mean I never had this experience of feeling close to someone who was married. It goes against . . . everything. So I fight it."

He said something like, "I wouldn't put you through the . . . the mess. The midlife mess." He went to his desk and picked up a folder of information he'd assembled for her about charitable work with the local hospitals. For years he'd coordinated ways for big businesses to present gifts of magazines and flowers and toys to those who needed comfort. "In here," he said. "You'll see how I did it." Instead of handing it over, he sat down across from her and met her eyes. "My wife and I are separated. We live in the same house but not . . . you know, together. We have to stay together because of the election—so my handlers tell me." For some reason, he added, knew to add, "She's . . . seeing someone. I have to put up with it, and of course that's tough."

"Oh, no. You mean she's . . . Has it been for a long time?"

"Long enough." He moved to sit next to her again and began rolling the manila folder instead of handing it over.

"Being governor wouldn't be worth it."

"Oh, don't say that. There are too many people hoping we can pull this off."

"Don't they care about you?"

"They want me in there. For their own purposes mostly—please don't quote me on that, please—and if not now, definitely in four years." He shrugged and noticed what he was doing to the folder, which he then straightened.

"Lieutenant?"

"No."

"Why?"

"Too slow. Somebody could be in for three terms."

"Interesting. So interesting."

"It is."

He can see it, hear it, months later, the whole conversation.

"Are those pet projects good things in the long run?" she asked.

"They have to be or I wouldn't play ball."

She wore a simple brown dress that crossed over—a wraparound. He remembered his wife describing that kind of dress once, so he knew the name. It was meant to be modest, but on her it wasn't. She was a creature with bedroom eyes, bedroom mouth. Is that what he couldn't stop thinking about? Or was it the way she carried herself, intensely alert? Or the surprise of her laugh. Or plain need in him for the adoration she provided.

He wanted to see her relax. There was that, too. He handed over the folder. She took it, closed her eyes, then opened them wide to look straight at him.

"Don't care about me," he said. "Don't. You have boyfriends?"

"Plural? That would be something. I don't even have one."

"And why not?"

"I never like anybody enough."

"Why not?"

"I just don't."

He leaned over and kissed her. The promise in her eyes and mouth was true; she was a sensual creature. Her family, she'd told him, was very religious. She'd had a strict upbringing and was even home-schooled for a time. "Oh my God," she said. "Oh my God. I wanted this, I thought about you that way, and now here I am and I don't know what to do."

"Do?"

She started to cry. "I'm stupid. As bad as Monica Lewinsky. Falling in love with the wrong person."

"You could make purses afterward," he teased. Then he sobered up. He couldn't do this, not with her. "Don't ever tell anyone I kissed you," he said. "You understand? They would misconstrue—or exaggerate. It would ruin my life. It would ruin all my chances of getting elected. Can you . . . not say anything?"

"I won't say anything."

He kissed her again and began touching her body.

That was in May when she came to work for the firm as a paralegal. She was a hard worker. Her name was Cassie Price.

He watched her out of the corner of his eye, so to speak, overheard her talking about wanting to buy a house, and steered her to a friend of his and a real estate company selling properties in the Oakland area. He enjoyed her excitement when she described the house to others in the office—a dinky thing that she planned to transform, a starter house that needed a lot of work.

She was on the verge of a new phase in her life. She was starting law school in the fall.

The thing in the air between them continued. They subsisted on the idea of it for almost a month before they did anything serious about it. At the office her assignments were not always about the political part of his life but included other aspects of the firm's business and some of his charitable work. She was interested in *everything*. That was May.

IN AUGUST, THE PARTY organizer came to him as he did at least once a week to jaw about the progress they were making. They sat in his office, him on the sofa, Todd Simon on the chair in front of the sofa. Todd spread out a map of the state on the small coffee table between them. He explained which districts were coming along and which ones weren't, which local party chairmen were likely on board and which were difficult. "We don't have a long time," he said. "And we need more bucks. You're going to have to lean on a few of your friends." He pulled out and lit up a cigarette even though he knew Michael Connolly hated smoke. "I can't raise the bulk of it on my end. I can only do my thing."

"Right."

"You'll get on these friends in the next two weeks?"

"Yes."

Simon unearthed an ugly plastic ashtray from his briefcase, one that had some logo on it and notches for three cigarettes. He blew smoke in the direction of the door, away from Connolly. Then all of a sudden, Simon said, "How many women in your life? Currently?"

"What do you mean?"

"Don't be dumb. I'm told you mess around. Or have. We're at a crucial juncture. You want to tell me anything?"

"No."

"Who are the current squeezes?"

"You don't need to know that."

"I sure do. Believe me, there are people looking to find out."

"Who?"

"Press, donkeys, my bosses."

"I'm very careful."

"Tell me. Let's start with current."

He stared out the window for a long time. He supposed he would always feel there was a camera on his every move. "There's a young . . . one of the paralegals here. And six months ago one of my wife's . . . friends."

Simon laughed. "Some friend. That's it?"

"Yes."

"And in the more distant past?"

"You don't need that."

"Yes, I do."

"A woman who used to be in the firm."

"She could be trouble."

"She's married. Lives in Dallas. She's content with her life."

"How do they leave you when they leave you?"

"Happy. I'm nice."

"Who else?"

"A woman I met at a fund-raiser about ten years ago."

"And where is she?"

"Somewhere in the city. I ran into her, say, three years ago and she was all friendly. No grudges."

"You must do and say the right things. How many more?"

"A couple."

"You don't look the type. Which is good, I guess."

"What does that mean?"

"You look like a guy who wouldn't."

He gave names and addresses. It galled him.

FOUR DAYS LATER, Simon was back. "You only have four paralegals. I could have figured out which one—not a doubt in my mind—without a name. I'd say she looks unreliable." This time Simon didn't sit down.

"What makes you say that?"

"Emotional."

That was true. She was emotional.

"Guilty."

That was true. He hated Simon.

"Where do you see her?"

"Motels."

"Where?"

"Thirty miles out, sixty, a hundred. Never the same one."

"Who pays?"

"I give her cash. She books the room."

"You ever go to her house?"

"Never." It occurred to him afterward that Simon had said "house" and not "place" or "apartment."

"That's good, anyway. And your wife?"

"We're . . . okay. The usual stresses."

"She knows?"

"No."

"Or like she's seeing anybody herself?"

"No, she would never."

"Well, it does happen. Sure?"

"Absolutely. Why? Are you telling me something different?"

"No. No. This little girlfriend of yours. I watched her get into her car one day. She was crying. See? She was crying?"

What could he say? He'd seen the waterworks. They made him nervous, too.

"Tell me," Simon said. "Remember, I'm on your side. You are our boy. A lot of people are putting up a lot of money on you. I need to know. The worst."

"Once she said she was going to call my wife and suggest we all meet and hash it out."

"Hash what?"

"Who ends up with whom?"

"So she's completely nuts. She doesn't get it, does she—what's at stake for you?"

"She's religious. She's upset. She needs to talk to somebody, I think. She doesn't know how to put it together."

"She thinks she's going to end up with you?"

"Yeah."

"And—you want that?"

"No. No. I want to keep things as they are."

A long whistle came out of Simon.

TWO

THURSDAY, AUGUST 13

LATE AFTERNOON, SIMON was getting into his car in the lot. He'd made sure he parked it near Cassie Price's car. Just as she was getting into her little Focus, he muttered something and looked up at her and gave a big smile. "My cell phone is out of charge." He smiled again.

"Don't you have a car charger?"

"I forgot it. Would you be willing . . . I'm sorry. I know who you are. I've seen you up at the offices. I'm the party man for—"

"Oh, I know who you are, too. I've seen you up there."

"Yeah, yeah. Meeting with our boy. He's fantastic, isn't he?"

"Yes." She handed over her phone.

He punched in a number and walked away, pacing a bit a few yards from her. Finally he said, "Simon here. We need it. I'm telling you we need it yesterday. Call me. Any time tonight." He ended the call—the noncall. He went back to her, handing over her phone. "Thanks. Is anybody ever at the other end of a phone these days?"

"Not usually."

"Thank you. Would you . . . What a day! Would you be willing to go someplace for a few minutes? Have a drink or a coffee?"

"Oh, I really couldn't."

"Too busy?"

"Very busy."

He made a halfhearted gesture of acceptance. "You see, I'm . . . kind of worried about our boy."

"Oh!" she said, and then she pulled back and tried to ask casually, "Why? The campaign?"

"Yes and no. His health."

She froze. "He's not well?"

"Maybe I shouldn't have said that. It isn't his physical health."

"Oh."

"He said . . . you needed to talk to somebody. I'm a friendly dope."

"He said that?"

"He . . . confided in me. An hour? Give me an hour."

"Yes, all right. Where?" She looked around the parking garage as if to suggest they lean against a wall.

"I have to have a drink."

"Okay."

"A bar near your place? Which end of town do you live in?" He knew perfectly well.

"Oakland. Parking is terrible in Oakland up where the bars are. It's not much better in Squirrel Hill. There are bars there that could be okay, but—"

"Hmm. Parking—you're right. How about that Shadyside—you know, Highland Park—area. You know where Casbah is?"

"I've seen it. Highland, right?"

"You got it. One car or two?"

"Two," she said definitely.

He got into his Saab and followed her Ford down the ramps and out the gate of the lot and then into the city. She drove competently, not fast like he wanted to drive. When they got to Casbah twenty-five minutes later, he parked quickly and watched her fuss with a lot of back-and-forth adjustments to get her car evenly between the lines. He played out possible scenarios while he waited. He went to her and led her inside.

"It's dark," she said.

"That way no one will hear us." He winked.

When they'd settled on a padded banquette and he'd ordered a Scotch for himself and persuaded her to try a cocktail, she frowned at the fancy ones on the menu while she picked at the snack mix on the table.

"You like salt?"

"I do."

"How about a nice margarita?"

She shrugged.

He tipped a head to the waitress, who went off, and sat back and looked at her for a moment. "Oh, you are so beautiful."

"I'm not. I know that."

"That's why you're gorgeous. Because you don't flaunt it."

"You said—"

"I know what I said. Sit back. I want to do this slowly. I want to say everything accurately. Let's wait till we have some liquid relaxation—"

The waitress carefully put down cocktail napkins, glasses, and a fresh dish of cocktail mix. She asked if they wanted anything else. Simon shook his head.

"Drink up," he said easily to Cassie, who was sipping and making a face.

"This margarita is . . . I mean I tasted one before, but this one is somehow different."

"How?"

"Better. More salty. But tell me now. I can't stand this. You're worried about him?"

"And you. What do you call him? Our boy, Mick?"

"Michael. Mike."

"Hm.

"I wish you'd say what it is. You're making me nervous."

"In time. Sit still. Timing is everything. Breathe. We both need to be very patient. Tell me, the margaritas you had in college or wherever—was there much of that? Partying? Our Mick has the impression you didn't do much partying."

"I didn't. I maybe sipped a margarita once. I didn't go to parties until my senior year and then not very many."

"What did you do with yourself?"

"I studied."

"I see."

"What does this have to do with . . . Mike's health? I'm being patient. I just don't see the point of beating around the bush."

"It's the whole picture. He worries about you, and that makes him vulnerable. He'll never get elected if anybody finds out about you. You understand that, I know you do, and yet you keep seeing him. You are willing to stand in his way."

She stiffened and didn't say anything for a long time. "It's not like I'm forcing him." He smiled at her. She returned it with an angry scowl. She took a sip of the drink, then another. "Which is more important," she asked, "real life or the election?"

"The election."

"I beg to differ."

"So you will stand in his way!" He said this with as much outrage and alarm as he could manage in a whisper in Casbah. He could already imagine the jumble of things party bosses were going to fling at him in some meeting in some out-of-the-way bar with no customers—*thought you were watching, all that work, all that money, all this time and goodwill and a little two-bit intern or whatever she is gets away from you.*

"I love him."

"That isn't sufficient reason to kill him."

"Kill him?"

"His career."

"He loves me."

"He doesn't." He went very still for a moment because she did. He watched as she digested what he'd said, blinking.

"He does. He's going to leave his wife as soon as—"

"He's never going to leave his wife."

"Oh, yes—because—"

"He's not going to. Why do you think he asked me to come talk to you?"

"What are you saying?"

"How old are you? Think. Think. Be a woman."

"He wouldn't do it through you."

"What else is he going to do? You cry, don't you? You make a sign of yourself for everyone to see."

"Never at the office. I hold it back."

"What is he supposed to do? Come on. You're a woman of the world now. Be that. You like the nooky. Have it. Have plenty of it. Have it with me! Just not with him."

"You don't understand at all."

"My dear, I understand more than you can imagine. Let me try you. Have a sip first." She did. "Have another. Tell me if you can feel it, you know, the buzz in the knees, any of that?"

"Yes. Yes."

"Man. I might be in love with you."

"No. Don't make fun of me."

"Men fall in love with you. They do. Just looking at you. A little conversation and it's instant. That's what happened to Mike. You had some meeting, some conversation, I don't know what it was, his work on Veterans Affairs or the fund-raiser for the leukemia kid, whatever, you were impressed by him and he saw that and he wanted more of you being impressed by him. Then you, not having a lot of experience of shitheads, I mean *men,* and apparently ignoring your peer group culture totally, decided it was love. Nothing like love. It was not just lust, I know that, I'm not stupid, I know it was more than lust. It was imagination. Hope. A small fiction of an alternate life to the one you're living. What are you, some poor student? Living in a falling-apart house. All your college mates a year ago thought you were a dork because you weren't living it up when they were. Suddenly in your mind, you're better than any of those idiots, you're in the

governor's mansion. You're in the newspapers. You're known for doing good works."

"No."

"When you say no, I fall out of love with you—when you play
dumb."

"Please. I can't stand this. He didn't send you." She reached for her
handbag. Her hand dropped weakly.

"I'm afraid he did. Take a drink and grit your teeth. We're going to
laugh about this later, you and me. I promise you that. He doesn't love
you. He doesn't. He is worried about you—because you cry. That's a
different thing. Are you gritting your teeth?"

She nodded. Her eyes welled up.

He leaned over and kissed her on the forehead. "Good girl." When
she didn't say anything, he moved closer and put an arm around her.
When she didn't resist, he gave it a squeeze, a fatherly hug.

"I'll talk to him tomorrow," she said.

"I wouldn't."

"I don't care if the whole office knows."

He kissed her on the brow again. "That's the point. You can't let
anyone know. Ever."

"They'll know when he leaves his wife." She paused. "After the
election."

"He's not going to leave his wife. Ever. You make me say things I
don't want to say. I like you. A lot. But you're being very difficult."

"She's having an affair. She wants out, too. I could call her, meet
with her. We could work it out. Women can be very logical."

"She's not having an affair. He told you that, didn't he?" Then
Simon took the leap. "He always says that. Always. To women." He
moved the drink toward her. "Here. Don't worry, you'll be fine tomorrow." He kissed her cheek.

The waitress came to them, grinning as if she had just witnessed
true love. "Ready for another?"

"Oh, yes."

Then he told her about all the other women in Mike Connolly's life.
He didn't give names, but he painted the general picture. Perhaps he

exaggerated some. He called him Mick now so that she would understand she didn't know him.

"He's not like that."

"You don't believe me."

"I know what love is. I'm going to marry him."

"You come from a religious family."

"Very."

"He told me."

"I need to talk to him." She took out her phone.

"Please. May I ask one thing? He asked you not to call him, didn't
he?"

"Yes."

"Don't make an enemy of him. He's in the bosom of his family
tonight. They're all being photographed at dinner, at play, the whole
gamut of pub photos so that we can all have him as our guv. After
the photo shoot, he has meetings. With high-level bosses. You probably know that—he got called to Harrisburg tonight. A phone call
will ruin him. If you love him, if you really love him, would you do
that to him? Can't it wait until tomorrow?"

She looked at her phone sadly, put it away. "Will he be in late
tomorrow?"

"Probably. They usual have early breakfast meetings—well, by
now you know that."

"You've really upset me."

"I know. But who else should tell you? Right, right, okay, he
asked me to talk to you, and . . . all right, I didn't give him a fight
because I *wanted* to talk to you—you intrigue me. Honestly, I could
fall for you just like that." He snapped his fingers.

"Quit it. How dumb do you think I am?"

"Not dumb, honey, just afraid of your own powers. Which are
significant, let me tell you. Men are going to be crazy for you. Get
used to it. It's okay that you did everything you did. You should have
been doing more of it all along. And—hey, what's so wrong with me
while we're at it? I'm insulted you don't take me seriously. I could take
you wonderful places, delicious places. You could date me to get over

your heartbreak. I would do things to your gorgeous body our Mick never dreamed of. I could make you feel such pleasure, such top-of-the-world glorious pleasure. I'm good at it. Believe me, I know how to make a woman happy." He made a comic leer. "What, you don't like how I look?"

She was almost laughing. How he hated her.

"What," he teased, "you won't date a Jewish boy? You don't like my nose? Remember Cyrano, my love. I am the real lover. Mick only happened to notice you after I raved about you. 'Who is that delicious one?' I asked him."

He got a hand on her breast. When she moved it, he let it fall to her lap.

The drinks arrived. He tried to imagine how he would report this. They were tough. Going to have his hide if he couldn't deliver Mick, unblemished.

"I feel like I died," she said.

"No. You are just beginning to live." He kissed her cheek.

"This is not who I am."

"Turned on, you mean? Unfortunately it is."

"I have to talk to him."

He thought for a long time. Finally he said, "If you behave, if you really behave, I'll get you home safe and I'll set up a meeting with him and I'll call you."

"You don't have to set up a meeting. I'll see him at work tomorrow."

"Wouldn't it be better if he could come away from Harrisburg tonight or early tomorrow before work? To your little house. So you could really have some time with him—to talk, to cry, to work it out."

"You said he had a breakfast meeting."

"Maybe I can get him to can it, cut out of Harrisburg at midnight."

"He's never come to my house . . . I have a house."

"I know, I know, he told me. Wouldn't that be better? A little time in your place? I'll tell him you're *not* overemotional. I'll promise him you won't go into work looking like a basket case. Everything you said to me, you can say it all again. You can ask him questions. Work it out."

She appeared to rehearse all she would say. Was it absently—she took another swallow of her drink.

"You have values," he said. "You've persuaded me."

"Not stupid values. Real ones. I look around. I watch people. I know what's what even though you don't think I do."

"And what do you make of me, then?"

"Only half of what you say is true."

"Fifty percent?"

"If that," she said firmly.

Top of her class, a rising star, and stupid, stupid, stupid.

"I'll make sure you get home okay," he said. "You need a shower and a nap. You want to look good tonight in case I can get him over there. In any case you want to look good tomorrow at the office, right?"

She nodded. She had a hard time walking a straight line, coming out of the bar. She weaved a bit driving home. He stayed two or three cars behind the Ford Focus. *Buy American,* he said to himself. He saw her house up ahead, which he'd scoped out a couple of days ago, but she didn't park in front as he assumed she would. She went around the block to the back, and he followed. He watched her park there. He slowed down enough to see her walk to the back door, and in his rearview mirror he saw her talk to a guy who was working on her porch, sawing something or other. They seemed friendly with each other. He didn't want to linger. He kept going.

He called his bosses and made his report and took an order that came at him in cryptic terms and that he made them repeat even though he wasn't surprised by it. Still, even though he expected what he heard, it hit him in the gut, and he threw up everything that was in his stomach, Scotch and all. His face felt funny—his eyebrows descending like a Neanderthal's over his eyes. He brewed a pot of coffee, strong.

He was supposed to use a guy named Frank Santini. But who was this guy? Todd had thought it through a million ways. He was prepared for exigencies. He didn't trust anybody else. He trusted himself. Simon flicked his television on and off a few times. Pregame this and that. He couldn't concentrate on the news. After a few cups of coffee, he went out to a payphone and called Santini. He didn't like the way the guy sounded, so he said, "I'll call you back if I need you." It was only seven thirty-five. He made a decision. He called a woman he saw sometimes and made a dinner plan. He paced for a bit and then he called Cassie to tell her the little date with Mike was set up. He said Michael would come to see her when he got out of the meeting in Harrisburg. He warned again, "The meeting might go until twelve, one. Will you hear if Mike taps at the door? He wants to come in the back door, okay?"

"I'll hear. I'll sleep on the couch," she said.

He pictured Mick being photographed all this time, smiling at the camera, arm around his wife's waist. A good dinner. A drive to Harrisburg. Smiling and easy.

He called Haigh in Harrisburg and asked, "Connolly's staying overnight, right?"

THREE

FRIDAY, AUGUST 14

COLESON AND McGranahan had had a run of junkies and bums and drive-bys and not much of anything else for a good four years, which rendered them second class in the homicide squad. Coleson was more philosophical about it than McGranahan, who tended toward bitterness. They were eating their lunches at their adjoining cubicles and talking about the latest shootout (Artie Dolan was the principal on that one; drugs and gangs and whatnot in Homewood) when they got a call. They fully expected their victim to be a junkie or maybe the barrel-end of a holdup, especially when dispatch said they were needed in lower Oakland.

They carried their lunches to the fleet car and got moving as McGranahan continued to get information by phone from a patrol car cop who was already there at the crime scene.

Coleson drove.

McGranahan listened and let out a surprised grunt.

"What? Clue me in, for God's sake," his partner said.

McGranahan ended the call, tucked his phone in his breast pocket where he liked it. "Guy who works there called it in. Found the body. Said the woman is a student—law school."

"Anything else?"

"Cop says she's gorgeous."

They both paused to think about the goodie that had come their way: Christie was not back from vacation, Dolan was working the Homewood shootout, Greer and Potocki were off on some cold case for the afternoon, and here it was, finally, luck.

"Parkview. Not a bad street," McGranahan said. "Sometimes students do live there, though, mostly undergrads I thought. This one was going to start law school. She had a job, too, apparently. She was supposed to be at work today."

"Patrol knew to hold on to the guy who called it in?"

"Oh, yeah. We'll be talking to him, all right."

When the phone rang again and McGranahan answered it, he was hardly surprised that his rotten luck had so quickly made a reappearance. It was Christie, his boss. What kind of vacation was the guy on? What kind of radar did he have? They'd only got the case minutes ago.

"Commander! Good to hear from you," McGranahan said.

Coleson hit the heel of his right hand to his forehead, hard.

"I just happened to call in to the office," Christie said. "Heard there was something doing."

"Seems that way so far. Are you in town, then?"

"We're on the road. It's storming up at the Cape, so we left early—is it raining there, too?"

"Not today."

"Well, anyway, we were vacationed out, or I was, Marina and the kids not so much, but it was raining, so we cut it short by a day. I'll be back late tonight. If you need me, feel free to call. Anytime."

"Sure. Thanks, Boss. We're just getting to the scene now. We'll be thorough."

"I know you will."

He hung up. "Cripes. Let's be miracle boys. We have about three hours to enjoy ourselves."

"Three?"

"Well, maybe six, seven."

McGranahan called for a Forensics team even as they spotted the small brick house.

Two patrol cars were in front. Neighbors gathered in groups, talking.

The patrol cop met them halfway up the sidewalk. "She's in the living room. The back door was open when the guy found her—he said. Her car's parked out back."

They went inside.

It was the cleanest murder they'd ever seen. Orderly living room, newly painted. Perfectly clean kitchen. No blood. Young woman in a white nightgown on the living room floor. Marks on her neck, and her hands up as if she'd been fighting it, and a tear in her nightgown at the sleeve. That was about it. Otherwise you'd think aneurism, some freak thing.

Coleson said, "Call in the others. We're going to want Dolan and Greer and Potocki at the very least." He listed, using his fingers: "People she worked with. Neighbors. People at the law school. The guy who found her. You said thorough. Let's be thorough. Oh. And I choose Greer to tell the parents. I understand she hates doing it."

"Okay by me."

"The vic has a computer upstairs," the patrol cop said.

"Those are useful. You touch it?"

"No."

"I'll go look," Coleson said.

"I'm coming, too," McGranahan said.

Before they got away, the patrol cop hurried to add, "Nothing is messed up, but the purse it looked like she used? It doesn't have a wallet."

Clearly the kid hoped to move up to detective in record time. "Thanks." The two middle-aged detectives tromped up together to look at whatever there was to see—still life with computer. Then

Coleson said, "Let's peel Potocki away from Greer and put him on the computer."

McGranahan assented. "Probably what Boss would do."

They went back downstairs, studied the body, walked around. Coleson said—and he was aware of channeling Christie—"I don't like it. This was one anal robber. Door isn't bashed, no windows broken. Of course she might have been careless, left the door open, heard something, then she came down, found somebody . . . That would fit, but I don't think so. Somebody with a key would also fit."

"Couple of wood shavings," McGranahan said. "Not much. Almost a token."

"Somebody's going to know something. Between the neighbors and the people at the office. Right?"

"Oh, yeah."

McGranahan was already on the phone, calling for some help.

CHRISTIE HAD FELT his blood spike at the news of the murder, and he had the unmistakable wish to be there, working the case. He tried to talk himself into letting it go to others on the squad who wanted and even needed the credit because after all, he told himself, driving along, he was officially still on vacation; everybody needed a break; Coleson and McGranahan were good, not creaky like Nellins and Hrznak. Marina watched him. He knew she was reading his thoughts.

"Who's the victim?" she asked finally.

"A young woman. A law student."

"Sad. Hard case, easy case?"

"Can't tell yet. I caught them just as they started for it."

"Vibrations," she said.

He told Marina, tipping his head toward the backseat, where his daughter had been staring out the window, slack-jawed, and his son, who wore ear buds, nodded his head to something he was teaching himself to like, "I should go in tonight after I get them to their mother's house."

She bit her tongue.

"You have to work *tonight*?" Julie asked, coming alert. He wondered what kinds of things she thought about on the long drive. What did she notice, what did she see?

Marina began arranging the things around her seat. She was always good for keeping paper towels, tissues, water, and treats handy. He knew she was thinking about his habit of hovering over the other detectives. It was a fault, yes, but he didn't feel like changing it.

He picked up speed. Somehow he refrained from calling in to the office immediately again and, well, hovering. He counseled himself that it might be all over by the time he arrived.

The rain had stopped.

"It's nice now," Julie said. "We should have stayed."

"Only to leave tomorrow morning when it was nice. That would have made us sad."

MARINA KEPT changing her position—it was hard being a passenger, not in control, *and* also not being able to move her body. She tried knees up to her chin. She tried crossing her legs. She felt tearful. Her husband hadn't liked Cape Cod and she had. He didn't even understand what a coup it was to get a house for half the usual price in Truro, right on the beach, absolutely fantastic. She'd snagged the house because she knew an actor who had an aunt who only rented to friends or relatives. She'd just spent two weeks in an amazing house and she'd probably never get to go again.

Richard was eager to get home.

He was a good man, a good husband, and an accepting person. He wasn't so much uncomfortable on Cape Cod as bored. When they went into Provincetown, which they did twice, once on a rainy day to join the throngs on the crowded streets, he tolerated the happy gays, the galleries, the tacky shops, the bumped umbrellas, leaking slickers, and thick crowds with as much good humor as he could manage. He said, "I wasn't meant for vacations. I like our backyard."

They'd laughed companionably about his being a curmudgeon.

But still, he wasn't romantic with her. He made love to her only twice in two weeks and distractedly at that. She didn't know how to win him back. Sometimes she wasn't even sure she wanted to. Why couldn't she take off for a glorious place like the one she just left and enjoy it without worrying about him? She loved his kids, but she had more than occasional fantasies of a life without cereal and backpacks.

She looked over at her husband and he said, "What?" and she said, "Nothing."

He'd warned her at the start that they were different and that she would get bored with him. She was intellectual and an artist—creative on good days, effete on bad days. He always said he was a working-class drudge, more ordinary than dirt. Anxiety seized her heart. Boredom wasn't it. She wanted to be let in. She sighed deeply. Police wives were always second. Work was first.

"Easy?" he said, as if they'd been speaking. "My guess is no. They'll call most everybody in to work on this one because it's newsworthy, high profile."

ARTIE DOLAN CAME off the shootout for the rest of the day and took a couple of juniors with him up to the law offices where Cassie Price had worked.

Dolan liked this case lots better than the shootout, a fact that made him feel guilty. The anger and defensiveness and poverty he faced in some of the black neighborhoods wore him down. Yet he knew other blacks looked at him curiously, sometimes bitterly. He was small, but trim and always beautifully dressed.

He felt at home in the law offices—or told himself he did. The thick Berber rug, the utterly new-looking desks and credenzas, the perfectly painted walls, even the artwork hit him as superimpressive.

The secretary who greeted him trembled when he showed his ID and told her to call everyone into the largest room they had, which turned out to be two conference rooms with the connecting wall folded back.

Some of them hurried in, some sidled in—he couldn't tell who belonged to what class of employee right off the bat except that the elder men were probably high up on the ladder. With the women, he guessed stilettos were the secretaries and scarves were the attorneys, but he knew he might be wrong. Some, it occurred to him, might be clients.

"Is this everyone?"

People looked around. "Tom?" someone said, and someone else said, "No, he's here."

"Cassie?"

"She didn't come in today."

A small ripple went through the room. They thought something. Then they banished the thought as too horrible. Then the thought returned.

"Pete? What about Pete?" A woman's voice had asked that.

"I'm here," said a guy in a nice suit, hurrying in, fastening his belt. Everybody laughed.

"This guy has an old lady's bladder," another man explained.

Then, when they were all gathered, Dolan made his announcement about the death of Cassie Price. One woman fainted. People collapsed—that is, they held on to desks, chairs, other people. He'd seen shock before, but he'd never seen it in posh surroundings, and there was something a little different about it, choreographed, like a big crowd scene in an opera. A tall handsome man took a chair and put his head in his hands.

An older man stepped forward. "I'm John Connolly. I'm the senior partner. This is my firm. You can speak with me."

Dolan said evenly, "We need to speak with everyone. In turn. We'll set up a schedule. We'll ask that none of you leave today until we've finished. We need information, and we must ask for your co-operation. There are five of us. I can assure you we're very efficient."

"It's already three o'clock," said the man called Pete, the one who had hurried in from the men's room.

"I know. We'll go very fast."

"Can we do our work?"

"Yes. Refrain from conversation about the murder."

"Are you sure it wasn't random?"

"We're not sure of anything yet. This is strictly routine."

Dolan took the ones who had worked most closely with Cassie Price: the other paralegals, the secretaries, and Pete—Peter Winkel, whose cases she researched—as well as the CEO, John Connolly.

Four juniors with him, Denman and Hurwitz, Harris and Wolf, had strict orders to take copious notes and to report to him before anyone was released.

Connolly. Dolan thought about the name. It had been in the news lately. Why? He tried to dredge up a memory.

The elder Connolly led him to a conference room and led the four others to small offices. Dolan asked for rosters of all employees, three copies, one for each room, so they could check off people as they talked to them.

He started with one of the paralegals, a plain young woman who looked uncomfortable in her jacket and heels, as if she had worn only jeans for ten years and now this terrible uniform constricted her. Would she opt out of courtroom duty and find some odd corner of the law that allowed her to work in jeans? Her name was Jessica Olmeda.

"You were friends with Cassie Price?"

"Yes. We went to lunch every day."

"Did you talk about your personal lives?"

"Not so much."

Dolan pricked up his ears. "Really? Why was that?"

"Well, everybody was nervous here about fitting in and being professional. We kind of keep a guard up."

"Did she ever come in late?'

"Oh, no, early; she was almost always early."

"Did she call in to you about today about not coming in?" Everyone in the firm was going to get that question.

"No. No, we had no idea."

"What did you think when she didn't show up?"

"I didn't know what to think."

"Did you think she'd turned it into a vacation day?"

"No, she wouldn't. She was all work. I thought maybe a parent was ill or something, like some emergency."

"Did anybody speculate about it?"

"Just like you. You know—running ideas—did she take the day off, did she oversleep, did something happen in her family, is she sick?"

"Nobody called?"

"We did call. At around lunchtime and again at one or so." She started to cry. "If we'd gone looking, would we have saved her?"

Time of death was not supposed to be revealed just yet. Dolan placed his hand over hers and said, "Don't think like that. Probably not."

"It's just—"

"I know."

"I can't get it through my head."

"Tell me about her boyfriends. Whatever you know."

"I don't have a name."

"What do you have?"

"Just some guy she was seeing. I don't think they went out so much as just saw each other."

"Why was that? It wasn't serious?"

"I don't know. I got the impression it was kind of serious for her. She said he was different. Not educated, not like her, but sweet."

"But you don't have a name?"

"No."

"Anything you know about him?"

She appeared to think about it. "No. It was like she didn't want to tell me but she did. Somehow."

"Thank you very much. Would you just take a look at this list? Is all this contact information correct?"

She used her finger to scan the line. "Yes."

None of the other paralegals or secretaries knew anything about the boyfriend, and they had little to add except some facts about Cassie's background. Cassie Price had been homeschooled up until halfway through her junior year, when she persuaded her parents that she should try the public school for the experience of it. After that, she went to Westminster, aced all the prelaw courses and exams, and got into Pitt, where she was supposed to start next year.

The single male intern, Brandon Marciano, said, "She had this thing about wanting to buy a house as soon as she got to town. She said the economy was going to bounce back up and she wanted a place to live that was all hers, no roommates, she was sure she wanted to stay and practice in the city, and she wanted the equity. She was very determined."

"She sounds driven."

"Yes. She was."

"Did you know anything about who she dated?"

"No. Nothing." The fellow blushed.

"You never dated her?'

"No. We went for coffee. I treated. That was it."

"Did you ever ask her out?"

"Yes."

"But?"

"She said no."

"Did she say why?"

"She was polite. She said something about not right now, she was seeing someone occasionally and needed time to figure it out."

"What did you think? Was it true?"

"I don't know about that, but I knew she was brushing me off."

Dolan smiled. "Did it make you bitter?"

"God no. If I'm not used to it by now, I'm not used to anything."

Dolan thought for a moment, then extended his hand for a shake. He predicted a happy middle age for Brandon, who was likely to be grateful when love came his way, but he knew Brandon couldn't project himself into that future life just yet.

The CEO, John Connolly, was stiff, affronted by this negative attention coming to his firm. He gave the impression the young woman had been an unfortunate choice in that she had brought this on them. "I don't work closely with the paralegals," he said briskly.

"Why do I think I've been hearing the name of your firm in the news? Have you been in the news?"

Connolly shook his head. "Not me. Not the firm. My son. He practices here. They're running him in the primaries for governor."

"Ah. That's it."

It was well before five when Dolan and the other detectives met to compare notes.

Ryan Harris and Harry Wolf were both young and clean-cut. They made quick detailed reports on the forty people they had talked to, people who had supposedly known Price peripherally or not at all.

Dolan turned to the next two.

Denman, originally from Georgia, was tall and fairly hefty. Dolan had run into him once at Home Depot wearing bib overalls, an image that stuck and that Dolan kept seeing through the inexpensive chinos and jackets Denman wore to work. He had the open face and manner of a country boy, all the more so in the mahogany surroundings. He still had a drawl. Hurwitz, as urban as they come, including the stains from fast-food lunches and the smell of cigarettes on him, was medium-sized in everything except his exaggerated facial features. His clothes were of a decent quality but well worn and in need of dry cleaning.

"Not much information to go on. I think the firm is going to come out clean," Hurwitz said.

Harris and Wolf had the same impression.

Denman said, "These folks are truly shocked. I think they're broken up about her death. The girl doesn't seem to have enemies here. They keep wanting to ask questions, and I had to keep telling them that we ask the questions."

Dolan liked to hear Denman talk. *Ah think* and *dudn't*.

"Who kept pumping you?"

"The younger member of the family in the firm. Michael."

There were three Connollys on the roster, Dolan saw: the father, John, whom he'd interviewed; the elder son, Evan, who looked older than his years; and the younger one, Michael, who'd got all the good genes. Denman had had the two sons on his list of interviewees.

"What did he ask? This Connolly?"

"How did it happen, what did we know, who would do such a

thing—all the usual questions." He looked at his watch. "He has some kind of photo shoot. He tried to get out of it but that caused a big fuss, so in the end he wanted to know if he would make it."

"What do you think?" Dolan asked.

Denman opined in a sweet drawl, "I think it's okay to release these folks. We can come back to any of them later, if the thing doesn't look random."

Ah think. Dudn't.

"You?" he asked Hurwitz and the others.

"Ditto," they said.

"Anything about a boyfriend?"

"No," said Wolf and Harris.

Hurwitz said, "Nobody knew anything except they thought there might be one."

"Hmmm, sure enough," Dolan said. "I got a hint of it. The old meat and potatoes of a homicide." He started to gather up his papers. "Oh. Anybody here in the offices who isn't on the rosters?"

Denman had one, a client. He showed the name.

Hurwitz had one, a party organizer who was going over district maps with the younger Connolly son.

That was it.

ELINOR CARRIED THE bag of trash out to the back deck and to the shed below. On the grounds, four men were working to make each flower stand out as if sculpted. When they were finished there would not be a weed or a weak plant anywhere. Each hedge was already trimmed to look almost unreal, like those pictures of gardens in England. What a misuse of labor, Elinor thought, to make a hedge look like a horse or a church spire.

The photographers were coming *again.*

Yesterday the team that arrived had taken a few pictures and run some video, but then the head guy said they needed to extend the shoot. Mrs. Connolly looked like she was going to spit bricks, but the director told her husband they had to glamour up a bit because the whole shoot was costing a fortune and they had to get it right. "We want movie stars," the director said.

So Mrs. Connolly had gone to have her hair done today as well as toenails and fingernails. She was more than okay looking, a teacher, sociology, at Duquesne. Yesterday she'd let her boys, the twins, play all day, feeling they should be photographed as they were, real. Today she caved in and scrubbed them.

Elinor nodded to the men working the grounds and went back inside. She knew every inch of this place, and she kept it clean as anybody's whistle. She set out the cheeses, napkins, wineglasses.

She had worked for one or another of the Connollys all her life. She was especially fond of Michael, but she found herself secretly hoping he didn't get elected governor because she liked her life as it was.

The twins came down the big stairs, looking miserably clean. "No fighting," Elinor teased. "We don't want blood all over those clothes."

"What are we supposed to do while we wait?"

"Watch TV?"

"I guess. Man, yesterday was bad enough." They galumphed into the family room.

She took out of the refrigerator the foods the caterers had brought. The canapés in dough were hard and cold to the touch. Some were spinach filled. Others had crab and shrimp.

"This isn't enough food," she told Mrs. Connolly. "I could have made something good."

"I know, I know. They said we won't stop to eat. They said quick finger foods were okay." Elinor had fed the twins a big late lunch so they wouldn't get hungry between six and nine. After that she had sandwiches ready for them.

Everything else was in order. Elinor wiped up the moist smears from the caterer's packaging.

Monica Connolly came down the stairs and into the kitchen, where she pulled out a chair but didn't sit. She looked pale. "My husband might be late. Something terrible happened at his office. He wanted to cancel, but that director, Jack Cain, said we couldn't. Said the photographers were paid for and we had to compartmentalize. How we're supposed to do that, I don't know."

"What happened?"

"A college girl was killed."

"How? A car?"

"A homicide, he said. At her house. She lived down in that area where your son does, in lower Oakland."

Elinor liked to think the area was safe. Her son had insisted on moving out to be on his own. She'd listened to Mr. Connolly and let Cal buy a house there—the Connollys' firm supported a guy who had a real estate company that snagged some government financing to sell properties there with the idea of getting stable residents in.

Mrs. Connolly looked anything but ready to smile at a camera.

"I can't believe the photographers won't reschedule if you tell them what happened."

"I don't think it's up to them. It's Cain."

"Tell me what I can do."

"Just be here. Keep the finger foods coming. And the wine. And let's be done with it."

Elinor's cell phone rang. She was embarrassed to take the call while Mrs. C was in the kitchen. She said, "I'll get that later."

It turned out to be much later when she got to her phone, almost two hours later. She'd got caught up helping the crew with what they needed for different backgrounds. The whole thing was slickly managed, like a real movie being made, and Elinor found it interesting.

It would turn out well. The glamorous couple smiled, Michael put his arm around his wife's waist, and they joked and teased. Still, if you knew them, you could see they were preoccupied.

When the crew began to pack up some of their equipment, Elinor opened her phone. Her son had called her.

CAL THOUGHT THE detectives' names were something like Colton and Hanrahan, but he wasn't sure. He wanted to ask, but that felt awkward. The skinny one put a McDonald's burger and Coke in front of him. He reached for the burger. He *was* hungry.

"Take your time," the bigger, chubbier detective with dark hair said. Colton? "When you're done we'll want to hear it again from the beginning."

He thought he would go crazy if he told it again. He took a bite of the burger.

"Good?"

"Good but not good for me," he chanted.

They laughed. "Why is that?"

"Everybody knows. *Fast Food Nation.*"

"What's that?"

"It's a movie," he said miserably.

"I think it was a book, too," said the skinny guy.

Cal shrugged. He didn't care what it was. Suddenly he got an image of poor Cassie on the floor of her living room and he couldn't swallow. He felt tears coming to his eyes. She was nicer to him than anybody ever had been. When he worked there, she made him coffee or tea. Once she made him a sandwich. But that wasn't it—it was the way she did it, like she truly liked him.

Once before last night he found her crying. "What's the matter?" he asked. "Did something happen?"

"Oh, nothing. Just life. You know. Life in the big city."

"Someone was bad to you?"

"Oh no, no, no. Troubles with love."

That time he didn't know what more to say, so he just patted her shoulder. Then yesterday he saw from the porch where he was working that she cried again while she moved around her kitchen, and he didn't know what to do, and he wasn't near her, so he just worked a little longer than he'd intended in order to keep an eye on her. When she made herself something to eat, he thought, Good, she's going to be okay. He listened to the crackle of meat in the skillet. He saw her take out bread and something else that looked like a vegetable. He called, "You need anything?"

"No, I'm just going to have some dinner. Thanks."

"Are you sure?"

"Yeah. Don't ever drink a margarita."

"Oh." That made sense of the odd way she moved. He kept an eye out for her. When she seemed more steady, he went home.

He hadn't told about her crying or what she said, only about seeing her eat dinner.

"Did she have a boyfriend?"

"I think maybe."

"Why do you think so?"

"I don't know. Just she was pretty."

"Anything else? You ever see the guy?"

"Never."

"Nobody came to the house."

"I never saw anyone."

"Kind of funny, huh? A pretty girl like that."

"Yeah."

"Did she like you?'

"Yeah."

"You were her boyfriend?"

"No, no, she liked me. She was nice to me."

"Did you wish she was your girlfriend?"

"Yeah."

"Why wasn't she?"

He put his burger down in frustration and heaved a breath that hurt the whole way going in. "I'm just a worker. She was going to be a lawyer. Besides I have . . ." He pointed to his head. "I had an injury."

"What kind?"

"Concussion and damage to my ear."

"When did that happen?"

"Long time ago. I was a little boy."

"Uh. I see. That must be hard."

"No. It was a long time ago."

"So now, tell us again about today, about finding the body. You were, what, painting?"

"Making a porch railing."

"There's one there."

"But it's bad. I was fixing it."

"I thought you said you were painting up the street."

"I was, but I wanted the white paint to dry before I put on the blue paint."

"Okay, so then you heard something?"

"Yeah."

"What?"

He had told it eighty times by now. "Something beeping. But I heard it . . . sort of heard it like in the background somewhere and I wasn't sure of where." This time he added, "Everything beeps these days. Phones. Coffee machines."

"You're right about that."

He was pleased to be right about something.

"And then what?"

"I noticed after a while that the back door was open, so I went in. And I found her."

"Where?"

"In the living room."

"Then what?"

"I screamed. I went outside. I used my phone to call 911."

"Did you touch the body?'

"Her foot, her arm. They were cold. I put a finger to her neck. No pulse." He heaved big gasping breaths. It was horrible to remember.

"Did you think it was odd that her car was parked out back?"

"No."

"Why not?"

"She didn't always take it to work. Sometimes she took a bus."

"Any pattern?"

"I don't know any pattern." He thought. "Except maybe more like she took the car on Thursdays or Fridays."

"This was a Friday."

"Not every Friday. Just sometimes. Maybe there was no pattern. I don't know."

He was so tired. He just wanted to go home and cry in private.

When they left him alone, when he needed a friendly voice, he called his mother, but she sounded so alarmed, he was sorry he'd bothered her.

MONICA TOLD ELINOR, "Go ahead. Go."

"Are you sure?"

"I can clean up."

She studied Elinor's face. The woman had a bony sort of good looks. Elinor was a light-skinned African American whom most people thought of as white. She worked for the Connollys because her mother had worked for them. She was about fifty-five and had been with the family for a long time. Mike had grown up with Elinor as a second mother/older sister. She'd actually lived in the house for a time. He'd had the inevitable crush on her.

When it came time to raise her son, whom everybody thought of as white, Elinor had moved out of the house to a small apartment in East Liberty. She still came to work every day, changed her street clothes to a black dress or a black skirt and white blouse. But Monica knew Elinor dressed, when she wasn't at work, in a bright, almost preppy style.

There was something wrong with the son. Cal. Monica had met him a few times. He was sweet tempered but just a little slow on the uptake. An injury, Mike told her, had done this to him.

"Take care," Monica said to the departing Elinor, aware that the woman was very upset.

Monica took over in the kitchen. It was a comfort, doing something as ordinary as filling the dishwasher.

Her husband came into the kitchen. "What are you doing in here?"

"Putting things away."

"Where's Elinor?'

"I let her go. Her son is the one who found the . . . the girl from your office."

"Oh . . . I didn't see the news. All they said to us was that a neighbor found her."

She shook her head. "It was Cal. I think he did it."

"What makes you think so?"

"Elinor's face."

He sat down heavily on the kitchen chair. After a while he said, "Leave that. Sit."

"I'll just be a minute." An ice cube skittered away from her, fell on the floor. She bent to pick it up and began crying.

"What?"

"For Elinor. For that girl."

He got up and lifted her up and held her. They embraced for a long time.

"We'd better watch the news," she said. Then angrily, "We should have canceled all that picture taking. I don't care about the money. I couldn't concentrate."

"There were deadlines. Contracts with the press and video company. I'm told what to do."

"I don't like it."

He left the kitchen abruptly.

She could hear the twins upstairs, thumping, probably fighting, on the floor.

She left the dishes where they were and sat at the kitchen table, which held four half-full wine bottles. If only she were a drinker—

All that smiling and ridiculous hand-holding and looking at zinnias and all the while she couldn't love him. Why was it everyone else could love him? People called him day and night; the boys adored him; Elinor loved him. Monica was supposed to be thrilled with her life, the big catch, the handsome senator-governor-who-knew-where-it-would-all-end, and she didn't want any of it. She didn't love him. They were past tense.

And she was trapped.

They had sons, a life. Expectations.

She poured a glass of white wine and forced it down. Her head began to throb. Her body went numb. She had to figure out how to magically resurrect the feelings she had for Mike at the beginning—

feelings stored somewhere in the bank of memories in her muddled head.

She got up and finished rinsing glasses—fast and sloppily. A glass fell into the sink as she grabbed it too hastily. Oddly it didn't break.

She took the rest of the bottle of white wine to her husband, who sat in the TV room, changing channels and talking on the phone. He ended the call.

"Who was that?" she asked.

"My father. The idea is to keep me out of any news reports or commentary. Low profile."

"But did you know her?"

"Only a little. Passing in the hallways. I had trouble remembering her name."

"Cassie."

"I know it now."

"It's very sad."

"Yes. Totally . . . disturbing. I can't believe it."

"You didn't know her?"

"No. Not really. And . . . you think Elinor's son . . . ?"

"He must have said something when he called Elinor. She was very upset. This Cassie lived near him?"

He nodded. "Paul Wesson's properties. People who are willing to commit to fixing them up."

"I remember."

He kept switching channels. The ten o'clock news came on.

The woman was pretty. Beautiful. The police wouldn't reveal anything. They did that police-speak, saying the investigation was just under way.

Her husband cried.

CHRISTIE HAD DROPPED the kids off, then Marina and various pieces of luggage, and then gone to Headquarters, where he picked up a few facts by reading the early reports on his computer.

There wasn't much there yet, only the bare facts of the case: 911 call from Cal Hathaway, who'd been working on the porch, then the alarm clock beeping, then the discovery of the body.

"What's up?" he asked Janet Littlefield, who was at her desk.

"Coleson and McGranahan are questioning this guy Cal Hathaway right now," Detective Littlefield told him. "They've been at him most of the day. They told me, 'He doesn't play with a full deck.'"

"Which room are they in?"

"B."

Christie fought with himself. He didn't want to intrude. He *did* want to. He passed into the viewing room and watched his men question a young man who was wide-eyed, seemingly polite, very shaken.

Coleson and McGranahan, as if they sensed Christie, announced a break. They came to the viewing room to greet him.

"It's going okay?" he asked.

"We're being thorough."

"Tell me about the woman."

"Getting ready to go to law school," Coleson said. "Pretty."

"Who told her family?"

McGranahan said, "I sent Greer to tell the parents. She's getting good at that sort of thing."

"She's here?"

"Yeah, I have her questioning some of the peripheral people down in the conference room."

"You suspect this Cal?"

"I do," said Coleson. "We're checking out his house. He had a case on the girl."

"Hmm."

Christie found Colleen Greer in the conference room writing up notes between witnesses, so he said, "Tell me. What happened? You saw the parents? You told them?"

"Oh. Yeah. I went in the late afternoon." She made a face.

"It was awful?"

"Yes. It turned out there were also three younger sisters to tell. It was tough going. They were nice people," she said. She sat back in her chair, smiled at him. "If Bible thumpers are ever nice, these thumpers were nice. They fell apart, and it was . . . upsetting. Then they all clasped hands, kind of like a prayer circle. The younger sisters were all gorgeous. Every one."

"That'll make the media happy."

"Yeah. You got that right." She gestured toward him. "Wow, are you suntanned. You got a lot of sun."

"Yep. Then it started raining."

"You must have relaxed."

"In my fashion."

"We didn't expect you back until Monday. We thought you'd get in Sunday night."

"We left early because of the rain."

"Bummer."

"I pushed and did the whole drive today. Fourteen hours."

"I'd say you're pretty tired."

"I am."

"You got curious about this case." She laughed.

"You know it. *You* have any ideas about it?"

"No. Wallet is missing. Also apparently a cell phone. The usual theories. In spite of the theft, which might not be a theft, of course, Coleson and McGranahan are pretty hot on the handyman."

"So long as you all run everything. Cover all the bases." He yawned.

"I think they will," she said carefully. "You should get some sleep."

"Right. Couple of hours will do wonders. I'll check back in the morning."

Christie wondered if he was losing his smarts, his instincts. He'd always relied on his intuitive abilities. Cal Hathaway. Was he wrong about him? He'd only seen him briefly. What, twenty seconds. Hathaway was supposedly *slow*—a person who needed a longer processing time than most people did. He knew nothing else about him.

He went home and climbed into bed. Marina had managed to put the kitchen things away, but the suitcases and other beach paraphernalia sat in piles in the living room. She was out. Exhausted. He counted some sheep, worked on the family budget by calculating things in his head, which he was still good at, thought about how happy his children had been playing in the waves, that is, when they could *get* waves—which wasn't all the time, Cape Cod being less surf-friendly than New Jersey.

He managed to drift off.

ELINOR SAID TO THE woman at the desk, "I need to see my boy. Calvin Hathaway. I called his house. He must still be here."

"Yes. He's here. I'm Detective Littlefield. Are you a witness to the investigation?"

"I guess I am."

"Did you see anything?"

"Nothing like that. I was at work. Cal is my son, and I'm worried he's not all right."

"How do you mean?"

"He can't take stress. I'm serious. He can't take it."

"It isn't easy on anybody."

"That's not what I mean."

"I'll call the detectives. Would you sit? Can I get you something?"

"No, nothing."

"Water?"

"Yes, water."

Elinor watched the lady detective pour water from a cooler. The woman brought it to her, patted her hand, and said, "Now you wait just a moment."

Two men wearing ties came out of a room. Was that where her son was? Elinor stood to walk toward the room, but they stopped her. "Just a minute. Are you Mrs. Hathaway?"

"Yes."

"We're glad you came. We want to talk to you."

The woman detective who had greeted her told them, "Greer is finished. Conference room is free."

"Good, good. You have water?" The man who asked her this was trying to sound polite. He looked tired. "Follow me."

The other man had a less polite look. He slumped as he walked. If they were tired, what did it mean for Cal? Had they been grilling him all day?

The conference room had a large wooden table and vinyl upholstered chairs that were on rollers.

"Sit, Mrs. Hathaway."

She sat. Her chair rolled, making her grab the edge of the table.

"The floor slants some," the larger detective said, smiling. "You've come to tell us something about your son? Is that right?"

"I've come to make sure he's okay. He can't handle stress. He probably won't tell you that he can't handle it, but I'm here to make sure somebody knows it."

The detectives stared at her. "What exactly are you saying?" the skinny one asked.

"That I want to talk to him. In private. Not"—her hand swept the room's ceiling—"not with some listening device."

"There isn't anything like that in here," the big one said, looking first at her, then at his partner. "We could let them talk in here."

The other one grunted. He turned to her. "He called you?"

"He did. Am I supposed to get him a lawyer?"

"Is that what he asked for?"

"He didn't ask me anything. He just said he was having a bad day. He found a body and he was upset that he couldn't get out to go home. Why . . . why are you keeping him here?"

"He's a key witness. He found the body. He's a witness."

"Did he do it?" Everything stopped moving. Her words hung in the air.

"We thought perhaps you were here to tell us that."

"I won't let him be bullied. He's had a hard life. He—did he tell you he's deaf in one ear? Did he let you know he doesn't always hear what you're saying?"

"No, he didn't mention that."

"It slows him down."

"We thought it was something else."

"There are other things."

"Can you tell us?"

She studied them. She didn't know what to do except explain. So she began. "When he was a boy, he got beat up at school. Badly. He had a concussion that . . . did not reverse, or whatever, right away. And after that he got a seizure one day at school, and so the same boys beat him again. Nobody should have to go through that. The boys got away. Nothing ever happened to them."

"I'm sorry. That's terrible."

"Yes, it is. He fought to make a comeback. He did okay in school in the long run, but he's never been totally . . . confident. The doctor said a brain injury is . . . tricky."

"What are you trying to tell us?" the skinny one asked, and again she felt afraid of him. "That he has excuses for certain—"

The other one quieted him. "Just a minute. I'm interested in this injury. How is he not okay? Can you be specific? Seizures?"

"Just the one to my knowledge."

"Did he ever sleepwalk?"

"I don't think so."

"Black out?"

"Yes."

"He did?"

"For a couple years he had memory problems. Things he just didn't remember." It was the truth. Would the truth help him if he did it or would they just hold it against him? "Please don't batter at him. I'm afraid for him. A seizure is a terrifying thing."

The two detectives sat for a long time as if thinking. Finally the friendlier one said, "I'm going to let you talk to him while my partner and I talk to each other."

"Thank you."

"Should I—" She stood.

"No. You stay here. We'll bring him to you. Maybe you can get him to tell us what happened."

It seemed to her she waited a long time, though it was probably four minutes. She couldn't sit. When her son came in, she stood and hugged him for a long time.

"I'm sorry I bothered you," he said.

"Just a minute." She waited until the detectives left and closed the door. "Are they being hard on you?"

"Yes. I'm tired."

"Did you eat?"

"They fed me once."

This froze her blood. If they fed him, they must be *keeping* him, booking him. What did they know?

"Can you remember today?" she asked.

He looked at her, puzzled.

"Everything. Finding the woman. Can you remember?"

"I remember okay. At first I thought she was sick. But then her nightgown was torn. Then I realized . . ."

She didn't know what to think. "Did you get near her?"

"I touched the body—maybe I shouldn't have, maybe that's what they're on me about, but I needed to know if she was dead for sure. Then I called 911."

"How did you know she was dead?"

"She was cold. No pulse."

"Did you black out?"

"No."

"So you remember everything?"

"I said I did. You didn't need to come here." He looked about ir-ritably, almost as if he wanted to go back to the others.

She couldn't help herself. She asked, "Did you go over there last night, to see her?"

He frowned, giving her a hard look. "No."

"Could you have gone and not remembered? Blacked out?"

He shook his head.

"You are so upset. I can see how upset you are."

He winced. It was almost a smile. "I felt good around her. And now she's dead."

Elinor was afraid to ask him anything more. She thought there might be a listening device in the room after all. She wanted them to know at least that he had a kind heart and a serious medical condition, that the two of those things together might have mixed him up, and that if they did, he was a creature not in control, a victim of bullies from twenty-some years ago.

THERE ARE MANY phone calls coming at Mike Connolly up to midnight. "Keep you out of the news. Do only one interview, just one, very sober, and use it, talk about crime, cleaning up our cities, wiping out drugs, getting jobs for people. This is your one good clip or sound bite or whatever. You understand?"

"Yes."

"But not multiple appearances."

"Okay."

"They'll play the one good clip over and over. Rehearse it."

"Right."

"Fine. Any questions?"

"There's going to be a funeral. I'm going to that, too."

A pause. "Important. Of course. I was going to move ahead and talk about the funeral. One visit to the laying out or whatever it's going to be if we deem it necessary. There are going to be news people around. But probably cops. And you can't control the coverage. It wouldn't look good if some cameraman got a long shot of a cop bugging you."

"I already talked to the cops at the office."

"You never know. They're not *smart*. Let me think this out. We could maybe make something of it. No. No. Just go with your wife to the funeral home or whatever, go once, be prayerful. And then ditto the funeral. No staying after and chatting over the meal."

There probably wouldn't be a meal, he thought. The Prices were poor upstate people, highly religious, private types, not people who entertained. He tried to work out if he should do something, pay for a meal, but he never proposed it to Haigh. He heard the message, all right: Keep it simple. One key light appearance, a glorious quiet song, then exit.

He didn't want white wine, which was what Monica had brought to him. She was running back and forth, putting the kids to bed, checking on him, catching bits of the news. He wanted bourbon. The good stuff.

There was a concealed bar in the TV room, for the purpose of keeping the liquor from the kids. He had to use a keypad and a code to unlock it. It was new—well, only five years old, and still felt new. He touched in the code. The mirrored doors slipped aside, and he had more than a few choices. He went for the Booker's. Oh, there were going to be gifts handed to him constantly, much fancier bourbons than these, but this would do the trick. He poured about six ounces into a bistro glass for a start. If he didn't get rid of the voices he would never sleep at all.

He left the compartment doors open. The sliver of mirror showed him his haggard face. If he looked this bad during the shoot, Jack and the video crew were going to be back for another try—all the time bellyaching about the huge amounts of money they'd lost.

He heard Todd's voice in his head even after he got half the bourbon down. When they'd hovered over the maps, before the detectives came to talk to them, he asked Todd, "Do you know anything about this?"

"Not a thing. I mean, I liked her. I could see why you liked her. I went out for a drink with her. She was funny—though she's a shitty drinker. I talked to her seriously. She was sad, but she agreed to back off. She said she would do what was best. She said law school was going to take up her time, and when she wasn't up here at the offices anymore, she wouldn't find it so hard."

"She said all that?"

"She's an awfully smart girl. Practical, I thought."

It didn't sound like Cassie. But Todd's face was open, innocent-looking. He seemed suddenly gloomier. "I used the present tense," Todd said. "I made that mistake people make."

"It doesn't add up."

Todd's face had hardened. "You have to forget you ever knew her that other way. You have a campaign to think about. Get it in your head how you have to react—she was an employee here. Likable and smart. You hardly knew her. Back it up three months and you have the reality you need."

The detective was nice, a young man, nice. Treated them well. Denman.

Connolly almost pointed to Todd, said, "Ask this man. Take him in." But he didn't.

When the detective left, Todd lifted the campaign map. His hands shook. Did that mean anything? They had shaken before. Underneath the good spirits he projected was a nervous guy. Well, he had a nervous job. He was rattled. He kept scratching at his neck irritably.

Mike kept at the bourbon. He heard bits and pieces of things Todd had said before he took his leave of the office. "Death is always sad, always. I don't care who it is. She was young, and that makes it really blister."

He was shocked by the ideas that had run through his head all evening.

Now there was this idea that Cal did it. Elinor's boy.

He switched channels back and forth.

There it was again—video shots of the neighborhood, people on the street. An older woman identified as Iris Mender, a neighbor, saying, "She was young and dignified. She was lifting up the neighborhood." You could tell the woman wanted to say something else, but the cameras moved off her.

Monica came into the room, looked at him, then at his glass. "That's not going to kill it," she said.

IRIS HAD FORGOTTEN to eat, what with all the excitement and her being on the news. She'd taken three phone calls from people who went to her church and two from her daughters saying they saw her on TV. One of the stations had apparently had her at six o'clock, but the two others played her little bit at eleven.

"Did I sound crazy?" she asked Corrine Corrigan, who played bingo beside her most Tuesdays.

"No, you sounded smart. I liked that line about the girl being dignified."

"Well, she was. She wasn't trashy at all."

Iris made herself two pieces of toast and began to scramble an egg. She had her appetite back these days so it was wild that she'd forgotten about food until now, except for snatching pieces of candy from the box on the end table. Give her chocolate, she wasn't going to complain.

During the fuss in the afternoon she was asleep in her bed. She was recovering from bypass surgery, and her whole system was a *mess*. It was surely the anesthetic—given a choice she would have refused it, not that that was possible—because after the surgery something went wrong with her melatonin, from what she could tell, turning her schedule upside down as if she lived in Egypt or Russia or somewhere. She was on a six- or ten-hour delay. Instead of getting sleepy at midnight, she got sleepy anytime between six and ten in the morning, depending on what she found on TV to entertain her throughout the night. A thriller at four in the morning could juice her up quite a bit. And for a while, she'd even lost her taste buds.

Her daughters worried about her because she sat on the glider on her porch so much of the time. She'd been amused that they thought some drug-addicted college student was going to bang her on the head, go in, find her wallet, and leave her for dead after she'd been through all the trouble of surgery. It wasn't funny anymore. This very thing—the break-in, the theft, the violence her daughters had feared—had happened to Cassie Price. Tomorrow her daughters would be here again trying to persuade her to move to the suburbs. But she had her friends, her church, her house, her porch, and the funny thing is, she wasn't frightened. She knew the students who went up and down the street—to see them anyway. They drank, she knew that. They lived in student messes, most of them. That didn't bother her. That was what young people did.

She made it to the news, and so did Cal Hathaway, the guy who worked on houses, and one student, an Indian guy, and one black man who owned his house, didn't rent. The media had wanted to show a variety of types, she supposed. She felt she'd won an audition, being the only white woman they chose.

She carried her scrambled eggs and toast to the front porch and sat on her glider.

The news guys were nice. The cops thought she was a ditz. She said, "I can tell you two things. Cassie was driving down the street yesterday and some guy in a gray car was following her. He wasn't right behind her, but I could tell."

"How could you tell?'

"Because of how the car moved."

"How was that?"

"Kind of—I can't explain it. If a person was walking and another person followed. The pace or something."

"The rhythm?"

"Yes! The rhythm."

"What kind of gray car?'

"I don't know the makes. Foreign, I think, not American."

"Why do you say that?"

"The shape."

"Okay. And what's the second thing?"

Then she'd hesitated. All she said was, "In the middle of the night, somebody was in the back alley getting into a black car."

"So a different person?"

"I guess."

"Make of the car?"

"Small. American. That's all I know."

She didn't say the part about how the person getting into the car looked like an astronaut. Because her kids were worried about her visions, her mind. They said she had a thing called "surgery brain." Like the time she fell asleep in the living room chair and woke up and saw the dog she used to have that died seven years ago, just standing there looking at her. "He was coming to get me," she said, "but I told him I didn't want to go yet."

The daughters looked at each other, those sideways glances, and even though she was miffed, it made her laugh to think how every-one got old (if they were lucky) and how you couldn't understand old when you weren't there. When you *were* there you knew the world was mystical and strange. Maybe the astronaut wanted Cassie Price. One way or another, he got her.

FOUR

SATURDAY, AUGUST 15

RICHARD CHRISTIE sat on the side of the bed to answer the phone. "Christie here."

"Commander?"

He saw it was midnight, no, 2:00 A.M. "What is it?"

"You said to call," McGranahan reminded him. "So. We questioned our man. It went fast. It went easy. Cal Hathaway. He confessed."

"McGranahan," Christie began carefully, "are you saying all the rest of it stacks up?"

"It does. You want to review?"

He saw Marina had opened her eyes. "Sure. Yes, I do. Thank you for letting me know," Christie said. "I'll read the files in the morning." There was a pause. Christie stepped in to fulfill the expectation he heard in the silence. "Good work."

He hung up.

Marina asked him something from her half-sleep. He interpreted it to mean, from the upward lilt, "You okay? Everything okay?" In spite of the fact that she was probably still down under, he answered her. "Sometimes I get it wrong. The guy is—"

A delicate snore. No. She was asleep.

Last night, the kids yammering in the backseat, they made it to the parkway just before ten. Christie had done all the driving; his legs were all wonky the last time he got out of the car to take a bathroom break, and he had to hold on to solid things because of a landsickness, which was not unlike seasickness—the body fighting to right its balance system.

Now, 2:00 A.M. on Saturday morning, he still felt a slight vertigo. It forced him to want to lie down and let others do what they did.

HE SAW THE ADMITTING officer write down Caucasian on the form, but he didn't say anything. He was too upset to get into it. The right term for him, he'd learned, was quadroon, one black grandparent. He'd gotten beat up because of it when he was seven years old. Those boys at school wanted him to *look* black, they said. They said he was trying to pull something off. They asked if he bleached his hair and skin. At first he thought they were joking and he laughed, but he learned later the laughter had infuriated them. They said alternately that he must have white parents who didn't want him because they obviously dumped him off on an old black woman. They meant his grandmother who walked him to school. She'd stopped working for the Connollys because she was sick with something that had turned out to be cancer. Some of the boys taunted him that he had an old black mother. He didn't try to correct them. It took him a long time to realize that everything about him, his pacifist personality, his mild answers, the color of his skin, made them crazy.

Now he didn't correct the police. All his life people had written down Caucasian. Hospitals, schools, jobs, insurance, driver's license. There were years when he was relieved by it—it helped him get by. But something had happened lately; the drift of the country, politically, got into his heart. He wanted to be fully what he was.

He had dirty blond hair. It was uneven in color with natural blond streaks from working outdoors so much. His skin was still white. He'd burned from working outdoors, then tanned. Even so, he looked white.

He had green eyes, a sort of green/hazel that occurred fairly often in mixed-race people. His eyes were wide spaced, not large.

They kept ordering him around. They made him sit in a big chair that was like an electric chair. It did something to him—like an X-ray, they said when he tried to protest. "It won't hurt you. Sit still." He had to stand for a long time in a line, and then he had to sit for a long time in a room with a lot of other people, most of whom seemed to be drunk and unwashed. He tried to sleep, sitting, standing.

He'd had that thing they call arraignment. It was in a funny dark room with a video camera and a person asking him questions on the screen. That person, a tired old man, asked him if he had any money, to which he replied, "Not much." The man said he would get him a public defender.

Then they took him to another line where they even made him strip and examined him every which way. Somehow it reminded him of being born—scrubbed and slapped and pushed to breathe on his own.

They were folding up his clothes, everything he owned. "I want to keep my watch with me."

"Can't," they said. "We're supposed to take it."

"Take it? It's mine."

He gave up his clothes when they pulled the basket away from him, but he wouldn't give up his watch. He accepted the limp bed-roll with its toothbrush, paste, tiny towel, red uniform, blanket, and that was about it. He was made to shower and use a special shampoo. They made him put on the red prison suit with white lettering.

When the officer walked him down the corridor of the jail, he heard murmurs of "Who came in?" "White guy. Must be drunk." "Guy can hardly walk."

He didn't think fatigue could be this bad. He couldn't care about anything.

The cell smelled of urine. The bed was a metal bunk bed with a thin mattress. He got one knee down on the lower level, crouching, and then let himself fall the rest of the way. He still wore the wristwatch he had fought hard to keep. "Be my guest," the man with the uniforms had said finally. "It's only going to cause you trouble."

Before his head dropped on his wrist, he noticed it was five thirty in the morning. After I sleep, he told himself, I'll tell them, everybody, the public defender and everybody, why I said it, how I just wanted to sleep. I'll tell them the truth about my mother making me angry because she thought I did the thing. And then about how I couldn't stand those guys coming at me and at me with their questions.

He knew there would be a large mark on his face from the watch, but he couldn't move to adjust his body. Everything went black.

FOUR HOURS AFTER the phone call from McGranahan, Christie sat at his kitchen table studying the newspaper while Marina poured him a cup of coffee.

The reporter had written it with only the early details of the story, not the confession, which had happened late at night. The article, which had made it to the front page, carried the expected shock value. A pretty young woman was dead. Her name was Cassandra Price. She'd come to the city from a town so small it had only eighty inhabitants. She was twenty-two, finishing up a summer job as a paralegal at a prestigious law firm and getting ready to attend Pitt law school. Friends and colleagues reported she was extremely serious about her studies and worked all the time, reading law and about law even in her time off. The murder had happened at her house, a property in Oakland, a fixer-upper that had once been rented to students. She had wanted to own something herself instead of renting a place, as most students do. Neighbors said she was happy to spend her evenings working on the house. People from the Connolly law office reported that she was thrilled to have a little backyard, a chance to garden. The reporter managed to convey an image of a promising young person just coming up in the world, just blossoming. The final paragraph of the article stated that a man doing repair work for

Ms. Price had sensed something wrong at the house and had found her body. The placement of the paragraph managed to imply the handyman was the answer to the reader's questions.

Christie couldn't wait to go into the office.

"You're beating yourself up," Marina said. "We deserved to go on vacation. You deserved it."

"I know that."

He was dressed and driving to Headquarters only minutes later. Once he got there, he felt like himself again. He popped on his computer and started to read the newest accounts of the investigation. He read through the interview notes for the law firm and the neighbors. His five men, headed by Dolan, had done interviews averaging ten minutes each at the firm. You could get a lot in ten minutes, but they'd come away with little more than what was in the paper.

He read Coleson's and McGranahan's notes again and thought over the facts. Cassie had been strangled. She had been wearing her nightgown. Her wallet and cell phone were missing. In her house the detectives found the morning coffee prepped and ready to go. They found the bleeping alarm clock set. Her clothes were set out for the next workday.

Someone had entered through the back door. The lock looked a little rough, but it wasn't absolutely clear it had been tampered with. The photos of it were vague and didn't make particular sense. The crime scene was strangely devoid of evidence. The Forensics staff looked for hairs, footprints, all the usual, and it would be a while before they analyzed most of it. But, good, they took samples of what they could get.

The pathologist had reported early on that the marks on Cassie's throat were consistent with manual strangulation. Coleson and McGranahan had surmised as much from their first visual inspection.

Christie read on. While Coleson and McGranahan talked to the boy, the young man they eventually arrested here at Headquarters, other detectives helped Forensics to comb the crime scene. One of the young detectives was the one who picked up a pair of work gloves from Cassie's porch, just outside her door. The gloves had hair in them.

Christie next went down the hall to watch the video of the interrogation.

"Did you want her wallet for her photograph, perhaps?" Coleson was asking.

"No."

"You didn't want to look at her? Did you like looking at her?"

"I'm not sure what you mean."

"Oh? I mean did you think she was pretty?"

"She was beautiful."

"Did you like her?"

"Yes. Of course I liked her."

"Did you wish she was your girlfriend?"

"She wasn't."

"Did you wish she was?"

"I don't know."

"Did you wish she could be?"

"But she wasn't."

"Would it be nice, though, if she could be?"

"Yes."

"Who *was* her boyfriend?"

"I don't know."

"Did you see her go with anyone?"

"No."

"Men at the house?"

"No."

"Never? A pretty girl like that?"

"I don't know. I didn't see anything like that, men at the house."

"Was she nice to you?"

"Yeah."

"We found some things at your house."

He blinked, puzzled. "My house?"

"You want to go home, to your house?"

"Yeah."

"Okay, then just answer what we have to ask. Did you kill Cassie Price?"

A stunned expression. "No. No. Oh, my God."

A knock on the door. For a while, a series of murmurs.

"We're going to take a bit of a break," says McGranahan.

"Can I go home now?"

"No. No. Actually no. We'll be right back."

Cal fidgeted on the tape. He cried. He shook his head woefully.

When the detectives came back in, they said, "Calvin Hathaway. We are taking you into custody in connection with the murder of Cassie Price. You have the right to remain silent. Anything you say may be used in evidence against you. You also have the right to an attorney. Would you like to have a lawyer present?"

"I didn't do it."

"Would you like to have a lawyer?"

"Why? What does it mean if I have one?"

"You are allowed to have one by law. I'm assuming you don't have a lawyer . . . Is that right?"

"I never used a lawyer for anything."

"You are allowed one phone call. Who would you like to call?"

"I don't know."

"Get him a phone. Want to call your mother again, let her call someone to represent you?"

"I don't want to bother her again. It's late."

There was another break in the tape. That was 11:29. The tape started up again at 11:47.

"Would you state your full name and where you live?"

"Cal Hathaway."

"Is that your full name?"

"Calvin. I never use it much."

"That's okay. And where do you live?"

"I told you before."

"Just for the record."

"On Child Street." He gave the number.

"That's the name of a street?"

"Yes."

"Is that behind Parkview?"

"Yes. Behind and one street over."

"Do you know who I am?"

"Police."

"Do you remember my name?"

"No."

"I'm Detective McGranahan. Homicide. Can you say who I am?"

"Detective McGranahan. Homicide."

"Have you had a pretty good summer?"

This getting-friendly talk that detectives are supposed to do appeared to confuse Cal. He squirmed, put his hands to his mouth. "No."

"No?"

"Not now."

"Okay. Just listen and answer our questions. Can you tell me what you do for a living?"

"Work on people's houses."

"Doing what?"

"Roof. Porch. Painting. Different things."

"Do you recognize these gloves?"

"I think . . . Are they mine? See, I have a lot of pairs." Long pause. He looks around. "I can't tell."

Another break.

When they come back, it is 12:52. Cal Hathaway is visibly nervous.

"I don't have to talk," Cal says. "Is that right?"

"That's right. You don't have to, but we hope you do. We're tired. We know you're tired. Just relax for a minute and tell us what you know about the death of Cassie Price."

"I found her body. I already told about that."

"Do you know how she died?"

He appears to think. "Strangled?"

Coleson jumps a little, and so does McGranahan.

"How do you know that?"

Cal scratches his chin. "I could see. I mean, at first I thought she was sick, but then I could see there wasn't any blood anywhere and there were marks on her neck."

"You looked at the body for how long? Before calling police?"

"I don't know."

"Did you move anything?"

"No, I said before. No."

"What was she strangled with?"

"The gloves?"

"Why do you say that?"

"You showed me."

"If a person did it, when do you think it was done?"

"Middle of the night."

"How was it done?"

"Strangled." Cal starts to cry.

"Why are you crying?"

"For her. Because it's sad. She's dead."

"Any other reason?"

"I'm tired."

"Did you strangle her?"

A strange look comes over Cal. Anger. His face scrunches up and he looks as if he could blow fire. "Yes. Maybe. Maybe I didn't know what I was doing. I didn't remember. I don't remember."

"You said yes."

"I don't know. Maybe I was dreaming. Or went crazy."

"You said before that you liked her a lot."

"Yes."

"But you killed her."

"Am I done?"

"Almost. You said yes, you did."

"I'm really upset. I need to sleep."

"You killed Cassie Price?"

"I just want to sleep. That's all I want. I want to put this day away and come back and be able to think."

"I'm going to have you sign something." McGranahan looks to the clock and says to the camera: "One twenty-nine A.M."

ELINOR TOOK THE BUS to work even though she had called the station in the night and knew her son had confessed. The only thing she could think to do was go to work, be useful. She blamed herself for everything, not being able to protect her son, not knowing how to. He was a good boy, a loving boy, but he'd been so unlucky—that whole terrible trauma of his childhood. Will she always be unable to help? She'd been at work, didn't know a thing, the day he almost died. Her mother, who lived with them, had gotten word that Cal was beaten and lying in a ditch, dead, and her mother had run down the street and found him on the pavement, bloody and unconscious. She screamed for help. Then somebody made a call to the police, and finally there was an ambulance, everything so slow, her mother said, so slow, and Elinor didn't know a thing about it all that time, thinking it was just a normal workday at the Connollys'. They were good to her then, during it all, insisting she take time off, and even paying medical bills that weren't covered.

She looked around the bus, noting familiar people among the strangers, feeling they might somehow guess her connection with the man arrested last night. All of it seemed completely unreal in the light of day. Something must have sparked her son's anger at the young woman. Elinor couldn't imagine it; anything she tried to come up with didn't make sense of the son she knew. How had the school counselor put it when he was in middle school—all that gentleness, given what he'd gone through, there must be wells of anger in him underneath.

She would have to talk to someone. Surely he had been provoked. And *surely* he had blacked out. He didn't remember doing the murder or he would have said when she asked him. The bus she rode came to a stop on Fifth Avenue. She was up and moving and getting off the bus as she had done every day for so many years now.

She started up the hill, winding her way. She could have taken off today, the Connollys would have let her, but routines had always kept her sane. Today on her list was getting the boys' school things ready. They needed gym clothes, swimming trunks, goggles, fins, tennis and racquetball rackets.

On Woodland Road, where she walked, everything was beautiful. The grounds, the trees—gorgeous. Mostly to the right on this lane were the buildings of Chatham University and mostly to the left were private houses like the one she worked in. To think young kids got to go to college right here, right on this road with the old mansions and the lawns and trees that were like a park.

She couldn't think what she could do for her son. She fought through the numbness.

When she found a moment, she would use her cell phone to call the police and find out about next steps and when she could see her boy.

She entered the house, using a key, disarming the alarms. It was quiet, nobody up. Elinor checked her watch. She was ten minutes later than usual, but it wasn't her fault, the bus was late this morning. Because she hadn't eaten, her stomach felt very strange.

Then she heard a sound. A voice. Low. She went through the downstairs and saw there was a light on in the TV room. It was Mr. Connolly. He was half asleep, with a liquor glass in his hand. He was dressed for the day in linen pants and a light lime green sweater. "It's about your son," he said. "I'm sorry."

He clicked the remote to turn off the TV.

"I know about it. What are they saying?"

"Just that phrase about 'arrested in connection with.' You don't have to be here. Go home."

"I want to work."

She said it so harshly that he seemed stuck for a reply.

The phone rang and he answered it, gesturing to her to stay. He said into the phone, "Of course I'm up." He put a hand over the mouthpiece, turned to her, and said, "I could use some coffee."

And strong, she thought, real strong.

●   ●   ●

TODD SIMON CLICKED off his phone and sat at a kitchen table, not his own, drinking coffee and smoking. He ran his hands over his face. *Damage control* was the phrase running around in his head. Mick, the idiot, wanted to volunteer to represent that kid, Cal, or to find someone who could. Said he *knew* him, knew his family. Of all the stupid ideas . . . Simon had used his calm, easy voice to tell him, "No, no, do not do that, conflict of interest aside, now is the time to back away, to stay out of it. She *happened* to work at Connolly and sons. Period. That's your stance."

He stubbed out a cigarette with a force that rocked the table. How was he supposed to protect a guy who couldn't protect himself? Give him a Machiavel any day over a simple man. His Mick had *a face* they all liked, he *made friends* wherever he went, he did a zillion charitable works, and, as the muckety-mucks explained to each other in Harrisburg, the guy had the goods to be a star.

But he needed sense.

Mick did well with the women—in every respect. Votes and fund-raising and bed partners, the latter of which he would have to give up in order to run for office. Simon did not envy him. It was *the* great pleasure in life. It was what our Lord, in a jolly mood, gave us to make up for the piss-poor mood he was in the rest of the time. Simon himself had five on deck a year ago. One didn't mind sharing him and knew he had several others. Pat. One was very dumb and frighteningly young. Mindy. She let him come and go once or twice a month without coming up with the courage to ask him for anything. He was down to three lately, and one of them was getting to be a problem. It was always something: She wanted his phone numbers or wanted to know where he was when she hadn't heard from him. Carola. She had come to his house bearing a tray of lasagna, as a "surprise" she said, and had been inconsolable when he wasn't pleased. She was, well, maybe not on deck any longer. All he said when she stood there with the lasagna was, "I can't talk about why I can't stay home tonight. I'm needed somewhere. And it's confidential. And it's governmental. If you can't handle it, I'm sorry." She went fuming into the night. He had managed to get the lasagna out of her hands, though, and it was good stuff. She'd call soon, wanting her pan back.

Pat he could always go back to if he wanted. Rita and Fredericka were still on deck.

He had chosen very carefully who to spend his last couple of nights with. She was a woman who wanted a little more from him than he was giving but wouldn't admit it, even to herself. She didn't cook for him, in fact forgot to cook for herself most of the time, eating whatever she could grab fast. She was a big (not fat) woman— and tough. She had a crew that worked for her renovating houses in places like Lawrenceville, wherever there was old property with some treasure to be preserved—old fireplaces, tin ceilings, stained glass windows. She knew her stuff. It's all she talked about—floor joists and stress points.

He'd first met her at a crowded restaurant. She was alone at a table and he was alone, and they were aware there were thirty people waiting to be seated. She was wearing jeans and a paint-stained work shirt. "Do you mind?" he asked, indicating a place at her table. And she said, "No problem. Go ahead. Sit." She announced that her name was Fredericka but that she went by Freddie. He really thought for a while he wasn't interested in her, but the more she talked about her work, the more animated she got; her eyes sparkled. He liked her. People generally did. She was very likable and upbeat. And definitely all woman in bed.

He chose her. It was tricky, though. He'd neglected her. He said, in the phone call from a pay phone, "I dreamt about you last night. I've been groaning all day."

"Ha. Sounds like a fun day."

"What do you mean?"

"Arousal is fun. It's . . . exciting. Where the hell are you? I hear traffic."

"Yeah, well, my phone was out of charge and I was thinking about you, so I pulled over to call."

"Oh, you are in a needy state."

"Freddie, don't torture me."

She let a very long pause go by.

"I'll bring you takeout from somewhere," he said.

"I'd rather go out. I need to see some life."

He thought hard. "I've been on the road all day, and you know what would be a big treat . . . Would you be willing to drive?"

"Sure."

"Really?"

"Sure."

"Okay, deal. Where do you want to go?"

"Well, here's the thing. I really want a big, sloppy pasta of some sort, but I also wish you would take me someplace nice, like Soba, even though what I really want tonight is old-fashioned spaghetti. Like Big Jim's."

"Big Jim's tonight, Soba tomorrow, how's that? Okay?"

"That sounds really good."

He plied her with liquor, made sure she was good and full, though he didn't have to push her to eat. The restaurant had two TVs going, and the Steelers preseason game was on, which they watched. Between plays, Freddie talked about five stained glass windows she'd unearthed in a house in Highland Park. She explained how she'd been tapping on walls and *knew* there was space behind the walls. She went outside and studied the brickwork, noting where the quality of the bricks changed slightly. She came back into the house to tap some more. Then very slowly she began ripping walls down. Encased, preserved, with brick on the outside and plaster on the inside, she said, were perfect, glorious stained glass windows that would rival those in a fancy church for detail. These, she explained, were not human figures but scenes—mountains and streams, deer, flowers.

She was comfortable with her body—statuesque, solid, and physically strong. All that goodness showed in the cropped pants and low-cut top—maroon or dark red, he wasn't sure what he would call it. He'd never bought her anything. He wondered if he tried to buy her a top, how to choose, what size to order. Her hair was light brown, tossed back, not so much styled as combed out of her face, and a good idea since she had a pretty face, very regular features and skin with a lot of color. She blushed a lot, which didn't go with the personality she was putting on. He let her talk. He pretended to watch the game from time to time. All the while he planned and planned in his head, thinking of what he would do, of all the things that might go wrong.

Now he was sitting in Freddie's kitchen and smoking. She liked him a lot. Women did. He made them laugh a lot, he opened them up sexually, he played a who's-chasing-whom game for a few months, then he was done with them and he went away and they never minded much—they still liked him. The lasagna woman, Carola, was a bit of an exception.

In high school, college, after—same thing. He lighted down for a night, flew away. And they let him. Most men don't know the truth— women might want to be tied down, but they also equally wanted this other thing: teasing, joking, laughing, sexiness that isn't going to last or cost them anything.

He's slept in Freddie's bed for two nights in a row—a break in his pattern. It feels practically like . . . marriage.

Last night, after Soba, she watched the news with him. She was trying to talk about ice cream, windows, old wallpaper. He shushed her, riveted by what he was seeing. He thought, as he watched, Look at the handyman, let it be the handyman. The thought ran repeatedly under all other thoughts, like a prayer. Now this morning, he's seen the early news and seen his prayers answered beyond his hopes.

Then a few minutes ago there was damned Mick on the phone, all worried that the boy was being mishandled by the police. Mick gave a long-winded explanation about how he knew the guy slightly and the guy was not well. So Todd kept thinking the phrase *damage control;* it was his prayer for the day. That and telling himself *stay easy*—which was more a matter of making others believe it was so.

Pacing in Freddie's kitchen, he thought for a moment he might just get into his car to keep watch over Mick. He could telephone Freddie later when she was awake. Or leave a note.

But then he heard a noise. She was up. Moments later, she was kissing him in the kitchen. And he thought, This is damage control, too.

IT WAS ELEVEN IN THE morning when Colleen Greer, John Potocki, and Artie Dolan dragged into the office. "I want you to watch something," he said. "This way."

He took them to the dark small room that held a DVD player and put in the interview disk. "Just watch. Tell me what you think."

"Where are Coleson and McGranahan?" Dolan asked, but with a tone that suggested he knew.

"They have the day off. They closed this."

"Uh-huh," Dolan said.

Then they watched the DVD. They didn't discuss what they saw in between sections of it, but waited until they'd seen the whole of it.

"All right, now, talk to me," Christie said.

"He did say yes, that he did it," Colleen ventured.

"Did you believe it?"

"I don't know. I wanted to."

"Because?"

"The tension. I wanted him to be able to breathe."

"Hmm. Artie?"

"They must have had something, Coleson and McGranahan. They're okay, usually."

Christie nodded.

Potocki said, "No detail. They were tired, I know, but they didn't get the detail—how he did it, what he saw. They didn't do the quiz."

"You get the A-plus," Christie said.

Colleen and Dolan grumbled at the same time that *of course* there was no detail, that that's *why* they had pointed to the tension of the confession and the fact that the detectives must have had physical evidence.

"They were tired," Christie said. He didn't say that they wanted to hurry it up before he got back to work and rained on their parade.

The idea that his men were trying to escape him made him feel awkward and ogre-ish. "Well, then, let's get the detail. Let's be sure. Artie and I will go to the jail and talk to the kid—why I say kid, I don't know. He's grown, twenty-nine." He shook his head to clear it.

"You were bored on vacation," Colleen teased.

He gave her a sharp look. She clamped her lips. "You and Potocki go back to the neighbors. Meet back here late afternoon, see what we have."

"Autopsy?" Dolan asked.

"Detailed results tomorrow."

"Forensics?"

"Monday, Tuesday."

"How . . . how do you want us to talk to Coleson and McGranahan when they come in Monday—Monday, right? They'll see we've added to their reports."

"I'll talk to them. I'll tell them I insisted on more detail for the hearing. It's on me."

"What do you think of the kid—the suspect?" Potocki asked. "He's supposed to be a bit slow. Sometimes he seems it, sometimes not."

"I agree. I want to meet him, see for myself."

"Surprised you didn't go into the interview last night," Dolan said slyly.

Christie just raised his eyebrows.

"What do you want from the neighbors?" Potocki asked.

"Anything that might reasonably explain this guy's confession. That's A. Then anything that might point a finger to an alternate suspect. That's B. If you come up with a C, that's okay, too. I don't want this going to court with this many holes in it."

WHEN CAL AWOKE, IT was to a voice yelling, "Trays up!" and then a bang and a series of clangs he soon understood as the doors to the cells opening. He sat up in bed. Two men stopped in front of his cell. "You coming?"

"I don't know."

"Got his beauty sleep."

A voice came over the speaker, saying, "You two in front of 205, get out of there. Get moving."

But one of them, a guy with long dreads, didn't hustle off. Instead he spoke toward the ceiling where speakers presumably could pick up his voice: "How's he going to know the drill if we don't tell him? He missed breakfast."

"That's his business. Get going."

The guy with the dreads moved finally, but he called back toward Cal, "A prisoner could starve himself in this place as a protest and nobody would know to save his life."

Suddenly a man who seemed to be a guard stood in front of Cal's cell. "You want to eat, the mess is downstairs, see."

Cal was hungry, but he didn't want to be around so many people. He peered out at the hallway and the stairs to the bottom floor of the pod. The process last night took hours, and by the time he had got here, he hardly looked at it.

"Come on," the guard said.

Cal tripped out to the corridor. The guard stepped aside, then moved to behind him. He went down a set of stairs made of netted steel. The sounds—the harsh metal sounds of everything—bothered him, especially in his bad ear, which hummed.

"See that there line. You get in line. How come you have your watch?"

"They said I could."

"I wouldn't leave it out of my sight if I was you."

"Oh. Keep it on me?"

"If I was you. Your girl give it to you?"

He shook his head. His mother had actually given it to him for Christmas a year and a half ago. The sentiment he felt about it came from imagining her choosing it, wanting something of quality for him. It was the year he was striking out on his own, buying his place.

Cal took his place in line, third from the last. He picked up his tray.

The guy behind him said, "What did you did?"

He turned slightly to take in the long braids and the wily smile of the same young man who had urged him to eat. He didn't say anything.

"You ain't going to answer. That's bad manners. Bad manners get you trouble."

"Nothing."

"Right," the guy laughed. "Least you know what you supposed to say. Some people already saying you totally green."

Last night is a blur. He remembers coming in through a garage and having to sit in the boxy chair he thought would electrocute him just like that. Right. Yes. The man who worked it just kept telling him to sit tight, but some woman told him, "Think of it like an X-ray. We're checking out your insides."

When the episode with the chair was over, he told her he still didn't understand.

She relented. "Guns, knives, razors, drugs. Hidden anything."

He held out his hands.

"Right. Clean as the day you were born."

Yes, he does remember. There were rooms with people peering out at every turn. Some were waiting to be arraigned, as he was; some were waiting to be released. Everybody was curious, looking at him. There was a big desk, like at a school or a . . . hospital with workers behind it. They took his photo. They took his fingerprints.

Yes. No blackouts. He can remember. They made him sit in one of those rooms with a bunch of other people. He tried to listen to everything to figure out what the officers were doing. Checking arrest history. Checking fingerprints. Checking his name. He was pretty sure they said to each other he wasn't in the system, some phrase like that.

Now he looks at the men in line ahead of him. What did they do to land in here? Not just drunkenness and fighting and drug possession. These guys up here on his pod looked rough.

They all wore red uniforms just as he did.

Right. Last night, before the harsh soap and delousing liquid, the man who issued uniforms tried to take his watch. He lied and said it was worth only thirty bucks, so they let him keep it. He remembers.

Now Cal got his tray and sat down at the only seat he could see at a quick glance. There were small white metal tables around the pod floor—each seated four men. The man sitting directly across from Cal was middle-aged, white, or looked white, and he was neat looking about his person, and alert, but at second glance that alertness was the nasty sort. His eyes glittered. His smile was mean. He said, "Nice watch."

Cal didn't answer. Lunch was two hot dogs on a bun, a pile of greasy fries, and some kind of Jell-O thing that seemed to have fruits tumbled in it. Cal began on the meal, planning to eat it all because he wasn't at all sure he wanted to come out of his cell for dinner. For a long time now, he'd been a solo guy, doing everything on his own. All these people talking and looking at him made anxiety rise in him. It took the form of a ball of anger and nervousness making its way up his digestive tract, fighting the food that was on its way down.

"So this is the badass came in last night?" The question came from the man to his right. He was large, pale, and sloppy, with messy long hair.

The man who had commented on his watch said, "Can't you tell?" The two laughed.

"He doesn't want to talk," said the guy with the dreads, passing. "I tried him."

"That's Levon," said the man across from him, pointing. Cal could see Levon went to sit with other African American men. There were significantly fewer white guys here, no surprise.

"I'm Sidney," the man continued. "This here joker next to me is Boreski. Some guy named Shiron is going to come up to you sooner or later and ask what you need to buy. Whatever you buy, I get half or the whole. I watch out for you. That's all you need to know for today. Otherwise you'll be overwhelmed."

The two men laughed.

There was a lot of noise, but Cal was pretty sure he heard Sidney ask, "You ever think you'd end up here?"

"No," he said.

"And we know already: You didn't kill that chick."

Cal shrugged his shoulders.

"You don't think you're better than anybody else, or do you?" Boreski asked. " 'Cause that doesn't go down real good."

Cal thought, I am in grade school all over again and I am going to be beaten.

"You can tell him your secrets," Boreski said to Sidney. "This guy don't talk for anything."

Cal liked hot dogs. These were not particularly good—he wasn't sure why, maybe something about the way they cooked them. In spite of the fact that they didn't taste particularly good, he kept eating. He looked forward to downing the Jell-O and getting back to his cell. The whole place reminded him of a gray playroom for oversized children with its two TVs mounted up high and the "easy" chairs made of blue plastic and the sets of white tables and metal chairs for everything else.

"See all them buttons," Boreski pointed. In one corner a guard sat behind a large station with a computerized console that had a thousand buttons. "Colonel could pick you and push a button and kill you if he wanted, just like that. Gas your cell."

He nodded. They laughed. It almost seemed true.

No need for batons or guns.

When he sat on his cot, not ready to lie down, his stomach in knots, he tried to think about Cassie Price. What was her life about, the parts he didn't know? When she came home Thursday, day before yesterday, she had been drinking. Even if he hadn't guessed about the drink, she didn't hide it. She said, "Oh, Cal, I'd better get something to eat." She was not even quite to the porch when she turned around to look at the alley. Was she looking at the gray car going by? Was this the person who hurt her in love?

He can't remember exactly everything she said. Why can't he remember that part? Did he black out later in the middle of the night? Did he hurt her? If he did, he deserves to die in hell, anything they do to him, he deserves it. If he could reverse time, he would choose to die rather than hurt her. The battle in his mind makes him leap up, move around in a tiny circle, trying to remember something about the middle of the night, anything. He hears a voice on the speaker system but pays no attention until there's the sound of his door opening. The same officer is there. "I'm the escort. You hear me? Visitor. You're going to the interview room. Move it. Christ, these idiots."

POTOCKI WAS RELIEVED he hadn't been put on computer today and would be out among people, working with Colleen. So, out for the afternoon, they did one of the things they did best— grabbed a lunch to eat in the car before they talked to the people of Parkview, Child, Swinburne, and Dawson streets. The lunch they grabbed was from the Original, the O, a place that had once long ago been a tiny hot dog shop known for its "dirty hot dogs"—you didn't want to think about them, you simply wanted to enjoy—but was now a huge place, expanded so many times that the signs now advertised everything from pizza to cheese steaks to veal parm sandwiches.

Potocki knew that Colleen Greer, in what she referred to as her youth, had eaten the veal parm sandwiches, but now she made hex signs with her fingers when he asked if she was going to order one. She counted off what was wrong with them: oily veal, tons of cheese, thick white bun, a mound of fries so dense it must have come from ten potatoes and could easily feed ten people.

After parking illegally, they went into the hot, already crowded place. The clientele always consisted of a few students and many people who either already knew or would soon know the jail system— long greasy hair, track marks, the whole ball of wax. "Why did we want this?" she asked Potocki.

"Fast, I think. And a memory of when we were young and could handle it."

They each ordered a single hot dog with lots of stuff on, skipped the fries, and promised each other not to do it again soon.

They ate in the car on the way to *lower* lower Oakland.

"Together or split?" Potocki asked. He was driving today.

"Let's see how we do together. If we run out of time, split."

This conversation, like most they had, carried a subtext of being about their personal relationship, but, as usual, they only heard the impact once the words were out of their mouths. They had agreed to pause, to examine their relationship as they worked together, to *decide* if they wanted to see each other intimately, and *if* so, to announce it to Christie, who would insist they split up as partners.

This was a hard decision in that they really liked being partners. They had a blast working together. The big problem was, they were also attracted to each other. For Potocki, it was a decision already made. He wanted her in his bed. Or to be in her bed. He wanted to wake up and have breakfast with her, to snuggle on a couch in front of a TV at night, to go out to a romantic dinner with candles and expensive good food, to go on vacations. Even though it meant giving up the days together.

She was deciding.

She looked great today. She always stood and sat tall, as if stretching herself. Good posture was half of attractiveness, and she knew it. Once they watched some sort of award show together on TV and she pointed out how many women sank their chests in and rounded their shoulders, as if ashamed they had breasts even though their clothes hardly covered them. She pointed out how many men led with a paunch or a forward-thrusting head. She said, "Look at Cary Grant in his movies. The way he stood. The way he wore his clothes. Plumb line from the tip of his head to the heels of his feet."

In the car, she opened her notes to use as a plate beneath her.

The area they were supposed to canvass consisted of similar small, modest brick houses with cement front porches, tiny front lawns, and awnings (mostly aluminum, some cloth); inside they all had living rooms, dining rooms, kitchens on the first floor, and two or three bedrooms on the second, everything sized by builders during the twenties and thirties—small squares, not at all spacious. The backyards would also be scaled to this modest idea of home ownership.

"God, I love a hot dog," Colleen said. "You know what I read? Even

Marcella Hazan loves a good hot dog. Can you believe it? So much for gourmet cooking, huh?"

He finished his own with a flourish of crumpled napkin. "About done?"

"Um, yeah."

" 'Cause here we are."

They consulted the list.

Cal Hathaway had worked for three families on Dawson and also for the Orthodox church there. Four households on Parkview. One on Swinburne. Two on Child Street.

They started with Dawson. These four jobs had all been painting work—outside windows and doors, mostly, some porch railings, in one case the porch cement; the other Dawson job was the inside walls in the basement social hall of the church. The first place the detectives visited had three screaming children and a woman who looked like she wanted to bag it and leave town. She said, "Yeah, he painted our stuff. I can't get over letting a killer near my kids." She appeared to stop to reconsider this. "I don't want to be a broken record. You hear it all the time: 'He didn't seem the type.' Well, he didn't. So that just shows how you don't know."

"Did you know the victim?" Colleen asked her.

"Not at all."

"You know anything about the accused?" Potocki had chosen his words carefully.

"Just he told me he was partially deaf. I thought he was retarded when he didn't hear me, but he wasn't."

"How long have you lived here?"

"Twenty-five years."

The detectives moved on to a second house. There was nobody home.

They went to a third. Husband and wife were both home and eager to talk about Cal. "Painted. He did real good," the wife said. "And he was cheap."

They dittoed all that the first woman had said.

"How long have you lived here?"

"Just three years."

"How do you feel about living where a lot of students rent?"

"That part is hard. But we bought through the Own Oakland program. The price was unbeatable."

"What's Own Oakland?"

"Oh. It's like a clean-up-Oakland program. Get rid of slum land-lords. Have real people live in the houses. Families. People who take care of their properties."

"I've heard of it," Potocki said. He tried to come up with a name. "Who runs it?"

"Well, there's the real estate company we worked with. Paul Wesson Realty. They advertise they're part of Own Oakland."

"That's it. Paul Wesson. Thanks."

They left and consulted their lists.

"Swinburne?"

"I want to see the church first," Colleen said. "You think anybody will be there?"

"Let's give a holler."

It turned out to be easy. There were two women cleaning the church. The altar was as glorious as Colleen had guessed it would be, all gold and icons and stained glass. "Orthodox. See, they put that cross with the little bar at a slant, and they're very big on pictures of the saints."

"I see that," Potocki said. He was studying her hair, which he often did. She had one of those looks like, should it be combed or did she mean it this way? He knew her well enough to be sure it was purposeful. He'd seen her fluff up the blond tufts so they looked casual, quirky. Cheerful hair.

The cleaning women pointed the way to the church office, which could be accessed through several doorways leading to the rear of the property. They said the priest was in.

The priest was a tall, good-looking man with a beard and a bit of weight on him. He wore black pants and a black shirt and his clerical collar, but on his feet were white running shoes. He was going over something that looked like a spreadsheet and probably was.

"Detective Potocki, Detective Greer," Potocki said. "May we have a word with you?"

"I didn't do it." The priest smiled.

"We'll be the judges of that!"

Everybody had a nice laugh. Then they got down to business. When the priest, Father Charles Mansour, heard that it was about the murder of the law student, he sobered. "You know, the boy you arrested worked for us," he said.

"That's why we're here. Anything you can tell us?"

"I knew so little about him. He was very likable. Very . . . humble."

"Did you ever see him lose his temper?"

"No."

"Did you ever know him to black out or have memory problems?"

"No," he said, disheartened. "He's in jail?"

"Yes."

"I'll make inquiry. If he doesn't have a priest, I'll visit him."

"What's giving you the headache?" Potocki asked, pointing to the spreadsheets.

"We got roofing problems. We got flooring problems. And our parishioners don't have extra to give in a lot of cases."

Potocki nodded sympathetically. At least the priest didn't seem to think the Lord took care of everything.

"Thanks for including me," the priest said.

And that was that.

They learned on Swinburne and Child streets that Cal could also build a deck and replace a window sash. They examined the work. It looked good and it had continued to be cheap.

Child Street was where Cal's own house was. His next-door neighbor was a man sporting a wife-beater and suspenders.

"I didn't talk to him," the man said proudly. "He minded his business, I minded mine."

"How long have you lived here?"

"Ten, twelve years."

"Did you purchase through Own Oakland?"

"What's that?"

"Never mind, then. It's connected to a realty company."

"Oh, I don't know about that."

The man reminded Potocki of a fellow he'd seen on TV who feared anything labeled liberal. "It's all gittin' like comm'nism," the man said. This man was his brother under the skin.

"How long did he live here?"

"I think almost two years."

"Not so long. Police ever been to this house before last Thursday? I know last Thursday they came to search the place—ever before that?"

"Nope. We don't like that kind of thing going on."

"What kind of thing?"

"Searching. Questions. Trouble."

"Nobody does."

"So fry him and let's be done with it."

"We know you're kidding, sir," Potocki said. "Take care now."

Colleen poked him appreciatively as they walked away.

They walked to their fleet car, which, for this canvassing job, they kept parking and reparking.

She fluffed up her hair. Potocki smiled at the gesture. They were going to have to land on a decision soon—

Oh, they talked. They talked all the time. He knew things about her. He knew she'd had an abusive uncle who'd assaulted her and tried to rape her. He knew she had never confronted her flaky parents about the time they left her and her brother *with* the horrible uncle. The confrontation was always just around the corner. She avoided it. She knew things about him, too, how confused he'd been when his marriage crumbled.

They'd saved Parkview for last. It was where Cassie Price lived and where they hoped to get something meaty their boss would like.

They stopped in front of Cassie's house. It was a plain place, well kept, but you had to look past the police tape and the bouquets of flowers and the notes and the children's toys people had placed in front.

"A little something to take across the River Styx," said Potocki.

"I suppose we should read the notes," she grumbled.

"On our exit from the street? In case something new arrives?"

"Fine. I always think it seems wasteful. Give the money to a women's shelter or something. Okay, now, this Iris Mender," Colleen said, reading her notes. "Two down from this place. It'd be that one with the crowded porch. Mender employed Cal, and she talked to the police that day. Let's see her."

They parked and approached a modest house that looked pretty much like all the others. They knocked on the door and woke Iris Mender, who was sleeping on the sofa.

CHRISTIE STRUGGLED with it—how to meddle. He was *still* officially on vacation. Coleson and McGranahan were sleeping or out in their yards or playing golf. He decided on phrasing—he would say he was cleaning up a few rough edges. He'd call a squad meeting either tomorrow or Monday. Monday was cleaner. He'd be officially back, Coleson and McGranahan would be on duty, autopsy report would be complete and forensics report begun. Still it made him nervous, working in a kind of limbo. No, he decided suddenly, tomorrow. Get it over with.

He and Dolan went to the Allegheny County Jail while Greer and Potocki talked to Cassie Price's neighbors.

Dolan was his usual chipper self. Today he wasn't dressed formally, just a crisp white polo shirt and sporty pants, not jeans. He carried his dignity in his walk. He said, and it wasn't much of a joke, "Fifty percent of these guys are going to know us. Watch out for projectiles."

They explained their business to a sallow guy at the desk who did nothing to disguise a mood both sluggish and grim. He called for an escort to take them to the interview room on Cal Hathaway's pod and for the escort on that pod to bring Cal to them.

A murmur that was surely the beginning of some idle speculative gossip started up as soon as they came in sight of a few cells.

Christie wondered all over again if he could have the strength of mind to make a life out of a prison sentence or if he would simply go mad.

Dolan said, as if hearing him, "Unfortunately it's the ones who don't know how to spend a day who end up here."

Christie had to laugh at their like-mindedness. They entered the interview room and sat at the small metal table that was bolted to the floor.

Soon Cal came in. He was shaking, clearly terrified. He dropped into a chair.

Christie began carefully, "I know you went through all this yesterday, but we need to keep very good records. Let's try to get comfortable and take our time. I'm Commander Christie. This is Detective Dolan. We're part of the same squad as the guys who talked to you. Understand? We need to ask you some questions."

"Okay."

"First of all, are you doing all right?"

"Not really."

"Why is that?"

"People here want to talk. I don't get into that."

"I don't blame you," Christie said.

Dolan added, "You have to do a little bit just to keep them off you, right?"

Cal nodded.

"So," Christie said, "I just want to start with something simple, but direct and important to your situation. The discrepancy. You said one thing, then another. Last night you said yes, you had killed Cassie Price. Then later, when you were booked, you said no, you hadn't. Can you explain that?"

"No."

"Why did you change your mind?"

"I don't know." Both detectives paused, waiting. They did the twelve count. When they were about to give up, Cal said, "I don't know what to think. What if I did?"

A little shiver went through Christie. "Are you saying you don't know if you did?"

"Yes."

"How can that be?"

"It's hard to explain."

"Drink? Were you drinking?"

"I don't drink. I'm not against it, I just don't, unless I go to some event and everybody has a beer."

"What kind of event would that be?"

"There aren't too many. Like there was one with the company that sold me my house for all the Oakland owners. It was a party. I handed out my work fliers. I had a beer there. I just never think to buy it."

"Did you have anything to drink last Thursday night?"

"No. I'm sure I didn't."

They let some time go by again.

"See, I used to have blackouts. That's the problem. I haven't had any for a long time. But what if I had one and didn't know I did?"

"I see," Christie said. "When is the last one you remember?"

"Two years out of high school. I had two in high school, and then the two after that, but then I thought they were gone. For good."

Christie looked to Dolan, who said, "If you did have one, let's see, you would have walked over to Cassie Price's place? Or what? Driven?"

"I just live a street away. I would never drive. But why would I go there?"

"Can you think of a reason?"

"If I got mixed up and thought I should be at work. I don't think I ever mixed up day and night before. But they asked me if the gloves were my gloves and they were. They were mine." He was still shaky. He looked at his hands as if they wore the gloves.

"That is puzzling. You keep the gloves with you, then?"

"No, no, well, I might sometimes, but these old ones I just left there. The weather, it's been dry, and I was working on her porch."

Christie gave Dolan the nod to speak.

Dolan said, "Tell me, what kind of thing about her would make you angry? About Cassie?"

Cal heaved a big sigh and knuckled his mouth. Christie studied the fellow. He was not bad looking. Just the slightest bit unusual—the color of his eyes, green he supposed, and something about the way the features went together that was arresting. He flushed, but it didn't seem to be Dolan's question making him angry—he didn't look angry; the guy had blushed before in what seemed like typical shyness.

"Nothing. She was a friendly person. I never got angry with her."

"Never?" Dolan asked.

"No."

"This is a puzzle, then," Dolan said lightly. "Unless you were in love with her and she didn't love you back, that kind of thing. That can cause anger."

Cal sat straighter. "I liked her. I felt . . . love for her. I worried about her. I never thought of her as loving me back."

"Why was that?" Dolan asked in his honey voice.

"She loved somebody else."

"How do you know? She told you?"

"I saw her crying. I . . . saw that."

"I've seen some guys," Dolan said easily, "that can't stand a woman crying. They need to, you know, stop it. Did you maybe feel that way?"

"No."

"Hm. Who was she in love with?"

"I don't know. She didn't say."

"You have any ideas?"

"No. But she came home . . . that day, Thursday, she'd been drinking. I never saw her like that. And . . . there was a car going down the alley, kind of checking on her."

"Oh. You didn't tell this to the others. Why?"

"It's easier to talk to you. They . . . I didn't feel . . . it was right to let people know she was unhappy in love."

"How did you know she'd been drinking?"

"The way she walked and held on to things. And she said, 'Don't ever drink margaritas,' or something like that."

"Why did you not say these things before? About her drinking and being with someone?"

"It felt private. She kept it private."

"I see. You really did like her."

"Yes."

"What kind of car?"

"Um, not sure. Small to medium. That's all I saw."

"Would you do us a favor?" Christie pushed a legal pad over. "Write me a description of the car. Or draw it. Either way."

He didn't draw. He wrote, *small or compact, hatchback shape, gray or silver.*

They watched him take a pen, write, hand things back.

"Tell us again, where did you see this car?"

"In the alley. Back of the house. Checking, probably, did she get parked and up to the house okay."

"You didn't get a good look at it?"

"I didn't see it at first. I was watching Cassie. Then I saw somebody go kind of slow, then fast. That was it."

"Hmmm," Christie said. "We might be back. We appreciate your cooperation. When do you see your lawyer?"

"I don't know anything about that. Do you know?"

"Probably not till Monday, but we'll look into it. There'll be all kinds of people coming to see you. That priest you worked for—he said he might pop up. If you like him, you can put him on your list."

"I like him. I don't know anything about a list."

"They'll give you one."

When Christie and Dolan left, they retraced their steps with the corrections officer going ahead of them. In a quiet voice, Christie asked his partner, "What did you see?"

Dolan said, "He's either really really slick or he's potentially innocent. He's got me thinking about this other guy and the margaritas. Plus. He's either faking it or he's actually left-handed."

"Ditto." They'd seen the close-up photos of the dead woman. The suggestion the photos made and the coroner corroborated right off was that the perp was right-handed.

In silent agreement they shut up for the rest of the walk in case the corrections officer was listening in.

When they got to the lobby, they found the grim desk guard arguing with a woman, stating, "Those are the rules. Accept it. See these detectives? They just saw him." The desk guard turned to them. "She says she has to be sure her son's okay. He's okay, right? This is the mother."

She was a very neat woman, dressed in gray pants and a purple jacket with a bright white top under it. Cal's green eyes had come from her. She looked at the two detectives pleadingly. "I don't have much time off. I need to see him. I called and they said visiting was on Saturday."

"Whoever told you," the guard said, "forgot to tell you he has to fill out paperwork for who can visit him. Nobody did that yet."

"Tell you what," Christie told the man. "She was next on my list to interview. We can go sit outside with her while you get the paperwork done."

"Today?"

"I would if I were you. It's not onerous. It's simple. It's human to let her see her son."

The guard's jaw dropped.

"It won't take you a minute," Christie persisted. He waited until the man began to pull out paperwork. Christie wasn't trying to be a saint. This simple intervention had clearly already bought the mother's cooperation and gratitude. It was two o'clock.

IT WAS TWO O'CLOCK when Greer and Potocki woke Iris Mender.

Iris Mender was a slightly plump woman whose hair—not too recently dyed a medium brown—exposed gray roots. She insisted she didn't mind being awakened because sooner or later she hoped to get her sleep patterns back to normal.

"You want some iced tea?" she asked, bleary eyed.

"No, thanks, but you go ahead and have some. Take your time."

"It might perk me up," she said, going to the kitchen.

Greer and Potocki looked around her pleasantly disordered place. They sat together on one of two sofas, the one she hadn't been sleeping on, after they moved a sweater and a few pieces of mail aside. On the table in front of them was an empty plate with crumbs, several boxes of chocolate, and plenty of newspapers and magazines. Not surprisingly, the common sedative, TV, had probably put Mender to sleep. It was on, tuned to a movie station. Karl Malden being a priest. A good one.

Iris Mender returned to the living room. "I did talk to some police yesterday. Did they tell you?"

"Oh, yes, we read the report of the interview. We thought it was interesting that you knew both the victim and the accused. You apparently hired him to do some work."

Mender worked to finger-comb her tousled hair and to bring herself fully awake. "I . . . had him replace all my windows. See?" She pointed. "I liked him a lot. I don't know what to say."

"Did you know of any relationship between him and the deceased?" Potocki asked.

"She was only two houses over." Mender pointed to her left. "I could see he was working there. From my back porch and whatnot, from my window, too. That's all I know. It's a terrible thing. Are you sure he's the one?"

They hesitated and checked with each other. Colleen took the question and rolled it in police-speak. "Let's just say the investigation is ongoing. These things are complex and take a long time to dot all the i's. We need to eliminate certain other possibilities. Do you have any idea of anyone else who would want to hurt her?"

She made a series of faces as she worked through the question. "No."

"You hesitated. Why?"

"Would you like to sit outside? I have a glider."

"Sure!" Colleen said. "I always liked a glider."

When they were settled, Potocki on a lawn chair, Iris Mender said, "It may be I'm a little crazy. I know that. I have dreams that seem so real." She sighed.

This is an epidemic, Colleen thought, people not knowing sleep from waking. "Is this about the gray car following her? You told our other detectives."

"No. I was right out here. I saw that. I know I saw that."

"Show us where?'

She pointed down to the corner to her right, saying, "Came from the boulevard, *she* did, and then this other car."

"Who was driving it?"

"A man."

"Can you describe him?"

"No beard or anything like that. Just a guy."

"You said there was something else? Is this about the black car?"

"Yes. That's the part that was like a dream. I didn't tell the others everything. I hate it when people tell me I'm nuts."

"What was it you saw? Just tell us again."

"There was a black car in the alley in the middle of the night. Behind her place. I couldn't see the car until it left, but I saw a man going to the car. The only thing is I only saw him at the last minute and I can't swear where he came from."

At night, and two houses over. And maybe coming from somewhere else. Colleen asked anyway. "Could you see the man clearly?"

"This is why I hate to say it. Why I didn't tell the others. He looked sparkly. Kind of like an astronaut. All white."

Colleen tried not to look surprised.

"And you feel sure this same person is the one who drove the car away?"

"He went around behind her garage and I guess got in the car there. But I could see the same something that reminded me of an astronaut in the car window."

"Describe it for us. And the car. As well as you can."

Colleen felt happy. She liked wild improbability, the chill down her spine, the puzzle to be solved.

•   •   •

ELINOR HATHAWAY sat on a bench outside the jail next to Christie. Dolan stood, so as not to crowd her. She kept looking inside, no doubt to see if there was any activity on the paperwork.

Which there appeared to be. Christie said, "Let's be hopeful."

She turned searching eyes on him. "You said you wanted to talk to me."

"If you would. I was wondering, could you give us some history—where your son worked before he started doing handyman jobs, where he lived, that kind of thing."

"He lived with me over in East Liberty until two, almost two years ago. Then he told me he wanted to go off on his own. I was glad for the most part. This was the right thing for a young man to do. He'd been saving some money. I'd been saving, always did. He wanted a house, he said. He told me he always wanted to fix up a place. He even thought he might fix up places to sell once he got established—you know, how people buy up properties and work on them, then turn them over. That was his idea."

"Had he always worked on houses for a living?"

"No. He was always handy, doing things for me and for other people. No, he worked in a restaurant for a couple of years out of high school. Got tired of it, and then for a while he helped with the grounds at the place I work—for Mr. Connolly. He was good at it, too. This one landscaper wanted to hire him permanently, but he didn't go for it."

"Why?"

"He just wanted to be on his own, not have any kind of boss. That was that."

"Did you know the woman, the deceased?" Christie asked.

"No, I never heard of her. I gather he worked for her."

"Did he never mention her to you?"

"No."

"Who else is he close to? His father?"

"His father left when Cal was two. He's dead now."

"Can you tell me some more about that?"

"I asked him to leave because of his drinking. I couldn't take it, watching the money drain away and him falling apart like that."

"Did he leave when you asked?"

"Oh, yes, he didn't give me a fight. He couldn't beat the alcohol. He died not long after." She seemed sad.

"So Cal never got to know him?"

"No. Two-year-olds don't remember much, it turns out. Cal's father was nice when he wasn't drinking. That was the shame of it."

Christie studied her, puzzled. Something about her voice, her syntax, kept making him think she was African American, but she was light-skinned and green-eyed. "Was his father white or black?"

"White." She considered Christie's question. "Did Cal tell you he's got African American blood? He sometimes likes to explain that. He's a quadroon."

"No, he didn't mention it."

"My mother." She said this and everything with a tightly held dignity.

"About the idea that he might have blacked out. Can you tell us anything about that? Is there an illness in his background?"

"Other boys were the illness." Then she explained about her mother running down the street when she heard about the beating he took, the slow medics, the concussion. Dolan paced back and forth, distressed and moved. Christie found himself losing his objective edge, wishing things would somehow go the boy's way for once, the mother's way.

THE FOUR DETECTIVES met back at Christie's office at five. They had caught up midafternoon by phone and then gone off to dig at other sources.

"Do Coleson and McGranahan know we're on this case yet?" Colleen asked uncomfortably.

"I called them." Christie looked through the others, then past them. "It wasn't easy. You can be sure they're on the phone to each other. Where are we now?"

Artie Dolan spoke first. "Just came from East Liberty where he used to live. Nothing. No violence. No prior fuss of any kind. Everybody liked him, all that."

Christie said, "I talked to the behavioral people. They're going in to see him Monday. Psychological portrait is going to be important. The guy was battered badly in his childhood but shows no anger. What's it about?"

Dolan worried the palm of his hand, shook his head. "Sainthood, I'd say."

Colleen told about the late-afternoon visit she and Potocki had made to Paul Wesson Realty. "He wasn't there. His secretary told us he's been at this cleaning-up-Oakland project for about five years. There were signs all around the place. OWN OAKLAND. CLEAN IT UP. TAKE BACK THE CITY. GOOD HOMES FOR GOOD PEOPLE. She told us where the guy lives, so we went to see him. Here's the thing. It gets really interesting. He sold to Cal Hathaway. He sold to a bunch of people, but Cal Hathaway was once of them. So was Cassie Price."

Christie and Dolan perked up. "There's a connection?" Christie asked.

"Connection? Yes. This Own Oakland project is part of an urban renewal initiative that Connolly works on. Maybe the whole law firm gets behind it. For sure the young Connolly does. He was into it as congressman, then as state senator. He's big into public service and attention to cities. So what happens is Wesson sells these places for pretty low prices on the condition that the owners will stay and improve the properties. He said Connolly recommends him to anybody who might even be thinking of buying a house."

There was a collective "hmmm."

"What does he do for Connolly?"

"Money for the campaign? Status? I didn't get the impression it was anything sneaky."

"Potocki?"

"At the risk of sounding naive, Wesson seemed like an eager beaver. Like he'd discovered doing good. He straight out admired Connolly."

"Tomorrow morning at eight," Christie said. "I'll call everybody in. Let's get some collective wisdom going. Forensics won't be ready with details until Monday's meeting, but we'll have some basics."

AT NOON ON THAT DAY, Mike Connolly had taken his phone to one of the chairs on the deck near the pond. He was sick of talking to people, which he had done all morning, and he fantasized, briefly, of throwing the phone into the water, but he didn't do things like that. He had had so many instructions to stay away, to remove himself from the mess, that he felt almost invisible. The drink hadn't helped. Or the lack of sleep.

On a normal Saturday he would have worked in his home office or gone into the firm or traveled to Harrisburg, but not today. His life was on hold. Elinor brought him lunch, a thick chicken salad sandwich with a side of chips. On the tray was also a tall glass of iced tea.

"You've got to eat."

"Thank you. But . . . go home. You don't have to be here."

"I wanted to do a few things here. Now those things are done and I'm going to go see to my son," she said. "Mrs. Connolly said to tell you she ordered flowers to the girl's hometown, the funeral home."

"Thank you."

He watched Elinor go back to the house. He couldn't imagine how she held on, working, when her son, whom she adored, was in jail.

He ate the sandwich gratefully, realizing how much he had needed to put food in his stomach. Outdoors, in his private patch of natural world, he entered a different zone, felt a Zen-like acceptance. The trickle of water from the fountain he had installed at the pond comforted him.

It was going to hit eighty today, though the sun didn't feel direct. It was already moving toward its autumn position. After he ate, he walked over the deck and down the path through the trees to the pool. The twins were in the water, horsing around. Monica sat at the side of the pool, using a pink marker on a huge textbook. He felt uncertain about everything. Go upstairs and make himself work? Play with the kids? He dropped into the water. He was still exhausted from not sleeping and not at all happy he'd put so much drink in him.

The cool water jolted him. His limbs went almost numb as he moved into a water-tread. In a moment the twins were on him, grabbing him around the waist, dunking him. He slithered away and swam a lap, making them chase him. They were fast, sloppy swimmers, and they caught up to him easily. He turned quickly and thrashed back to the deep end. They yelped with pleasure.

One more time, for the boys, he told himself. He pushed off, swam back to the shallow end, and let them grab at him for a while. They wanted rough play, but he hugged them tight and kissed their wet hair.

"Are you depressed?" Christopher asked.

"No. Sad. I'm sad for the young woman who died."

"Did you know her?"

"Not really. Just to hand projects to, to say hello. Still, she worked for us."

"Did you know Elinor's son did it?"

He nodded.

"Why?"

"We don't know."

With that he climbed out and toweled off.

Monica asked, "What's next?"

"Nothing. Thanks for sending the flowers. I'm allowed to go tomorrow. Up to wherever she's being laid out." The boys listened to his phrasing. "Will you go with me?"

"Yes. Of course."

Then he walked back, keeping the towel around his shoulders, to his secluded spot near the pond. Again his limbs were heavy as he dropped, almost out of control, to the chaise. He closed his eyes. He thought, I can't give her anything now, except that I can think of her.

Lying there, he could see the scenes in the office so clearly. The first kisses. The way she walked. The way he heard her explaining in the outer office about the sublet she had taken with a student from the business school. She said she wished she could afford her own place because the roommate was not a neatnik like she was. "Oh," the others said right on cue, turning to him. "You ought to tell her about Wesson Realty."

So he did.

She'd been so happy.

She let him know she was happy when they were alone. Publicly . . . no, she acted aloof. "I'm on it," she said, all the while hand-numbering the pages of something she was working on. "I'll check it out."

"You have to commit for ten years. That's part of the low price. There are some legal loopholes. Marriage. Major job offers."

"It's worth checking out."

What could explain how good she was at dissembling in public? A natural talent. "You're a possible . . . politician," he teased in private. "I see a future for you."

No, she said, she wanted to do public service law. In private she was utterly frank with him and not always so cheerful. If he'd known in advance that she really was a homeschooled, dyed-in-the-wool virgin, would he have continued? He wanted to tell himself no, but the answer was yes. He simply liked her. He felt good around her, more than good, invincible and worthy.

Finally—the lunch, the swim, the sun did its magic on his body and he slipped into a half-sleep, the best kind, a drowsy in and out that he had no control over. In this state, he both thought about Cassie and dreamed about her, sketches of dreams in which she was still alive. The memory, when he was half-awake, was of their long flirtation. He got her to come in to work in the evenings, and when the last person left, he brought her into his office. They held each other, murmured about not doing anything, all the while building the arousal to an aching that made him feel alive, young, something of who he used to be. He asked her into his office in daytime, too, but only briefly, and she always left carrying work. Oh, he knew she was a good fake—she told him she sometimes grumbled about the work he gave her or looked perplexed and asked for help. But in those few minutes together, they kissed and touched, more and more.

In late June he said, "Would you meet me for dinner on the road, away from all this?"

"Yes."

"No. I must be going crazy. Someone might see me. My mug's been in the paper. Would you pick up dinner and meet me in a motel?"

"Yes."

"Something might happen."

"Yes."

He knew she was ready. He did not want to believe it was her first time—nobody got to be twenty-three these days without—but it was her first time. The responsibility he felt terrified him. He thought, No more, never again, let her go, let her down easy. Put it behind me.

In his first half-sleep, in the dream that he manufactured, she was still alive. He was happy to see her, tried to say something about the scare she'd given them all. She smiled slyly and walked away toward something—a door? In a motel? She looked like herself, totally, very alive. Loose curly hair, brown he always thought of it, but in some light it seemed almost blond. Trim. Thin, some would say. He followed. He said, "Don't run." She said, "I know we have to be careful, but I want to stay in a better place." The dream got more abstract with a long scene of puzzlement, faces making expressions, his trying to read himself and her, and all the while, time passing. "A good hotel," she said finally.

He woke with a jolt.

Christopher was standing in front of him, holding out a bottle of water. "Mom says you're getting dehydrated."

"I guess I am. Thanks."

His watch on the table beside him told him it was very late afternoon. His son climbed onto the chair with him. The wet swimsuit and damp skin on the boy sent a chill to Connolly's warm sun-drenched body. He uncapped the water, drank a bit, and then embraced the boy. Slowly their temperatures merged. He kissed his son's hair again.

"Why do you always kiss me in the hair?"

"The head. I'm kissing your very good brain. Your alertness and awareness."

"Oh."

"If you don't like it, I'll kiss your cheek."

"Head is better."

"Okay."

Each time he was really kissing his son's heart, a long spiraling kiss, head to heart, the heart that was fixed and, knock wood, would be fine now forever. Christopher was still a little smaller than his brother, a little more sentimental, but in athletics and in school, he was caught up. No more gray skin, eyes, nail beds. No more congested lungs.

After the surgery, Connolly had sat with his son all day every day, playing games, reading stories, or watching videos. He kissed his son's head again.

They were going to be close for life, having gone through that.

After a while he caught himself in an aborted snore. Christopher wriggled out of his arms. He felt empty for a while but wrapped his arms around his own body until sleep came again.

It got to be six o'clock, in and out of sleep. The political bosses hammered directions at him in his dreams. It was like being in a roomful of fathers. Cassie entered and exited the room; for some reason she was serving food, like a waitress. She seemed serious about doing the job well. He kept wanting to say something to her, but the others didn't notice her at all.

When he woke again, it was to Monica saying, "I hate to wake you, but dinner is on soon. And you're going to have a hell of a night tonight if you keep sleeping the day away."

He stretched out an arm for her to pull him up off the chaise.

FREDDIE OWNS TWO vehicles—her Dodge truck for work and her little Sebring.

"Let me use your Sebring today," he had said, back in bed in the morning.

"Why?"

"Because I want to see how it rides. I might want to buy one."

"Don't kid me."

"I'm not. There's some pressure on me to buy American. I don't care. It's just a car. If it breaks down, I'll rent some other one."

"But there might not *be* any more Sebrings. It's an endangered species."

"Okay, make me beg you."

"Fine. Take it."

"You can drive mine. If you're not in the truck."

"I'm in the truck until about one. Then I need to shower and go shopping."

"So use mine for shopping."

"Where are you going?"

"Harrisburg."

"This murder?"

"Among other things."

"And you won't be—" She did some pantomimed math. "No, of course you won't be back by afternoon."

So he took the Sebring and he thought, Why can't she be a little stupider? Because he felt he'd better put on four hundred miles total or she might notice he came up short. Well, it could be worse. He had his three phones charged up. He could talk to whomever he had to talk to all day long.

The car definitely was American. Loose, cheap, cheerful, and pretending the road wasn't really there and bumpy, not at all like the tight European cars that moved almost arthritically, pridefully. It was all falling to shit, though, all the companies were merging and Europe was getting more American and possibly a little bit of vice versa was going on. But the direction was almost always toward the cheap, the mediocre.

He stopped only for gas, not for anything else. He skipped the turnpike so there would be no tolls to account for. He took Route 22 instead toward Blanchard, a dot in the center of Pennsylvania. It was where she had lived. Population 756. Did it excuse her dumbness? There must have been some worldliness in that town somewhere. Or a television. Or a movie theater. Or a book. It seemed somehow appropriate to go in that direction, where she'd lived, though he couldn't explain it. Not that he'd go the whole way. He'd stop short. Find a country road, some woods.

Funeral in Millheim, Pa. To go or not to go. Probably he'll get orders to go in order to keep an eye on Connolly.

Undo the thing with Freddie. Unlatch. Say work, work, work.

Freddie was nice. Neat and clean. Organized. Big and American and sexy and friendly. That was Freddie. That was Freddie.

His phone was not ringing. One big collective breath was being held all through the party. It would all be okay. He knew how to work it.

After nearly two hours he took an exit. A small country road. Shit. Seen. Passed a guy with a tractor. He had to pretend to be looking at a map on the passenger seat, so no wave of hello would be necessary. Kept going. Found another dirt road. Chose it. Nestled his car into a thicket. Dug with his hands and one of the large spoons from Freddie's kitchen drawer. Then unearthed the paper bag from his briefcase. It held plastic gloves and her wallet and her phone. He put the plastic gloves on. Not able to help himself, he looked inside the wallet again. Driver's license. Photos of her family. God, four beautiful girls. One going down into the dirt.

Shit, shit, shit, shit, shit. He felt his stomach rising and hurried to a different patch of ground to empty it. He wiped his mouth and leaned against a tree.

When he returned to the hole in the ground, he made sure the cell phone was off and dropped it into the grave. He took the cash out of the wallet, a mere thirty-six dollars, and stuffed it in his pocket. Lunch some day. Or give it to someone. Then he made himself drop the wallet into the hole. And he covered everything up.

After he was finished patting down the ground, he imagined a scenario in which he needed the wallet again—or the pictures. He hoped not, but he had to mark the little grave in some way. He studied the trees, then counted his steps to the road where his car was. He used the spoon, scraping and scraping to nick a tree at the edge of the property. Then he retraced his steps, checking his count. The same. He nicked the tree closest to the hole he'd dug. And one more time walked to the car, counting. Good, good. He turned the car around and studied the road carefully, set the trip odometer to zero, and drove out to the dirt road where he'd seen the man driving a tractor. Ha, a name, Shell Pond Road. He could find it again if he needed to. The odometer read 1.7 miles.

He was more careful than Connolly could ever be. Smarter, too. Even better with the ladies—he got away and left them happy after all.

Once he was sure he could return in his sleep, he drove for a while aimlessly, calming himself. When he noted that he'd put enough miles on the car for a trip to Harrisburg, he got back on the same roads he used to come here.

The afternoon was beautiful. Gorgeous.

The money. Might hold prints. He stopped at a gas station that had a bathroom. He tested the toilet to be sure it flushed well. Then he got rid of the money in one quick flush, waited, and when nothing came back up started to throw in the gloves. No. Too dangerous. If there was a clog, someone might remember seeing him. He carried them with him in the brown paper bag for another few miles until he saw a roadside rest stop with a large garbage can. He tossed the bag as if just dumping the remnants and wraps of his lunch. Nobody saw him. Nobody was looking.

Now he had to get his own car back and unwrap himself from Freddie tonight.

FOR ONCE THE CHILDREN are at their mother's house and Marina can have time, precious time. She's going to be teaching in a week, not much, just one course as an adjunct, Acting I, but there's talk that she'll be acting in a production at Pitt as well and coaching the young actors. The butterflies that have been dormant for so long fly crazily at the thought of these upcoming activities. Today, though, tonight, is still vacation, whether Richard knows it or not. He went to work today. She did laundry, unpacking, and then sat in the backyard, polishing her nails, reading, waiting.

At six she hears a series of noises, doors opening and closing, keys dropping, as he makes his way through the house and toward her. "Hey," she says.

He comes out back, looking curious. "What time is it?" He looks at his watch as if it might be broken.

"Because I'm not in the kitchen?"

"I guess," he answers a little sheepishly. "No good smells to greet me."

"That's because we're eating out."

"Oh. Fine." He looks all juiced up, alert, not tired at all.

"You had a good day?"

"I felt useful."

"Can you talk about it?"

"A little." He sat, looked to see if any neighbors were in their yards, and continued in a low voice to tell her of some of the doubts he had about last night's arrest. She listened carefully, admiring him for the care he put into the job even while she resented the voluntary time away from her. "I just want to be sure he doesn't go to Rock-view if he didn't do it."

She shuddered. The hanging, the chair, the needle—they all were wrong, violent, the latter improvements not improvements at all. Yet that young woman had suffered a terrible death, as bad as the noose, the chair, the needle could give her killer, possibly worse with the fear and panic. Shakespeare would say all that was behind her now, all that struggling. Over and over he prized the idea of rest. He must have been an insomniac.

"Where are we going?" her husband asked curiously.

"We're having a date. I'd be happy with Casbah for scaling up. Or Tessaro's. Even Del's if we're going down and dirty."

She watched him consider. Shower and clean shirt? Or well-worn polo and jeans? He was undoing his tie. She let him off the hook. "Del's is fine so long as we're together."

Family togetherness had been the goal in Cape Cod. Neither one of them would have considered leaving the kids in Truro with a takeout of fish sandwiches so that they could go to an intimate dinner. But that left tonight and tomorrow night.

She took his hands, smoothed her thumb along his skin. "Thank you," she said.

"Of course."

They needed a good fight. This was bad, thanking him for noticing her for a few minutes.

POTOCKI AND GREER both stayed late, typing reports, keeping each other company. The clocks ticked, phones stopped ringing, and they were still there.

"Well," Potocki said as they finally walked to their cars, "I'm ready to set a date." Colleen squinted at him. "You know what I'm saying."

She did. They had to make a decision. Every day was fraught with wanting to touch each other. "After this case," she said. "Soon as we're done with Cassie Price, we'll tell Boss to repartner us and we'll—"

"Are you sure?"

"I'm sure."

"This is great. We should celebrate. Tonight."

She had to laugh. She wasn't that good at saying no under normal circumstances, and they'd been building up to this conclusion for a while.

"Come on," he said. "We have control."

"Maybe you do."

"Dinner somewhere."

"A work dinner. Something, you know, low profile. We can talk about the case. So no fault, no guilt." She sure didn't feel like going home and eating alone, and she liked Potocki so much it scared her.

"Two cars." He shook his head. "We are wasteful."

"I know."

But they stood in the lot for a moment and didn't revise the plan. "Okay, what's your pleasure?"

"Del's. I think Del's."

"Del's it is."

A VOICE ON THE loudspeaker says there is trouble in the kitchen and trays are going to be late. Cal thought he wouldn't want dinner, but his stomach is growling, so when the voice on the loud-speaker says, "Trays up," he engages in a short battle with himself, then descends the stairs. He puts himself in line. The guy with the dreads that are partly braids looks frustrated, trying to catch up with him and missing. Levon. Each tray holds meat loaf, mashed potatoes, carrots, cake. His mother would say that's not a summer meal. She talked about light foods and heavy foods, not that he expects the prison cooks to care about any of that. Luckily he has a strong stom-ach. He sits down at the first empty table he sees, and soon after, three black guys join him. The first one to speak is a big guy, bald. "Somebody told us you might be looking for something sweet?"

A panic hits him. What does that mean? What did he do to make the guy ask? He tries hard to think of something to say. The long preparation for a reply seems unbearable to him. He tells him-self, Don't take any shit. If you take it now . . .

"Okay," he says. "Thanks." He takes a piece of cake off the one guy's plate. The three guys look surprised. Then one says, "You ain't that dumb."

"It was a joke," he says. "Here." He puts the cake back.

"You killed that girl," says a third man.

He knows they watch TV all day. He's not sure about newspapers. But there are visitors, like his mother. The word must have spread fast about him. "They say so."

"They got evidence?"

"They must."

"Then you have to prove how they got it, it was wrong. You know, illegal."

This turn toward helpfulness from the third guy is confusing. Cal doesn't want to talk. He wants to eat his mushy meat loaf and go straight back to his cell.

"But only trouble is, this one ain't never going to live that long," says the second guy."

The men snort and guffaw. He doesn't know how to answer. One moment they seem nice, the next minute not. How is he to know?

"Tell me something," the first man asks. Big, bald-headed, and muscular. "Tell me something I don't know."

"I'm part African American."

"Don't try to shit me."

"My grandmother."

"And you think that buys you what?"

"Nothing at all. Only it was something you didn't know." He shovels large portions of meat loaf plus potatoes into his mouth.

"You eat like you like it."

He considers. "I don't hate it."

"Want to know where it's better?"

"Sure."

" 'Sure!' He's like fucking, 'Sure!' "

"So tell me."

"Somerset. State prison. I got a friend there. Sounds like you might be going there or someplace state. They get like the same kind of food, except better. Here we got Aramark. Them fuckers do hospitals, colleges, ballparks, and us. They must bid low like you wouldn't believe. You probably eating squirrel meat loaf. Horse meat loaf. But you might get that good stuff in State sometime soon." The man laughed. "Or not. Heard some priest came to see you. Last rites perhaps?"

Cal looked at his food. He was sweating. They said he would not make it out alive. All the while he pretended he was not scared, and definitely willing to fight back.

"When you getting a roomie?"

If someone was assigned to his cell, he would never be able to think, probably wouldn't get to sleep.

"You ain't going to make it," the big guy said. "Here." He handed over the plate of cake. "I watch my weight."

The others laughed.

Cal thought, He slipped a razor in. Something.

"Eat it. I ain't moving till you eat it."

Small bites. Careful chewing.

"WE'RE CAUGHT," Potocki said when they dawdled at the restaurant to let Boss and his wife leave.

"Can you believe it? The man has some sort of radar? God!"

"It's sort of funny."

"Sort of. Let's go to your place. It's not even quite nine o'clock," she whispered. She felt young again and sneaky.

If Potocki holds her, if he kisses her, it's all over. She has no STOP button. She remembers a lecture she had to attend in college. The woman said, "There is no such thing as being carried away. It's always under your control. It's always a decision. You must always weigh consequences."

Right. If you're not a romantic. If you don't value thrill, the game.

THE RESTAURANT food is just about killing Christie. Marina has forgotten how hard it is for him to eat sauces and such, but because everybody else was hitting up the pasta at Del's, and drinking, he did, too. He popped a double dose of Prevacid when he got home. "While I digest," he teased, "let's watch something."

For a while Christie and Marina channel surf aimlessly before settling on a film with Tommy Lee Jones. It's good. It occupies him. Sort of. Not really.

What a mess for everyone, running into Potocki and Greer, who tried to pull off a just-working excuse. There was no choice but to all eat together. Marina sighed good-naturedly and kept a hand on his thigh for half the meal.

Christie understands what is expected of him tonight, and he wants to do it. He loves Marina, and there is no doubt about the fact that she's totally gorgeous.

Now she snuggles in close. In his mind, he experiments with an alternate life in which he is married to Colleen. In this alternate life, Colleen teases him unmercifully, calls his bluff on everything. All of it, this future unlived life, is extrapolated from ordinary work exchanges—the look on her face when he gets too serious, the glimmer of amusement at him.

She blushed when they all ran into each other.

Well, we can't live all our lives.

Potocki is such a good guy, too. Deserving, both of them, of something good.

He thinks off and on throughout the movie of the time he met Marina, how hard he resisted taking up with her. He was strong until she spoke about how she felt, until she touched him. She was officially married then. And he was, too. The memory arouses him.

FIVE

SUNDAY, AUGUST 16

IT'S SUNDAY, IT'S morning, and the squad is irritable, cross-eyed with sleep. Christie notes that Colleen and Potocki enter separately and move to opposite corners of the room only to move back together five minutes later. Coleson and McGranahan elbow their way to the front of the room, implying they will present their case right along with Christie. Not quite, not quite. He wheels the chalkboard into position, sips a bit of coffee from the thermos he has brought. "Kill a few minutes," he tells them. "Jim Meakie has agreed to come by. And a rep from Forensics, even though they've done hardly anything detailed yet." A few of the detectives move about; some lean back, close their eyes. He adds, "Sorry our two guests are late, but we'd be better off waiting so we don't have to repeat." He sits and gives himself over to thinking.

A couple of people go to get themselves coffee from where it is brewing. Coleson and McGranahan sit back, chatting together, legs crossed to indicate cool, but it doesn't take a practiced eye to see they are bristling.

Finally Bobby Baitz, the rep from the lab, comes into the meeting room, and soon after that Jim Meakie, the forensic pathologist who'd been on duty Friday night, arrives. Christie stands, signaling the meeting can start.

He says, "I know it's Sunday morning. I just need all of you to help with this. It's got some complications, and we don't want to take it to a hearing with any rough edges. We need detail. Some of the evidence fits. Some doesn't. So we need to make sure we've covered all the ground. This is not to criticize Detective Coleson or Detective McGranahan, who worked long hard hours. It's . . . the nature of the case."

Coleson's brow is furrowed; he doesn't quite believe the case is unusual.

"I would like to let Bill Coleson speak first. Just to give us the basics of what he did."

The man flushes and stands, arching his back, his good-boy-in-school posture.

He begins, "We classified it as a homicide. Justifiable or excusable or criminal or without intent, we did not try to decide straight off, but we ruled out suicide. The back door was open, her nightgown was torn at the shoulder, she had marks on her neck. There was no wallet in her handbag." Coleson stops. He says lightly, "My wife tells me they're called handbags and not purses." He is gratified by the smiles he gets. "We did a walk-through of the house. There was nothing untoward. Most signs in the immediate crime scene indicated criminal homicide. We proceeded from there. We called in Forensics. We have photographs, sketches, and our notes. They're in the report. I expect you've all . . ."

"I asked everybody to be sure to be caught up," Christie says. "Go on."

Coleson takes a pristine white handkerchief from his back pocket and wipes at his forehead. "We had no trouble identifying the victim. The man who called in the 911 did the preliminary ID, but then the father drove down later in the night after Greer went up to talk to the family, and so by ten at night we had the next-of-kin ID—though there was no doubt in our minds. There were a couple of photographs around in her house, things like that. And she sure resembled the photographs.

"In terms of motive, it looked like robbery. The door had some slight chip marks around it. But we also considered that strangling is very intimate for a robbery. We were not sure of motive. There were no documents of any interest, though we did take her computer and we did a quick check of e-mail and such. We sent detectives to canvass neighbors and talk to people from her work.

"Our best witness was the accused. He was distraught, but he had called the homicide in. He was willing to talk to us. He had been working for her. We took him to Headquarters and asked him to stay close and he did. He was cooperative for many hours, but after a while he started asking about going home. Eventually his mother came to the station, and we talked to her. It had been apparent to us that he was a little odd. She explained that he'd been badly beaten as a boy and had sustained some brain damage. He had experienced blackouts as a youth. We found his interest in Cassie Price and his proximity to the crime suspicious. We questioned him further. Our boys noticed there was long blondish hair in the work gloves on the porch. We asked if those gloves were his. He said yes. In no uncertain terms. The gloves were his. He eventually confessed."

"Thank you," Christie says. He does not remind Coleson that the identification of the gloves was not quite so sure at the time. For all intents and purposes, the gloves were almost certainly Cal's.

Christie does say, "For the record, let me say that the accused man, Cal Hathaway, also retracted the confession afterward. So we have a yes and a no. I saw the tapes. Detectives *did* administer Miranda, and there were no improper pressures or anything of that sort. I *will* say everyone was extremely tired, including the accused. That could eventually play some part in this. Now, when Cal Hathaway confessed, he did not say how he did the killing, so we don't have the details we need for a hearing. Then, of course, he retracted the confession, so we need to get those details on our own. And we need to prove those details exist." This is the careful phrasing he practiced through most of breakfast. "Let's pause and hear from Dr. Meakie."

Meakie has very closely cropped hair, more like a layer of fur. With a large nose and protuberant ears and large glasses, he seems like an intellectual insect or bird. He stood when Coleson sat. He says, "Victim definitely died from strangulation. There was struggle evident in the torn clothing and the position of the body, there was no rape, and death appears to have been quick. The position of the marks on her neck suggest the perp was most likely a right-handed man who faced her and strangled from the front. We estimated death to have occurred between midnight and 6:00 A.M. I think the median, 3:00 A.M., is a very good bet for a more specific TOD. This time corresponds to the level of rigor and to the remains of food being digested. She was a slow digester, so there were remains."

Coleson raises a hand. "Accused reported that he saw her making a hamburger. He was working on her porch."

Meakie looks thrown by the interruption. "Well, yes, that fits."

"Had she been drinking? Could she have been drinking a margarita?"

Meakie thinks, nods. "Alcohol would have evaporated, but there were acidic remains consistent with a margarita."

"Anything else we should know?"

"A couple of things. She was apparently sexually active. She was fitted with an IUD."

"So she didn't work all the time," Dolan says. "A couple of her colleagues got that wrong."

Everybody laughs a little.

Meakie continues, "There is one other thing, an unusual factor I'd like to add at this point. My assistant reports he found a chip, a small sliver of wood, thinner than a bit of toothpick, in her neck, in the back. It didn't do particular damage, but it stuck."

"Wood?" Christie says.

"Yes."

So, wood, yes, that would come from the gloves. It doesn't prove Cal's guilt, even though it seems to.

"Anything under her nails?" he asks.

"Something powdery. We don't know what. We scraped and sent to the lab. No blood. She didn't bleed."

"Thank you." Hands begin to go up. Ideas. He hates to cut off anybody who has interest, passion, but Christie says, "Just if you can give us a tiny minute. Hold on to those thoughts. I want to hear from the labs in case these good people have to go before we do." Which was never if you were police, but he doesn't say it.

He turns to Bobby Baitz, who wears shorts and a T-shirt and looks younger than his thirtysomething years. "I know you don't have much time. I'll try not to hold you."

"Kids are in the car," Baitz says. "I'm taking them to Lake Arthur. Forgive the clothes."

"Forgiven. If you would just tell us the few basics we have at this point and then what you might expect to get down the line, that would be helpful."

Baitz takes a long pause. "Well, DNA down the line, of course. We picked up a lot of stuff, the usual stuff. Most of it will probably not be anything. We don't have all the prints identified—hers and the accused for sure around the house, plus a couple of other faded ones. We found some powder on the floor. We got scrapings from the lock—the lock was meddled with, probably using some kind of knife. No footprints other than those of the deceased and the accused. The big thing, the main thing we have at the moment is the work gloves that were outside the door on the porch. They had her hair in them. A couple of strands from the roots. And then also—this is important—there were a few splinters in the gloves. Just small, but it looks like a definite match for what Meakie found in her neck and a clue as to the means of murder."

"Murderer wore the gloves," Christie says evenly.

"I'd say so."

Coleson and McGranahan balloon happily in their seats.

Man, it looks bad for Cal Hathaway.

Christie says, "Normally we would have to try at this point to ask Hathaway exactly how he did the murder—the kind of details that would stand up in court. Since he is now saying he is unsure he did it, and remembers nothing of doing it, we might not ever get to that stage. So. Here is what I need from all of you." He pauses for a considerable time. "Let's play devil's advocate and list all the things that suggest the possibility it *was somebody else.* Anybody. So we can examine that list, consider it, and then shoot it down if we so wish."

"Somebody else could have used the gloves," says Hurwitz.

Christie writes on the board, *Gloves: Other user.*

"Why would the murderer put the gloves back? He or she?" asks Denman. "Anybody with any—"

Hurwitz interrupts. "Right. If I did it, I'd figure it was too obvious to leave them with the body."

"—sense would have taken them away," Denman finishes.

"Right. That would make sense." Christie writes under gloves, *Too obvious.*

McGranahan, who has been grinding his teeth, speaks up finally. "Well, I happen to be the rep who went to Wecht's symposium on evidence. He said most of what we gather is unreliable." He turns to Baitz and grimaces an apology. "Because, he says, most of everything can be argued this way and that, except, *except* DNA. I'd say we wait for an analysis of what's *inside* the glove." McGranahan folds his arms.

Christie says, "Thank you, we will DNA the gloves. But if we could just continue to list the glitches—"

"Any particular glove markings on her neck?" somebody shouts.

Baitz answers, "No. Just the typical bruising from manual strangulation."

The detectives appear to digest this fact. They *are* working their brains, in spite of the day and the hour, Christie is relieved to see. He looks to Dolan, but before Dolan can interject anything about their visit to the jail, he is interrupted.

"Wood shavings were *inside* the door, not outside." This is Potocki.

Nice. Christie wondered who would be the first to come up with that.

"The pattern is odd, as if to make it *look* like a break-in. Also," says Potocki, "taking a wallet is an easy feint. The first thing a person would do who wanted to get us to think it was a robbery. I hear there is a cell phone missing, too, but I'd say the same thing about that."

Christie writes on the board, *Robbery possibly not motive.*

"Somebody could have had a key," murmurs Janet Littlefield. "Do we know about her relationships?"

He writes, *Key used for entry?*

"If somebody faked the robbery, that person might have faked the gloves."

"That means a certain amount of . . . premeditation." Christie writes the word on the board.

"I'm wondering, who did she have a margarita with?" Littlefield continues. "Maybe a person she gave a key to?"

Margarita partner, he writes. He says, "Very likely someone in a gray car. We have a neighbor reporting a gray car following Cassie in the street in front of her house, and Cal reports a gray car following her in the alley until she parked." He writes, *Gray car.*

Colleen Greer says, "The woman in the neighborhood who reported seeing a gray car also saw a black car in the alley at roughly the time of the murder. This woman says she's often up in the middle of the night. She says the person going to the car reminded her in some way of—hold on, guys—an astronaut."

"Oh, good, now we're really getting somewhere," Coleson mocks. "Is this somebody we talked to? I know who it is, right?"

"Yes. Iris Mender. She told your man the part about the black car, but she saved the part about the astronaut for us."

"Needless to say," Coleson continues in his light tone, "astronaut, alien, the woman knew who to confide in."

"Some of my best colleagues are aliens!" Colleen retorts.

Christie writes, *Unidentified visitor?* while everybody talks at once. Then things settle down.

"The powder on the floor? Drugs?" one of the juniors asks.

"We did a presumptive," Baitz says. "Not drugs. We don't have what it is yet."

"And then," Christie says, "Dolan and I have something bugging us. Tell them what we noticed."

"Perp was almost certainly right-handed. *But* when we visited Cal Hathaway in jail, Boss handed him a pad, a pencil, asked him to write some stuff down. He used his left hand. We wondered if this was purposeful."

Christie nods. "So, we went back to the video, the part where the primaries handed him a pad and a pen. Left hand is what he used repeatedly. He's a lefty."

"I'd say he didn't fake it," Dolan asserts. "Totally natural."

"What do you make of that?"

"Could he have used the weak hand for some reason we haven't figured, like maybe he needed the stronger hand to restrain her?" the same junior detective asks. "Is there more of her hair in the left glove?" Eager fellow. Name? Yes. Melanowsky.

Coleson and McGranahan brighten.

"Maybe," Christie says. "It's unusual, but believe me I will consider it." He turns to Baitz. "Anything else for us?"

"We used luminol at night. Saw a spot of blood. Very small. Got excited. It turned out to be a mosquito full of dinner. We took it in case."

"Any evidence of a bite on the deceased?"

Meakie shakes his head slowly. "No."

"Hm." Christie goes back to Baitz. "You can DNA it?"

"Yes, sir."

"Before the hearing?"

"That would be pushing it."

"How hard would it be to push it?"

"Very hard, sir."

"But of course being a good guy . . . you'll try." He smiles.

Baitz shrugs helplessly.

Of course one way or the other defense will say the mosquito blood doesn't prove a thing. If it's Cal's blood, why couldn't the mosquito have bit during working hours? Christie doesn't say these things aloud, but he makes a note to have a medic at the prison look over Cal's body.

He dismisses Meakie and Baitz and gives his detectives their assignments. Some of them he dismisses for the day. Coleson and Mc-Granahan he puts on the search for more particulars on the black car—"Get me everybody Cassie Price knew who drives a black car."

"Yoy."

"I wanted to give you time with the astronaut," he jokes. "In other words, neighborhood plus black car is your search term."

Somebody whistles. "Hey, Commander, you're getting better at this computer thing."

"Getting literate," Christie says. "Denman and Hurwitz, same deal, see who she worked with that has a gray car. There'll be plenty. Once we have the list, we'll work on alibis."

He points to two others. "All the recent robberies in the neighborhood. Any break-ins. Especially anybody who takes just the money. Or targets phones. All of Oakland."

He says to Potocki and Greer and Dolan, "I want the four of us to work the funeral home today." Colleen's eyes roll back in her head. She hates death. Can't stand it. Which is really funny when you consider she opted for Homicide.

"Littlefield, what do you have on Price's computer?"

"I was at her e-mail yesterday and this morning. Dull isn't the word. Totally boring so far."

"Well, go through it and report tomorrow."

COLLEEN IS DRIVING this time.

"You were gorgeous last night."

She feels suddenly shy. Men will say anything. Shameless.

"Really. The way you move. Everything."

"Well, thank you." She squints at the road as if the glare is bothering her, which it isn't since there's cloud cover.

"Need your glasses?"

"Oh, yes, thank you."

He roots around in her bag without looking. "What do you think? Boss is going nuts this morning or what?"

"I think he has a strong feeling Coleson and McGranahan rushed it. And I kind of agree, but between the *for sure he did it* column and the *not for sure,* we're about even. If it were my case, I'd go with the not for sure. And the other thing . . . like he said last night at dinner, he doesn't know if Cal Hathaway can survive in prison. Or even in county jail. Whether he killed her or not, he's not a fighter. There's something gentle about him."

Potocki finds the glasses and hands them to her. "This is a three-hour drive. Plus three, maybe. Visiting hours start at two. We might end up with time for lunch. I wonder what kind of place we're going to find up there. If traffic is smooth and we're sure we have time, we should maybe stop in State College, where they have a lot of restaurants."

"That would be great, but—"

Potocki's phone rings.

"As I was just saying, it's going to be a four-way lunch," she whispers hurriedly before he answers. "That'll be our invitation."

"Hey, Artie," Potocki says, winking at Colleen.

Her prediction is right—Boss saying they might as well talk while eating lunch someplace when it hits twelve or one, get their ducks in a row.

They stop in State College, all four of them.

Lunch is totally cheerful, but all the while she's thinking they could have driven up in one car, so why didn't they? Was Christie letting her have time with Potocki or simply not wanting to be around them for the full three-hour drive? Maybe it's all work—two cars, two options for escape.

She feels nervous. She isn't at all sorry she slept with Potocki last night, though it makes her predicament at work worse. She's a bad liar, so there's no sense pretending to Christie, who sees everything, that she and Potocki are *not involved.*

•　　•　　•

CAL HAS BEEN STARING at the ceiling all morning. After breakfast he twisted a bit, trying to block out the sounds of voices, TVs, speakers, and metallic echoes until he succeeded and all the sounds whirred like machinery, a big factory of voices.

All the morning long, he's thought of Cassie, as if thinking could bring her back to life. Still, hours later, he tries to remember anything that suggests he got up in the middle of the night, got himself dressed, walked up the road to her place. But the blackouts of his youth were significant. He'd lost whole days or parts of days.

And so with the voices and TVs chattering, he tries to create a scene in which he did the awful thing. In his mind he gets himself dressed and up the road. But then what? Perhaps he didn't understand the time of day because he was dreaming. Perhaps he started working on the porch, frustrated there was not enough light. What if he tried to get into the house to turn on the porch light and he frightened Cassie. But he would have *run*, wouldn't he? Backed off? Apologized?

He forces himself to imagine it. What if she screamed or said she was calling the police. And that . . . scared him enough to try to stop her. What if?

He shudders. The tears begin to form again.

He thinks hard. He wore the baggy jeans and a blue shirt on Friday. What the day before? Then he remembers. A striped jersey. Yes, and the older jeans! Yes, he's sure. He is so happy with this memory, he ignores the fact that he might have donned the blue shirt and baggy jeans twice, once in the middle of the night. He lets his mind turn over and over. He remembers the priest just sitting with him, asking if there is anything he can do. Nice. It makes him cry. He falls into a drowsy wakefulness.

"Trays up," goes the call.

He thinks, No, I won't eat.

Levon passing his cell, says, "Come on, man."

He gets up. "Roast beef for lunch," he hears someone say.

He moves out of his cell and gets into line to get his roast beef.

•   •   •

THEY ARE LINED UP, the sisters, like contestants in a beauty pageant. They stand next to their mother, who is not particularly beautiful but is clearly a vessel for beauty. In their faces, combined, are the ingredients for Cassie's face.

There are flowers everywhere, and the workers keep carrying more in until it's clear there simply will be no room for them all.

In the Price family the grieving process has only begun, the ravaged expressions just being hinted at. The pretty sisters standing in a row are wide-eyed, stunned or in denial.

"This is hard, I know," Colleen murmurs to the girls, repeating herself a few times. "I'm going to go outside for a while. I'd be grateful for the company if you take a break."

She gets a flicker of interest from the older sister, so she reaches over and squeezes her hand. Then she passes back through the room toward the exit, toward the outdoors, hoping. Potocki is sticking with the father and the males in the group, especially anyone that looks like he might be or had been one of Cassie's boyfriends. Christie and Dolan are talking together in a hush, but both of them are observing those who come and go.

There is a minister holding court in the hallway, many mourners gathered around him. Colleen picks up a card from the table in the hall. It is filled with Bible quotes and a list of prayer services that will take place in the next day and a half—a significant number of them, amounting to a royal send-off in religious terms. The funeral is to be on Tuesday morning.

Outside is not exactly comfortable. Although it's sunny, it's also eighty degrees and Pennsylvania humid—a condition that just sort of hangs over the state for days and keeps the dehumidifiers running in most basements. So she's hot and she dabs at her forehead. And she wonders about those sisters, all of them sexy looking. Is the homeschooling a way of keeping them in check?

There are three media cars. Some of the crew are inside scoping the crowd; the others are outside wielding cameras and waiting for something to shoot. They recognize her as police and take a few minutes of film, especially when she stops a group of young women going into the building and later when she talks to two others coming out. Friends from high school, friends from college, some crying, all thinking, thinking about this thing called death. From them she extracts facts she already knew: Cassie was gorgeous. She worked like a demon. She had the best grades. She was very religious. She was uptight. (Well, they didn't put it that way. They said she wasn't interested in dating, that she was "very strict with herself.")

"Golly, weren't boys calling her all the time?"

"They were," one girl says. "I think she had secret crushes. I don't know. She wasn't mean to the guys. I mean they liked her a lot. I think they always ended up thinking it might work out."

"It sounds like they didn't get angry at her for being unavailable."

The girl says, puzzled, "No, they didn't."

The conversation is interrupted by Colleen's awareness that the media has come to attention, one running to a camera, some adjusting cameras surreptitiously. All for one particular car. Who are the celebrities? Cadillac limo and all. The car pulls up to the front door. A gray-haired man and woman emerge. Then a middle-aged couple who look uncomfortable. Then a handsome middle-aged man and woman, and with them a solo man who has a lively, cheerful look and might have been brought along to keep the jokes flowing.

"Senator Connolly," one newsman says, addressing the handsome one, "could we have a word?"

"Not now." His refusal is kind, even regal. "I'll make a statement in a bit if you'd like to wait."

"Yes, sir. I'll be here."

They watch him walk into the building, shooting of course all the while in case it's all they get.

Colleen sidles up to the newsman who spoke first. "Senator?" she asks. "Ex, isn't it?"

"Yeah, but you can't call out 'ex-senator.' The word is, it might be governor soon."

"No fooling. You think we're going red-state?"

"That's the buzz. It could happen."

Man, she's got to pay more attention to politics. She determines to make herself read about it every day. She mainly manages to digest what the Steelers are doing, who killed whom, and the mixed blessing of the G-20 coming to town. She's heard all cops, all of them, of every stripe and rank, will be in meetings every day starting any day now and will be on call through *all* of the G-20. There's talk that they have to carry a toothbrush and jammies to work and to load in food. It's kind of like preparing for war, just in case.

After the next governor and his entourage go inside, things seem dull. She talks to the newsmen for a while in hopes of something good, but they don't have much to add to what she knows. They dismiss the Pirates—pitching bad, relief pitching worse—and land on the Steelers as a safe topic. The offensive and defensive lines are looking good at this point, and fingers are crossed to keep the players healthy and crime-free.

Colleen entertains the guys with a story she heard. "You know Troy Polamalu is married to a Greek woman and he goes to the Greek church? Well, I heard the Greeks love him so much they decided he simply must be Greek. Here's how they explain it. 'Look at his name,' they say. 'Troy. See. Troy. And Pola-malu.' Anyway, I can't say it the way they do. But they say it means 'many hairs.' Multiple hairs or something like that. So they've decided he's Greek!"

The cameramen laugh, but the laugh is not as hearty and gratifying as the one she got from Potocki, who loves wordplay.

When she is just about to give up and go inside, she is rewarded by the appearance of the oldest of the remaining Price siblings. The girl comes right up to Colleen. "I couldn't stand it in there," she says.

"Let's take a walk. Get away from these bozo paparazzis."

"Are they being awful?"

"No. Just doing their job. But I hate to be bothered, you know. Let's walk." There is no place to walk except a small-town block, but it's something. Colleen starts moving. "You're Carrie, right?"

"Yes."

There is a funny thing about their names. Colleen thought her hearing was tricking her at first. It was Cassie, Carrie, Caddie, and Cammie. "Why are your names so similar?" she asks now.

"My parents liked the idea. They're a little weird."

Colleen laughs. "All parents are a little weird. Are the names all shortened?"

"No. Mine and Caddie's aren't. But Cassie was Cassandra and Cammie is Camille. I'm really not Caroline or anything, just Carrie. We could never tell which one of us was being called to set the table—that's sort of a joke. We have a schedule of tasks on the refrigerator. But anyway, we started to call each other S, R, D, and M just to be silly. Get it? The middle sound." Her hair glints in the sunshine. It's a luscious light brown with blond, slightly lighter than Cassie's. This girl and her sisters have beautiful suntans. They could sell hair products, swimsuits, makeup, just about anything.

"You must know you and your sisters are very beautiful. You have to be aware of that if you're going to stay safe."

Carrie swallows hard, but doesn't say anything. Survivor's guilt, Colleen guesses.

They pass a series of houses in silence before they turn a corner and begin talking again. The real estate has turned commercial. A bank, a coffee shop that's closed on Sunday, a camera store.

"Do you know anything that could help us? We're not quite done putting things together."

"Oh. Well, the guy did it, right?"

"Are you talking about Cal Hathaway?"

"The newspaper said so."

"Yes."

"You don't doubt it, do you?"

"I would like more information. Facts. Did she ever talk about him?"

"No. She just said some guy was working on her house. That's all. I guess I heard his name from her, but I'm not even sure about that."

"Do you think she was involved with him?"

"No." Carrie almost laughs. "No, she wouldn't be. She always liked guys who were a challenge."

"A challenge? Really, like who?"

"Oh, you know, like the president of the class. Or her English teacher. Or people who had a lot going for them."

"I see. She had little romances with these people," Colleen asks offhandedly. "Or crushes or something."

They turn another corner. "She was always in love. She had a lot of love to give. Then some jerk just got rid of her."

"Maybe the person who killed her was in love with her and they had some sort of relationship . . . Maybe she just didn't tell you."

Carrie shakes her head. "That can't be right. I'd know."

"You're sure?"

"Yes."

"One of her co-workers thought she was seeing someone who was, let me think how she said this, a simple fellow, humble."

"She would have told me," Carrie insisted.

"On the other hand this fellow, Cal, thought she was in love with someone else."

The girl draws in a breath. "He said that?"

"Yes. He thought she was sad because of it."

"She wouldn't tell him. She wouldn't tell someone like him, just a worker, about her personal life."

"Maybe . . . maybe he observed. Do you think she was sad?"

"No. She was happy."

They turn the corner back to the funeral home, and Colleen asks more urgently, "Do you know who she was in love with? We should talk to this person."

"I don't know who he was."

"But wait a minute, you said she told you things."

Carrie shakes her head. "She told me there was somebody, but she wouldn't tell me who. I got mad at her because I could tell there was something big going on in her life—we had a fight." Carrie starts to cry. "What if she died thinking I was her bitch of a sister?"

"I'm sure she didn't. I'm sure." Colleen hands over a handkerchief. "You were a good sister to her."

"How do you know?"

"You talked to her. Right? You cared?"

"I got jealous."

"That's totally normal." After a while Colleen says, "I wonder who this guy was. He could maybe shed some light."

Carrie shakes her head. "I don't know. It had to be from work. She never went out otherwise."

"Was the relationship very developed? I'd better not mince words. Were they having sex?"

"Um . . . I mean she didn't exactly say, but I'm sure."

"Was he older?"

"I think so."

"Well, I'll be very discreet. I'll try to find out, and I promise I'll contact you when I do."

"Thanks."

"How often did you talk to her? I guess she called you."

"No. We never talked like that on the phone. My parents could have heard. She'd come home on Saturdays."

"All the time?"

"Not at first but lately, yes. She'd get in about noon on Saturday and then stay through church on Sunday."

Not Friday night, though, because once she got to her parents' house, she couldn't just leave. Colleen feels a trickle of excitement at this new information.

"But the handyman . . . he did it, right?"

"Probably. We don't have all the facts lining up just yet. Are you able to keep a confidence?"

"Yes."

"I'd appreciate it if you'd keep this particular conversation we just had between us. We can do our work way better if you do."

The girl nods.

A risk, saying this much to Carrie. Colleen had to take it.

A married man. If Cassie wasn't talking, it was a married man. All Colleen has to do is imagine herself in Cassie's life and she zeroes in on who it would be.

THE CONNOLLY ENTOURAGE has paid respects to the Price family and has turned, one by one, to the open casket. They are clearly upset. The women are crying openly, and the younger Connolly has tears welling up, too. All look lost. Stay longer? Talk? Go?

Dolan tells Christie, "We can help focus them."

"You bet." They approach the Connolly family.

Dolan says, "I did some of the inquiries up at the office. Detective Dolan. This is Commander Christie, head of Homicide. He was away on Friday, but he's back in town and on the case now."

"Good, good," says the elder Connolly vaguely.

Christie moves in closer. "It's good of all of you to come this whole way."

"But of course," says the elder.

"I don't mean to interrupt you here. I realize the media are after you, too. But I'd like to talk to each of you sometime in the near future. Let me know what's possible."

"Oh," says the senior Connolly. "I thought the case was closed."

"We need to build details for court. These things go on and on."

"Of course. Could you come to the office tomorrow? I could see you then. We need to get back to the city now." He looks at his watch.

Golf? Dinner party? Christie wonders. He feels a rare bitter envy of the privileged.

"Also," hand up as if in school, "that's best for me," says the older brother—a slightly sour-looking fellow, but it might not be mood coloring his face. It could be just the unlucky chance of his gene combination.

"That's fine," Christie says. He turns to Michael Connolly, about to ask, "You, too?"

But Mike Connolly says, "I could see you today. Here or—" He stops, no doubt realizing an interview would hold up his family. "As my father said, we need to get back, but I could go into the office tonight. Or you could come to the house."

"I'll come to the house." Christie looks at his watch. "About six all right? Or would you rather after dinner?"

"Before, before."

The eagerness is interesting. Puzzling.

"I could get to the Connolly offices tomorrow," says the man Christie has identified as Todd Simon. "If you want to see me, that is. Right now I'm more concerned that our boy has to handle the damned media."

"I understand. Go ahead."

He lets them go out to the hall, but he can see enough to see the handler, Simon, doing some sort of pep talk, coaching. It makes him curious about what Connolly will say on camera. He gestures to Dolan. "Let's go outside, watch the news being made."

They go outside, where they find Potocki talking to Greer while making notes in his small notebook. There is no time to confer because the cameras are setting up to catch the Connollys on the way out of the funeral home, and one of the reporters gestures to Christie to hold on.

Christie knows he always comes off well on camera. He isn't sure why, when cameras whir, he always finds the words he needs and seems utterly reasonable.

Even so, he is nothing compared to Mike Connolly, whose very exit from the building and entrance to the arena have star quality. For one thing, the man wears his clothing well, and it is surely very good clothing—tailored to thirty-seconds of an inch. And he looks sort of beautiful in his sadness, as an actor would.

He allows the microphones to come at him. He faces them square on, doesn't hide the moist eyes or the catch in his voice.

"This is a very sad day. We have lost a valued worker, a young woman who . . . was just on the brink of what would no doubt have been . . . a wonderful success in law school and after. Her life stood for something, and I won't let it be lost in vain. She cared about civic works. The city. Improving the city. I take that mission seriously, too. This is a sad day for all of us."

He made a move away from the microphones, but one of the newsmen said, "About the care of cities—are you still planning to run for governor?"

He pretends he hasn't quite heard, that he's busy getting to his family and getting an arm around his wife.

The newsmen follow him to his limo, asking more questions. "Not today," he says kindly. He allows them to film him, but he doesn't add anything.

"What did you think?" Dolan asks Christie.

"He's interesting."

"He's very interesting and very handsome," Colleen observes.

"You noticed," Dolan quips. "Is that really all women want?"

"Nonsense. I'd prefer the handler. He looks like he has more jokes up his sleeve. But listen. I've got something. It isn't surprising but it's important. The next-oldest sister told me in confidence that Cassie was having an affair with someone and wouldn't say who, not even to her. Has to be a married man."

Dolan whistles. "I like it."

"Lots of men in that law office," Christie ventures, but his eyes drift to where Connolly's car has just driven off.

"She liked them high up."

"Okay. We'll have to think how to proceed. Where was our next governor Thursday night, for a start?"

Potocki says, "Do we bother with these others? I talked to about ten guys who wished they were her boyfriend. She had opportunities for sure. These were guys from high school and college and two from work."

"Do some preliminaries on them? Just in case. We have to screen them, take a look. And go by and help Littlefield with the computer e-mail."

Potocki nods.

"I've got to get moving. I'm seeing Connolly at his house. I can drive Artie back."

Take Artie along to Connolly's? No, he decides. His gut tells him he should go in alone.

"YOU WANT DINNER when I finish up at the office?" Potocki asks.

"Oh, what the hell. We're in deep shit anyway."

"Tell me about the handler."

"I dunno. A glint. Something unusual. Something wild."

They watch Christie and Dolan drive off. She tweaks a pinch at his waist. "Don't worry. I'm not nuts."

EVEN WHEN PARKING in the roundabout and simply looking at the outside of the Connolly house, Christie feels like a rube. To think of living like this.

Marina would love this house and grounds—rolling land and stands of trees, everything attended to. Each matching flowerpot lining the driveway wall is so clean you wouldn't believe they held or sat anywhere near dirt. He can't identify the flowers—he knows the common ones, but these beauties are blooming in gorgeous shades of pink, orange, red, and white. He takes a quick, inadequate picture with his cell phone just to capture the colors.

He's always known the area was here—private homes bordering the Chatham University campus—but he's had no cause to be up here on Homicide business. He knows rich girls go to this school, but also some poor girls on scholarships. He knows all this because he listens to others at the office preparing to get their kids into colleges. He wonders how his own daughter, Julie, would feel ending up next to kids who have horses, convertibles, summer homes.

The campus buildings are mostly old mansions, converted. There are homes all over Pittsburgh that speak of this other, privileged life that flowered a century ago. Carriages, horses, chauffeurs, gowns with trains—he's seen the pictures. History interests him.

He uses his cell to call Marina. "I still have work. Give me two hours. Eat without me if you want."

"I'm okay. I can wait. Is it . . . something complicated?"

"I honestly can't tell. It could be simple and I'm making it complex."

"Where are you now?"

"Outside Connolly's house, about to go in. It's awfully fancy."

"I'll wait. You can tell me at dinner. I'm just marinating some tuna steaks. I'll eat cheese till you get here."

"I'll hurry. Pray I don't bump something precious."

"Move very slowly."

"Yeah," he laughs.

So he exits his car, taps a knocker, rings a bell, and is greeted by an open door more quickly than those sounds could have communicated his presence to anybody a room away. It's Elinor at the door, Cal's mother.

"I wanted to answer. I wanted to thank you," she says.

"I was glad to do it. Those people—" He shakes his head. "Nothing better to do than insist on a set of rules."

"Well, I thank you."

"How was he?"

"I'm worried."

He waits. It seems he waits a long time.

"He's in shock, I think."

"I'll make sure a behavioral person gets in there as soon as possible."

"Thank you. I'd better take you to Mr. Connolly."

He follows her through two large spacious rooms he would like to look at, but he's moving too fast to know what they contain except carved things and furniture that looks valuable, antique. The room he ends up in is a large cushy family room with a big flat TV and a bar. Connolly, in jeans and a T-shirt, is sitting on one of the sofas, making marginal comments in a file of papers. The national news is on. When he sees Christie, he clicks off the TV and stands.

They nod to each other.

"Thanks for coming here. It makes it easier for me."

124

"You're welcome."

"Please have a seat wherever you like. Can I get you a drink?"

Christie sees that Connolly has a drink started. It looks mighty good to him, but he won't accept a drink on the job. "Alcohol, no, but water or a Coke, I might take you up on that. It got hot today."

"Blistering at times."

Blistering. He watches Connolly at the bar top his own drink up and fill two glasses with ice, then one with water, the other with Coke. "I'm getting you both," he says.

"This is a big room. Will we be private? Not overheard?"

"You're thinking of Elinor. She's scrupulous. I told her we needed privacy. I banished my wife and the boys to the outside. They're all busy cooking hot dogs and burgers. They'll stay out there."

Hot dogs and burgers. Not terrine of pigeon and foie gras.

"I can get you something to eat if you want."

"No, thank you. I don't want to ruin my appetite. My wife told me it's tuna steaks tonight."

"I like them. Seared. Rare. About raw."

Christie smiles. He eats his tuna cooked medium, and it has taken him a while to get that far.

"Tell me everything you know about Cassie Price and Cal Hathaway. For starters, how did you know each of them?"

"Well, Elinor has been with our family for a long time. Her mother was, too. Her mother worked for my father's family, and then Elinor did when I was growing up."

"Here?"

"Yes, my father and mother used to live here, but then he wanted to move to Sewickley, but he and my mother didn't want to lose this place and my brother didn't want it and I did. That's more information than you need—"

"No, no, that's fascinating. So you love it? I mean, I don't blame you. It's wonderful."

"Yes, I do. I just do. Elinor didn't want to commute out to Sewickley and she didn't want to live out there, so I kept her on. I've never been sorry for a minute. She makes everything flow smoothly.

We don't even see half of what she does. Anyway, that's the long story for how I know her son. She brought him around every once in a while when he was little, but mostly we didn't see him until he was grown. For a couple of seasons he worked on our grounds under a man we use for landscaping. Elinor liked having her son around. She'd get to have lunch with him some days."

"Did you know him?'

"Not much. A little. In passing."

"How did both Cal Hathaway and Cassie Price end up buying houses in the same neighborhood?"

"Ah, yes. Well, one of the boards I'm on is the University of Pittsburgh. We would like to eradicate crime and poverty in the Oakland area. Well, eradicate might be going too far, but we want to reduce it."

"I'm pretty sure one of the reporters was trying to get you to talk about that today."

"Well, I'm supporting this organization called Own Oakland. They buy up properties and then sell them for very little—the idea being to get a stable person in there who will take care of the property and not turn it into absentee landlord student housing. We believe that's the trick to making . . . safe neighborhoods." He has slowed down considerably. "Yes, I heard what I just said."

"It's a horrible blow to the program, I would think."

"Probably. That's not the most important thing here. Two worthwhile young people are finished. One in prison and the other—" He can't finish the sentence. It seems genuine.

"Did you have the impression anywhere along the way that they were seeing each other?"

Connolly blinks and looks unfocused. "I never thought about it. I think I heard someone at the office said so, but I don't know."

"Okay, so now to how you knew Cassie Price. Can you tell me how she was hired, what she did there, and all that?"

Connolly winced slightly. "You seem like a reporter."

"Well, you might as well practice on me, because they're going to be at you as soon as they can be. So how was Cassie hired?"

"What she wanted . . . you see, she applied in a letter for an internship. But we don't normally have interns. We may have a lot of money in the family, but that's not the same thing as having it in the firm, and we don't run the firm sloppily, that's for sure."

"Maybe that's why you have a lot of money."

At first Connolly looked confused, and then he laughed. "Oh, the money doesn't come from the firm."

"It doesn't?"

"Oh, no, I mean, lawyers make a decent living, a very nice living much of the time, but my childhood, this house, my father's house . . . it comes from my grandfather, who married into U.S. Steel money, one of the daughters. My grandfather was a whiz of an investor to boot, and he was apparently really good at moving in the circles of the wealthy. I always loved hearing about him, how he wasn't born to it, but he fit better than those who were. One year he was a newly married man considered an outsider and not good enough, and by the next he was the center of a social group."

"Is he still alive?"

"No, he died three years ago. He was ninety-one."

"He must have been fascinating."

"He was. A little scary, too."

"Was he in politics?"

"No. Not at all. My father wanted to be in politics from the time he was a teenager—he talked about it often when I was a child— but he never could break away from the firm to do it. I guess he lit a fire. I found myself wanting to make a go at it and I had success."

"He's proud of you?"

"Very. It's embarrassing."

Christie smiles. "It's probably worse the other way. Parents have hooks. You might as well have a good hook in you."

"Are you *sure* I can't get you anything?"

"I'm sure. Really. So now about Cassie Price?"

"Well, my father mentioned this letter he got from a woman wanting an internship. I said no, my brother said no. We're not a boutique firm, but we're small. Not like Reed Smith or Kirkpatrick."

"Explain."

He made a face, took a sip of his bourbon or whatever it was. "Number of employees? Even the smaller one has about two hundred lawyers and as many other workers. They can afford interns. We used to be even smaller than we are now—oh, about sixty—but we've been creeping up some. We have about a hundred people altogether."

"That seems big to me."

"Believe me, it's nothing in comparison."

"So the next thing was I got a call from an old classmate of mine from law school. It turns out he was Cassie's professor at Westminster. He said, 'She's really really smart. Give her a chance.' I said I would see what I could do. Before I did anything, my father got a call from Pitt, one of the people he knew there, a guy who's been at the law school there, and the guy's saying how he just had an interview with her and she doesn't want to spend her summer pouring coffee because she wants experience in law. So finally my father and my brother and I said we could take her on as a paralegal, though we already had three hired and it was straining the budget. We decided we could pay her something equal to the others, and let her see how the whole operation worked. So she arrived."

"She was persistent."

"I'd say so."

"She did well?"

"She was that kind of hundred-and-ten-percent worker. Took it home, came in early. Proved herself."

"Did people at the firm describe her as beautiful? By her pictures she was startlingly good-looking."

"Yes. Yes, she was. Everybody said so."

"I met her family. They're very conservative and religious. Well, you met them yesterday. Was she like that?"

"I don't know."

Christie makes his move. "We heard from some sources that she was kind of a bit wilder than she seemed or than her family knew."

Connolly blanched. "Who said that?"

"I can't reveal it. People she worked with."

"Oh. I wouldn't know."

"They thought she had a teasing manner. Flirtatious, I guess you'd call it."

"I . . . I never saw that. It could be."

"They even—well, this is something I have to ask—they even intimated that she flirted a lot with you, and one of them intimated you had a personal relationship with her."

"My God, who said that?"

"So . . . nothing going on between you?"

"No. No. Absolutely not."

"Well, you see why I had to ask, though. I have to follow up anything like that."

"I see. No, I didn't have a relationship with her."

"It wouldn't be unusual. It's been known to happen. It's always on the news, it seems."

"I know."

"Yes. So. You know, I hate to hurry this up. This is the most comfortable sofa I ever sat on. In. But I should get to my tuna and you should get to your burger. So I just have to ask for the record just a couple of things. First, what kind of car do you drive when you drive yourself?"

"Lincoln. Town Car."

"Color?"

"Gray."

"You like a comfortable seat."

"I do."

"And I have to jot down your whereabouts from about six Thursday night to—just to be safe—noon the next day."

Connolly looked amazed, not to mention worried. "You actually want my alibi?"

"I'm sorry to have to ask it. Just to clear you."

"Okay. Six. Let's see. I came home. We had the second of two photo sessions. They wanted everything—still shots and video. I left the house at probably seven thirty, eight. Got to Harrisburg at around eleven something. Went straight to Haigh's house. We had a late-night meeting—there were seven people there—we were talking about me and the campaign. Got done at about twelve thirty."

Cigars and bourbon? Christie wondered. "What did they want to talk about?"

"The usual. Money. Hauling in certain districts. The competition. The truth is, I was still auditioning, constantly auditioning. They concluded for the tenth time I had a very good chance at this. The governor's race."

"Exciting. Okay, then?"

"What?"

"After twelve thirty?"

"Went to bed."

"Where? I have to ask."

"Right there at Haigh's place. In his guest room."

"And did you get up during the night?"

"No. My God, I can't believe what you're asking."

"I have to. Slept through the night and awoke when?"

"Seven. Talked to Haigh at breakfast. Left about eight-ish. Got into the firm about noon."

"Is there a night staff at Haigh's place?"

"Actually I don't know."

"I'll look into it."

"Commander, do you suspect me?"

"We don't think like that. We just cross the t's and dot the i's. We simply gather all the pertinent information at this stage. We're almost done here. Just one more question. Did you know Cassie Price was missing from work on Friday?"

"I didn't. I didn't notice. A hundred employees may not be big, but it's not small either. There are plenty of people I don't see on any one day and several I hardly know."

"I understand. I thank you for your time. I'm sorry I had to ask questions that upset you."

Christie doesn't dislike Connolly. In fact he identifies with him in some way that he can't quite explain in spite of the differences in looks, wealth, and experience. And the fact that Connolly probably lied.

As he gets into his car, he feels sorry Connolly no doubt dislikes him. He could imagine being friends across the money divide. He pulls out of the driveway and in his mind he is already home, having the bourbon he's been craving for the last hour, saying, "Hot day. Blistering," as Marina searches his face for answers.

HE FLICKS ON THE TV looking for replays of the Thursday night game. He finds enough other games in other cities to keep him watching. The pace of this contemporary world suits him—how strange to think that not so long ago if a person was not *at* a football game, that person saw nothing of it. Even with early TV you had to live in the vicinity of a team to actually see the game. Now you can live anywhere, you can see anything anytime if you have the money to pay for it. You could follow a team from Burma if you wanted to.

Dish vs. FiOS vs. cable. He loves it all, comparing, arguing.

At first she laughed. She said, "Where . . . why are you wearing that—" She didn't have a name for it.

"I was working," he said. "Pulling plaster. Ugly job."

And for a moment she paused, wanting to believe.

He had a long story made up in case she seemed different, in case she looked like a calm and logical woman, in case he was going to give her another chance. He watched a thought—a glimmer of the truth—cross her face.

"You can't expect this to go on," he said.

"What did you do?" she asked. But she was scared by then. "Who did you talk to?" Then she turned determined/flirty—that cute look she got. "You don't understand. I'm not afraid."

They wanted it done. They wanted *her* done and over with.

Shake it off. Don't think. Learn a new scenario until it becomes real.

He feels his stomach turning upside down again and so concentrates on the game. Games. The 49ers and the Broncos. The Vikings and the Colts. Airs out his secret wish that the Bengals will climb up out of their hole. Focuses on the games. Listens to the announcers saying what he already knows: skill, coaching, yeah, yeah, all have to be there, but swagger, confidence, that's the magic ingredient. It comes down to a head game most of the time—who dominates. Preparation, blah, blah, blah, and then the exercise of will.

He carried a crowbar, hidden of course, stuffed in his belt. In case he needed it. The other guy they wanted . . . it came down to trust . . . he couldn't trust anybody with it.

His heart jumps in his chest and feels as if it wants to be freed from inside him. His stomach turns again. He leaves the TV for a ginger ale. In his kitchen drawer, under some sample vitamins and other shit, he finds a bottle of generic acid reducer, ranitidine, and pops two.

Justifiable homicide: You are in danger and so you act quickly to defend yourself. Or your child is in danger. Or your property, therefore your life as you know it; your state, your country. He *felt* the danger. He understood it. They all did. It was visceral. It was destruction tromping toward them.

Ah. Think of nothing. Watch the game. And eventually get something into the stomach.

SIX

MONDAY, AUGUST 17

THE NEXT MORNING, the clank of metal again, and Cal is once more called to the interview room.

Someone whistles. "Mr. Popular." Is it Levon's voice? And even though he can't hear very well, he's pretty sure somebody laughs, saying something like, "Ever notice how much nicer they are to the murderers?"

Cal shuffles into the interview room, hoping it's his mother or the two detectives from Saturday.

A woman stands. He does not know her.

She nods for him to sit down. "Cal? I'm Dr. Beni. I'm with the behavioral unit. I'm here to see how you are and to do some record keeping on you."

He sits. What's the trick? What do they want him to say now?

"It's important to be relaxed and to simply answer my questions. The aim here is to be honest. Totally honest. I can help you best if you are."

About maybe fifty or so, this woman has a lined worried face and a small square body. Dr. Beni. She wears a jacket and skirt, nylons and flat worn shoes.

"Is this about making me confess?"

"No. This is about assessing your mental readiness to stand trial. I need to ask you a few simple questions. Try to relax, take a breath."

He tries.

"Do you know what day it is?"

"Monday."

"The date?"

"Sixteenth."

"Sure?"

"Seventeenth."

"Of what month?"

"August."

"Good. Did you have breakfast?"

"Yes."

"Do you know why you are in here?"

"They think I killed Cassie Price."

She paused, then wrote something down. "Do you understand why they think so?"

He worked to formulate his answer, what he had thought about as he lay on his cot. "Because I've always been different, because I used to have blackouts."

"I see. Could I back up for just a moment? When they took you in, did you understand why they were questioning you?"

"Because I found the body."

"Did you understand why they took you into custody?"

"They didn't have anybody else. Somebody broke in. They thought it was me."

"Was it?"

"No. Not unless I had a blackout and went nuts."

"Do you think you did?"

He couldn't answer at first. He shook his head. Then he said no, but his voice came out breathy and ragged.

"Why don't you think you did?"

"Because I don't remember."

"Could it have been a blackout?"

"No. Yes, I guess it could have been. But I had no . . . I always got along with her. I never got angry with her, so why would I . . . They told me it was my gloves that did it. I keep trying to imagine it and I can't."

"I read something in your records about a confession."

He has to nod yes. "I didn't know what else to say." He notices his hands are shaking.

"Can you explain?"

He tries to explain how tired he was, how the gloves being his and his own mother looking at him like he did it just all came at him and he allowed himself to think he must have done this awful thing in a blackout.

Under the worried lines of her face, Dr. Beni seems kind. Maybe it's a trick. Is he being dumb to trust her when they all just want him to say yes and to explain how he did it?

"Did they read you your rights?" she asks. "Mirandas go like this"—and she recites the whole thing, just the way they do it on TV.

"Yes."

"Do you understand your rights?"

"I guess so."

"So which part of it is why you're here?"

"Because of the glove."

"No. Not exactly. From the Miranda rights . . ."

He thinks. " 'Anything you say may be used . . .' That part."

"Yes."

"I have a whole series of questions I have to ask. Just relax. They can be kind of interesting."

Relax. It's not possible. His hands still shake. Now his knees, too.

"Here's an example. It's just a game of imagine. If you were trying to sleep and a dog was barking so long and so hard that it was driving you crazy, what would you do?"

"Put a pillow on my good ear."

"Would you get up, say anything to the dog or its owner?"

"No."

"Why not?"

"I don't like that kind of thing."

"What kind?"

"People being angry."

"If somebody shoved you a couple of times and slammed you into a wall, what would you do to defend yourself?"

"Is this because—um?"

"What?"

"Because of what happened to me?"

"I'm not sure I understand. Here? Are you saying something like that happened here?"

"No. Before."

"Would you like to tell me about that? We can come back to the questions at any time."

And so he tells once more about the three who were at him all the time in grade school, so bad he didn't want to go to school. He tells how he tried to make friends with them because his mother said kindness was better. The three boys didn't want kindness. They called his grandmother his nigger mother. Nothing he said got through to them. It didn't matter what he said to them, they kept making up his life. They kept wanting him to fight, but he knew he had no chance against three of them. They knew, too, there was nothing he could do. He can still see their faces, how excited they were, and scared. They tried to kill him. And came near to doing it. He went to the hospital for a year. They went back to school and nothing at all happened to them.

"Where was this?"

"East Liberty."

"Did you see them again?"

"No. My mother changed my school."

"Never?"

"Well, I saw two from a distance once, but they walked away."

"The new school—it was better?"

"Better, but I had blackouts. And a seizure. And my one ear never healed. I'm deaf in one ear. So I wasn't Mr. Popular."

Mr. Popular. Another joke, another taunt.

"What was your life like lately, these last years—before coming here?"

"Good. Nice. I have my own house. I like working on houses. I'm getting good at it, too. I like it way better than working for someone else."

"What is it you like about being on your own?"

"I don't get nervous. I tell the customers what I'm going to do, how much it will cost, and I do it. I keep my word and they like that."

"I'll bet."

He keeps thinking they're finished the way she caps her pen as if she's about to pack up. She uncaps it again.

"I see that your mother visited you. Are you close to her?"

"Yes." He thinks. "Yes."

"Where's your father?"

"Dead."

"Tell me about him."

"I never knew him. I saw pictures. That's all."

"Did you ever try to find him?"

He laughs. "No."

"Why do you laugh?"

"He died when I was like two or three."

"Oh. How did he die?"

"He was an alcoholic."

"Did he have an accident or . . . get a disease?"

"My mother said pretty much everything in his body stopped." His mother had told him when he was old enough to understand that his father had been a quiet man, not violent or anything, but a man who was so full of sorrow he was killing himself every day. She said it was as bad as if he stabbed himself repeatedly. He took all her money for drink. She couldn't watch it, and she couldn't keep supporting it, so she made him leave.

Dr. Beni is watching him, so he adds, "They were separated at the time."

"Do you remember him at all?"

"No. Sometimes I think I do, but I probably just remember things my mother said."

"Angry things?"

"No. No, she didn't get angry. She said he was . . . lovely. She meant as a person. In other ways. She still loved him."

"I see. Were there other adults in your life when you were growing up?"

He tells in stops and starts about his grandmother, who cared for him a lot of the time, and then he adds the thing about being a quadroon.

The lines of her face soften. "Me, too," she says. "There are so many of us around and people don't know."

Then something in her expression . . . she doesn't look like his grandmother or mother, but she reminds him of these women in his life all the same.

"SQUAD MEETING AT one," Coleson tells McGranahan.

"Why so late?"

"Waiting for the labs. We're supposed to review the tapes of the confession before we go in."

"Commander is just exercising muscle. It'll go our way eventually. I think."

"What do you mean, you *think*?"

"I woke up with doubts. Probably dreamt something."

Coleson stares at him. "Shit. If you start getting wobbly on me—"

"Well, we did stop looking fairly early on."

"We were logical."

"I know. It'll be okay."

What they have found and will have to report is that nine co-workers, all men, drive black cars to work. But Cal Hathaway has a dark blue Hyundai that could easily have been mistaken for black, though why he needed to drive a block to commit the crime is not totally clear. If he drove because he felt he could be more hidden, that makes it a very premeditated crime. They hadn't been thinking of him that way.

McGranahan paces. "What would energize Cal Hathaway to do the murder in the middle of the night? Hands around her neck? *Gloves on.* That's the part that bugs me. If he just went there, woke her up, tried to get it on with her, okay. She said no, he got angry. Or maybe he went there earlier, they had a kind of date. Hung out. Then they had an argument. But why would he put on his work gloves in the middle of the night?"

"Something needed fixing in the house?"

McGranahan looks skeptical.

Coleson says, "I see your point. We don't know the scenario; we don't have the details. But that's just because we can't guess what went on between them and what went on in his head."

"And he's left-handed."

Coleson's breathing makes a raspy sound. "I know he did it. Let's look at the tape. Maybe we can establish that he's ambidextrous."

McGranahan says, "Look, I don't want to get demoted over this."

"Okay, you've got me going, I admit, but it doesn't do to apologize for our work on this. What kind of clout are we going to have if we start backpedaling first thing?"

"I know."

"I'm going to get a roll and coffee and then we'll watch the tape."

Day-old rolls from Panera Bakery on a big platter in the entryway—McGranahan has seen them and passed them up, coming in. He watches Coleson take a roll and coffee. McGranahan eats little, and never the stuff that appears at the office. Almost all food is appealing to Coleson and almost none appeals to McGranahan, which, everyone jokes, makes them perfect partners, Mr. Convex and Mr. Concave.

* * *

HE CALLS A WOMAN named Rita who works for the party and is a point person on the campaign up in Centre County. Otherwise her days are spent in an insurance office up in Bellefonte. He met her ten months ago one night at some party-sponsored picnic and went back to her place. He left about three in the morning, murmuring endearments. She's not pretty at all. Which doesn't matter to him. He liked her. She needed a little excitement in her life and he provided it.

"What's doing?" she asks in a too-cheerful voice.

"Seeing people. Talking. It's what I do for a living."

"I know that." He assumes she's a bit miffed that he disappeared on her some two months ago.

"We've had a mess here at the firm—"

"I saw the news."

"It's nothing to do with us, but it's distracting as hell. Otherwise, things are going swimmingly. We're positioned well. We've got good people in the field. Like you. Are you going to bring in Centre County?"

"I don't know."

"Sure you are." He likes to say her name like *sweetah.* "Rita, Rita! I think you're just modest."

"If that means I worry a lot, yes, I guess so."

"Fretting is okay. The best people fret. You just have to make time for fun, too."

"I do."

"Good. You know, I didn't ask you straight out if you're seeing someone."

He waits out the little pause on the other end of the line before she says, "Nothing you need to know about."

"How about I come up and rescue you for a little meeting with me this afternoon?"

"I'm at work."

"I know. I mean, I called you at work. The thing is we're all pretty ragged down here over this killing."

"I can imagine."

"So, you can rescue me is what it comes down to. We can go for coffee and go over contributions and you can let me put my head on your shoulder."

"I guess. Yes."

"I have to stick to the office here for some to-do with the police trying to find out more about this woman who got killed. I could get there about when you're done with work. What happens when you quit work for the day?"

"What happens then is I will walk my dog."

"I will walk him with you."

"We take long walks."

"I can handle that." His phone rings through. "I have to take a call. I'll see you late afternoon."

He works one or the other of his three phones all morning, getting Connolly in position.

MONICA LOOKS UP TO see Sam O'Malley, one of her colleagues, at her office door, a hand on each jamb, expansive. "Hey, it's really you," he says. "I wondered if anybody besides me would come in early."

She had really thought *she* would be the only one in the offices. School won't begin until August 24, a week from now. The first event is an opening mass on August 23. "I like to get a jump on things," she says. "It's hardwired in me, always doing massive preparation."

He smiles at her. "I'm glad to be getting back. I got totally bored this summer."

"Most people don't admit that."

"Well, I'm not a golfer. I don't totally mind writing academic articles, but I don't like doing it alone. I'm a collaborator. Give me people."

She laughs. Is being dependent such a bad thing?

"Are you okay?" he asks. "I saw the news."

"I'm . . . okay."

"Did you know her?"

"I didn't. My husband hardly did. Apparently she really lobbied for a job, wanted to, you know, get ahead, be ready for law school, and look what happened. It reminds me of a person who fights to get on a flight and then the flight crashes—stories like that."

"I know what you mean. That's why I never try too hard. Or, maybe I'm just lazy."

Sam O'Malley loves his work. And he does write articles. Though what there is left to write about, given the huge interest in the social aspects of crime, and all that is written about it and shown on TV, she wonders. Well, it's a publish or perish world, the academic treadmill.

"Being lazy obviously works for you." She smiles. "Will your classes be full? As usual?"

"Yeah. There's a waiting list. It isn't me, it's the subject."

"Don't sell yourself short. I hear good things."

"Thank you. Are your classes full?"

"Full enough. The one is Government and Medicine. When I proposed it last year, I never guessed it would be quite so timely. Now I have to worry if violent protesters will take my class just to disrupt it."

"It's a mess for sure. Your husband probably has a lot to say about the whole health care thing."

"Somehow he avoids the topic. Pretty good trick, huh? He sticks to bringing industry into the state and getting rid of crime and creating jobs. Nobody is against jobs so far as I know."

" 'Too many jobs. Down with jobs!' " he chants lightly. "What's it like? Being first lady in waiting?"

"I try not to think about it."

"I'm a Democrat. Just so you know."

"I used to be. Maybe still am, underneath." She looks around her small office, just so, just exactly as she wants it—each book in order. She's imagined scenarios in which she gives it up and other ones in which she doesn't. Her future is a script in the making. She knew of a woman who hired a car to drive her the three and a half hours to work three days a week and used the time in the backseat as prep time, office time. It's possible she'll opt for that pattern.

"Want to go for a coffee?"

"Sure. Why not?"

Why not is that he's flirting and always has and that she doesn't exactly mind. She's never been unfaithful—unhappiness lies that direction for sure—but right now she feels a divided self, like a highway sign that shows a road splitting. Left lane straight ahead, right lane veers off. She feels the pull of the right lane, something else, something different from the straightaway of her life.

But she has two boys. Parents. In-laws.

She slings her handbag over her shoulder.

"I'm sorry you have this awful thing in your life, this tragedy. It must be distracting."

"Distracting . . . yes, yes it is. It takes up my thoughts. Mike is upset. And there's still the funeral."

He says, "Well, I'm sorry."

"At least they caught the guy fast. I'd like to interview him. I've been trying to get access."

"No fooling?"

They begin to walk down the hall and don't say much of anything until they're outdoors.

Sam says, "I'm going to use the case in my class, first day. They will all have seen it on the news—well, unless they're more out of it than I think."

Outside it's a bit cloudy, but otherwise nice, a good temperature.

"I feel like we're playing hooky," she says.

He laughs appreciatively.

SO NOW HE LIES ON HIS bunk and he reviews the conversation, trying to guess what Beni concluded about him, why she asked what she asked, what she will report.

"Do you have a girlfriend?" she asked.

"No," he said.

"Did you ever have a girlfriend?"

"There were girls I took out to a movie or to Kennywood. Just simple dates. In high school and after."

"Did any of them work out?"

He shook his head.

"Why?"

He looked down at his hands. He hated the fact that his hands and knees shook. "I need to change the type I'm attracted to."

"To?"

He shrugged. "Somebody who doesn't zip around at a hundred miles an hour."

She frowned. "Do you possibly prefer men?"

"No. No way. That's not for me." He looked at his feet and wondered if the group he had sat with had already started that rumor. "Is that what people automatically think if you're not dating?"

"Nice people just want you to be happy. Whatever you need."

"I'm okay alone."

"Don't you get lonely?"

After a pause he admitted it. "Yes."

"Do you attend a church?"

"Not since I was a boy. With my grandmother." This new tack in questioning threw him off. He'd got a message that Father Mansour wanted to come talk to him again and that was okay. He liked the guy fine.

"They'll have services here at the jail if you want to go. Do you have any questions for me?"

He couldn't think of anything to ask.

"Do you know why you're in the Allegheny County Jail?"

"You asked me before."

"Yes."

"They didn't have anybody else. I was easy."

"That's a serious charge."

"When you've had a bad history—I mean the blackouts—you can't get past it. It sticks."

"One thing I'm not clear on . . . when was your last blackout?"

"I *think* almost ten years ago. But the thing is I can never be absolutely sure. That's the thing."

She had looked thoughtful.

"Hathaway," the voice on the speaker says. His cell door opens. An escort appears.

"Where?" he asks boldly, his own voice surprising him.

HE WISHES HE COULD avoid the office.

The man at the desk in the lobby leans forward and says, "Good morning, Senator. I'm sorry for your loss."

"Thank you." They don't know what other term to use.

Connolly goes up the elevator with four other people who appear to be watching him, trying to find the opportunity to say a few words. Finally one after another of them ventures a phrase of condolence.

As he thanks them, he can't wait to get away, to be alone even though, when he is alone, it's worse, the way he can't control the meanderings of his own mind. *Don't think of the word "elephant."*

He has to step over flowers, bouquets of them stacked before the glass doors leading to his firm. If only this kind of effort, excess, could bring her back. He uses his pass card to open the door.

"How are you, sir?" asks the lovely model-ish receptionist with geometric hair.

"Upset . . . I know we all are," he says. She nods curtly. And that seems to satisfy her and the others at the front desk.

All this mess. For what? To feel the thrill, to be fourteen years old again? Hard-ons from eating a banana or turning a page or walking down the street, not to mention looking at breasts, legs, bums, stomachs, anything. The feeling of life.

His secretary, the one he shares with his brother, since computers have eliminated the one-to-one relationship of old, hands him a few pieces of snail mail, also a relic of another time. Almost everything of a daily nature—inquiries, drafts—comes to him by computer. This secretary is a well-dressed woman of about forty, with smooth, highlighted hair and good shoes. Her expression is that of sympathy, concern.

Who suspects him, then? Which woman or man up here told the police he was having an affair with Cassie?

He and she had worked out a story, a routine. She was supposed to make something up. She was supposed to allude to a guy she was seeing to satisfy any curiosity about her. When they lay in bed, teasing about it, she said, "Oh, he's young, younger than I am. Very handsome. A bit of an athlete—such a body. He's always eager. We polish off a bottle of wine together some nights."

For a tiny moment he thought it was true, she sounded so convincing. But then she looked depressed and said, "Is that good enough?"

"Well, no. You haven't answered why you aren't seen with him anywhere, why you don't go out."

"Oh."

"You'd better say he's married but, you know, make up everything else," he'd told her.

"I couldn't."

"Why?"

"I don't like that identity. I don't like being a person who would do such a thing."

That had stopped him cold since she *was* a person who was doing such a thing. How did she talk to herself? What was in her mind?

"I know," she said. "I'll say I'm seeing someone who is very shy. He doesn't like crowds or any of that. We're taking it slow. We don't run in similar circles, so we're just trying it out. I'll say I've met his family at a picnic and they are like him, simple and unassuming. I'll tell people I like that kind of person."

And did she? "Okay," he said. "That might float. What is it you like about him?"

"He's genuinely nice. In a world that's so full of rotten people."

"Of bullshit."

"Yes."

"Well," he said. "That's your story, then. Stick to it. And make sure to drop it every once in a while. Because people are going to be curious about you."

She always got to him when she wrapped around him, the way she held on to him. "It's torture not touching you at the office," she said.

"I think you're marvelous. I don't know how you do it. You move around that place as if you don't notice me and don't even like me that much."

"I care only about you," she said quietly. "I'm trying to give you what you need." She pressed tighter, as if she wanted to climb into him. "I care so much it hurts."

"I love you," he blurted. Since the words surprised even him he had to think about whether it might be true. The dangerousness of love, the doubleness of his life, hit him. He was alerted to danger that night, worried by his own words.

"I want to spend my life with you," she said.

He cursed his body for getting him into this. "Let's talk about work," he said abruptly. There was a tear formed at the corner of her eye, the way she was lying on her side. Her body made that perfect rolling-hills shape that painters loved. He traced it with his right hand, then cupped her chin. "Let's talk about work and get rid of sad thoughts."

"I will spend my life with you."

"How?"

"Because things change. They do. Your wife is undeserving and unprincipled—"

"Don't say that."

"And dumb."

"Please don't say that. It's complicated."

"But she loves someone else. Have you no pride?"

"I have pride. Don't accuse me like that." He got up. He left her alone in the bed. She started crying. "Just understand there are things you don't know."

"Like what. Tell me."

"Married life. People get bored."

"It doesn't have to be that way. My parents didn't get bored."

He thought, How does she know that? He thought, It's probably because they're boring people to begin with. He fumed and walked to the window of the motel room, pulling the heavy drape aside. It was bright evening out there still. Men were home at dinner with their families. Or off playing golf. Why did he need this?

"I love you. I'll wait."

"We must be extremely careful."

"I'll let you concentrate on the campaign."

"Thank you."

"I won't wait forever. I never did this before and I don't like myself for it and I want to make it right somehow."

"Just hang on. We'll figure it out." He suddenly needed to get out of that room, get his clothes on, and be away. Until the next time he saw her pretending to avoid him and wanted her all over again.

He shook off the memory now as he opened his mail. Ballet offering complimentary tickets, asking him to consider being on the board. He already had the symphony board and the Pitt board and the Cultural Trust. Could he take on another?

Request for money.

Request for money.

Why could she tease and tease like a pro and then turn gloomy? Did she actually like the simple fellow she made up the story about? Did she see him sometimes? Was it Cal?

He banished these thoughts and turned on his computer. His screensaver faced him with Monica and his boys.

He hated himself. He could go to the police, that nice one, the commander, and admit he had lied about his relationship with her. No more lies. Clean slate.

He would go to church. Next Saturday. He grew up on confession. *I took a baseball, I swore, I tricked my brother and got him in trouble, I stole money from my father's wallet, I masturbated eight times in one day.* Sin or adolescent behavior, it was a relief to seek forgiveness.

*   ●   ●

CHRISTIE STOPPED BY the jail to talk to the old gnome-like doctor who had scanned Cal Hathaway's body for evidence of mosquito activity. "There was something that could have been an old bite or a mild bite, I can't tell. Some people don't react much to a mosquito. Some swell up like crazy."

"Hm. I see. Not conclusive, then."

"Right. Not conclusive. He was pretty jumpy, shy. But I managed an exam. One of the stranger requests I've had."

"Keep it under wraps, would you?"

The doctor grunted a yes.

Christie spent the rest of the morning reading about mosquitoes until his skin itched. One site called them the most dangerous creatures alive because of the terrible diseases they could transmit. They were nasty little things, "little flies," looking for hosts and drinking vampirically. Could one be a little witness?

He decided as he started toward the squad meeting room not to bother the others with this particular obsession. He'd scheduled the meeting later than usual, one o'clock, since he was hoping for more stuff from Baitz.

His detectives trooped in a bit more alert than they had on Sunday.

Christie first asked for the report on black cars. He started writing on the board. There were thirteen altogether, four in the neighborhood and nine at work.

Then gray cars. Nineteen altogether.

"Unless we hear something to the contrary today, I'll want you to check alibis for those people."

"Yes, Boss," they answered in a syncopated chorus.

"Home break-ins in Oakland. Burglaries, muggings?" He pointed to the two detectives he'd had going through those files.

"More muggings than break-ins. Two hundred and fifty-two muggings over the last three months. Reported muggings, that is. Some were faked-up claims when cell phones and iPods got lost, etc. Most were real. Most were never solved. The few that were solved were the dumb ones who used credit cards. Three are in the county jail, two are in other facilities. We also checked with Pitt and CMU and Carlow on these numbers because sometimes the university police have their own records. We added auto break-ins on our own because they yielded good prints. We've gathered files of fingerprints from all the vehicle break-ins and are ready to turn them over for comparison to anything found at the Price house if that should become necessary."

Christie nodded appreciatively even though he heard the phrasing—*if that should become necessary.* Cal was such a perfect suspect. Who wanted to give him up? He wrote on the board, *Many muggings not solved,* and all the while he worried that he didn't have the full trust of his squad. *Jail and prison inmates off the list,* he wrote. "Make sure you delete these guys who are in jail," he instructed. "And now for home break-ins?"

"A hundred eighty-nine the last three months. Three twenty-two—when we went back six months. Reported. Seventy doors left open, about a hundred through windows, the rest were doors jimmied."

"How many solved?"

"About ten percent. Two of the jimmied doors were solved. We'd like to talk to those guys today. Both got released from jail early. They didn't take that much. So either of them might be at it again."

"Thank you. Yes, I'd like for you two to search those guys out. Bring them in here and question them." He wrote, *Question burglary suspects.*

Although he'd already talked to Potocki, Christie asked him to report to the group on the interviews at the funeral home. "Give us a picture of Cassie Price and her friends and acquaintances."

Potocki stood. "I found the interviews . . . telling and also puzzling. I talked to young men who went to school with her. They were noticeably upset, of course. No one came off as particularly suspicious. I asked them each if they had dated her. I kept getting a 'no, but if only I could have' kind of response. This was pretty consistent. I kept pressing. Did she flirt a lot, keep a lot of guys on the hook? Believe me, I didn't ask it quite that way. But they seemed to say yes, she was fun and flirty. But then they also said she was off-limits, highly religious. She must have driven them a bit mad, from what I can tell."

Dolan said, "I got some of this at work, too. The same thing. I'd summarize the personality as having some conflict about sex."

"Colleen?" Christie asked. She was known in the squad for her former job, a counselor. She had the psych degrees.

Colleen flushed and swallowed hard. She stood. "I get angry when men bandy about the term 'hysteric,' or 'tease' or 'cock tease.' So I want to be careful here. More harm has been done to women by men categorizing them as conflicted about sex. I don't mean this against any of you. I just want to make a caution for the record. Sometimes a woman just doesn't want a certain person, but she doesn't want to be mean about it. I think, to be honest, many men and women alike would, however, call Cassie Price irresponsible about her flirting, and that's that. She did not appear to want to engage in casual sex; she'd had that strict upbringing. Her parents will probably be shocked to find she was sexually active at all. But back to the point. Her personality was . . . defensive. She put a cheerful face forward, which made her generally liked. But she was secretive about sex. And apparently she felt she needed an extraordinary man to justify having sex. She was always in love, according to her sister, but it was always with someone in a position of power and not particularly attainable. I vowed confidentiality in my conversation with her sister, so I need for all of you to honor that. But the end result is important. It seems she was seeing someone she couldn't or wouldn't talk about."

"Her sister said this?" Denman asked.

"Yes. But her sister didn't know who."

There were murmurs.

Colleen sat.

Christie said, "We need to find out the who. It doesn't mean he killed her, but we will need to clear the man she was seeing." He considered saying he was pretty certain it was Connolly, but he held his tongue. It was awfully salable information. He didn't need the headache of a leak right now. "Littlefield. Potocki. You were looking at her e-mails."

Janet Littlefield reported, "She did a lot of work e-mails, and like I said they're ordinary—what reports she had received, when she would finish some project. There were some personal exchanges, but nothing about a boyfriend. One about shopping for work clothes that would look appropriate. Several when she bought her house—to the Realtor, the bank, her sisters. One with a friend who wanted her to go on vacation to the beach. She answered that she couldn't take the time off work because she needed the money for school. She did write to Carrie, her sister, to say when she was coming to visit. That was every Saturday except one in the last two months."

"Is there any indication in the e-mails of what she did on Friday nights?" Christie asked. "I mean, work was done for the week. Did she say in the e-mails what she was up to after work?"

Littlefield shook her head. "Potocki read them, too."

Potocki said, "No, nothing about where she spent her time."

Christie said, "And it's looking like she took her car to work on some Thursdays and most Fridays and yet didn't go to her family until Saturday."

Colleen said, "Even her sister thinks she was seeing the guy she was seeing on Friday nights."

"Just so we don't jump to conclusions, let's ask neighbors if maybe she came back home on Thursday and Friday nights. This is delicate. Potocki, can you do that? Ask carefully. You know how quickly rumors spread."

"This is a whole new ball game!" Hurwitz said.

"Maybe. At the very least there are people and events we need to clear."

The room felt electric with this new possibility.

"Are you saying," Hurwitz asked, "there's the possibility that the guy she was seeing went so far as to kill her and set up this poor shmuck?"

Christie shook his head. "I'm asking us to see what fits as a theory. What doesn't, we toss it out."

There was a knock at the door, and Baitz came in. "Sorry," he said. "Traffic."

"That's okay. We had other reports to make." Christie gestured him to the front of the room. "Go ahead."

"Well, I went in early this morning. Very early. I've been working on the powder. The powder on the floor and under her nails? It's almost certainly all plaster dust and paint. Like when somebody is scraping a wall."

Coleson and McGranahan practically jumped up into the air yelling, "Hurrah."

Christie felt a little wire of depression bore into his body, head on downward.

"And I've been thinking," Baitz went on, "about that astronaut idea. Look at a picture of an astronaut and what do you see? A guy all booted and covered up in white. Get it? You know what looks like that? One of those paint overalls. They're made of polypropylene and they're pretty indestructible. If we don't have any fabric traces on her and no blood under her fingernails, that could be an explanation. Those coveralls don't tear or shed."

"Holy Moses," Denman said in his very southern drawl. "We just went back to square one."

Christie stood very still. He let them watch him thinking. Finally he said, "Okay, let's get to work on Cal's car. Let's check it for matching plaster dust." He paused again. "Potocki. When you're in the neighborhood, would you also ask the people he worked for if he wore that kind of overall when he worked? Also, did he do any jobs that would kick up a lot of plaster dust?"

Coleson and McGranahan went glum again.

Christie sighed and knuckled his mouth as he figured out next steps. The others looked at him hard, but he couldn't read their expressions. "I want motive. I want a strong motive I can believe in. I'm not a hundred percent certain we have that with Cal Hathaway."

"Jealousy of her other lover," Nellins tries.

"Yes. Possibly. We can go back to Hathaway as many times as we want to try to establish guilt. But let's not miss anything else. Greer, Dolan, come with me back to the law offices. We can ask where she might have gone for that margarita."

"She could have gone almost anywhere," Colleen said.

"Don't I know it? Still, we can ask. I have appointments to see the father and the brother up there. Dolan, talk to all the married men who look like possible love interests for this girl. See who likes to go out for a drink. And Greer, you get to grill the women and the handler."

"I do?"

"You said something about liking him."

"I'M YOUR DEFENSE attorney," the man says. He's young looking, he wears a whole matching suit, and his hair sticks up in that style done with gel. He wears glasses. "What we say in here is confidential. You should feel free to tell me anything you need to tell me. How are you?"

"Terrible."

"I imagine."

"Can you get me out of here?"

"I doubt that. The bail is set very high. Five hundred thousand. You don't have that handy, I'm thinking."

"No. No I don't."

"You remember when you saw the magistrate in the middle of the night—let's call it Saturday morning. He told you then there's a hearing scheduled for next Tuesday. I'm here to prepare for that. We don't have to keep the date. That is, you can waive the hearing—"

Cal was confused, trying to follow the steps. "What does that mean? No trial? How would we—"

"No, this isn't a trial stage yet—next Tuesday. Just a hearing to see how much evidence there is and if we're going to trial. Okay? There are a couple of reasons people will waive a hearing like the one next Tuesday. If you've already decided to plead guilty—that's one reason." The fellow pauses and studies Cal closely. His glasses slip forward; he replaces them carefully, slowly.

"What's your name?" Cal asks.

"Oh, my God, I'm sorry. I'm jumping ahead. My name is Foote. Gerald Foote."

"Did . . . did they assign you?"

"They assigned me."

"Okay."

"So, to go on with how this all works, people might waive a hearing if they decide to plead guilty or they want to hurry things up or they want to avoid the publicity of a hearing. Do you understand?"

"Yes."

"Then we enter a plea. If we want a trial, we enter a plea of not guilty *or* not guilty by reason of insanity." He pauses, looks at Cal searchingly again. "Then the trial date is set. If, after the hearing next Tuesday, you decide you want to plead guilty, we avoid the trial and set a date for sentencing." Gerald Foote looks down at his blank notebook page and back up to Cal. "I know I'm doing a lot of the talking. Did you understand everything so far?"

"Yes. Um, more or less." Can he trust this man? Should he?

"I've read all the notes they have, especially Dr. Beni's. Apparently you've had some nervous episodes in the past, and that could stand in your favor if—"

"What's a nervous episode?"

"Blackouts."

"I think they were just blackouts."

"But apparently you've had some trauma in your background, and blackouts can be an indication of a nervous condition. Let me just explain. You do have the choice of pleading innocent, and then it's all up to the prosecutors to come up with proof. The detectives and the labs will all weigh in, and what they'll be looking for is *proof*. A trial is very difficult for anyone to go through—even people who have not suffered a past trauma."

Cal thought Gerald Foote was a pretty nervous person himself.

"Or you could plead guilty by reason of insanity, which gets you different treatment and a shorter term. Have you ever been institutionalized for your condition?"

"No, I have not."

"O-kay. Well, that isn't a reason to dismiss that appeal as a possibility. Keep that in mind. There is also another possibility. We could enter a plea of no contest. Nolo contendere. It basically means guilty, but the plea can't be held against you if the family wants to sue, for instance. It could mean many things—extenuating circumstances that you are unwilling or unable to explain, for instance. It's kind of like, 'Let's not get into this. Do what you have to with me. I refuse to talk.' Do you understand?"

"Sort of." It sounds like something that would be good for a Mafia boss, Cal figures. And he certainly would like not to talk, especially in court, but if it translates to a guilty plea . . . "The thing is," he says, "the longer I sit in my cell and think, the more sure I am that I didn't do anything to Cassie Price except find the body. The rest I can't explain—why they went after me."

Foote appears to study him. Cal can't read Gerald Foote's expressions—the way he grimaces and sucks on his tongue.

"I think—before I met you, reading everything over, I assumed guilty by reason of insanity was the best plea. Now I'm a bit undecided. You seem different from what I expected, more aware. On the other hand, you said you did it, then you said you didn't, which would be confusing to anyone. Why did you say yes?"

"It seemed they knew more about me than I did."

"Hm. If you could justify an insanity plea, we might be able to use that change of mind to your advantage—like you didn't know what you were *saying,* nor did you know what you were *doing.*"

"I'm not insane."

Foote writes something down. "So long as you know it's your best bet."

"What about finding out who did it?"

"I'm not sure what you're saying."

"I think it was whoever followed her home, whoever made her cry."

"Okay. Okay. Explain to me."

Cal heaved a sigh and once more he explained. He wondered if he seemed crazy to Foote. He talked, describing everything for the thousandth time.

Foote looked puzzled. "There's lots to think about. This is just our first meeting. There is also the possibility of plea bargaining," Foote said brightly. "That way, we could get the charge reduced to third degree or manslaughter."

"I didn't do it."

"You haven't been sure of that. There's the possibility of selective memory."

They left it that Foote would be back in two days.

COLLEEN HAD TO SEE the handler first because Todd Simon was in an anxious state about needing to be in Centre County later in the day. He asked if they could meet in the conference room at the Connolly offices. He worked in different places, he explained— he had an office in Harrisburg, he said, in the Republican reps quarter, and he had a title, but he was on the road a lot. They called him a campaign fund-raising czar. The phone chat leading to their interview made things seem informal. Colleen decided to go with that. She decided he was a person she could get to most easily by seeming to be doing nothing serious.

The conference room at Connolly was huge. All the chairs were upholstered in a brown tweed fabric that might have come from Ireland. It was lovely cloth. The chairs all swiveled and wheeled on miracle bearings that made it clear how low-end the conference room chairs at Headquarters were.

They sat at the end, him at the head of the table, her next to him. "I'm curious. What do you czar it over? Does that mean you look for funding irregularities?"

He made a face. "Would it shock you to hear I don't actually work at anything like my job description? Plus I tend to love irregularities. I'm a party organizer."

"And specifically a handler for Connolly?"

"Where did you get that term?"

"The media boys."

"Okay"—he put his hands up—"it's true."

"So how does it all work?"

"I try to get him money. And votes. I hardly ever land in my actual office. I'm always in meetings here and there."

"I see. Is he going to be elected?"

"You know anything bad about him?"

"No."

"He's a golden boy. He's going to be elected."

"He seems . . . more like a Democrat that a Republican."

He smiled. "I think that's good news to me. But what in particular makes you say so?"

"Personal style. He seems nicely loose. He doesn't have that strict part in his hair. You know, Republican hair. Neither do you, actually."

"Can it all be that simple?"

"Well, it probably wouldn't stand up in court, but there's a look and a manner. Come to think of it, you seem even more Dem than he does."

He swiveled back and forth in his chair, looking at her amusedly. "Well, I was once upon a time."

"Aha. Why the change?"

"I'm a complete pragmatist. I'm good at what I do. They saw that. They wanted me."

"Like an attorney. They paid, so you took their side?"

"Pretty much, yes."

"That's wild."

"Why?"

"I'm all about conviction. True belief and all that. Do you have a law degree?"

"No. Political science. Which has nothing to do with the real world, believe me."

"Interesting. Well, I know you have to go. I should get down to business here. Couple of questions only, just a little rumor we have to follow up. Ready?"

He opened his hands. "Sure."

"Did you actually know Cassie Price?"

"To say a hello. I saw her around the offices."

"Did you ever think she was in love with anybody up here at the offices?"

His expression got wary. He didn't attempt to hide it. "No. Was she?"

"I'm asking you."

"I don't know."

"Are you a married man?"

"No. I was. Once. A pretty long time ago. Then I realized I wasn't much good at marriage. Why are you asking?"

"Honestly, we just need to clear possibilities off the books."

"I'm sorry. But you have a confession in this case, don't you?"

She nodded glumly. "And no details. And so it means a lot of work for us, to eliminate all other possibilities."

"Oh, I see. Everything is always more complex than people know. Almost everything."

"Yes. It can be a drag, doing all the eliminating. So only two more questions. What kind of car do you drive—make and color?"

"A Saab. Color? I think they call it Light Pewter. No, let me think. That was some other car I had. Glacier Silver, I think."

"Fine. And where were you on the night of Thursday the thirteenth?"

"In my bed."

"Anybody to vouch for you?"

"No. Is that bad?"

"Neither bad nor good. It just is."

CHRISTIE'S INTERVIEW with the most senior Connolly, the head of the family and of the firm, was brief and unfulfilling. The man oozed importance and conducted himself with absolute restraint. He welcomed Christie into his office, a place of high polish and almost clear surfaces. It must have taken whole rooms full of files to keep things this free of clutter. Christie had passed other offices in which file folders were piled high on every surface, high and low, among family pictures, food, trinkets, mementos.

"I want to be helpful. What can I tell you?"

"Tell me how you happened to hire Ms. Price."

Connolly told the same story his son had. The son's friend called. Then his own friend called. Her name kept coming up. "By the time we had three pleas to hire her, it seemed fated."

"Tell me about Elinor Hathaway—her work habits, her family?"

Connolly Sr. frowned at the change of subject. "She used to work for me. I hated to leave her behind, but we talked it over and did what was best for her. I adore her. She is like a part of the family. I can't say enough good about her."

"And her son?"

"I didn't know him well. Like everyone else, I'm shocked that he did this murder. I always liked him. He seemed a lot like his mother, a salt-of-the-earth hard worker."

"Did you know he got badly beaten as a boy? Almost died?"

"I knew about that, of course. I hired a temporary worker to give Elinor time off."

Christie asked a few more questions. He asked formally for an alibi for the time of death.

"Me?" John Connolly looked at him strangely. "At home in my bed."

"Any witnesses to that?"

"No. More here than meets the eye, then," he said.

"Just routine."

"Let me know of anything we can do to help. And anything I can do to help the family."

Christie left John Connolly's office aware the man had not tooted his own horn, had not said he paid Elinor the whole time she was off and paid doctor bills, too. He found himself literally scratching his head. He watched Colleen Greer now leaning forward to hear something one of the secretaries was telling her sotto voce. He hoped Greer got something good.

So, no alibi at all for the elder Connolly. The youngest, Mike, had an alibi, but it wasn't airtight. A man could drive like a maniac from Harrisburg to Pittsburgh, do the murder, and drive back equally fast to make it to breakfast. It was unlikely but almost possible.

The other Connolly son was named Evan. He opened the door to his office almost eagerly.

"How are you holding up?" Christie asked.

"We have a lot going on. Issues with Aramark, Allegheny General, just to name a few, but of course we're all thinking about our paralegal."

"Thank you for making time for me."

"You're welcome." Evan's less than perfect face became more and more attractive as they talked. It reminded Christie of how John Malkovich's looks had seemed to morph on various screens from simply odd to simply fascinating.

Christie asked many of the usual questions and ended where he had ended with Michael—asking about the rumor of an affair at the office. "I have to ask if you were seeing her."

Evan was visibly shocked. "No, absolutely not."

"Do you know who was seeing her?"

"No."

Was there a flinch, a glance aside? "Just one more thing. I have to ask this. It's part of a routine investigation. Can you account for your own whereabouts on last Thursday evening and night—the thirteenth of August?"

"I can't think."

"Take your time."

"I went home. We . . . watched TV."

"How late?"

"Oh, eleven. The Steelers, the news."

"And then?"

"I slept the night."

"Can you prove you didn't leave the house?"

"No, I can't prove it. My wife would know that I didn't. She wakes with the drop of a feather. This whole question is making me sick to my stomach."

"I understand. I really do. I hate asking as much as you hate answering." So. No airtight alibis so far. He changed tacks. "Do you ever go out for a drink after work?"

"Am I being invited?" Evan asked with the first glimmer of humor.

"No. I'm not much for it. But do you ever?"

"I don't. I'm a boring homebody."

"Who from this office does go out?"

"God, I don't know. Probably several."

"Anybody favor margaritas?"

"A guy named Pruss does. He's one of our attorneys. I've heard him talk about the good tequilas."

"Okay, thanks. I forgot to ask your father and your brother if they ever go out after work. Do you know the answer?"

"The answer is yes, both. Always a business reason, though, when they need to oil a client. They'd both rather go home. They just play the game a bit better than I do."

"What's the best place for a margarita?"

"God. That I don't know. I can't help asking: Is that important in some way to the investigation?"

"We're just clearing the decks. Or the books. Whichever image you like. Simply building our case."

"I see. Oh. Well, I don't know where a good margarita can be found. I could ask Pruss."

"No need. I'll ask."

COLLEEN HAD BEEN talking to Olivia Della Vida, the middle-aged secretary whom Michael and Evan shared. Della Vida said, "I love working for Michael Connolly. He's the best." When Colleen asked about Cassie Price having a crush on Connolly, the secretary looked miserable, then said, "We're all a little bit in love with him."

Colleen pushed the envelope. "The truth is, it was more than a crush. Cassie Price was in love with someone up here. She told her sister. We're just checking the story. Was it Michael or someone else?"

"If you ask it that way, I'd have to say yes, it was probably Michael."

"And not just because everybody was. Because? What did you notice?"

The woman wrung her hands. "Am I going to get into trouble? Or get him into trouble?"

"No," Colleen lied. "This is simply routine—and confidential."

So finally Della Vida answered. "Because we all made jokes about how handsome Michael is and she never did. She avoided him so much, I thought it was unnatural."

"Did you assume they were actually *seeing* each other?"

"I hate to say it . . . I kind of did."

"Why?"

"The way I always made appointments for him for afternoons on Thursdays and Fridays in Harrisburg. I would think, if I were messing around, that's exactly how I'd do it. A real place to be, but some flexible hours in between."

"That's very observant of you. Does he have a second house somewhere? An apartment in town?"

"Not that I know of." The woman's face changed. Her eyes became cloudy. "I'd rather hurt myself than hurt him. Is he in trouble?"

"No, he's not," Colleen lied again. "People have secrets. All kinds of secrets. Basically we need to clear him."

"Good." But Della Vida still looked uncertain.

When Colleen met up with Christie, he said, "Connolly denies it."

She told him what she had found out and said, "Potocki was planning to ask the neighbors if they ever saw a tall, handsome, well-dressed man going to Cassie's house. I doubt it. My bets are he met her somewhere else. We need the where—hotel, apartment, somebody's house? Too many possibilities."

"A lot of possibilities. Still, I'll have you and Potocki or just Potocki working on that angle. You have any other ideas?"

"The parking garage? They might have cameras that would show which Thursdays and Fridays she brought the car. Could narrow it down."

"Go for it," Christie said.

*   •   •

EVAN AND MICHAEL have been at each other more times than not, the four years of age between them making for an awkward brotherhood—Michael trying to be like his older brother and friends, Evan resenting his younger brother's popularity, not to mention the free pass Michael seemed to get from parents, teachers, everyone. As Evan got older, he adopted a little wisdom and stopped being furious at Michael. But when he enters Michael's office, after the detectives have left, he has that look—almost crossed eyes, furrowed brow. He takes a seat without being asked. "What's going on?"

"They're gone. Is that what you mean?"

"I think you know what I mean."

"We should go get some lunch. I haven't had anything."

"I ate. I couldn't eat even if I hadn't. You haven't answered me."

"Look. I don't know what to say. This is a terrible situation, and I have my hands full with orders about whether or not I should appear in public or be seen as a candidate right now. My phone rings every thirty seconds—"

"So you were seeing her." His hands go to his face. He pushes and worries his skin upward.

"What?"

"You think I don't know you by now? When you won't answer a question, when you divert—I know you."

"There are things—we flirted a little. People might think she was in love with me. I'm sorry for that. Believe me, I'm sorry I ever flirted. It was harmless. Nothing happened."

Evan sat for a long time, staring at him. Finally he said, "You do understand, the way they're asking questions, they don't feel the case is solved. They're looking here. You do understand that, don't you?"

Michael can't think of what to say for several moments. "I'm not sure."

"I'm sure. Three of them up here quizzing us about married men? A rumor? We have to deal with it. I talked to Dad. I thought he was going to have a heart attack. This is serious. So you were seeing her, then. It's not a question."

Michael nods.

"My God." Evan drums his fingers against his thigh, keeping his eyes there. Then he looks up. "Did you—"

"Of course not. I may be a louse and bad at marriage, but—"

"Were you able to provide an alibi?"

"Yes. Yes, I was in Harrisburg. At Haigh's place."

"Did they accept that?"

"Yes. Look, I didn't kill her. I wouldn't. I couldn't. Why would I?"

Evan makes another of his scowling expressions. "I can think of scenarios in which she might be considered dangerous."

"Right. But she wasn't." Michael feels sick as he says this. In his head he is having a similar conversation with Todd, but he is the one who's asking, "Do you know what the police are asking? Do you know anything about this?"

"Did you go out for a drink with her that day? Thursday?"

"No. I never did anything like that. I was never seen with her."

"Believe me, somebody saw you somewhere."

"I don't think so. I was very careful."

"In a way that's more depressing than the other." Evan gets up angrily, leaves, and manages not to slam the door. Controlled, as always.

Connolly immediately calls Todd. The first number he calls is not answering, not even voice mail. Todd has some complicated system of turning off and on cell phones. He tries a second number and gets a hurried "Hey, man. You okay?"

"Of course I'm not. Come in to see me, would you?"

"No can do. I'm nowhere near."

"Where are you?"

"About where the Corner Restaurant used to be, Route 22. Just passed it. Why?"

"Because you know what the police were up here about. You know what they're asking."

"I figured it out, yes. We have to weather it. You have to keep a real clear true course."

"How long are you going to be away?"

"Well, the campaign isn't just going to stop. I have work to do."

"Where?"

"Centre County."

"Will you be at the funeral tomorrow?"

"I will be there with you. I will be there *for* you. I'll support you all the way. We'll talk there."

"That seems a funny place for a talk," Connolly says.

"One of the things I have to do today is strategize about the funeral. You did great on the news yesterday. Everybody agrees on that. Go with another sound bite, we haven't made up our minds. Somebody will call you tonight. Maybe me. Gotta hang. I'll call you later."

For the first time, he allows himself to think it. When he tries to stand, a dizzy spell grips him, the room starts to move, and he falls back into his chair.

JUST LIKE THAT, THE corrections officer's voice came over the intercom saying, "Cellmate for 205," and moments later Levon was at his cell door, which opened, and then Levon was inside.

"You heard it. You got me as a roomie."

"Oh."

"You been sleeping on the bottom. I'll take the top. No problem."

"Why'd they change things? I was okay with the way it was."

"The guy I was in with said I drove him crazy, talking all the time. Just between us I did it on purpose. I din like him either. So I just talked him to death."

"I didn't know they made changes."

"If people can't get along, or if you, you know, agitate. So here I am. I see you're neat." Levon opens the wire cage closest to the bunk beds and sees Cal's things neatly folded and lined up. He opens the other wire cage to put in his few things—the tiny threadbare towel, a Bible, another book of some kind, his Walkman-style radio player.

"How come you din get a radio? Somebody take it?"

"I didn't want one."

Levon says, "You should get a radio. It helps. You need to come down to Pod Central. You need to talk some."

"I'm not a talker."

"Better to learn how. You don want to make enemies."

Yeah, well, Levon had apparently made an enemy of his former cellmate by talking, so there was a fine line to tread.

"I just don't have anything to say," Cal murmured.

"Make up stuff. Everybody does. But here's the thing you need to know. They going to be at you—what your lawyer say, what your police say, who your mother know, what you did, what you going to plead, everything. But this is the trick. See, they be looking to pump you so they can sell what you say. So you can't give them anything. Not anything real. I give them a bunch of bull, so when they try to use it, they come out like liars. I heard that trick from a guy who made it through prison and came out the other side just fine. Told a whole bunch of hooey about being an airline pilot and a singer with two CDs out and all kinds of things. None of it true, so the people reporting on him looked stupid bad. You listen to me."

Cal began to say several things—all the while Levon watching as if to guess at the sentence that never came out.

"You want to know why you should believe me," Levon interpreted. "You want to know why I bother to tell you shit."

"Well . . . yeah."

"I don know. I do not know."

"You don't tell what *you* did?" Cal was curious, and in this he supposed he was like the others.

"I tell you what they say. Here is what they say. They say I took a gun that I bought illegal on the street and I went into this furniture store and I held up Mr. Weiss. He threw money at me like I was a animal, but all the time he was ringing alarms and I shot at him. I say I found the gun and went to scare him and shot to scare him because he was reaching under the counter. Now what is true? You can guess. Some things is true and some is not true. But Mr. Weiss, I will tell you this about Mr. Weiss, he is a ugly son of a bitch who charged my mother triple for some fucking bad furniture, then took it away when she couldn't pay this one month after paying all these years. He deserve to die slow. That's how bad he is. He out there cheating people, like, and laughing about it, and me, I'm in here. Believe what part you want."

"Armed robbery."

"He say I ask for a hundred thousand dollars. I say I asked for my mother's payments back. Who will the jury believe?"

"Him," Cal said plainly. He shivered to think Mr. Weiss might be the truthful one.

"Everybody want to know why you killed that girl. How you did it. Even I want to know why. If you want to be smart, you say knifed her if the truth was you shot her and you say shot her if the truth was you hit her, you get the idea. Mix it up. But you can tell me *why* you did it, right? It was like a sex thing, right? She say something ugly?"

"Never in a million years."

"Treat you bad?"

"No. Treated me good."

"What, then?" Levon looked sick. "Too damned good to live."

He didn't answer Levon, but he smiled so Levon would not hate him. Levon paced a little. "I'm going to go down and watch TV. You got your chance at the crapper. Oh, did you know some guys take the water out of the toilets so they can talk to each other between, like, the cells? I vote we leave the water in ours. Nobody I need to hear through the pooper. So I'm going now. You could come down and get used to the rest of us. It's not good to hold yourself apart."

"I'll come down in a little bit."

"Lay some cable, man."

Cal planned to stay just where he was. After a while, though, his own head got to him, and he decided he would prefer the buzzing of people like Levon and the folks on TV to the merciless fly inside his skull, so he went downstairs.

POTOCKI WAS IRRITATED with Colleen for so much as joking that she liked the handler, Todd Simon, even though she probably said it to deflect attention from them. He knew she loved him. He could *feel* it.

He was back in Oakland, looking up Iris Mender. He brightened when she answered the door. "Me again," he said.

"Not a problem. Where's your partner?"

"Other work."

"So it's just us?"

"Just us. You want to land on the glider again?"

"Sure, that's good." She half-opened the door to slide out, but paused. Was she afraid of him? He didn't think he was scary, nor did she seem easily frightened.

"I can bring you a beer or a Coke or whatever."

"Nothing for me." He brandished a bottle of water. "I come prepared." He saw then through the screen that there were papers on every surface of the living room.

"The house is a mess. I'm trying to put my life in order."

"That would be a big task for anybody."

"People keep sending me bills. I know I paid them. Why do they do that?"

He wondered if she had paid them or paid them twice. He explained, "There's a big gap between *when* you pay a bill and when they credit it. Statements are often outdated. Also computers are a problem. I mean, when the companies use computers instead of people, you can't ask questions."

"That's what I think," she said soberly.

"Do you have kids who could help you?"

"Yes. Yes, I do."

She opened the door and came out and gestured him to a seat. "I wish I knew something about your business," she said. "I wish I could bring the poor girl back."

The glider creaked as they sat on it and got their rocking rhythm going.

"That last isn't possible, but I hope you can help. It's a terrible thing when a young person dies." She acknowledged it with a nod. "What I really need to learn is what men were in her life. I'll bet you've seen something. Some visitors."

"No." She looked thoughtful. "No, I never did."

"Do you think Cal was a boyfriend?"

"I never thought so."

"Why?"

"They didn't act like a couple." She appeared to think about it. "They dressed real different from each other."

He nodded. "Just a couple more things. Did you ever notice her car being gone some nights?"

"Oh, weekends, yes, she went away."

"What? Friday to Sunday?"

"Yes, I think so."

"Car gone any other times?"

"No, well, Thursdays was her night out. She'd come home late most Thursdays."

"How late?"

"Oh, midnight. One A.M."

"Know where she went?"

"I always assumed either she had a guy or maybe had a girls' night out, that kind of thing. Young people can drink and get up the next day for work. That's youth."

"But maybe with a guy."

"I don't know, but I hope so. I always think it's a shame to miss out on that when you're young."

"Sure you never saw a tall handsome fellow coming and going?"

"Sorry to say, no."

"Do you happen to know if Cal Hathaway ever worked evenings?

I know this is a lot to remember, but would he continue working after suppertime, say?"

"The couple of times he worked for me, he did." She dipped her head down. He saw that she had colored her hair since the last time, roots all taken care of.

"Interesting. Hard worker?"

"I'd say so." She narrowed her eyes. "You don't think he did it, do you?"

"I can't say at this point. We're putting all the facts together to see what we have."

"Hmpf."

"What does that mean?"

"Nothing. Just thinking. I don't know what happened. Here I am, up all night, and no help at all."

"That's not true. I think you're a big help. I'm going to show you a picture. I want you to tell me if you think the person you saw in the alley looked at all like this." He pulled out of the slight portfolio case he carried a photograph of a polypropylene suit used for construction jobs and painting. He'd chosen the super model with a hood and booties—total coverage. He would have bought one and brought it to her, but the ones on the local shelves were the lesser models, just jumpsuits without the full coverage.

She stared at it. "Yes. I'd say yes. Like that."

"Thank you. When Cal worked for you, did he ever wear one of these?"

"Never did. No, he wore blue jeans and a T-shirt and if was colder weather a flannel shirt."

"Okay." He looked around at her street view. "You like it here?"

"I love it. I know my neighbors. It's not dangerous, no matter what people say. This killing was an isolated thing."

"I hope so. Just driving down here, though, I've seen a couple of porches with the mattresses and old couches and beer bottles—you know—a pretty sure sign that there are either deadbeat owners living there or college students renting."

"They're just kids. That's what they do."

"What's what they do?"

"Drinking, sex, sleeping late." She smiled. "Most of them grow up eventually."

You go, girl, he thought as he stood to take his leave. He said, "We appreciate your cooperation. You have my card. If you think of anything, give me a call."

"Okay." She rapped her head. "I wish there was more in here."

HE GOT TO CENTRE County just as Rita was leaving work. He came up behind her and put an arm around her shoulder. "So you see, I didn't interrupt your workday. Though I wanted to."

Her wavy hair, clumped unevenly at her collar line, was not exactly tousled on purpose—more in need of a cut. She was not into earrings and makeup. She wore dark pants with a brown and black patterned top that came down to her hips. Her shoes were brown with a small heel, sensible. He thought tenderly of her dressing for work, finding things that were presentable.

"I have to walk my dog."

"We'll do it together. Then I'm going to take you to dinner."

"I have a ton of leftovers. Half a chicken, corn on the cob, other vegetables I grilled. We might as well eat that."

"All right. I could appreciate eating in."

"You're awfully agreeable today."

"It's how I prefer to be. Things sometimes get in the way."

"Work?"

"Exciting job. Shitty job. Both."

She opened the door to her car, a white Toyota. "You remember where I live?"

"Absolutely."

He followed her home. What was it he liked about her—the dour way she had of believing in little, expecting little? Her grumpiness gave him a small tickle of enjoyment.

Her dog was leaping at her, ready to go as soon as she opened the door to her house. Todd, not even out of his car yet, watched the scene inside, this woman grunting at her dog, a tricolored corgi, big-eared and nervous. Rita quickly fastened a leash and let the dog lead her outdoors, where he went straight to Todd Simon, not fully out of his car, and commenced an immediate inspection of him. "He remembers you," she said. "Probably better than I do."

He found that funny. They walked for a long time. While they walked, he let her be the party worker he knew her to be. She reported clearly on each person in her district. "Roberts doesn't like it. Says Connolly is a pretty boy. He's pushing for Granger. Mundy is okay with it if it looks good for Centre County. I didn't know what to promise him."

"Businesses. Roadwork. Not casinos," he jokes.

"That's okay for Mundy. Roberts needs more than promises."

"Can you set up a meeting with me and Roberts? Breakfast. Something very eggy and greasy."

"Sure. When?"

"Tomorrow."

"I'll try."

He watched expressions come and go on her face. "What?" he asked.

"Why do I put up with you?"

"Because I genuinely like you and you know it."

"Maybe."

They came back to her place after about an hour of walking. This woman really gave her dog a workout. Then she took her time feeding the dog, but he wasn't put off by that. He came behind her and put an arm around her waist and felt her relax into him. He kissed her neck, her ear. When she didn't fight it, he began touching her breasts. "You're being nicer," he said.

"I like to know what's on the agenda."

"Dinner first or later? Your choice."

"Later."

"Way to go."

It was when they were lying there the second time, after the chicken, corn, grilled vegetables, and several beers, that he spoke slowly of the stress of the investigation that took police up to Connolly's offices. "You know how police are. Crude. It's terrible. And nobody has alibis. For God's sake, it was the middle of the night when it happened. We were all in our beds. If it drags on, I'm worried it will tarnish our boy."

"Does he have an alibi?"

"Sort of. He was at Haigh's place. You know how they think— did he drive away in the middle of the night and drive back?"

"Connolly was seeing her?"

"I don't know for sure, but it's how the police think. He's a good-looking guy. They worked together. Things happen. But look at the facts. Just look. They have a confession from that kid who worked on her house. So why are they bothering us up at the firm? I'm beginning to wonder if some Dem is paying them to smear us."

"Are you kidding?"

"No. I'm *not* kidding. It gets ugly about now. When people are announcing their candidacy."

"What can you do?"

"Nothing. Connolly and I will go to the funeral because we have to and then we hope it goes away." She had gotten him his breakfast date early tomorrow before the funeral.

She turned and adjusted her body, trying to find a good position in order to sleep. "It's worrisome," she murmured.

"If it comes down to it, if they doubt my alibi, what if I say I lied at first about being home alone and that I was here, with you? Would you perjure yourself for me? I can't have them at me."

"What would I have to say?"

"Just that I came up Thursday night and spent the night. That we're pretty private about seeing each other so I didn't give your name when they first asked, but I was here."

After a while she said, "I'll say it."

"Did you watch the Steelers?"

"Of course."

"We can say we watched the Steelers together. We can look up a schedule and see what was on after and say we watched that. In case they're nuts enough to ask. Maybe they won't. We'll be ready, though, no surprises."

He felt her tense up for a few minutes. But even he found the silence at her house, the ticking of the bedroom clock, peaceful. Soon he felt her relaxing into sleep.

SEVEN

FOR THE POLICE, THE funeral was a virtual repeat of the Sunday at the funeral home. The same cast of characters appeared, including the television crews. Connolly gave another sound bite, saying little more than that the death was a tragedy and that he wanted to give his time to comforting the Price family—all other questions about his candidacy off the table. Weeping boys and girls—well, young men and young women, but they seemed in their grief like children, stunned by the impossibility of death—followed the family and gave context to the funeral proceedings. No unexpected people showed up. Nobody looked suspicious. Cassie's beauty and promise went down under piles of rich soil. The sisters clung to each other.

Colleen could hardly get a moment alone with Carrie. Finally she caught up to her in the ladies' room at the church where there was a meager sandwich lunch Colleen didn't plan to stay for. "I'm so sorry," she said. "For you, for your family."

"Thank you," the girl said through the thickness of tears.

"If you think of anything else—"

"I'm sorry I told you."

"Why?"

"What good will it do? You'll just think little of her."

"The opposite. I feel all the more for her and what she was going through."

Carrie registered the comment with a sob. Colleen left her alone.

On Wednesday and Thursday the whole police force got stuck in a rut they got to know as the G-20. The world conference was coming to town, and everyone would be on call. The preparation was insane. From the top down—and that meant Washington, D.C.— there were orders about coordinating city, county, state, and visiting police as well as Secret Service. The city would be hosting tens of thousands of officers of various stripes.

"Man, why did we think we wanted the G-20 here?" Christie asked. Nobody could remember why. The whole next month was going to be a terrific time for criminals. The police could hardly do homicide investigation what with planning for unruly protesters, terrorists, and the large numbers of misdemeanor felonies to be accommodated in the local jails.

It wasn't until Friday of that week that Colleen was able to get the old man at the garage to give her surveillance DVDs for the Wednesday, Thursday, and Friday of last week and for the Thursday and Friday of the week before that. The disks would show only the entry and exit lanes. Nothing else was recorded at the garage.

First the man said she would have to watch in the parking office. Then he tried to tell her he didn't have them, that they'd been erased. She stared him down. Finally he handed over a set of DVDs. "Those cost me a few dollars," he said.

"I may need more," she answered. She waved the disks and left the place.

For a while she sat up at Headquarters, watching. She saw the blue Focus come in at a little before nine on Thursday of the week before the murder. Mike Connolly's Town Car came in at a bit after ten. She found herself watching for black cars, gray cars. At almost noon, a silver car caught her attention. It was that handler's—Todd Simon's. She watched that car leave at one that day. She saw Connolly leave at one thirty. Short workday—but no, he was going to Harrisburg, right? The blue Ford Focus left work at five. The young woman driving was alert, alive, listening to music it seemed, adjusting her belt to reach for the ticket machine, watching the gate go up, moving ahead. Cassie Price.

Christie came into the room that held the DVD player. "Anything?"

"Suppositions. Connolly left early Thursday the sixth and Friday the seventh. I'm about to start on the Thursday in question—the thirteenth."

"I put Potocki on her credit cards. He found something."

"Yeah?"

"Cassie Price paid for a breakfast in Breezewood on Saturday the eighth using her credit card."

"Breakfast?"

"He checked the credit card for motels, but nothing doing. We're guessing she was seeing Connolly somewhere—maybe they had a private place, a friend's cabin or something. What do you think?"

Colleen said, "So he goes to Harrisburg, has a real meeting in the late afternoon, suppertime. She drives to somewhere, let's say Breezewood. Gets there at seven. He drives back, meets her at say, eight, drives on home later. She goes home, too, on Thursdays. On Fridays she stays and goes to her folks."

"Could happen."

"They didn't have very long together," Colleen says quietly. "It probably made them all the more crazy."

Christie shuffles at the door between staying and going. "Potocki is going to call some motels."

"But nothing on her credit cards—"

Just then Potocki comes into the room, saying, "You're talking about the credit cards? I learned something a few minutes ago. Could help."

"Let's hear it," Christie said.

"Well, it seems the motels are supposed to keep a list of reservations or bookings even when a person pays cash because they're supposed to use a credit card to establish identity. So, the card company won't have any record, but the motels should. Might. If they're working as they should be. The only trouble is, some of them probably don't keep records, and there are a lot of motels between here and Harrisburg. It's going to be grunt work."

"And he could have been seeing her, yes, and still the killing was something else—Cal Hathaway losing it," Christie said. "I still don't think it was Cal. And I think Connolly is a nice enough guy—"

"Not too charismatic for you?"

"I think there's some soul there."

Colleen and Potocki both stifled the jokes. Their boss was getting into his priest mode.

"How are Coleson and McGranahan handling this?" Colleen asked.

"They look pretty sleepless. So does Connolly, for that matter. And we aren't terribly rested." Christie paused uncomfortably. "I have to go talk to the doctor from behavioral now. I'll let you know what she says. If you two could keep at the tapes and the motel connections . . . let's see what we have." He looked at his watch. "Be good." He left the room.

Be good? She felt like a teenager.

POTOCKI AND GREER worked well together. Christie knew it, but he'd have to break them up sooner or later.

He found Dr. Beni standing outside his office, practically tapping her foot.

"I'm sorry. Emergency."

"It's okay."

"Come in."

They settled in his office. "Thank you for coming," he said. "I very much want to get your take on Cal Hathaway."

"He's not easy."

"I know."

"All right. I read his history, and then I talked to him at length. Some people have thought of him as mentally challenged. I think a high school teacher called him 'simple.' He isn't. I went back yesterday and gave him an intelligence test. He's careful. He's slow. Deliberate. He takes his time out of some sort of *caution*. But there's nothing deteriorated in his intelligence. He's not a superhigh IQ but he's very competent. Math is fine. Reasoning is within the normal limits."

"What do you make of his confession?"

"He retracts it."

"I know. Does it strike you as a false confession—are you using that term these days?"

"We don't have any better term. It's hard to persuade judges and juries that a confession is false. They think if a person says it, it has to be true. Jurors think, 'I would never confess to something that I didn't do. Never.' But people do confess falsely—"

"I know that."

"Of course you do. I don't mean to be insulting. I think . . . I think I might be rehearsing for the hearing in case I'm needed. Cal Hathaway doesn't know why he said it. He felt pressure. He wanted to rest. Everybody who was coming at him seemed to think he did the murder. He knew he had experienced blackouts in the past. He broke. But in the cold light of day he can't make any sense whatsoever out of the idea that he would kill Cassie Price—he doesn't know why he would do it, *how* he would do it. He's at a loss."

"We may have other factors that point away from him . . ." He thought about the newest information, the labs saying they found some paint chips in Hathaway's car but no plaster dust, no particular match to what was gathered from Cassie's floor. "Would you be willing to say what you just said in the hearing? If necessary?"

She took her time before replying. "Yes." She rubbed one hand against the other, nervous. "Honestly, if I'm letting a psycho out, if I'm fooled, I don't think I'm going to forgive myself."

"I feel the same way. It's a big responsibility."

"Do you have a line on someone else?"

He nodded ever so slightly. "I can't talk about that just yet. The hearing is Tuesday. I really don't know what I'm going to do just yet. I see the DA on Monday. Be in touch?"

"Yes. Thank you, Commander."

"The thanks are mine."

AT SIX THIRTY COLLEEN and Potocki were still at the office. They caught something—they saw the silver car that belonged to Todd Simon leave the garage. They saw the driver look into the rearview mirror, put on his turn signal. Just behind him was the blue Focus. Cassie Price put on her turn signal. The silver car paused while she inserted her ticket. Then both cars turned left out of the garage.

"Ask Boss for the list of places where the good margaritas are."

"Could have been a bad margarita."

"True."

"Could have been anywhere." But Potocki was already on the phone to Christie for the information. "Some weekend assignment," he told her while he waited for Boss to answer. "Margaritas and motels."

The list of where to get a decent margarita included some of the upscale places downtown: Palomino, Eleven, Steelhead, Six Penn, Nine on Nine. It included the places on Mt. Washington. And the Big Burrito group of restaurants sprinkled throughout the city.

"That's too many drinks," Colleen said. "Even for us."

"Let's eat someplace first and then hit these places with our questions."

They ate crackers from their desk drawers to tide them over while they copied a dozen photos of Cassie Price to take with them on this tour of duty. Finally they got to the parking lot and decided to take only Potocki's car and to start with Six Penn for dinner, fancier than their usual, but not exorbitant.

Colleen ordered a margarita. "Can't help it. Got it in my head." When the waiter came back with it and a beer for Potocki, she ordered a skillet steak and he ordered a pork shank. Colleen dug out one of the photos and made her speech.

The waiters passed the photo around. Most looked puzzled, as if they hadn't paid attention to the news at all. Surprising as it was to the detectives who were working the case, Cassie Price and her fate were unknown to some and not on the minds of other Pittsburgh citizens going about their jobs.

She and Potocki spent an hour downtown and another in Mt. Washington, asking questions. Colleen refrained from ordering a second margarita anywhere. It was almost eleven when Potocki said, "Go for your car?"

She felt his hand on her back, familiar, not so professional. They were messed up, the line they had crossed was messy. "Let's make a last push. At least Soba, Casbah."

Of course, life being life, the last place they went, Casbah, was where one of the waitresses said, "Yeah, that woman was here. I remember her. I wondered where she worked. She was dressed really well, like she was rich. Some guy was putting moves on her. I figured it happened to her all the time. I thought she was rich. Then I saw on the news that she got killed and that she lived in lower Oakland and it made me think how we don't really know what we're seeing."

"You got that right," Potocki told her. "We don't always know how to interpret what we see."

Colleen took a careful breath. "The guy who was making moves on her? Can you describe him?"

"I can't. I don't remember him much—I mean not physically— but I had the impression he was cheering her up, you know, saying, 'It's okay, lighten up, I can solve your problems.' Like that kind of come-on."

"Try hard to remember him. Was he, say, very handsome and well dressed?"

"Well, no," the waitress said somewhat irritably, since she thought she had made that clear. "Not handsome, but okay looking. Sport jacket I think. Sort of uncombed hair. Way older than the woman, say in his forties I'll bet."

"That's useful," Colleen said. "I might come back with a photo. In any case, thank you. I think you've been very helpful."

They walked back to Potocki's car. He said, "She was here with Todd Simon. We need to talk to him again. Maybe Boss will want to. Or maybe he'll send me in this time."

"Yeah. So. That guy makes me nervous."

Potocki opened the passenger door for her. "You want me to take you back to your car?"

"Yes." She relaxed into the seat while he walked around to the driver's side. "Let's get my car. I don't want people talking. Then I'll come to your place."

He brightened.

She definitely didn't feel like being alone tonight.

EIGHT

SATURDAY, AUGUST 22

CHRISTIE'S KIDS WERE slumped in front of the TV. Christie stood in front of the screen and made what he hoped was a pleasant face—shutting it off seemed too autocratic.

"What?" cried Julie.

"Homework."

"I don't have any!"

Eric put his hands up. "I did mine."

"Already? When?"

"Last night."

"That's . . . unusual."

"Mom made me do it. She said she didn't know how we would spend our time here."

He laughed. What did she think, scrubbing floors? "Marina is taking you to a play."

"That isn't until two."

"Okay. Have breakfast with me. Help me work my case."

"It's Saturday," Eric said, frowning, but he looked alert, interested.

"Don't I know it?"

"What do we get to do?"

"Take a ride with me. Go pick up some phone records. Help me trace them. We could have lunch out."

When the children started moving, he turned off the TV.

"I'm coming along," Marina said. "I'm not that interested in laundry after all."

"I'm also meeting Artie."

"That's fine. I like Artie Dolan."

So she made French toast and then they drove to Headquarters and got there before eleven.

"What's the deal?" Marina had asked as they drove.

"Artie did his magic with somebody in New Jersey. We're expecting a fax—they said about eleven o'clock—of some cell phone records. Both the victim and the accused."

"They weren't easy to get?"

"Not so quick and easy. If you keep it clean, go through channels, it takes some doing."

"Where do they keep phone records?" Eric asked.

"In a computer somewhere. Both are Verizon—so legal offices are in New Jersey."

Marina said, "This is what I hate. Everything is like that. There is no such thing as local. You lose your luggage in Pittsburgh, you end up talking to somebody in Honduras."

"I think it was Puerto Rico."

"Whatever."

"Anyway"—he directed his attention to his kids, who looked interested in the task ahead—"we ought to get something from the phone records. The woman who died—well, her cell is missing, but out there in some computer, there's a record of her calls."

"No such thing as privacy anymore," Marina said to him. He was parking the car. The kids were out of their seat belts and walking into the building before he could stop them.

"No such thing."

When they caught up to the kids, Marina was saying, "I feel bad for the girl. All of us here to look at her dirty laundry."

Julie's face showed she was listening. She appeared to be turning over the phrase *dirty laundry*—

Artie greeted them in the lobby.

"Hey," Christie said. "Happy Saturday."

"To you, too." They went up a floor by elevator. Artie wore a short-sleeve madras shirt and jeans, but nothing ever looked quite casual on him because there was something of starch in the clothing as well as in his personality.

When they got to the copy room, Artie paced in front of the fax machine. "It better get here." He watched Marina and the kids poking their heads into the staff kitchen, then going to Christie's office, where Eric immediately turned on the computer. "You have an entourage today," Artie commented.

"For a little while. It's the only way I could spend any time with them."

"I hear you."

"Artie? Am I all wet? Be honest with me."

"I don't think so, but I sure do like proof. What if we see there were tons of calls from Cal to her or her to Cal? What if he called her that night? That's going to tell us something."

At eleven seventeen, they heard a hum and a click. They turned nervously toward the machine like two schlubs in a bomb flick. They watched page after page spit out, first Cal's wireless records, then Cassie's. They already had Cal's landline records, and there was nothing suspicious there.

"They sure used their phones," Christie muttered as he gathered up pages.

"Well, it's partly that and it's partly that I got us the deluxe service—we get the IDs of everybody along with the phone numbers. Good, huh?"

"Supergood. Poor Eric was all ready to do reverse phone lookup. He's going to be disappointed." He gestured toward his family to indicate they should leave the computer and follow him and Artie to the conference room. When they were in, he said, "Spread them out, Cal's first. Let's have a look."

Dolan flipped the pages down one at a time around the table as if prepping for a big board meeting. He had a listing of calls for the last four months. The whole group got in line and went around the table, studying. Christie could see Dolan was getting antsy, but the kids were entertained by this work.

"Elinor Hathaway called him a lot," Eric told his father.

"His mum."

"Boring."

"Hey."

"I thought maybe some hot chick."

"Hey. I might have to boot you off this job."

Eric cackled, then got serious. "He called a lot of numbers that start with 681 and 621. What's that?"

"Oakland."

Dolan said, "The names look pretty familiar. We'll have to check them all, but it looks like people he worked for. It'll probably check out as work related. I don't see any number called a lot. Where's Cassie's number?"

"There," Julie said.

"Ah, I see," Christie said, though he had seen it moments before she did. "Let's list how many calls and when. Somebody do the blackboard."

"Not me," Julie said. "I want to look."

"To detect."

"Fine. I will," Marina said. She stood at the board and wrote down what Christie dictated: *Hathaway to Price: June 7, June 15, July 12, July 22, August 10.*

"Not August 13," Dolan said. "Let's do the reverse."

Christie dictated, "Price to Hathaway: June 7, June 14, July 11, July 22, August 10, August 11. "That's it. Do you see any more?"

Julie kept looking.

"Nuh-uh," Eric said.

"So what does it mean? What should we conclude?"

"I'd hire him," Marina said. "He returns calls! And pretty much right away."

"Don't most people?" Eric asked her.

"No. They pile up jobs and keep everybody on hold."

"Maybe he didn't have enough work," Eric said.

"There's that," she conceded.

Dolan had already begun gathering the pages into an ordered pile. The rest of them waited patiently while he put them aside. Then he did the same with Cassie Price's phone records. "We know when she called Cal. What else are we going to see?"

They began their study.

"She calls some number in Blanchard, Pennsylvania, with the name Price," Eric observed.

"Family."

"Oh."

"No, wait, this is confusing," Julie said. But Christie, standing just behind her and leaning over the pages, saw what she saw at about the same time. "I thought this section was *to* her, but it's also *from* her. It doesn't make sense."

Everybody stopped and came to the place in line where Julie pointed, saying, "Like she called herself."

"This is good. Real good," Dolan said. "I like this. Now we have to go back to Verizon and find out *where* the other Cassie was when she called the Verizon Cassie." He raised his eyebrows.

"Poor thing," Marina whispered.

Julie pulled out one of the chairs at the table and collapsed into it. She rapped her head. "I wish I understood."

"Easy," Eric told her. "She gave her other phone to somebody, and they called *her*. Kids do it all the time."

"But why would she need two?"

"Different strokes for different folks," Eric said.

Christie and Dolan looked at each other and tried not to laugh.

Eric said, "Some kids have different phones for different friends."

"What about dates—let's record the dates."

Julie got up again, energized. "There are pretty many of them."

"Let's record other Cassie to Verizon Cassie."

They looked at their father and then got to work. "May 17, May 22, May 30. Then June 4—"

"Night or day?" Christie asked, even though he was hovering, looking, too.

"Night. Night."

"Evening," he amended. "Evening."

"June 4 and June 5," Eric recited. "It's almost always the other one to Verizon."

"Okay."

"Then June 18 and 19."

"Okay."

"June 26. On that day, Verizon calls the other number once at seven fifteen."

"Interesting," says Christie. "Getting bolder. Tell me just the Thursdays and Fridays—can you do the math?"

Marina kept the chalk poised, ready to write.

Since the children did not show any interest in doing the math, Dolan, who always had a calendar in his head, answered, "That's going to be July 2 and 3—"

"There's a July 2," Eric offered. He and Julie checked listings further on, and Eric reported, "Not July 9 and 10. But I see one, like July 7 and one July 12."

"Okay. Okay. Now go back to just Thursdays and Fridays."

The kids moved down the table. "Not until July 16 and 17." Christie checked the pages. They were right. He suspected a vacation with the Connolly family had interrupted the pattern.

"And then July 24. July 30 and 31. August 6 and 7. And now there are more calls going from Verizon to the new number. Lots more."

"Did anybody call her August 13?" Christie asked, but he was looking, too, and he answered himself. "Yes. Someone called. The notation says a pay phone in East Liberty. A pay phone. Eight P.M." He looked at Dolan.

"I still want to know what it means," Julie complained. "After all this work we did. Does this tell us what got the woman killed?"

"When I know for sure what it means, I will tell you, honestly I will. I won't pull any punches. But for now I'd say she was doing something sneaky, something she didn't make public, and that is not a good thing. If anybody ever wants to . . . to date you and they don't want you to talk about it to anybody else, I want you to run as fast as you can in the other direction. I'm very serious."

He didn't miss Marina's amused look. A sharp memory hit him of his first couple of weeks with her when he thought he would lose his mind with guilt and longing.

"We'd better get some lunch. Let's go. You coming with us, Artie?"

"Fine with me."

The others walked down the hall ahead of them.

Artie said, "I'm pretty sure the *Sp* means it's a Sprint phone. Who paid for that Sprint phone? It's not on her charges."

"Right."

"Plus: Where is it?"

FREDDIE HAD CALLED him—he looked at her number, surprised. She never called. She was not a needy type. He also felt a hot anger he knew was supposedly wrong—he only liked to make the calls, not receive them. Rita had it right, well, right in his book, which he understood was a wrong and bad book, but he liked the fact that she never initiated.

It was Saturday, and he was on his way to Harrisburg. He'd been on the road for an hour. His counterpart, the state party organizer, the person who had put him onto the problem of Cassie Price, wanted to see him. He was messing with his cell phone by opening it and closing it, when he dropped it accidentally in the slit between the seat and the center console. The Saab wiggled as he fished for the phone unsuccessfully, getting his hand jammed. The phone began to ring.

He couldn't reach it. It stopped abruptly after four rings, so he was pretty sure it hadn't gone to a message. Who was it? He wanted to know. He pulled off onto an emergency platform and saw that he was shaking.

For one thing, roadside stops had always frightened him—ever since he heard about a young woman who pulled over to safety only to have a confused driver assume it was another lane and plow into her, killing her. He looked behind him, got his hand out of the jam, and put the emergency blinkers on before, fishing with a tire gauge, he managed to nudge the phone out to where he could retrieve it.

He checked the CALLS MISSED menu. The number was not familiar to him. He'd try to trace it later—it might be a simple error. They were getting more and more common these days.

That's when his body gave him another instant signal. His late breakfast rose up in him and he opened the car door, taking deep breaths to keep it all down. He wasn't used to vomiting—hadn't in his memory since college binges, until a week ago when he lost it twice.

A car came dangerously close to him, blaring its horn in one long terrifying note. He brought the door closed with his left hand. His right still clutched the phone. And perhaps because of that, he began to think about phones.

If the police were messing around, still asking questions, clearing the decks as they said, to eliminate other possibilities, would they look at the girl's phone records? He got sick to think of course they would. But they'd be looking at Cal still, right? And any calls made from boss to paralegal could be . . . could be business calls.

He had to talk to Connolly, give him a program of things he could say about a work project.

God, the man was naive. Had he called her much? Todd hoped not, though a superposition lawyer had a right to call an employee whenever he wanted. Connolly couldn't be arrested for that.

Even if they cottoned on to the affair, it proved nothing, really. Still, it made him sick to think how careless Connolly was.

He had been given an impossible task.

But he did the impossible. And he did it well.

"JOHN! DID YOU SEE who that was?" Colleen asked. "Not the guy blasting his horn, the one on the side of the road, losing his cookies?"

"Oh," Potocki said, eyes widening. "Was it?"

"He's back and forth to Harrisburg all the time, I guess. It doesn't mean anything." But then she said, "Slow down some in case he catches up with where we are and we can spot him along the way."

"We're still going to need to stick to the motels in Breezewood. It's already a long day."

They would see signs along the turnpike soon: BREEZEWOOD, TOWN OF MOTELS. What a distinction. Breezewood wasn't actually a town; it was a *place* on the map. There were roughly ten motels and several fast-food joints. Breezewood was a place to stop briefly for something.

They'd get there at one, they'd need to eat something, then start the questioning and probably get done at four or so—a three-hour stop, probably.

She had a laptop with her, equipped for Wi-Fi but without a card. "There'll be someplace to use this. Probably any motel lobby."

After a while she saw the Saab moving past them, going at a pretty good clip. "There he is."

Potocki picked up speed. "Nice car."

"Would you describe it as gray?"

"If I were *me*, I would say silver. But if I were Iris Mender, I might very well say gray."

"I was thinking, if we put together what Iris Mender saw in the front of the houses with what Cal says he saw in the alleyway behind, it means the guy got her drunk at Casbah, comforted her about something, saw her home safe, but didn't try to go in, right?"

"Sounds about right."

"Kindly? Aware of Cal? Or casing the joint?"

"I choose C. He wasn't forthcoming about knowing her. He said he didn't. He never said he went for a drink with her."

"Right. Maybe it was someone else who went for the drink."

"Another dude in another gray car? What is your soft spot for this guy?"

"It's not a soft spot. It's fascination/horror." She added irritably, "And hating to be wrong about a person I might have liked."

Potocki reached over and took her hand for a moment.

They couldn't keep up with the Saab. They let it go and got off at the exit that pointed them to the town of motels, where they soon chose the Bob Evans restaurant for a road-style breakfast to be consumed as lunch.

Right after they'd settled in a booth and put in their orders, Colleen got a call from Christie.

"We have a pattern," he said. "Cassie Price got phone calls from another phone in her name on many Thursdays and Fridays."

"Interesting. Tricky."

"Do you have a pen handy?"

"Yes," she said fumbling for one.

He waited. Then he said, "I have some specific dates you can target. Evidence of the phone calls. Ready?"

"Yes."

He gave her a series of dates.

"Got it," she said.

"We don't know who paid for the phone. It's not on her charges."

"We're thinking Connolly," Colleen said glumly.

"Right. So, go for it with the motels, see if you can establish it was Price and Connolly anywhere. You know, the truth is, there's nothing to say they stuck to Breezewood."

She could hear Dolan in the background saying, "I'd mix it up."

"We'll check as much as we can check today," she told Christie.

She didn't tell him they were at Bob Evans. The Bob Evans wasn't where Cassie had used her credit card, but she might have gone there on another occasion. They could show her picture and ask if anybody remembered her.

"Good. The other thing that's interesting is that Connolly, assuming it's Connolly, made all the phone calls until late July, when she started calling him on that other phone. What does that mean? She got bolder. Antsy."

"Angry," Colleen says just as she hears Dolan say the same thing in the background.

"So, if we establish this, it doesn't prove homicide. We can't hang the guy for an affair."

"Yes, Boss. We . . . get that. Proof is going to be the sticker. I get three possibilities: Cal did it. Connolly did it and we have to break his alibi. He hired someone to do it. In which case it would make sense of Simon lying about one thing and another."

"Somebody called her from a pay phone on the evening before the murder. Probably not Connolly if he was on his way to Harrisburg."

Guy in a silver Saab.

MIKE CONNOLLY SITS in his home office on Saturday—as usual, on the phone. He played a game of golf this morning. He and Monica are having people to dinner tonight. He has to nap and shower and shave. Elinor is handing over her kitchen to the caterers from All in Good Taste. She looks worn out with worry. An hour ago, she came in and cradled his head as she used to do when he was a boy.

"Always on the phone," she said.

"And I don't even like phones."

He had been instructed to turn everything to advantage, and that is what he had done all week long. He was talked out. He had talked and talked.

When the news of the state budget impasse kept hitting the headlines, he told various people that the problem with the budget was solvable and he hoped that both parties would soon see wisdom. It was hard for him to get specific about where cuts could be made because he was on the board of the symphony and of Pitt and at the moment they were getting hit hard with proposed cuts and taxes and they were fighting back. But KDKA camped outside his office one day, so he got to make a brief speech about how, although he wasn't officially in Harrisburg this term, he kept in touch with some who were and saw bipartisanship as a key to solutions. Also, he said, if he could bring in just half as much business and industry as he had good reason to believe the state stood in a good position for, there would be no budget problem, no impasse. Pennsylvania would be flush. And that was a goal he intended to pursue.

"When are you going to announce your candidacy?" the reporter from KDKA asked.

"I'm talking to my family this weekend. If they give me the go-ahead, if we think we can preserve our family life and that I can still work on the causes I'm already committed to, I will agree to run."

"So something midweek next week?"

"About that, yes."

"You left the political arena because your son was ill with a heart condition. Is he all right now?"

"He's perfect now. Thank you. We had a lucky and happy outcome."

He escaped, as he always did, before he said too much.

Haigh and the other bosses liked his sound bite.

His father liked it, too. The old man called him immediately upon seeing the news. "I knew it. I knew you'd be good at this."

The compliment gratified him.

Most of the week he'd spent being a candidate. He had lunches and dinners on Wednesday, Thursday, and Friday with people that . . . mattered. He began to understand in a way he never had before that he was important to a lot of people. He was a connector. He was the link that gave people links to others. He introduced a banker high up in PNC to a builder of hotels. He introduced the head of the August Wilson Center board to the head of the symphony board. He went to dinner with the head of Reed Smith. He talked to the county commissioner four times, listening to what the current problems were. He drove to Philly for a dinner and drove partway home that night, stopping on the way back in Harrisburg, where he stayed with Haigh again.

The stop, the reminder of his old patterns, was only one of a hundred times Cassie Price leapt in and out of his thoughts like a dolphin breaking the crest of the water. He'd think, "I'm focused, I'm working, I'm okay," and there she'd be, looking at him. He could hear her voice. He could understand . . . what she was thinking. He could look into the blue eyes of the PNC man and see her eyes. It was awful. He kept working. He filled himself with work.

Last night, Friday evening, before he left the office for yet another dinner, this one at the Frick mansion, a thing some people had put together for him and in which he would be the center of a long chain of connections, his father came in unannounced to see him. The old man closed the door carefully and took a chair. Connolly was sitting at his desk at the time, on the phone, as always. He ended the call and faced his father across the desk.

"About this girl who died," his father began slowly, "I know about you seeing her."

"Evan."

His father nodded once. "Who else knows?"

"You, Evan, me, and Simon."

"Simon knows?"

"Yes."

"Did he—"

"He quizzed me until I gave it up."

"You know what I'm asking."

"I don't know the answer. I asked him. He denied it." Then he felt his whole body shake as if his heart literally did a somersault. He wanted to be a boy, to crawl to his father and rest a head against the old man's leg and be comforted by his father's hand on his head. "Should we press it? It means giving everything up."

His father looked at him steadily. "Are you strong?"

"I don't know what you mean."

"You were meant to be in high office. You look it, you sound it, you smell of it."

"I'm not so sure anymore."

"I've given this a lot of thought. There's being good. We are, you and me, pretty good men. Then there's the greater good. You have that dinner tonight?"

"Yes."

"And you are innocent, I take it."

"Yes."

"Is it worth giving up? I think not."

He had been shocked by his father. He would have sworn his father would choose the other way—come clean, personal honesty. But when he went to the dinner at the Frick, the way people kept referring to his father, the long years in the business of the law, the reputation for things done with class and dignity, he realized his father didn't want to spend his last days with his name smeared and the firm in disrepute.

Your father, they said, *your brother*—always liked working with them. The casinos, the budget, the fund-raising hurdles, the other potential candidates, the invitations to golf, vacations, everything he talked about had the subtext of who knew whom and how A could get into a conversation with B. He chatted with men and women in beautiful shoes and he watched an imaginary Cassie dressed up and trying to fit in, trying to make her way into this crowd. At times, he thought his eyes teared up, but he couldn't tell if others could see that.

THE WAITRESSES AT Bob Evans couldn't remember having seen Cassie Price. One of them sat down at the table with Colleen and Potocki, delicately moving aside their plates, which held unfinished bits of sausage and pancake under crumpled napkins. She stared hard at the picture. "What did she do? Prostitution? Fraud?"

"Neither. We simply have to trace her movements for a case."

The woman shivered. "Oh. I get it, right. She got killed."

"Yes."

"I have a daughter, came out beautiful. Who knows why these

things happen—you see good-looking parents with kids that got the worst of them and bad-looking parents with beauties . . ." The woman wasn't terrible looking at all, but she had a tired coarseness about her. She rubbed at her face in a manner a cosmetologist might have fainted at. Erasing the feeling of worry, Colleen thought. "They get something wrong with their brains when they come out too pretty. Mine thinks about things like whether models are parting their hair on the side or in the middle this year. She wants two hundred and fifty-nine dollars for jeans and seventy-five for a belt. She didn't get that way from me. It's because she can achieve a certain look."

Because she can. Clinton said the reason for Monica Lewinsky was simply because he could.

"And she doesn't notice the hungry way men look at her. She really doesn't. She's too busy looking at herself."

"Keep her locked in the house," Potocki said. " 'Lock up your daughters.' If I had a daughter, it's how I'd feel, I know."

"She's twenty-four."

Ah. Dependent and probably not that gorgeous, Colleen thought.

The woman tapped the photo. "Some guy killed her because he couldn't have her, plain and simple."

She and Potocki left the woeful waitress, who was no doubt codependent in the beauty game, to go to the motels of Breezewood. They hit it on the second try. A man wearing a turban did not recognize the photo and did not think he had registered Cassie Price himself, but he readily pulled up his ledger on-screen and began checking the dates Colleen gave him. "No, no," he said to June and July dates. When he got to August, he brightened. "Yes, yes," he said, "I have it here. Cassandra Price. She, yes, secured the room with a credit card. Let me see. She charged no incidentals and paid with cash. Does that help?"

"Yes, it helps enormously. Would you see if there is any room being charged at the same time to either of two names, Connolly or Simon."

The hotel manager handed over a blank sheet of paper for her to write down the names she wanted him to check. He liked the work of it, looking these things up.

Colleen told Potocki, "Just in case they were covering their tracks that way. Probably not. You never know."

"Nothing," the man said. "Not the day before or the day after."

She nodded. "Do you have a surveillance camera here?"

"I'm sorry. No. We cannot afford one yet. My friends tell me they break down and create one problem after another."

Too bad, too bad.

They progressed to the other motels, working out what the pattern was. "They motel-hopped," Colleen said. "Didn't want to be remembered."

"He was careful," Potocki said. "He could have booked a room in his name and stayed overnight, but he went home, late at night, probably. He was being careful. He had her make the reservation."

"I hope he didn't make her pay for the room."

"No doubt he gave her cash."

"She had to pay for her own breakfast that day."

"Yeah. That was early on. She probably didn't know how careful she had to be about her credit card. But you know, when you think of all the fancy places he could have afforded to stay—he could buy an apartment or a vacation home, but to see her, he was slumming. Motel bed, motel bathrooms. It's odd."

"What do you make of it?"

"Something in his fantasy life."

"Like what?"

"Like a god dipping down to kiss a mortal. He can't take her to the heavens where he'd be recognized. He plays at her hut."

Potocki was thinking of Zeus's exploits. Zeus's wife, Hera, was unhappy and vengeful.

"Do you think what's-her-name, Monica Connolly, got wind of it and hired someone to— It looks like a passionate murder, it looks like a burglary, but it sciences out like a premeditated murder."

"Totally agree."

As they worked through the afternoon, they found two more stays registered to Cassandra Price, both paid in cash, no incidentals. Three places admitted to having surveillance cameras. Only one of them was a place she had stayed. At that place, the tapes for July had been erased and rerecorded, so it was no good, but they had enough evidence to get the pattern.

"Enough for today," Potocki said. "Let's go home. We can establish the rest of the pattern with the phone calls." It was going to take lots more paperwork to pinpoint the locations of the callers when the calls were made, but that could be done, and Christie was no doubt already on phase two.

"Do you realize we have not one iota of evidence that it was actually Connolly?"

"Boss will find out who paid for the phone."

"She probably paid for it. She paid for it, she called herself, she went to a motel. It's sounding like masturbation."

Potocki laughed. "Don't knock it. It got me through a lot of bad times."

"I say nothing."

Potocki laughed again. They got into his car and started for Pittsburgh.

After they'd been back on the road for thirty miles or so, Potocki said, "I keep asking myself what this is like. Is this Clinton-Lewinsky, just a little fun with a cigar but the girl talks too much; is this Gary Hart—who can remember him?"

"Barely."

"Is this John Edwards, all Mr. Clean, but dumb as dirt when it comes to choosing a reliable mistress; is this Mark Sanford, hopelessly in love and in need of the loved one; is this Vitter or Spitzer, paying for it and happily because the transaction is needed for the kick; is this Ensign, who is just playing chess with people: 'I'll take this piece, you can have that'?"

"Most of them were already in office, so they had a throne to defend. Connolly is seeking office. Closer to Edwards."

Potocki appeared to think about this, nodded, squinting into the sun.

"You know who you forgot?"

"Tons of politicians."

"Yes, but what about Gary Condit? The girl died. She was killed violently. And he was blamed because she loved him and wanted him. All that time, I figured it this way: He tells somebody, a brother, an associate, somebody, 'Man, I'm in too deep. She's putting a lot of pressure on me.' And the associate quietly goes off to take care of it. I thought that's what happened. Now it turns out it's some Salvadoran immigrant—the Cal Hathaway solution, somebody out of the blue. The Salvadoran had been attacking women in that same park."

"The police look real bad in that one. They concentrated on Condit and missed the other," he said.

"We had guys who concentrated on Cal and missed the office affair."

"So we're somewhere . . . between Gary Condit and John Edwards and Mark Sanford—for explanations."

"Which feels like nowhere."

They drove in silence for a while before she dug out her phone and called Christie to report what they had established.

"We're moving," he said. "I already put in the paperwork to get the GPS on the calls. Take a break. Squad meeting Monday."

Again they drove in silence for a while. Finally Potocki said, "We're very much together these days."

"I know."

"I'd like to have dinner together tonight and spend the night at one or the other of our places."

"Stop at a market. I need to cook. I mean, I need to eat *in* for a change. I'll cook at your place. I'll spend the night. We won't talk about work. We'll just be normal."

Potocki didn't look thrilled. She knew there was something she'd forgotten to say, but she didn't know what it was.

MONICA WAS NEVER as happy with caterers as she was with Elinor. But tonight the pressure was on, with important people coming, to surprise and delight. The only thing Monica ordered from the caterer's regular menu was stuffed endive. She herself was always happy with a plain steak or a piece of fish or a pizza, but her guests expected something extraordinary.

Monica searched the house for her husband. Michael was lying on their bed. He looked like a corpse, hands clasped just under his heart.

"Are you awake?"

"Yes. Resting my eyes."

"Do you want to know what we're having?"

"Shoot."

"It's not so hot out, so I think we'll be okay. I've been worried about the heavier courses. Okay, he talked me into crab puffs and a good tapenade with bread, not crackers, and stuffed endive for arrivals and schmoozing in the garden. We almost opted for outdoors for the dinner, but we decided indoors. First course is a salmon mousse. After that a fairly straightforward salad with Asiago and fresh shrimp. Then cold vichyssoise. I struggled over that—I really wanted to do the caskets of love dish, but it works better in fall or winter, don't you think?"

"I guess. Actually I don't remember what it is."

"Caskets of love is that pasta dish—you liked it—where the outer pasta makes a basket and is filled with a thin spinach pasta, mushrooms, béchamel, and ham. They're like little bags tied with a pasta string."

"Oh, yes."

"You called them testicles." They did kind of look like that. They had the same size and shape. She climbed up on the bed. He hadn't changed position. "So anyway, I can order them another time if you want. I chose the cold soup instead."

"Okay."

"Then a little sorbet. Then rack of lamb with some sides of tiny potatoes and asparagus."

"I like rack of lamb."

"I know you do. The caterers are prepared with a quick vegetable something, a soufflé I think, in case we have any hardcore vegetarians. Sliver of mousse cake for dessert and some homemade hazelnut ice cream and some of those signature dark candies."

"Should be fine. Thank you for everything."

"He's using some of our white wines, but he wanted control of the reds."

"Now if I could only get some energy."

"You're tired."

"Yes. You need me for something?"

"Elinor sent two people to help with the setup, and she's coming back to join them later. She hasn't left anything unaccounted for. She went to see her son."

"Good. I'm glad."

"You seem . . . very tired. We have that cookout tomorrow. Should I cancel it?"

"That's mostly family. I can be a zombie."

She stroked the inside of his arm, tracing the veins. "I'm trying very hard."

"I know."

"I wish it were effortless."

"Almost nothing is."

"What's going to happen to us?"

"I'm so sorry I'm not what you want."

"I never said that. I'm not sure it's true."

"I'm trying to be realistic."

Her heart tugged downward. She got energized when she thought of leaving him, but a deadening defeat hit her when the same idea was his. Talk or not, they couldn't do anything. They were puppets of the political system. An intact, loving family was the only card that had any value, and so tonight, as on so many occasions—like the one with the photographers—she would touch his arm, smile when he spoke, tease a little, and pay enough attention to her appearance that at least some would envy him and nobody would call her a joke.

It made her furious. She started crying.

"Don't cry. Please don't cry."

"I can't help it."

"I'm so knocked down, I can't do any lifting."

He was. Very knocked down. Worse than ever. No room for her tears. The arena was his.

CASSIE WOULD HAVE killed to be at a party like this. When she asked him what he ate at home, which she did fairly often, he saw her mind ticking, as if she mentally rehearsed cooking those things. "How long does that take?" she asked of something once.

"I don't know. It was catered."

"Catered. Of course. No fuss, no bother."

Once he saw her studying one of his shirts and then later looking at the labels in his sport jacket. She asked him if he got his clothes from Tom James on Strawberry Way. The local store was a client.

He said, "No, why did you think so?"

"I've been reading about them. Fine custom clothing. Then I went by the shop to look. It's all hidden back behind everything. I figured it was a secret treasure for those who knew about it."

He said carefully, "It is. Just that. A lot of young up-and-comers use it. They pass the word, try to get a good fit. I mean they do get a good fit. They do fine. I have my own tailor," he explained. "Same one my father has. I've had to push him not to be stodgy, but I think he's good with fabrics and fitting." He didn't say his man was considerably more expensive than the tailors at Tom James, but he was sure she got it by the quiet that came over her.

"Things aren't important," she said later. "People are."

"I can't disagree with that. I'll take it as my slogan."

"Don't condescend. I don't mind being middle class. I dress as well as the budget allows. I don't want to be dismissed if I don't know about fancy things."

"Did you think I dismissed you?"

"No. But you sidestepped, condescended a little."

"Look. I'm as comfortable with poor people as I am with rich people. Maybe more so. After all, I married a woman who didn't come from a lot of money—some, not a lot. She's not a snob in any sense."

Cassie had looked miserable. "I don't want to hear good things about her. You shouldn't defend what she's doing to you."

He was again sorry he'd said the thing about Monica being off with someone else. It was the crack that allowed a crowbar in. It was the loose tooth. She was going to wiggle it and work it forever. He always had to say something like, "This is a precious time. Let's not spend it on things we can't solve."

But she got more and more distraught. It was awful to see. Only holding and kissing her calmed it. The funny thing is, it didn't disgust him or turn him away. It just was what it was, an unhappiness he'd caused and had no way of solving.

She was so lovely. And he could always work it so that she was teasing and playful again, so playful that she persuaded herself she was happy enough.

He can't bear it—his suspicion. Tonight he will be smiling and shaking hands as his father recommended. At midnight, when everyone is gone, he will imagine going to Christie and saying, "I think I might have caused it."

Then of course the world as he knows it tears to shreds. He's dishonored. His father is crushed. His brother gloats. He has nothing— no prospects, no hopes, no friends, no reputation, only money in the bank. It's almost a joy to think it.

THERE IS HIS MOTHER through the glass. Cal makes a funny little wave to lift her spirits. There are lines on her face that he never noticed before. She's fiftysomething years old and he's landed her here.

He lifts the phone. "Hi, Ma."

"How you doing, honey?"

"I'm okay."

"There's something going wrong with the money for the commissary. I put in a hundred and fifty dollars at the start. They had to show me how to use the machine, but they said it went through. Couldn't you get it? All the money is still there."

"I don't need anything. I'm okay."

"They said there's candy and stuff like that. You could get a radio thing, like a Walkman. Did they tell you?"

"The guys told me. I didn't use it. Things get stolen."

"They do?"

He nods. He doesn't tell her about the watch. Levon had been downstairs in the pod yesterday, watching TV when Cal went to the shower. After a rapid soaping and shampooing, Cal returned to his cell to find the watch was gone. His first assumption was that Levon took it. He looked through his cellmate's things. Levon came back up and said, "Look, man, I know what happened, and I know the how, see, but it could get ugly to prove it." Cal sat on the bed and looked away from Levon, who he still thought was lying. The simple fact was, the watch was gone and not among Levon's things.

"You look okay," his mother is saying. "Are you okay? Eating?"

He can't help but smile at this. Eating is about all there is to rely on. Three times a day. He has not skipped meals since the beginning. "I eat," he says. "Unfortunately it isn't home cooking." She watches him as he pauses to think what to tell her next. "They have an exercise court. It's mostly basketball hoops."

"Like teams?" she asks, surprised.

"I don't think I'd get chosen if they were doing teams. I never was great at that kind of thing . . ."

She says, "Don't put yourself down. You can do anything."

That's when he starts to cry—when he's reminded how much she loves him. He chokes it back. His tears have triggered hers. "But I take my turn down there. I go down there and I shoot baskets."

"Oh," she says, eyes brimming. "Exercise is good."

"I know . . . For me, it was working on houses that gave me the movement." He flexes his body to illustrate.

She says, "Yes."

He looks around to see who might overhear him. He says, "You think I did it. I don't think I did."

She is stuck and doesn't know what to say, but then she's weeping openly—tears streaming. "I'll do anything for you. Tell me what to do."

"Believe me. That's all."

She listens, alert.

"Believe in me."

"Oh, Cal, you know I always . . ."

"I mean . . . on this. Believe in me on this. Other people do."

She is stunned. "I thought you told them—"

"Erase that."

"Okay."

"Put that away and start fresh."

"Okay."

They both take a moment to pull themselves together.

"Tell me something else. Anything."

"Big party at work today. You wouldn't believe the food they're having. People can't possibly eat that much—I don't think they can. It's moderate portions, the way they do it, but there are so many courses. And then they waste. I hate to see how much food comes back not even touched. I wish I could bring it to you. Of course, it's not allowed."

"Nothing's allowed. Almost nothing."

"Is your bed okay?"

It's pretty terrible, he thinks, but if he tells her it's a plastic-covered hard futon, she will cry again. "I manage to sleep," he says. "My body just tells me to sleep."

A guard nods to him. He replaces the phone. She leaves weeping again, and turns back to wave.

Cal hates that the guard and one other inmate have seen him crying. A quick swab to his eyes with his forearm, and he is headed back to his cell. Levon is sitting there inside, trying to read the Bible. "I'm getting religion," Levon says, smiling. "It seems to go far here."

Cal lies down, facedown. After a while he says, "I want my watch back."

"Oh man, he is the worse. I don want you beat up. He do this. It's what he do."

Levon explained yesterday that when Cal went to the shower, Sid had Boreski and one other guy bug the hell out of the corrections officer at the control station, asking every which way about their commissary funds and distracting him. Then Boreski pushed the button for Cal's cell and Sidney went up. Levon said the officer saw but it would be too messy to do anything about it—to admit he didn't have control of his station. He said Sidney also took Levon's two candy bars. At first Cal didn't believe the story. But last night after dinner, almost everybody was downstairs watching baseball. That's the way it was—sports. Tonight they will watch football. In the whole jail, if football was on, *everybody* watched and nobody said *anything* except to cheer or boo in four-letter words.

Baseball—sometimes people muttered other things.

Sidney had a thing he did—insisting somebody play him chess *during* a game—when he knew they all wanted to watch TV.

At one point last night, Sidney lifted his pant leg. In the momentary glimpse, Cal saw his watch, the band stretched around Sidney's calf. Then Sidney let down the pant leg.

"I'm going to get it back."

ERASE AND START over. Can she?

Elinor stands at the mirror in the visitor restroom on the first floor. She dressed to cheer him, not her bright colors, but nice black pants, a patterned black and white top, sandals with a small heel, black-and-white button earrings. She brushes away tears and dabs a little makeup on.

She doesn't have to wear a uniform at the Connolly house. They allow her to come and go, to be independent, but she tries to respect them by wearing something uniformlike. Today, she has two people from her church coming to help with the setup and the cleanup. They asked what to wear. She told them black pants and black top. She will change out of her top to a white shirt and a feminine white vest; there will be no doubt who are the guests and who are the workers.

There are times she studies the shoes and hair and clothing of the people who come to the Connolly house and tries to figure out what about those things costs so much money. The black dresses she will see tonight, the sundresses, the sandals with decorative knots or jewels, cost a week's or month's salary. But she's not always sure those things are pretty, that's what bothers her. When those people look at her clothing, do they see the price tags, twenty dollars, thirty dollars, or do they have no experience of shopping for bargains?

A mirror at the jail restroom shows her that she still presents a good appearance.

Several other visitors enter and congregate, talking rapidly and loudly about what they will buy their imprisoned family members. They vie for the mirror, stretching and examining.

What is she to think—he says now he didn't do it. All this week she has tried to get her head around a death sentence, a life imprisonment, but mostly inside her head is a constant prayer, Keep him alive, keep him alive.

She leaves the restroom, wondering who these rough-tough women who elbowed her aside are visiting and how Cal will defend himself against their offspring.

Outside the ladies' room are hordes of people, families with small children, many of them coming to see a papa or an uncle here in jail. Some folks are white. Most are black. They come in two styles, it seems: overly humble and defeated or loud and insistent. This world, she thinks, this country. How many people in this one town have done bad things—taken what they shouldn't take from someone, killed, tried to kill, sold death in the form of drugs. And after all this time being good, her efforts to keep her own nose clean and her boy's nose clean have come to nothing.

Three little kids follow her outdoors. They run in front of her and make a barrier of their bodies. They look like criminals in the making—their eyes, calculating, their expressions sardonic.

"You have any money?"

"Why?"

"We need candy."

"Where's your mother?"

They point back. She turns to see a woman who looks totally

dead in the eyes. This woman doesn't care what her kids do. One of them tugs at Elinor's handbag.

Speeches fly through her head. Begging is wrong. Work for a living. Don't expect help. Help yourself. You can do better. But none of these speeches take form. She is crying again. The tears that began upstairs are only the beginning. There are buckets of tears behind them. Her face vibrates with the need to cry and cry.

Elinor reaches into her bag and pulls out a five.

A boy of about four practically rips it from her hand. Before the kids have run very far an older sister takes the money from the boy. The second oldest, a girl, begins pulling at the older one.

Elinor owns a car, Toyota Celica, which she takes good care of. She drove it to work today because she knew she wanted to make this quick trip downtown to the county jail and didn't want to tangle with buses. It was a mistake. There is a parking ticket on her windshield.

What else?

The Celica is tough like she is, clean, too, well kept. It hums into power, ready to go. She'll have to find a place to park it back at the Connollys' so that it doesn't block the driveway where valets will take the cars of the people coming to dinner. The huge and wonderful dinner.

Her people are going to want to take food home—that is easy to predict. They will look at the untouched food and get a little crazy. When the time is right, she will turn her head.

AT THE DINNER PARTY, Connolly becomes the great connector, introducing people who don't know each other, making golf dates, lunch dates—all of them to be firmed up when someone's secretary calls his secretary on Monday.

The TV is on in the family room/bar inside. Most people drift in, watching the Steelers. "We're ahead. Can't lose this one," one woman says. She's married to an upper-level guy at PNC.

"It's only preseason," her husband reminds her.

"It counts. It's psychological," she says with conviction. "Gotta win every one."

"That's my gal," he laughs.

Monica looks good. She's had her hair done and wears a new, elegant sundress that she says is inspired by *Mad Men,* very retro, very sixties, a flattering look. She takes his arm, pats his wrist, moves through the crowd. He has done her wrong. She wants out and she doesn't even know the worst of it.

His father carefully works the crowd—gesturing toward the back garden, getting people to sit, acting easy. "I loved living here, too," Connolly hears his father say. Then the talk turns to Chatham University, its elegance. Only in the quick blink of a glance does Connolly see his father's determined concern that this last week disappear, that the future he has wished for be allowed to happen. One of the caterer's servers, a beautiful young woman with deep black hair tucked back in a braid, tendrils of curls sneaking out to frame her face, comes up to him with a platter of tapenade spread on thinly sliced bits of baguette. "Thank you," he says to her eager offering. They look at each other a second too long.

Sick, he makes himself sick. He loathes himself.

That gesture Monica made, arm through his and then the pat of his wrist with her own extended hand, it almost felt real, it almost felt as if she loved him.

He's heard of men who disappear. They go off to be monks or something. Take a bit of cash and start a new life. As he smiles and talks to people, he plays out this fantasy.

No, he wants to be governor. He has ideas. He's built the base. He would be able to do wonderful things. Die with a highway named after him. Or a road. Or a building.

COLLEEN HAS MADE clam linguine. And a salad. Potocki has opened two snack tables and put them in front of the sofa that faces the TV. He still doesn't have a lot of furniture, only the basics: beds, sofas, TV, and a few tables of various sorts. The condo has a clean spare look—a divorce look. He's having a beer. She's having red wine, preferring it to white, no matter what the meal. She brings in the platters of pasta, putting them down on the tables to go back to fetch the salad. "It isn't a classic football meal," she calls out.

Football. Seems to call out for meat, blood. He's pleased that she's willing to watch. It's what he would do if he were alone, but now he has the double treat of the companion of his choice plus the game. He's feeling good.

In Washington there are hordes of Steelers fans. The stadium is awash with yellow towels waving in the air.

How great it is to put everything aside, all the things you're worried about, and just give in to the contest that doesn't really matter at all but only seems to.

Everybody symbolizes. If the Steelers win, our case goes well, if the Steelers win, our relationship goes well. Has anybody done a study? Who knows if there mightn't be a connection way under the surface? A scary thought in many ways. He does know that crime is up—particularly domestic abuse—when the Steelers lose.

"We ought to be able to beat the Skins," one fan says when the microphone comes to him in a bar. "We rock."

"We kill," says the guy behind him, pushing into the camera.

"Ben isn't playing. I dunno," says another. "Batch is good but Ben is *ma man*." He points to his own number 7 jersey.

"What's Connolly doing tonight?" Colleen wonders aloud.

"He's singing, 'What Do the Simple Folk Do?' He's wishing he had no problems and clam linguine."

"Maybe."

"We shouldn't think about work. We have to learn to put it aside."

However, if they let Christie separate them as partners and then come together of an evening, they will be hungry to talk about work. How awful his last few years with Judy were—him holding everything in, her not caring or understanding.

The pasta is good.

Even when the Steelers fall behind, he doesn't care. He is so happy.

CAL GOES DOWN TO the common area where everyone is watching the Steelers. There is this new guy on the team—trying out for it—that everybody wants to be. Logan. He makes it look easy the way he runs, slipping past everyone. *Getting away. Getting out.*

Whoa, Logan, fucking Logan, see that Logan. You gotta see this. Wait, they'll run it again.

Sidney is playing chess again, watching the game with part of his attention. He has a worn, irritable look.

"We're going to lose this fucker," someone cries out.

Sidney bites out, "No way we can lose to the Redskins. We'll pull it out." He stretches back, thumbs his opponent away from the board. Sidney won. He always wins. He is running out of people who will play.

"I'll play," Cal says.

Everybody who is watching the game hears, looks up, puzzled. Really, can the slow kid play chess? Is he like one of those geniuses?

Cal is a terrible chess player.

Levon is shaking his head.

"We play for stuff," Sidney says. "What you got, boy?"

"Loser has to wear the gold watch on his calf."

"Huh? What kind of offer is that?"

"My offer."

The guard stops watching his TV and stands to hear better.

Sidney says, "Make a real offer."

"Okay," Cal says slowly as if thinking hard. "Loser has to wear the watch on his calf and take two candy bars off the hands of the winner."

"What are you talking about, simpleton?"

"Taking on the burdens."

Levon is shaking his head.

The Redskins score again, and that interrupts things for everyone. The Terrible Towels waver and collapse. When the fuss is over, Cal takes his seat at the chess table.

"Go on, play," Boreski says. "Beat the shit out of him. We'll get the watch back tomorrow."

"I'm done playing tonight."

A couple of guys boo, and it isn't at all clear it has to do with the Steelers. Cal doesn't turn or look but begins setting up his end of the board. "I might need some help. I don't know if I remember all the moves," he says.

"He ain't going to make it to death row," someone says.

Most of the men go back to the TV, irritable and furious that the game isn't going their way.

Sidney makes a first move.

Cal stares at the board. He really can't remember the moves.

"What you think you're doing?"

"Playing for my watch," Cal says. When he doesn't think, it's easy. Words just come out.

Levon has stopped shaking his head and is leaping around nervously.

"Boyfriend give it to you?"

"Not yet," Cal says. He concentrates on the game and plays as hard as he can.

NINE

SUNDAY, AUGUST 23

THEY LIE ABED READING the papers. She seems happy, really sprightly this morning, Potocki thinks, watching her.

His son is coming over today. Scott has met Colleen before, and even though he suspects she is more than a colleague, that is not a conversation Potocki has been ready to have with his son—one reason being that the relationship has been so off and on.

"You have Scott today," she says, reading his mind. "I ought to go home and clean."

"Cleaning can wait. How bad can your house be?"

"Bad enough."

"Talk to me."

"What?"

"What is this to you?"

"I think I like being alone."

"You don't and I know it."

"How do you know?"

"I know."

"Oh, the great mind reader." She twists to look at the clock. "If we're not going to work today—"

"What work? We have no new assignment."

"You could dig up stuff on Connolly. We could go to the Sprint stores with her picture, Cassie's picture. Dolan says it's Sprint."

"Dolan is doing that. Boss pretty much told us to take the day. It's okay to be normal."

"Maybe it's just lazy. Anyway, I'm going to go see my folks. I haven't seen them in a while."

"I could shoot your folks." They both jump at the words that have popped out of his mouth, but he's angry with her parents, no matter that he hasn't met them.

"What are you talking about?" she grumbles, getting out of the bed.

"For what they did to you. Or didn't do." He knows about how her uncle assaulted her. She was left to run through the woods for hours, frightened and lost, before making her way home—or rather to her uncle's place. Then the creep told his wife some lie, and the wife treated Colleen like a siren who tried to take her husband away. And Colleen, too afraid to tell her parents.

"I don't blame them for anything."

"Why not? They were the parents. That's what a parent does— protects the young. That's the definition."

"Well, I'll let you protect Scott today. You can protect him from me. I'm going home."

"They dumped you with a pedophile because they just didn't want to know."

"Easy answers. Easy answers. They were allowed to have a vacation. You're the one who goes on and on about people needing to relax."

"Why are you turning me into the enemy?"

"I think you're being overly sensitive," she says huffily.

"The fact that you never told them—think about it. You didn't trust them to be on your side. That's scary."

Before he knows it, before he has his shirt on, she is dressed and gone. Her car door slams too hard. Just like that it's falling apart.

CHRISTIE ARRIVES AT the Connolly house at noon. This time he studies the flowering bushes arching partway over the driveway. Trained on wire? Can he get this effect in his little Bloomfield garden?

He goes to the door, and again Elinor Hathaway answers. She's out of uniform. She wears light purple linen pants and a darker purple top. Her earrings are somehow these same two colors. That would take some serious shopping, he thinks. "How are you doing?" he asks.

"I'm glad to be working. It's hard wondering what happens next."

"Have you seen Cal?"

"Yesterday."

The house is eerily quiet. "Anything you can tell me?" Christie asks.

"He wants me to believe in him. He says there's no way he did it."

"He's been pretty consistent, then? Since after the night he was arrested."

"I think so."

Christie can see she wants to ask him something. "Before you show me in, go ahead. What is it?"

"You being here? Does this have something to do with . . . with the case?"

How to phrase it? "Peripherally. As we trace the movements of the girl and others who knew her."

Her face lights. "Is there another suspect?"

"Not at the moment. No."

"Oh."

"I'm here to see Senator Con— I just did it again. It's hard to call him mister."

"It took us all a while to get used to it."

"He expects me."

"Oh, yes, he told me. He's in that TV room."

Christie grimaces. The room is large and unprotected. He won't have the privacy he likes. On the other hand, it is his fault, not calling Connolly to Headquarters to talk. Obliging the noble and not the other way around—that's what he always thought "noblesse oblige" meant until Marina instructed him otherwise. Even now, his definition seems more correct.

When he arrives at the family room, there is Connolly on the phone, looking up to acknowledge him. Various Sunday newspapers are spread on his lap and at his feet.

Connolly ends his call quickly.

"You get several newspapers," Christie comments.

"I could spend all week trying to keep up. I'll study Philadelphia and a few others online."

"It's interesting to see another life, how it's conducted."

"You could sum mine up as 'talking.' In person, on the phone, at the podium."

"How are things at the firm this week?"

"People are still devastated, of course. I think we think about it all the time." Suddenly his tone changes to a more abrupt one. "What can I do for you today?"

"I need to ask you a few questions."

"All right."

"Are we private here?"

"I had Monica take the kids out of the house. I could . . . Just a minute, let me check something." He gets up and leaves the room, his tall, lanky frame awkward at first, then fluid as he gets his bearings. He is gone for a few minutes.

When he comes back, he says, "Elinor is the only one working today. We have a cookout later this afternoon for about twenty people. She's outside getting the tables ready. I'll be cooking the meats. Elinor and Monica did everything else."

"I thought you said you had this party last night."

"Oh, no, that was a whole other thing, more formal."

"Do you ever get tired of hosting?"

"Yes. Don't repeat that."

Christie smiles. "I won't."

Connolly sighs, then waits.

"This will be brief. We've had to check on the movements of Cassie Price as a matter of course." Connolly visibly blanches. "One thing we know. She is reported as not much of a drinker. Yet she had been drinking fairly heavily the night before she was killed. We were able to trace her whereabouts to a particular bar."

"How? I mean, no, she didn't seem like a drinker. This is something I didn't know about her."

"I see. Well, that might lead to my next question. We're tracing a good deal about her movements and who she spent time with. For instance, she often went to motels."

Connolly looks sick—give him credit for that.

"Witnesses put her in a restaurant with a man having these drinks. Given the rumors at work, we need to know if you were that man."

"No, I wasn't."

"Do you know who she was out with?"

"No I do not. Are you thinking that has something . . ."

"We're thinking nothing except to establish her pattern of behavior, who she was with, who she talked to."

"Are you saying it wasn't Cal Hathaway?"

"He's part of the whole picture we're establishing. You don't know who she might have gone to motels with?"

Connolly shakes his head.

"I see. I think that might be all for now. I will need to talk to a few more people from your firm. Let me see—I suppose I should just come up to the office. But the one fellow, your campaign manager, is not always up there, not usually up there, and I need to talk to him. Do I have a phone number for him?" Christie looks at various pages of his legal pad. "I probably do, but if you have it handy, that would save me some time."

"I do. Just so I don't get it wrong, let me go up to my office and write out his numbers. This will only take a second." He does the gangly rise from the cushy sofa and seconds later can be heard climbing the stairs.

His cell phone is in plain sight. Surely the number is on it—speed dial surely. Mike Connolly is upstairs giving Todd Simon a heads-up.

CONNOLLY WATCHES from the front doorway as Christie drives away. He lifts a hand in farewell. Then he goes inside. Why did he not say it was Todd who had the drink? Why did he not admit to being the person Cassie met at motels? The words would not come.

He paces to the back of the house where Elinor has laid out the paper plates and silverware, mustards and other sauces. Her sadness is evident no matter how she keeps at the work. What if Cal didn't do it? Connolly may be a louse in many ways, but he won't let a man languish in prison for the rest of his life if he didn't do the crime.

He has to talk to Todd—all he could manage was leaving voice mail messages on Todd's cell and at his home. He said quickly, "Don't answer a call from anyone until you talk to me." But Todd has not called him back.

He could have told Christie that Todd is coming to the house for the cookout.

His father, Todd, Haigh, all tell him to be strong. Business as usual.

He's falling into a deep hole he will never dig out of.

Elinor looks up at him. He gives her the okay sign for the good job she is doing.

COLLEEN IS AT HER parents' door and, turning the knob, finds it locked. She knocks. What is this? They are always home. She peers into the darkened interior at a still life: newspapers, coffee cups, scissors, slippers.

Right. Their car isn't in the driveway either. There is a garage, but it's always used for storage, not for the car. Great. She finally gets a moment for a visit and nobody's home. She should have called. So much for happy surprise. But all is not lost. Her brother lives in the apartment above the garage. He must be home, for the windows are open and there are clattering sounds mixed with the music of a rock group she doesn't know. The entrance to his apartment is an outside stairway that wraps from the side of the garage to an upper door on the alley side. She takes the steps and voilà, the door opens to her turn of the wrist. "It's me!" she announces.

Her brother looks up. "Hey! I didn't know you were coming!"

"I didn't call. I wanted to be a surprise."

"Like the first time." He makes a pregnant belly.

"I guess. I've been told we never change." Then she catches herself. She wants Ronnie to change and she's just handed him a discouragement. "But that of course is not any truer than anything else," she says awkwardly as he studies her.

"Is something wrong?"

"No. I just had a minute. Where are they?"

"I don't know. I heard the car go about an hour ago. Food shopping I guess."

"Well, you're here."

"Here I am." He inches forward on the sofa. "These are parts to an old CD player. I might get it working for them."

"Nice."

"You need anything to drink?"

"You have a Coke?"

"Yep."

"It's okay. I'll get it." And she does. One corner of the room is a kitchen separated from the rest of the space by a waist-high wall— good for using as a surface to hold things that are too difficult to carry in one move. Her brother is a fairly orderly housekeeper as divorced bachelors go—not as orderly as Potocki, but then much more depressed than Potocki ever was. His studio bed is put back together, the old mahogany coffee table in front of it. The four chairs are tucked in place under the dining table. "You have two Cokes," she announces. "Want the other one?"

"Nah. You can have both."

She looks at him, wondering if maybe he didn't open up his bed at all last night. Between the pop of the tab and her first sip, she manages to ask him, "What's the news? You, I mean. Seeing any-one?"

"No. You?"

"Um . . . yes."

"You're not sure?"

"I argued with him today. Maybe he won't be too welcoming when I'm back."

"Who is he?"

"A guy I work with."

"Is that okay? I mean allowed?"

"No. It's *verboten.* But human beings, you know, don't follow the rules too well."

"That's for sure."

Ronnie was such a lively kid back in the days . . . She wishes she could get that spirit back for him. He's a pretty good-looking guy, about six feet tall, high forehead, brown hair slicked back—an old-fashioned look, a CEO look, but in his defeat, in his shabby T-shirt and jeans, he is anything but top of the heap. He works at Walmart and smokes a lot of dope. "You think they'll be back soon?"

"Probably. They never go anywhere. Ever. Not to a movie or any-thing."

"Hm. As if they knew I was coming."

He laughs. "Yeah, you are scary sometimes."

"Ronnie? You remember that time we went on vacation—to Uncle Hal's?"

"Kind of. I mean I don't remember a lot about it."

"He didn't assault you or abuse you or anything?"

"Christ, no. You know something about him? I mean I was al-ways uncomfortable around him, but no, he didn't touch me."

"Good."

"Um, I think I hear you. Is that what you're saying?"

"Yeah, he did. And he was married to an evil woman. She knew it. She let him."

"I never liked her." His face worked worriedly. "If he was alive, I'd kill him."

"Thanks, but I'd be first. And I might opt for torture."

"What did Mom and Dad do?"

"I never told them."

"Wow." He turns this over.

"Until today."

"Why now, then?"

"I'm on assignment."

"Thinking about it now, you're bringing it back. He was always hanging around you, right? Those two were both creeps."

"Yeah. They were."

"There's the car," he said. "See, I told you they never went far."

"I didn't hear it."

"I'm used to the sounds around here."

There are overlapping cries of joy outside. *Is Colleen here? That's her car. Hooray. She came to see her old folks.*

Out the window she can see her two stringy parents looking up. This in a nutshell is their relationship. She, looking down, is the goddess who bestows her presence and needs nothing. They, her humble servants, want to serve, but briefly—and not get close.

She will make them dislike her this afternoon, but it has to be done and she knows it and has always known it. She knows all the lines. They will drink to buffer the blows, but maybe they will hear her. *Where were you when I was little and growing up—when I didn't know up from down? Why could you never notice things? Why did you dump us with two creeps and pretend not to know what they were made of? Why were your heads always in the liquor bottle? A parent protects. That's what a parent does.*

CONNOLLY, MANNING the grill, keeps looking up, checking his phone, and having distracted conversations with the people who come up to him to watch the ribs and the sausages getting brown. Todd has not arrived yet.

Dexter, the county commissioner, with whom he is friends, is here with his wife and two daughters. So are the head of city council, also a friend, with his wife; a neighbor who is high up in the party with his wife and one daughter; two other prominent party members, one with a teenage son in tow and one with a girlfriend on the way to being a second wife. Of the guest list, only Todd is missing.

Connolly instructs his guests to make the bar their own. It's hidden away outdoors—a small, discreet structure that houses a sink and microwave and refrigerator but is extremely well stocked. "You want me to mix something for you, I'm happy to," he says.

But most of them dip in for beers or soft drinks. Some take advantage of the pitcher of Tom Collinses.

"Ribs look good," says Dexter.

"Elinor baked them for hours to get them ready. That's how she does them to get them really tender."

"Where'd you find her?"

"In my nursery. She's been here for as long as I can remember."

"That's going some in this world. A person like that, staying in service. I thought those days were gone."

Connolly doesn't say anything. He's uncomfortable with the whole conversation about service. He's even from time to time tried to think how to do without paid help, but there is no way around it, not so long as he's in this house, at the firm, running for governor.

Finally he hears Todd's voice from the house, rising, cheerful— saying something jovial to Monica and laughing afterward. Did the man listen to his phone messages?

The jolly act continues when Todd comes out to the grounds. He's glad-handing everybody, introducing himself to the ones he hasn't yet met and doing such a good job of circulating that Connolly wonders if he will get a word alone with him at all.

"I have had the laziest Sunday," Todd tells a few people. "I took the papers out to my yard. I have a hammock strung up. I can almost never get in it without tipping over and breaking a few bones, but I managed to get the balance just right today and the papers put me to sleep . . . and I didn't want to get up. I mean I woke that little bit a couple of times and thought, No, no, just go back under."

"You won't sleep tonight," says the wife of the neighbor.

Todd flashes a trademark smile. "Maybe not. It was kind of worth it."

The woman smiles back, asking, "Won't you have to work tomorrow?"

"Oh, I might screw a few things up."

One of the party people, the one with the girlfriend, says, "I thought you were going to stop at 'screw,'" and the girlfriend hits him while the neighbor's wife looks abashed to think she handed him the straight line.

Simon continues to smile easily. He takes a seat on one of the chairs with plump cushioning.

"Drink?" Monica asks.

"Oh, sure. Whatever you have going. Anything is fine."

"Personally I think beer works best with the ribs and sausages, but I can make you a martini or . . ."

"Beer is great."

Monica goes to the bar to fetch him a beer. She looks very strained today. She's doing her best, but she hates all this socializing and she gave most of her best last night.

Connolly keeps turning the ribs. It's four thirty now. He made the invitation for three o'clock and hopes they all leave at six. Elinor brings out the bowls of potato salad and slaw, then the dense good rolls she ordered in.

"Ready to eat," Connolly says. "Bring your plates to me."

By five o'clock he's served everyone and put the extra meats on a platter. He's even eaten a little himself, though the food won't go down. It's stuck somewhere high in his esophagus.

At nearly six o'clock—some guests have left—Todd says, "Show you what I mean about the seats. I'm just around the side of the house."

Connolly follows, fuming. "Why didn't you call me back?"

"I'm thinking. I'm working things out."

"Look. That Commander Christie was here today. They have a lot of questions." Todd stops momentarily in his tracks, then continues toward his car. Connolly says, "This thing isn't over by far."

"What's his problem?"

"He wants to know who she was having drinks with. You told me it was you. Why didn't you tell him?"

"Look. I know what you're asking me. Yes, I took her for a drink. I had orders. I was supposed to talk her down from being in love with you."

"Orders? That means you were telling people about me?"

"They told *me*. Don't be naive." Having arrived at his car, Todd opens the door, pops the hood. "There you have the guts of it. Have a look."

Connolly has wanted to ask why all this pretending and subterfuge if he's not guilty, but that question gets knocked out by the surprise of what Todd has just said. "Who told you? Told you what?"

"See," Todd says patiently, "when I asked you about women, I was on orders to get you to talk about Cassie Price. Haigh and his men knew. What do you think? They weren't going to get behind you without some detective work. They had a detective follow you for a couple of weeks. They saw the motel stops."

"My God." He looks about distractedly, fixing his attention on the guests in the distance, laughing and talking. "Oh, Christ."

"Now I need to ask you some questions. If it's heated up, I need to know—*how* did you call her? Because they're going to be tracing phone calls. What did you use?"

"A phone. I bought her a phone. I sent her to buy one and I kept it to use."

"I'm thinking."

"What?"

"If they trace it—"

"My God. No, it's okay, it's in her name." Suddenly Connolly realizes that he's being sidetracked. "Look, what do you care about the phone? I asked you—"

"Because if they trace it, you'll have to cop to the affair. You have an alibi, so you didn't kill her. Maybe they'll keep it quiet."

"Do you have an alibi? I want the truth this time."

"I have an alibi. And you have the whole party on your side."

"If the kid didn't kill her—"

Todd's eyes narrow. "They're saying that?"

"They don't have to. I can tell by the questions they ask."

"I'm thinking. I'm thinking. I will definitely admit to the drink with her. I was supposed to find out what she was made of. That's all. I was supposed to see if she was reasonable. That was my job. That's all I did. I won't tell them that. I'll tell them she was a hottie and I tried for her. We have to beg the police to leave reputations intact—yours I mean. And we have to protect Haigh and the party in case . . ."

"If you think Haigh . . ." He couldn't say it. "I can't stick the Hathaway kid with it if something else went on."

Todd looks at him with the eyes of contempt. "The kid will get off on mental issues. I've been asking around."

"So Haigh did . . ."

The side door to the veranda opens, and three kids, Connolly's two boys and one of Dexter's girls, come out, running to the front of the house, around the veranda, and past them at the side of the house. The screams are a relief—kids having fun.

Connolly closes his eyes, wishing Todd away. When he opens them, Todd is still there and he is saying, "Don't get into that. Don't let yourself think it. If he did anything, and I doubt it, it's in the past. You have a bigger responsibility to the . . . people, the state."

"She was young. She was naive."

"Not very."

"She was beautiful."

"She was a bitch."

MONICA—HER FACE TIGHT from smiling—had gotten a little relief from watching the children cavorting about the grounds, running through the house and then back out again. At one point, when she was inside and they were running through, she followed them out the veranda door, about to yell, "Be careful," but something caught her attention and she never yelled. It was her husband's voice only a few feet away, around the side of the veranda. She heard a few words. Only a few words. She went back in.

She poured herself a tall glass of water and drank it down.

"Are you all right?" Elinor asked.

She nodded. "The sausage."

Walking unsteadily she climbed the stairs to her bedroom. There were a few guests lingering, but she didn't go back downstairs. *She was beautiful. She was a bitch.* Is that what they said? It was, wasn't it? Her husband, then Todd. *She was beautiful. She was a bitch.*

COLLEEN CALLED Christie on her way back from her parents' house. "Boss? I'm all at odds today. Should I be doing something?"

"You can relax. Where are you?"

"Went to see my folks."

"Good, good."

"Not so good." Did he think all interactions with parents were positive? "I'm on my way back."

"Are your folks all right?"

"You know that conversation you told me I needed to have with them?"

"To tell them about your uncle? Yes."

"I had it. I mean I knew I'd tell them one day and I did."

"Okay."

"It wasn't easy. I got angry and I said some things about how they were always drinking and into each other and not noticing me or my brother. It was ugly. They denied it and got all hurt. I think they hate me."

"No. Probably they hate themselves."

"Yeah. Drinkers do. So. Put me to work."

"I've been thinking. I want you to be the one to talk to Simon."

"I thought you'd want to. Or Dolan."

"We think we'd scare him. He'll probably think he's getting around you—and you can trick him better."

"Maybe."

228

"After the squad meeting tomorrow when we can have somebody shadow you. Okay?"

"Okay."

"Take the evening off. It's all right. Where are you headed?"

"Just home."

They hung up. He sounded . . . relieved when she said home. He didn't want her going to Potocki's house. But when she got to the Squirrel Hill exit, her car seemed to make the decision for her. It just kept going past the exit to her house. Potocki might boot her out or fight with her while his son watched; Scott might be either pleased or alarmed, or maybe, being a kid, simply curious. Oh, her life was very messy today.

WHEN THE CALL CAME for "trays up" at suppertime, Levon told Cal, "Something going to happen tonight. He ain't going to let you go."

Cal swallowed hard. He had made it through breakfast and lunch wearing his watch on his leg though he didn't let anyone see that's where he had it. Sidney sat one table over and kept laughing at him, calling him all kinds of names under his breath. He felt again and always like a little kid in school, with that dumb rhyme about sticks and stones going through his head. He understood, though, that he could not back down, not this time, if it came to a fight and even if he was being beaten again. He tried to think what little he knew about fighting. Eyes. Side of the head. A hit to the nose stuns. Duck low. Go for the knees. He didn't much like to think about it.

He and Levon pulled out chairs at another table, and one more guy took a seat with them. Cal didn't know his name. Kipper, Kippler, something like that, small guy.

"Hey, Chessman, I think you should sit at my table."

After too long a long pause, Cal said, "I think you should sit at mine." He's aware of a couple of the inmates laughing. Talk faster, faster, he tells himself.

"That's 'cause you aren't too swift. We've been giving you charity here. So far, that is. Most of these guys aren't pussy, didn't take it out on some young girl who didn't want them." Sidney gestured: dumb, hopeless. "So she didn't want you. And that's how you took care of it."

"We had a good time when we were together," he blurted. "I played my guitar for her. Then we were playing Scrabble."

"Fuck that. Scrabble? Then you killed her?"

"Nope. Somebody else stabbed her. I was home in my bed."

Sidney laughed. "She let you visit her? Scrabble? Dumb pussy like you?" Sidney's eyes are bright.

"Yeah. She won, though. That time."

Levon's eyes were round, trying to figure out where this was coming from.

"In the middle of the night, huh?"

"No, it wasn't middle of the night. That's just what the news said. It was like ten, eleven o'clock. We had the TV going. It was a Steelers night." He took a quick breath. "How come you want to know? I don't like talking about it."

"I don't want to know. You're just running off at the mouth."

"Seems you give me a lot of thought. Supercurious."

"No. Not true. I don't give you two seconds."

"You're welcome to come over here and sit. If you have questions."

A small pause and Sidney said, "You're really asking for it. You want to give up that watch?"

"What watch?"

"What you took from me."

"I don't know what you're talking about."

Sidney looked at him pityingly. "You make it worse and worse."

The food was a tough couple of pieces of chicken and a bunch of vegetables. Cal thought his mother would know how to doctor it up to make it better—butter and oils and flavors. Chopping it and putting it in something else. How she'd hate this food he was eating, how she would worry about him. He loved his mother. He needed to make her understand that he knew his own mind sometimes. She protected him too much.

"You going to play chess with me tonight?"

He looked up at Sidney. "Not in the mood."

"You going to watch the tube?"

"No. Not tonight."

The calm that he felt was something strange—as if talking faster, answering without thinking, making up lies, eased things inside him instead of the other way around.

What Cal really wanted to do tonight was go to the basketball court, but it was too dangerous a place to be caught alone with Sidney. Sidney running the roost was a puzzle to him. What was his power? Levon was even more nervous than he was, eating rapidly. And Sidney was looking at Levon like a snake ready to strike.

Suddenly and without any warning whatsoever, there was a quick flicker of lights and then the whole place went black. Even under the first shouts, Cal had heard the whirring-down sound of power dying, appliances shutting off. All lights were out.

Bells started ringing, and now more voices joined: *What is it, hey, power's out, do something, what's going down?*

Cal slipped off his left shoe, reached down and pulled off his watch, put it on his wrist. He felt his legs go out from under him and his head hit the floor. Somebody socked him in the stomach and started feeling around his left leg. There were shouts from the command desk of "Everybody stand. Hold your places. Name and cell number *in order*."

Before he heard the whole of "Mike Pitsger, 201," the lights came back on.

Most men were standing. He was on the floor with Sidney, who was grappling at his leg.

Somebody laughed.

"Stand. I said stand."

Cal got up, trying to catch his breath. Sidney was staring him down, his eyes drifting only to the watch, which was in plain view on Cal's arm.

The other inmates were busy looking around trying to figure out the reason for the outage.

"To your cells."

"What about dinner?"

"To your cells. Immediately."

The sally port guide came in, weapon drawn, and everybody moved.

Soon Cal and Levon were back in their cell and the door clicked into lock position.

"You are one lucky son of a bitch. How you do that?"

There was something to be said for luck.

TEN

MONDAY, AUGUST 24

CHRISTIE DIDN'T WANT to tell the whole squad yet about the Connolly connection. A blunder there would cost. So he was relieved to see that two cases—a homicide and an attempted homicide—required a good number of his detectives. He decided to narrow the pool of people he confided in to a few. There was going to be a need to let everybody in on some aspects of what he was calling the Price case—or they would wonder why the case was faltering. Christie weighed his bits of information and moved his few chess pieces around.

"Let's quick start with the new cases," he said.

Two of his oldest detectives, Hrznak and Nellins, reported on the attempted homicide. They had a white male in Allegheny General, near death, of a series of gunshot wounds. The man claimed he didn't know who shot him or why. He had been watching the Steelers game in a bar on Saturday night; on the way home he was shot. That case was already taking some intense looking at neighbors, friends, bar patrons, and a history of the victim. Hrznak and Nellins had started it, but because they were working on a Sunday, finding people was slow. Also, those two detectives were slow. Christie wrote on the board, *Kolkowski*, who was the victim, and he put eight men on the case, including several of the best young detectives because the primaries needed the boost.

It was his great luck that the clearer homicide case had fallen to Coleson and McGranahan. It would keep them busy. The crime was committed (apparently) a full twenty-four hours after the game, but still connected. A guy had stabbed his brother twelve times. Both men were in their twenties. An uncle called it in, though all the talk in and around the incident was confusing and not consistent. The perp had been bingeing on drink and Ecstasy. But so had the victim. And it was probably the uncle who was the seller of the drugs.

People needed a high from something. Sports ecstasy was one way (Marina told him it was universal, a need for communion, an attempt at a world soul, and he supposed she was right). Sometimes it was just face paint and innocent revelry. At other times that great feeling of brotherhood led straight to violence and insanity.

Christie put six people on that case.

"Catch you up on Cassie Price," he told his squad then. "Dolan has traced the phone that made some calls to her, but it was registered in her name. Go ahead," he said to Dolan.

"She had a second phone. Prepaid. Sprint. Cash payment. That's all we have except it was registered to her. She gave it to somebody to call her. We don't know who. Could have been her sister."

"Not her sister," somebody barked. It was Hrznak.

"Well, we're looking into it," Dolan said mildly.

"Also," said Christie, "she got a call from a pay phone in East Liberty the night of the homicide. We're looking into that, too. It was a short call. Could have been a wrong number."

"Maybe she was—"

"She was not turning tricks," Christie said, and the room went silent.

Coleson and McGranahan, now clearly off the case, looked at the toes of their shoes.

Having brushed by the phone evidence, and sidestepped the Connolly connection, Christie said, "Plus. More evidence. Our friends at Forensics have done the impossible. They have come up with—way ahead of the schedule—a bit of the science. Here are some surprises. One: There is no plaster dust in Cal Hathaway's car. Two: There was powder inside the work gloves. The powder was the sort that is used on those plastic gloves. Latex gloves. The kind you buy in multiples in a box or a bag. It seems the person who killed Cassie Price wore *both* plastic gloves and the work gloves. That fact suggests a certain amount of premeditation." He paused.

He waited for somebody to say, "If not framing."

"That points away from Hathaway, you mean?" Hrznak blurted, trying to get right with his commander.

"Yes. It looks like. So far there is no evidence that Cal Hathaway ever had or used plastic gloves. Or polypropylene, if you recall." He paced, studying them. "Add that to the funny position of the lock shavings. Add that to the lack of footprints—again this might mean premeditation. And of course the wrong-handed strangling." Dolan gave him a subtle thumbs-up. "Add one more thing. Our friends at the lab did push for some DNA evidence. This is interesting. There was nothing much on the floor or on Cassie Price's clothes. The perp was covered up—we think. There was nothing to examine. Again—premeditation in the lack of trace evidence."

"I love this case," Dolan said. "Just a side note."

"Yes, it has its puzzles. The lab hasn't worked on the clothes in her closet yet. That's a big job. The only other thing they could test quickly for us was the spot of blood that turned out to be a dead insect. If you're still counting, here's number three: Mosquito, you remember? They expected to find either Hathaway's or Price's DNA on that blood sample, though—this is important—the prison doctor never did find a clear bite on Hathaway, and the medical examiner says Price did not sustain a bite. Here's the thing. The DNA is somebody else's. Nobody we know so far. That's it. So I consider this case still under investigation. I don't see a clear conclusion yet. How we're going to trace some of this other stuff I'll let you all know as I figure it out. Those of you on the new homicides can go and get started."

That left him with his team of six, handpicked: himself, Dolan, Potocki, Greer, Denman, and Hurwitz. When the room had cleared, he said to his select few, "We're going to have a mini squad meeting. I have some sensitive material. We have to keep gathering information. I've called the DA to tell him the way this looks. I might recommend we don't charge Cal Hathaway tomorrow."

"He's listening?" Dolan asked.

"He was skeptical, but he listened. Let's see what we can learn today."

Denman and Hurwitz both turned to look at the door, presumably to see if anyone lingered. They both looked swelled with pride to be among the select.

"The confidential material I am about to tell you—if it leaks at this point . . . Let's just say it would ruin the career of anyone who leaked it." Having made everyone terribly nervous, he continued. "It's likely Senator Connolly—I don't know why I keep calling him senator—"

"Try governor," Dolan wisecracked.

"Yeah. The problem in a nutshell. It seems likely he was having an affair with the deceased. He had a lot to lose. I need some surveillance on him. Nothing obvious. I also need surveillance on his handler, Todd Simon, who is the guy we think put the margaritas in Cassie Price's system. I need Potocki on computer"—he saw Potocki grimace—"to check the history of both men in terms of any sexual harassment claims that maybe went away with a little money. I need Greer to go solo with Todd Simon to face him with the evidence of the date he had with Price. I'd go in with her, but my gut tells me he will talk better to her alone. He might assume she's a pushover for his charms."

"Thanks," she quipped.

"We know better. He doesn't. Besides, you liked him."

"I found him *interesting.*"

"That's magic in my book. Pin him down about the cocktails. Also see if you can break him down on his alibi—I hate this home in bed all night stuff, though unfortunately it could be true." He paused. "Depending on what he says, I'm back to Connolly to get specific about the phones."

Hurwitz and Denman looked restless.

"You two," Christie said, "need to tag Connolly, get his patterns of movement down. Dolan is going to Haigh to check on Connolly's alibi. I'll shadow Greer while she talks to Simon. When Potocki is finished with all he can find by computer, he can take over the shadowing and he and Greer can tag Simon for the rest of the day. It could be terribly boring. Gear up for that. Saturday I put in the paperwork to get the locations of the phone calls. I'm betting they were made from the road, most of them, in proximity to the motels, but I sure would like to have the paper evidence. Might have it late tomorrow. Cal Hathaway's hearing is tomorrow at ten thirty. I could request an extension, but we might be ready."

They stared at him. They were asking in silence, "You're going to get him off?"

His motive wasn't totally pure. If Cal Hathaway was released from custody, one way or another, that news would shake things up. Somebody would get nervous.

COLLEEN, SITTING IN her office cubicle, took a deep breath before she pressed in the numbers for Todd Simon. She was so prepared for a runaround, for voice mail, that she was taken aback when he answered. She identified herself, saying, "We talked in the conference room."

"I'm not likely to forget."

"Names. People forget names."

"I don't. I'm in the business of names."

"Right. All right. Well, we'd like to talk to you again. We have a few questions."

"Ask them."

"Not over the phone. Do you want to come to police headquarters? Or do you want me to come up to the Connolly firm?"

"Actually I wasn't going in today. I was—oh, you don't want to hear my day."

"Sure I do. More travel?"

"Yes. More travel."

"Well, what works? I'll get to where you need me to be. Where do you live?"

"Regent Square, but in a few minutes, I have to be in Shadyside."

"A restaurant there?"

"How about a coffee shop?"

"Done." They chose the small one on Ivy. If it was crowded she'd insist on moving to another or sitting in her car. She told Christie, and he promised to be close by. They tested her speed dial—he was number nine. It rang in five seconds. He could get to her in twenty-five seconds or so. Neither one of them thought Simon was the sort to do anything wild in a coffee shop, but still, they had to be ready.

Simon was standing outside, smoking, when she arrived. "I can't go long without smoke," he warned.

"I used to love the stuff. You should quit."

"I suppose so. I'm romantic about it—the old movies with pols smoking all the time. It's dumb, believe me, I know."

He dropped his half-smoked cig and ground it out. They went inside.

Simon insisted on buying her coffee.

"This will look like bribery. We're not supposed to accept it."

"But when a guy can't help it—"

"I know."

"I was brought up to pick up the tab. I can't get my mind around going dutch."

The shop was very small. There were two people on laptops at small tables. There was only one table left and some comfortable-looking sofas. She forced herself to choose the table. She saw her choice register briefly on Simon's face, but he was smiling when he returned with the coffees.

"Love this stuff," he said.

"And cigarettes."

"And booze, too. I'm a cliché."

She sat up straighter and assumed a formal manner. Her assignment was tricky. She'd got it because she was a good flirt, but she had to balance the flirting with a harder police manner. "Thank you for taking this time," she said. "I'm going to speak quietly just because of where we are. I have two specific main questions for you and probably some follow-up questions."

She studied him again—not bad looking. Not bad looking. And there was still, even under the evident worry he let her see, an irrepressible something, a need to have fun and the rest be damned. He punched one hand into the other. "Okay."

"First. Witnesses put you in Casbah with Cassie Price on the Thursday of the night she was murdered."

"My God," he groaned. He made a pained face, which she somehow didn't believe. "Long arm of the law."

"Tell me about it: the whys and wherefores and why you didn't mention it before."

"I'm embarrassed. I came close to mentioning it, but I didn't because I'm getting up there in age and she was a young thing and I was trying my luck with her."

"Did you have the impression she was interested in you?"

"I thought so. She said she had this sort of going-nowhere thing with this guy who wasn't her type and she didn't know how she had gotten herself entangled with him. She pitied him in some way. She was thinking to break it off. I told her I would be in the wings, waiting. She didn't fight me off."

"Waitresses thought you were comforting her."

"Well, I was. She was a mooshy drinker. Two sips and she was telling me confidences."

"Who was this guy?"

"She didn't say."

"You're sure she didn't say?"

"I'm sure."

"Had you seen her before?"

"No. Not outside the office setting."

"I see. And you went home with her after the drinks?"

"No, I didn't. I followed her to make sure she got home safely. I thought to let her have her own time. Besides, there was a guy on her back porch when she went into the house. I didn't want to get into anything crude."

"Was the guy the boyfriend?"

"I don't know. I just don't know. It sounded like that on the news. It fit what she told me."

"What?"

"Just the two different worlds."

Colleen felt the ground shift. He was very persuasive.

"Okay. Question number two. Your alibi." She had to lie to ask this one. "My colleagues asked around. Apparently, one of your neighbors said you didn't come home that night." There had been no neighbor's report, but she saw him blanch. "You told us you were home in your bed."

"Oh. This is really embarrassing." He closed his eyes. "It's going to make you dislike me a lot."

"Because?"

"I wasn't at home. I was with a woman I see. She lives up in Centre County. She works for the party. She's superprivate . . . maybe even, to be honest, old-fashioned; she gets nervous when I stay the night. I don't know who she worries will think less of her. Anyway, I didn't see any need to bring her into it."

"Her name."

"Rita. Rita Sandler."

"Jot me down her information." She handed over her notebook and pen. "Believe me, I don't like prying into personal lives any more than you like talking about it. But you have to tell the truth in these situations. Discrepancies call up a big red flag."

"I see that." He took his coffee cup and hers to the counter and turned back. "Want more?"

"No. Thank you, no."

Then he came back to sit. He hadn't written anything down yet. "Look. Let me explain something. I was married once, a long time ago. I've lived what many people would call a perfect bachelor life since. I've had a lot of fun. Just lately I'm torn between the old me with the temporary liaisons and something new that surprises me—a wish to get settled. I don't know where I'm going to land."

"And you're saying?"

"Both impulses were at work that day. And I'm smart enough to feel a little shame. I made sure Cassie got home, then I went straight to Rita."

He ignored the pen she'd pushed across the table and pulled out one of his own. He wrote down Rita's particulars without touching the notebook.

CHRISTIE PICKED UP his phone. He was parked a block from the shop and not happy about sitting in a car, motor running for the air con—like a rookie detective.

"Got him," Colleen said. She quickly gave the relevant specifics. "He gave me a lot of rigmarole about being embarrassed. But. He wouldn't touch my notebook. Not giving up one jot of his DNA no matter how careful he was at the scene."

"Don't worry. We'll get it."

"But if he did it—and I think he has a lot to hide, so I think it's highly likely—was it out of his own anger at her for rejecting him or was he protecting his candidate? That's something I can't tell yet."

"Guess?"

"Both? The anger. The carefulness." The more she thought it through, the more right that seemed. "Still, to work up to a strangle . . . Where are we, then?"

"We have the gray/silver car detail. We still need to solve the black car," Christie murmured, thinking. "We can get the DNA one way or another. The big question, to my mind, is whether Connolly ordered it or not. Or even knew it."

"Yeah," she said, deflated. "How do we get there from here?"

"Baby steps."

"So next, what, I go see this woman in Centre County—where he maybe spent the night? Rita Sandler."

"Yes. We're honing in on alibis now. I sent Dolan to talk to Haigh. I don't think Potocki is done with his research yet, so I'll follow you to Centre County. Will she be home?"

"My understanding is she'll be at work. You think we need two cars?"

"Here's my thinking. Simon might be going straight to her. I had my eye on his car, but he got too far ahead. If he's there, I don't want you going in alone."

"Ah. Got it." Colleen was already moving.

It was close to noon. She knew that somewhere on the road, she would get a call from Christie, suggesting they stop for lunch. It would be nice to spend a little time with him, but she worried he needed her more than she needed him. It made her sad that she'd stopped thinking about him in that sexy way. It made her want to put an arm around him, kiss the back of his hand, his cheek, old pal kisses.

DOLAN CALLED IN later that day, saying, "Haigh is a good good old boy—he defines the term."

"And?"

"He says he had Connolly staying there and that he has security cameras at his house. He turned over the DVDs, said if the guy left in the middle of the night, we'd see him get into his car. So probably Connolly's alibi is going to hold up. This guy Haigh was pretty mad. He said, what were we doing smearing an upstanding man, how ridiculous it all was, all that. Lots of fun. How is yours going?"

"I'm tracking Todd Simon. Don't know whether to believe him that he was going to Harrisburg today or whether he's going to hightail it to his alibi, this woman, Rita Sandler. Why don't you hang in Harrisburg for a bit, keep an eye on Haigh, see if anything is up. What were you doing? Eating?"

"I was just about to get on the turnpike coming home. Okay, Boss, I'll grab a takeout and go back."

SIMON WAS ON HIS way to Harrisburg. While he drove, he called Rita Sandler at work. "I'm pretty sure," he said easily, "the police are doing that check of alibis I told you about. Remember how we watched the Steelers together?"

"I remember," she said. "Mind like a trap."

Rita was a good soul. He felt secure about her.

It was Haigh avoiding him he was worried about. After repeated calls to Haigh, with quick assurances and speedy hang-ups, he was finally getting an audience. He drove fast. A little over three hours later, he was there.

A young fellow wearing a black shirt and pants opened the door. Simon had met him before. He did secretarial work for Haigh.

"He's expecting you," the guy said.

Simon started up the wide staircase to the office he knew was on the second floor.

"Oh, sorry, I forgot to say . . . You should just wait in the front room."

"Oh." He descended again. Front room. A parlor. What did that mean? Not welcome upstairs?

Soon enough Haigh was down the stairs, pulling on a sport jacket over his suspenders and white shirt and well-rounded belly. He had a bluster in his voice when he said, "Those judges are going down, down. Good news for us. We'll use it."

Simon hardly cared about this bit of political news—a couple of corrupt judges using the juvenile courts to further their own financial endeavors—but he cheered halfheartedly. This was public conversation, something the secretary was allowed to hear.

"Go for a drive?" Haigh asked, but it wasn't really a question. "My car. It's right outside."

They climbed up into the Explorer. Todd thought about how the high-up cushy seats, roomy interior, and noisy engine compared to his closer to the ground, more sophisticated European compact. The two cars just about summed up the relationship between the men.

"Where are we going?"

"Just to find a road, any road. We stop, get out, then we talk."

"Christ."

"Yeah."

Todd said, "Why the elaborate—"

Haigh interrupted. "Tell me about those judges. Tell me you can use the topple."

"Sure I can. I use everything."

Haigh said, "Tell me about Centre County and Luzerne County. Tell me about Esposito and his pals."

Todd thought, I am the employee; he wants a report, I have to give it. He managed a rote recitation about the people and districts Haigh wanted updates on.

It took twenty minutes to get to a park area. Haigh nosed the SUV around to a more or less secluded spot. "Let's walk," he said. He got out of the car.

Todd had to laugh. He pictured Haigh carrying a gun, bam, no more worries for old Todd. But it wasn't going to happen. Todd's car was back at the house. The secretary knew they were out together. Plus—he had to laugh—the Pittsburgh police were very aware of his existence. So. He squinted a hard look at Haigh, who was already puffing before they went ten feet. The poor guy was not a walker. For Haigh it was a significant exertion just getting up and down his stairway.

When they had walked some thirty feet into a wooded area, Haigh stopped. He turned to Todd. "Okay. Show me you're not wearing a wire."

Todd, aghast, almost hooted at the question. "Are you—? You're not kidding?"

"It's a necessary precaution."

He took off his jacket and handed it to Haigh. "Examine it. Pat me down."

He continued to be surprised that Haigh actually examined the jacket, taking his time. "When are you going to tell me what this is about? We could have talked back at your house."

"This is safer." Haigh patted him down.

He wanted to hit Haigh—it was that simple. He gritted his teeth, felt the blood rising to his face. When he saw Haigh point to his shoes, he took them off and watched his old mentor examine them, lifting the inner soles, for God's sake.

"Okay," Haigh said while Todd struggled back into his shoes. "The hearing for that kid is tomorrow. Is it going to stick? The police are everywhere asking questions. I just had some Pittsburgh cop up here asking me about Mickey. What is going on? How is it they are still asking? Why the hell didn't you use Frank Santini? I offered him to you. If this falls apart—"

"If it falls apart, it's not my fault. It could be Mick being stupid. Nobody, but nobody, could have thought it out like I did. I chanced a lot for you."

"Did you, huh? Doing it yourself?"

"Tell me when Benton gave me orders he was speaking for you. Tell me that."

Haigh pursed his lips. "You might have to go down. DNA and all that. If you do have to take the fall, I want an airtight story. I want you to keep Mick out of it. We'll get you the best, somebody to get you off on a technicality. Do you understand?"

"I figured all that. I'd want a lot more than that. I'd want some serious money. Whatever you were going to give to poor old Santini. And more."

Haigh stared at him. "I want you to ask yourself, Which is better? You take us down but stay in prison for some period of time and come out without money or work? Or you shut it and we get you out? Which is better?"

"Don't talk to me like I haven't figured the angles. I'm light-years ahead on every count."

"Tell me. From A to Z. I need to know."

"Okay. I took the bitch out for a drink the day . . . the day it happened. I really worked her. I was totally sure she would *not* keep quiet. I know you told me to work on her for a couple of days, to send this Santini in if she got impossible. But she was already impossible. She was reckless and dangerous. So I had to act fast, before she went back up to the office and made a scene. I let people see me with her. That was on purpose. Just in case there is any DNA of mine at the scene. I'll say something must have rubbed off earlier in the day. But they aren't going to find any DNA. Want to know why? I figured it all. I saw this worker kid outside her house, working on the porch. I said to myself what a very good suspect he would be. I thought it. I borrowed a full-cover painting gear—that thick paper shit which is honest to God impenetrable. I was covered. I even wore plastic gloves. Who else could have come up with that in two hours of thinking?"

Haigh made that funny move—finger and thumb squeezing his nose as if to stop breath—that he sometimes did when he was thinking. "Okay."

"I used the kid's work gloves. I was hoping they'd make a print on her neck. I don't know if they did. I took her cell phone, I took her wallet, I made like the place was robbed. Or like the kid tried to make it look like the place was robbed."

Haigh nodded. "Not exactly what I told you to do."

"What?"

Haigh gave him a steely stare. "You heard me."

Suddenly Todd thought, Shit, shit. He's recording this. He said, "So, tell me, are *you* wearing a wire?"

"Don't be ridiculous."

"Prove it." He started slapping at Haigh's clothes. It was an odd feeling, like hitting your father and realizing he was only made of flesh and blood and bone. He felt no wire, but he kept at Haigh, who started to hit back. Soon they were grappling at each other. Haigh's glasses fell and then he tripped and soon after that, both men were on the ground.

After a while Todd started laughing. "I ought to do this more often," he said. "I used to scrap a lot when I was a teenager. I forgot how good it feels."

Haigh grunted something like a laugh. He stood up, winded, and brushed himself off. "Where's the stuff? The stuff you took from her?"

"Buried. Gloves thrown away. I was careful. I know where I buried the phone and her wallet. I know how to get to them if I ever need to plant them."

"How do you figure that?" Haigh gestured him toward the car.

"In case it doesn't stick with the kid. I'll find a way."

"You *have* thought of everything."

"Yes."

"And you're loyal, right?"

If Todd heard any word thousands of times from Haigh it was that one. Loyal. The most desirable of traits.

"THEY SEEM TO HAVE gone someplace together," Dolan was saying. "Simon's car is here, and they just came back in Haigh's SUV. Simon isn't going into the house. They're shaking hands. I have to keep moving. I think, yes, Simon is getting into his car. You want me to follow?"

"From way behind. See if you get a direction at least. Let me know. We're partway to Sandler's house. We had a quick bite."

"I had a quick bite in the car. Not my style at all. I dropped mayo. How did I get sloppy?"

"It comes with age. You ever noticed old geezers? They have spots all over their clothes."

"Just what I needed to hear."

Christie was laughing. He liked ragging Artie. "Can't you laugh?"

"I'm laughing a little."

"Good."

"Is Greer in the car with you?"

"Two cars. I want to be around if Todd shows. Otherwise I want her to soft-pedal it with Sandler."

"Got it. You unpartnered her with Potocki?"

"Not yet. It's something I have to do."

"I'd say so. The vibrations are heavy-duty."

"Yes," Christie said. His tone didn't disguise his irritation. He missed having Greer in love with him. Well, real life was full of losses. You could even lose fantasies.

She drove fast. In the car ahead of him, she bounced with music—presumably music. She answered her phone. It wasn't a call from him.

RITA SANDLER SEEMED miffed to be bothered at work when Colleen introduced herself and showed her badge and announced that she needed a little of Sandler's time.

"I never take time away from work," Sandler said.

"This will take only a few minutes. Really."

"It's . . . What is this about?" Her fakery showed. It was clear Simon had called her.

"Do you have a conference room? Or we could step outside."

"We could go outside."

It was muggy. There were squat trees in a row outside the insurance office. Cars went by slowly.

Rita Sandler was a surprise, not the person Colleen had pictured Todd with. She'd been sure she was going to see a long-haired, short-skirted young thing in heels. This was a down-to-earth woman wearing pants and a top without much style. Her hair, a thick wavy brown, looked as if she ran fingers through it much of the time. If she wore any makeup it was virtually invisible. How could Colleen have guessed so wrong?

"How do you do both? Full-time job and all the politics?"

"It isn't easy. I'm always tired."

"I'm going to need your address and phones and all that." She handed over a notebook. Sandler propped it against the outside wall and wrote.

"Do you live alone?"

"Yes. With my dog. Not really alone."

Colleen smiled. "And you have a relationship of some sort with Todd Simon?"

Sandler paused. "It isn't serious. But yes."

"Oh. He thinks it's serious."

Sandler frowned.

"He's talking marriage."

The woman let out a surprised laugh. "Poor fellow. I'm not the marrying kind."

"Neither am I. I'm with you there. How often do you see him?"

"Oh, once a month. Maybe three weeks."

That was a lie, so clearly less often. And Todd's concern about privacy and protecting the woman's reputation made little sense. "Are you nervous about people knowing you see him?"

"I never advertise what I do."

"You're very private."

"You could say so."

"He seems like a pretty devoted fellow."

Sandler paused again. "He's a lot of fun."

"So the question I have is when you last saw him."

"It was about a week ago."

"I think you know the night I'm asking about. Did you see him on Thursday, August 13?"

"If that was the night of the Steelers game, yes, we watched the Steelers together and one of the talk shows."

"Which one?"

"Letterman. He had Paul McCartney on." The woman looked toward the street as if there were help there. Colleen followed her gaze but saw only Christie, way in the distance.

"And you would swear to this in court?"

"Yes, of course."

"By the way, what time did he get here?"

"Oh, seven or so. But why are you asking about him?"

"Because the night that for you is only memorable for a Steelers game—and a McCartney interview—is the same night a woman he had cocktails with only hours before was murdered. What time did he arrive?"

Sandler froze. So she hadn't known about the cocktails.

Finally she rallied. "Look, I don't remember what time he got here. We watched most of the game, but he wasn't here at the beginning. If this is something to do with smearing the party, I won't stand for it. I'll blast it open."

Colleen steadied herself. "This is a homicide investigation. Nothing less than. And it has its own protocol and rules. We may be in touch with you again. You need to stay available to us for questioning. That's it for today. Thank you for your time."

Christie was pulling out and passing her before she got anywhere near her car so as not to give the impression he was there for her or following her. But as soon as she was in her car and around the corner, her phone rang.

"She was a surprise," Christie said.

"Yeah. I thought he'd go more for Cassie's type. He talked about possible marriage to Sandler. To keep her from testifying?"

"Interesting. You have her home address?"

"Yes, of course."

"You go to her house. I'll wind back to the business. We'll give it an hour and a half, no more. Dolan said Simon was getting on 322. So he's probably coming here. I want to see whatever I can see. If he goes to the house, call me. We'll go in together. Give me the address so I have it."

As she did, he said, "What did we ever do before GPS? I can't even remember."

Two hours later, Simon hadn't showed, and so they went back to Pittsburgh. Christie rehearsed mentally for a squad meeting at eight the next morning and the hearing for Cal Hathaway at ten thirty.

CONNOLLY GOT HOME from work earlier than usual. He went straight to the chair he liked in the yard and sat. He needed to do something, something, but he didn't know what. Haigh had called him midafternoon. "Stay cool. I know they're checking your alibi. You're fine. We have to hope this goes away before any of the news media make it smear."

"Look. I really want to know what happened to that girl. I can't talk to Todd. There's something funny about the way he talks."

"Look. All I know is some guy killed this unfortunate young woman. You need to keep clean, watch your nose, and talk about *other things,* for God's sake. We have a lot of money and labor in so far. You're not going to pull out. Gotta go. Call you later."

Haigh sounded just like Simon. Nobody was talking straight.

He heard a noise behind him. It was Elinor.

"Mr. Connolly. I heard you drive up. I have to tell you, I won't be here tomorrow morning. My son's hearing is tomorrow. I need to be there."

"Of course. I totally understand. How . . . how is he?"

"He's trying to be brave around me."

"What does he say about the charges?"

"He feels they pushed him—those police—talking about blackouts. He tells me he didn't do it. He says he doesn't believe he had any blackout."

Connolly stood to talk to her. "I know this is horrible for you."

"I keep thinking of the bad luck of it, how once those boys beat him up, he never was the same, and now this. There's violence in jail. I don't know how he's going to make it through."

He took her hand. "Let me know if there is anything I can do. I'm very concerned."

"Thank you. I'll probably be here by afternoon."

"Don't worry about tomorrow. It doesn't matter."

He thought for a while after she went back indoors and then punched a number into his cell phone. He had to do something, something. What good was he if he couldn't help a woman like Elinor? His call was to the courts to find out which magistrate was on tomorrow morning. A clerk gave him the name and the time of the hearing.

He'd met the guy once. Only once. He asked for the number even though he assumed he'd have to get it some other way, but the clerk simply gave it to him, and he dialed it as soon as he terminated the first call.

The magistrate answered. His name was Lord, which was sort of funny. When he heard who his caller was, his brusqueness faltered only a little. "What can I do for you?"

"You have a case tomorrow. A person I'm concerned about. His mother works for me and *has* for nearly forty years. She's quite a wonderful person."

"This is the Hathaway hearing?"

"Yes. Her son is someone I know and . . . and a gentle creature. She's obviously concerned about him. He's not tough. He's not a fighter. He's not particularly social. If there is any way to make his experience more suited to his temperament—" He got stuck. What was he asking? Semisolitary with kindness thrown in?

There was a long silence. "I'll be aware of the character reference," Lord said drily.

They ended the call.

In his heart, he doubted Cal Hathaway had anything to do with the murder at all. Probably less than he did.

He was corrupt, corroding. He felt filthy.

Monica came into the yard and up to him. He put an arm around her and rested a head against her belly. They stayed that way for a long time. "Let's go somewhere," she said. "Let's talk."

"MARRIAGE," RITA SAID. "What do you take me for? What makes you think I want that?" She began taking pots down from a counter.

"Maybe I want it. Maybe I need it, to stop running, running, all the time. To be with one person."

"It's in your nature to run."

"Why do you bother with me, then?"

"My life is very dull. I need excitement now and then. I lied for you. That's a form of excitement, but not exactly what I prefer. Don't worry. I won't go back on it. But I would surely appreciate it if I didn't have some police detective looking at me with suspicious eyes." She banged around for a while. "All I have is the makings of an omelet and some red potatoes."

"We could go out."

"I don't feel like it. I had a long day. I have to walk Keeley."

"I'll go with you. Then I'll take you someplace for dinner."

"No. I *want* to stay home. It's eggs and potatoes or nothing."

"Fine," he said. He didn't plan to stay, but he was looking for a way to make things nicer between them.

She was silent as they walked. He tried to put the rough meeting with Haigh away in some side pocket. He concentrated on facts. Haigh was sending that secretary of his to court tomorrow morning. The secretary was to pretend he was sitting with the family to write a book about their daughter and them. God bless America—hearings were public. They would all know a lot more tomorrow.

Todd congratulated himself that he had not stopped working today. He had taken and made calls to various county chairmen as he drove away from Haigh. He had stopped and had a big meal—he wasn't the least bit hungry—with a drink midafternoon, not at all his usual practice, which was more like a piece of pound cake and several cups of coffee. He had driven down the country road where he buried the evidence, and he had done it to test himself—his grit, his memory—and to be alone. He found his markings. He found the bit of earth. He didn't dig. He just looked at it.

WHEN MONICA ASKED to go out, Connolly thought she meant to dinner. She said, "No. Someplace where I can cry. Someplace private."

It was funny. He couldn't think where to go. She couldn't either.

Finally she said, "Let's walk over to the campus. Use their chapel. If it's locked, we can go into one of their other buildings. Let's just go."

He still had his briefcase with him. He put it in his car as they walked down their drive and off their property.

When they got to the chapel it was empty. "It might not stay empty," she warned. "We might be interrupted. We'll have to chance it."

He felt a great dread pulling at him. He thought he would go through the ground, he felt so heavy with it.

"I heard you and Todd talking. Tell me about Cassie Price. You were seeing her."

After a long while, he nodded once. "I'm so sorry."

"I'm not the worst victim here. Did you love her? Do you?"

"I think so."

"I can always tell when you're falling in love. The way you talk to me, the way you hold me. The absence of lovemaking. Some men, you know, make love to their wives even more when they're straying."

"I'm sorry."

"Am I so unattractive to you?"

"No." He didn't say her toughness made her unattractive sometimes.

She had begun to cry. She had promised to cry and here it was. "I am what I am. I'm middle-aged and I like to work. That's . . . that's not what I wanted to talk about. It's what's going through my mind. It's about that girl . . . woman. She was a young woman. How did she die?"

"I don't know."

"Please don't lie."

"I'm not lying. I don't know."

"I believe you. You didn't do it, right?"

"I didn't do it."

"Somebody who cares about the election did. Who was that? Haigh? Todd? That's what I think, Haigh or Todd."

"I've thought it and thought it. They deny it. Then I think, Well, maybe Cal did it after all."

"Maybe it was convenient that Cal happened to kill her? Nothing is ever convenient."

"I don't want to lose you."

"Oh, I don't know about that. We're very far apart. We've been just a couple of people smiling for the cameras for a long time."

"Don't give up on me."

She shrugged, wiped her eyes. "You've made me be . . . guarded. I don't like how I am any more than you do."

"Do you want to call Christie? Do you want me to call him? I go back and forth. There's nobody I can talk to. I try talking to Haigh and Todd—and it always comes down to the hordes of people already counting on me to get elected. If this comes out, it's going to mean no more election. And shame. For my father. The whole firm. Our kids. I'm totally, totally stuck."

She began to hit him with her fists. ". . . for what you do. For touching someone else's body. I've given up everything for you. I don't want this, any of it. And all the while you have to fuck somebody else."

He tried to grab at her hands. They were in a chapel. He tried to tell her it was important to wait twenty-four hours, to see what happened at Cal's hearing. Maybe their worst fears were wrong; he prayed they were wrong.

"BUZZ SAYS YOU HAVE a hearing tomorrow," Sidney said, taking a seat at Cal's table. "I take an interest, see?"

It was hard to get food down with Sidney there, but Cal had thought it important to choose a seat on his own. He had instructed Levon to sit somewhere else, which the kid did, but now Levon looked nervously over at Cal's table.

The next person to sit down was the man who had made him eat cake. And then, in the fourth chair, that man's friend.

"Let them eat cake," Cal said.

The man who had made him do just that laughed a little, saying, "What's that from?"

"Some history class in high school."

"Yeah, I always heard that."

They all kept at their meat loaf. Cal swallowed hard to get his down his gullet.

"So there are bets going down," said one of the newcomers—the big bald guy. "I put money on you, Cal."

"About tomorrow?" Sidney asked. "When he comes back whipped? What kind of odds are those? Everybody knows what's going to happen. He's just fucking stupid, making an ass of himself."

Cal felt his face flush—would he always be thought stupid?

In a tone of clarifying, the big bald guy said, "The bets are about whether he's a brother. I decided it's true."

"You want to claim him?"

"I think he was telling the truth is what I'm saying. We have our network out there, looking into it."

Cal kept eating—forced himself to swallow. He understood that the bald man and his companion looked more favorably on him because of the chess game. He also understood that they would be careful not to pull Sidney down publicly. It was interesting. He thought if he stayed in prison forever he would like to be a whatever, counselor, liaison, whatever job there was that figured out the dynamics.

"Well, it doesn't matter," Cal said, "what color I am. I'm the color you see. But I had a real good grandmother. She was dark-skinned and she came from slaves."

"I don't care about that," Sidney said. "You can be green. You're going to be dead soon. I mean it."

Cal wondered if he could possibly live through whatever Sidney did to him.

"What do you think of that?"

Cal shrugged. "Time to be with my grandma," he said.

ELEVEN

TUESDAY, AUGUST 25

SOME HEARINGS started on time and some started late. This one was late because the eight-thirty case had started late and gone overtime. There were, apparently, complications. Christie waited in the hallway where he had waited multiple times in the past. He didn't see Cassie Price's family, but he understood they were there, waiting in one of the empty rooms so they didn't have to face reporters or Cal's mother. The printed page on the courtroom door was interesting: COMMONWEALTH OF PENNSYLVANIA VS. HATHAWAY, LORD PRESIDING.

If only.

Magistrate Lord was going to ask why it wasn't Coleson and McGranahan in court. Christie would have to do his word magic. He scanned the group of people gathered. Elinor Price. He nodded to her, then went to her and said a few words of polite greeting. He wanted to comfort her, but in this setting, no, he needed to hold himself apart. When the DA, James Ray, arrived, Christie and he sat on a bench as far from the others as they could.

"Sorry I wasn't able to take your call earlier," Ray said. "Is there something new?"

"There are some new items I can't give away inside." He nodded toward the two reporters he knew and the other person he
didn't know, the nervous-looking fellow with a laptop. "The evidence continues to point away from Hathaway. If his counsel is any
good at all, the charge won't stick down the line. So far as I'm
concerned it's still an open investigation. Our job is to get Lord to
understand."

"Small matter of the confession."

"You got it."

"I thought defense was leaning toward mentally incompetent."

"Before they met him, they had their minds made up. But he
doesn't come across as incompetent. He's careful in his speech, deliberate, but he seems to be picking up flow, less self-conscious, as he
gets used to us. Unfortunately or fortunately—however you see it—
he's coming across as sane."

"So. Okay. I'm going to ask for an extension. I'll just say we don't
have enough at this time and the investigation is ongoing."

Christie said, "And you'll have me agreeing."

Suddenly an officer opened the door to the courtroom, and another appeared with a wand to scan the participants. In seconds, as if
a bell had gone off somewhere, everybody was in line, and that included the whole of the Price family, who materialized out of nowhere. Everybody in line submitted to open purses, open briefcases,
and the wand. In seven minutes they were all inside.

On the left sat the family and the one reporter fellow—no, he
wasn't a reporter. Christie watched him. He was too pleading when
he talked to the Prices, shifty-eyed, up to something. On the right
were the mother, Elinor, and a woman who appeared to be a friend
holding on to her elbow. The actual reporters took seats in the back
on the right. Christie, then the DA, then the defense council, then
Cal lined up in their places at the front like two teams supposed to
do combat. Cal wore his prison reds, letters splashed across his back.

Lord looked back and forth to each of them for a while before he
said, "Let the proceedings begin."

Jim Ray began. "I would like to ask for an extension. This case has not produced the conclusive evidence that would be necessary to continue."

The magistrate rifled through notes he had. "It was my understanding that you had a confession." He looked back and forth from one side to the other.

The defense attorney, Gerald Foote, said, "Your Honor. The confession was brief and partial. The suspect felt a great deal of pressure, and he was exhausted with the long day of having found the body and making himself available to police for extended questioning."

"He retracts the confession?"

"Yes, he does."

A quiet cry of "Oh, no" came from the Price family. Christie turned to see it was the daughter next in age to Cassie.

James Ray gave her a gesture of prayerful hands that suggested she be quiet, a gesture that meant, "Please wait until I can talk to you."

"Is there a videotape of the confession?" Lord asked.

"There is. It shows clearly that the accused was exhausted. When the detectives asked him if the gloves used in the homicide were his, he said yes. He interpreted the detectives' words to mean that he had had a blackout and had used them without knowing it. Cal Price had blackouts in his past as a result of a bad beating at his grade school."

"In the past means what?"

"Until he was almost twenty."

"How old is he now?"

"Twenty-nine."

"Nothing since?"

"No. In his fatigue, he let himself be persuaded he had blacked out again. When he was rested, he indicated that he saw no reason to believe the blackouts had returned. He had a friendly work-oriented relationship with the deceased. He was doing work on her house." Gerald Foote fiddled with his glasses, then took them off. His eyes were soft, worried.

Lord made an odd, humming sound. "Do you have any evidence that this crime was done by someone else?" Lord asked Christie.

"We are in the process of establishing another suspect. Evidence at the scene suggests premeditation. And the labs identify the per-petrator as right-handed. All tests show the accused is left-handed. There are other pieces of evidence being accumulated—phone calls and things of that nature that suggest we look at other suspects."

"Plural?"

"Probably not, but it's difficult to say right now."

Lord's eyes drifted over to Elinor Hathaway and back. He sighed and fiddled with the papers before him. "Do you determine the sus-pect to be a flight risk? I want to hear from each of you."

"No," said each one in turn.

"He has a stable family?"

Gerald Foote answered. "His mother is in the courtroom. She is his only family."

"He has a job?"

"He's a private contractor."

"She has a job?"

Christie could tell by the way the magistrate asked the question that he already knew the answer.

"She—I believe she works for Senator Connolly."

Christie thought, I know what's coming. This is amazing. The wheels of justice might grind slowly, as the saying goes. And the path-ways to justice are circuitous much of the time. But this—

"Are you requesting a reduced bond?" Lord prompted the defense council.

"Yes, Your Honor, we are."

The magistrate looked through his papers again and stacked them. He studied the face of Cal Hathaway, who stood straighter than Chris-tie expected and looked more worried than frightened.

"I'm ruling for a ten percent bond in good faith. And house arrest. No window to go to work—the job is too unpredictable. I will man-date psychological testing and sleep-study testing, and I will approve a window for those things."

Gavel down.

Christie was astounded. Nobody got out after making a confession.

Well, maybe twice in his whole career, and those were minor cases. As glad as he felt for Cal and his mother, who wept openly, he was sorry for the Price family, who had come expecting closure. They were having a hard time.

Christie watched as the man with the laptop approached the family, tucking the computer in his shoulder carrier. He told them he was writing a book about Cassie. Christie followed behind as they started out the courtroom. "Who is the other suspect?" the man whispered to the sisters, who were huddled together.

"Leave us alone," Cassie's father said. "Get out. Vultures. Vultures."

The young man withdrew with his hands up, then got out his cell phone and walked down the hallway talking hurriedly.

Christie wanted to follow, but he was interrupted.

"Commander?" He turned back to James Ray, who said, "I knew from the start it was something big. The way you jumped on it. Who are you looking at for this? I have to know."

At that point Elinor, exiting the courtroom with Gerald Foote, raised a hand to Christie. "Thank you. Thank you."

He gave her a quick nod. Right now the wheels of justice were turning in Cal's favor. Anything could happen. He turned back to Ray. "Would you be too surprised if I said I have to look at Connolly and his group? I'm sorting information."

James Ray shook his head, but his eyes were wide.

Christie'd started all this by muscling in on the case. He was about to ruin a political career and a reputation. He hoped to hell he was right.

ELINOR HAD WANTED to cross the barrier to touch her son, but the guards whisked him away. Gerald Foote had followed a few steps behind those officers, saying something to Cal, but then he came back to Elinor. Her friend Olive, a woman who felt like a twin except that she was dark and Elinor was light, held on to her elbow as Foote then ushered them out of the courtroom and as they passed Christie.

Foote now explained the next steps. "You got reduced bond. That means you'll have to come up with fifty thousand."

"I have it in a retirement account. How do I get it out?"

"Could be cash. But it could be your property, too. If you owned a house or if your son did . . . ?"

"We both do. We both own."

"Excuse me," Foote said, a hand to his forehead. "I didn't think I was going to get my way. I'm still adjusting. Do you owe much on your house?"

"It's paid off."

"Excellent. We need to get its assessed value."

"Sixty-five thousand. That's the tax assessment."

"You are home free."

"I have to sell it?"

"No, no, just put it up. Let's go meet with your son and then with a bondsman."

If Olive let go, Elinor felt she would collapse. "This is good," Olive was saying. "This is real good."

"How long does this take?" Elinor asked, expecting the answer to be "a week."

Instead, Foote said, "If everything goes smoothly, we'll have him out today."

"What did you do? How did you do it?"

"I don't know for sure," he said vaguely. "I . . . we had a good deal of cooperation from the prosecution, but I think there must be an angel I don't know about."

Elinor studied him. She tried to guess who the angel was.

TODD, KNOWING THERE was a hearing on Tuesday, kept himself busy working from his home while he waited for word. He wandered from kitchen to living room, one or another phone to his ear. He found that gossiping about the judges from Luzerne County continued to be a good icebreaker—he'd make a few jokes, and, like a comic, count his laughs.

When he was sure his contact was having a good time, he got the subject around to money for Connolly. "Let's think Labor Day picnic."

"People are going to be away."

"Don't give up before you try it. Start asking around, man. People like free food. Feed them and they'll cough up something."

When his phone buzzed, interrupting, and he saw it was Haigh, he said, "I have to take this."

A second later, he listened to Haigh saying, "Cal Hathaway is out of jail."

He heard the words and had to separate them and put them back together. "How did that happen? They don't believe he's innocent, do they?"

"I should have sent somebody other than Walter. He's excitable. He can miss details. But what he's sure of is that the police are looking at somebody else. Phone calls are a part of that."

Phones, phones. He was thinking.

"Walter says everybody who was there was surprised by the magistrate. It's house arrest. Reduced bond. The guy isn't off their charts, but he's fading from their view."

"I see."

"You have an idea?"

"I have a fix. Don't worry."

"You'd better tell me what you're—"

"Don't worry. I've got it. I promise."

He pressed the END button. His hand was shaking. He'd sounded good. He could do that—hearty voice, confident manner. If he hadn't learned anything else in twenty years, he had learned how to produce that voice, and even Haigh calmed when he heard the take-charge attitude.

His fingers fiddled with the phone again. He called Freddie's number.

"What is it?" she answered. "I'm tiling a floor. I can't let the grout sit for—"

"Okay, I'll call you back sometime."

"What is it?"

"I don't know. I felt like calling."

"That's new."

"You'll be home this afternoon?"

"No. I'm here all day. Probably need to keep at it until about seven. These people want to move in, like yesterday."

"You're home tonight?"

"I'm seeing Old Reliable tonight."

"I hope you won't forget me."

"You're not very forgettable. I'm not always sure I like you, but you are memorable."

"Can't you get rid of Old Reliable?"

There was a sound of scraping, like sanding over the line. "I'm not sure I want to. We might be thinking of something more permanent."

"You and some old guy."

"I never said he was old. Only reliable. I can't believe it. You're jealous."

"I am certainly not jealous. Only," he said in his jolliest tones, "I hope you'll keep me abreast of your relationship . . . status."

"Tell you I'm getting hitched before I do it. Sure, I can do that."

Bitches. All of them. It didn't matter. He felt fine. And he certainly didn't need to be tangled with a woman tonight. He went out to his car and patted it—his doggie, his friend. He liked his car.

He got into the driver's seat and started up. He was right to mark the grave of the wallet and cell phone. Nobody, nobody, could have remembered and worked out everything as he had. And his brain was still ticking.

CHRISTIE PULLED HIS small squad in—they went to a conference room and shut the door. Christie said, "I have a dilemma. I don't know if Connolly is involved in this convenient death. There's something about him—naturally innocent. I like the guy. He might be blocking out the truth."

Everybody was quiet.

"Denial isn't . . . innocence," Colleen said.

He felt himself drift. He had a religious background—Catholic, an almost conscription into the priesthood. "Isn't it? I don't know. Talk to me."

There was discomfort in their shifts of position.

"Politicians get away with too much," Potocki said. "We can't contribute to that."

"Boss, you see something in this guy. Are you . . . Republican?" Even though Greer used a light tone and pretended to be joking, there was a challenge in her gaze.

Everybody got more nervous. Hurwitz tried to lighten things. "Oh, he's likable, but I personally can't fall in love with a Republican. Just can't. It's bred into my DNA."

Christie laughed. "I'm an Independent—"

"Big surprise," Dolan said.

"Who happens to lean Democratic most of the time—and I didn't have to reveal that." Greer was mouthing, "Whew," and he ended up laughing again. "So. Connolly is just a person. A rich person. Depressed, I'd say. All about being good and doing good deeds and underneath, pretty darned depressed."

Colleen said, "What do you want us to do?"

Christie looked at her, then at the rest of them. "Stick to surveillance." He turned to Hurwitz and Denman. "You two continue on Connolly. Unobtrusive. A couple of cars. I don't know how many vans we have available."

Surveillance was hard. It was boring. Detectives fell asleep. "I'm banking on somebody behaving oddly. Which means we also need to keep an eye on Cal."

"He's not on house arrest?" Dolan asked, but it was rhetorical.

"There's a window for him to get medical testing. It could be interesting to see if he departs at all from the program. Artie? You could start and I could join you."

"Got it."

"Again I'm not sure what our vehicle situation is."

"I could check that out for you," Potocki volunteered.

"Thank you. Potocki, Greer. You two will need a van. You get Todd Simon. Full surveillance drill. I think I have money on him. Anyway, somewhere, somebody is going to give something away, right?"

Then they were all standing, gathering their things, preparing for a long night.

IN MIDAFTERNOON, Todd Simon was already on the country road that led to the evidence. He had stopped only to buy a packet of latex gloves at a Rite Aid.

It was about eighty degrees and muggy, Pittsburgh muggy, steam pressed between the hills. The evidence, when he dug it up, would be like hot coals in his hands; he didn't intend to juggle them for long and he'd be wearing the gloves while he did.

Freddie would be out all afternoon, she said. And she had a nice backyard. Better to stash things there than at his house or in his car where police might eventually look.

He drove, trying to make himself think of other things. New carpeting. Diana Krall. Haigh's fat belly. Good jokes. The hours spun by with these diversions. He got the whole way to Shell Pond Road.

Oh. Hilarious—the guy with the tractor, same guy, same tractor, idling down the same old road. Todd stared straight ahead, slack jawed, mouth open, because he remembered that he had dived down to his right before. It wouldn't do to repeat. Hopefully the geezer did not have a memory for cars. Todd kept his jaw dropped, his eyes wide, hopefully sending the message that he was just a dumb rich guy in his nice car driving along on his way to an early dementia.

Should have ditched his car before doing this task. Soon, soon, he must get rid of this car, probably for good. If he hasn't traded it in by the time he does the deed, he will have to get himself something else, a cheesy rental if necessary, but there are risks in that, too.

He passes the man.

He finds the dirt road. The tree. His little Cassie Price grave.

Brilliant. The step count was perfect.

He digs. There it is. All there. He removes the rest of the gloves, another eight, from the packet and puts them in his jacket pocket. He lifts the wallet and phone gingerly and drops them in the plastic bag that held the gloves. He is not sick at first but then he is, so he works on his deep breathing. Almost throws up. Doesn't.

He drives back home to Pittsburgh and to the supermarket lot that's two blocks from his house. He needs a breather. As he buys a few groceries, he calls the lasagna woman, Carola. She doesn't work. She teaches part-time, a couple of evenings, if you call that work. Family money keeps her in bread. She answers the phone.

"It was delicious," he says.

"You have my pan."

"And I was planning to bring it back. Are you home?"

"Not for long. I'm meeting a friend for dinner."

"Should I know about this? Are you telling me something, I mean, that kind of friend?"

"A woman friend. For dinner."

"I could drive you. Pick you up. Wait for you somewhere. I could go have substandard lasagna."

"Look, I'm kind of mad at you."

"I gathered."

It's strange, the charmed life he's led up to now. No woman ever said no to him, not that he can remember. Now they all want him to vamoose. He needs to get his mojo back.

"Later, then. You have a good time tonight." Screw Carola.

He hates Haigh for ordering the killing, and he hates Cassie who made it necessary. And while he's at it, he hates people in general— they always seem to be in his way. But he doesn't hate himself. He always knew it would come to this one day. He is a server, born to grease wheels, pave paths and make things happen and unhappen. Connolly—bless his damned stupid soul—is the golden boy they've all been hoping for, perfect, perfect. If only this were Europe, the thing with Cassie Price would have gotten no more than a few knowing smiles and winks. But here they are, in the Bible-thumping U.S. of A. where men are supposed to go to bed saying prayers and when they slip from the straight and narrow everybody pretends not to understand.

POTOCKI GOES BACK to his cubicle for a moment to work out which cars and vans are available for Christie and the others and for him and Greer to watch Todd Simon.

He feels bad for Christie. Everybody wants Greer. She's great, just right out there, says what she thinks, gets enthusiastic about ideas, people, food, enjoys humor, and is wonderful to look at. She has a bright face most of the time. You can see her get tired and then pow she's back again, bright eyes, glowing skin. Sleep renews her. Food renews her. She wears her hair in a slightly bed-head style, just enough to advertise a bit of whimsy.

They hit a turning point on Sunday after she stormed out, went to visit her folks, and came right back to him. He had thought it might take a few days for her to cool off, but there she was, saying, "Sorry I flew off the handle." And then she just came in and stayed for dinner. She played Wii tennis with Scott—didn't beat him, but she took it seriously, and his son respected that. They all talked easily at dinner, and Potocki knew for sure this was what he wanted, the kind of blessing he hadn't thought he'd have again soon. He was a family man. He liked peace, humor, easy times.

Colleen was over Christie. He could tell.

He jotted a few notes. Then he went to her cubicle. "Take all the newspapers and a couple of books along," he said. "This could be a long one. We're going to be in the Jensen twenty-four-hour plumbing van. We don't have another driver, so one of us has to drive and then slip into the back."

She pulls out of a drawer a cap that says PNC PARK and a pair of huge sunglasses in case she needs to be out of the van at any point.

"Here's the plan: You go home, rest up, eat, gather what you need, I'll get the van ready. I'll come get you around seven, seven thirty. You can precede me in your car. We'll park your car a street away from Simon's place, you get in the van, go in back, but if we need a car, we can get to yours fast."

"I don't think I have anything to eat at home . . . I'd better get to a store and cook us something."

"No problem. I'll pick something up."

"Thanks. Buck me up. I hate surveillance."

"Two of us in a darkened van. It could be worse. I'll run some ideas by Commander about Cal's house, what his options are. A van on Child Street—seems to me it might get too much attention."

"He's awfully worried."

"Sure. The political takedown—if that's what it comes to—could get really ugly."

CHRISTIE SITS IN HIS office, head in his hands.

If Connolly cops to collusion, accessory, it's easy to figure out what to do, he'll take them all down. But if he determines Connolly didn't know what was happening . . . where are the lines in this murky case? One way or the other, prosecution is going to end up reveal-ing Connolly's relationship to the dead girl. And the guy is ruined. Mike Connolly.

He has an e-mail from Marina—*Home tonight?* It was her first day of teaching, and he knows she would like to talk about it.

He is about to answer her when Potocki comes in with the sur-veillance plans. "You can have the van that says BUG OFF. 24/7 SER-VICE. But you probably don't have to use a van," Potocki is saying. "Look at this little map. St. Regis is directly across the street from Cal's place. You could hole up in there, I'll bet. Room to breathe. If you like the idea, I'll call the church for you."

He likes it. "Wow, thanks. Yeah, try to get me and Dolan into the church. That would be great. Van for Hurwitz and Denman?"

"No need. They can have two cars and the coffee shop and office building across the street."

He writes back to Marina. *I can be at home until 7:30. Then back out.*

CONNOLLY AND HIS wife sat in the yard again, this time together. She looked strained. He could hardly believe in the midst of this, she went to teach. "How did you manage to go to work?"

"What choice did I have?"

"People call off."

"Not the first week if you hope to have a good rapport with a class. Not that I think I did a good job. My mind wouldn't stay tacked down." She sighed heavily.

"Do you remember when we met?"

"Oh, yes."

"We neither of us could work?"

"I remember. What did you see in me then that kept you coming back? Sex, yes, of course I understand we had that. But . . . that was everywhere to be had. That was easy."

"You were nice."

"Nice? Ugh."

"It's all right to be nice. I mean, *kind*. Aware of other people. You still are. I see how you are with Elinor. And other people."

Between them is a pitcher of tea Elinor made yesterday. It's odd, not having her around, but the process of getting Cal released has taken up her day.

"Nice doesn't get a girl anywhere. Or does it?" She sounded bitter again, flinty.

"Attraction is . . . I don't pretend to understand all of it, but an idea takes hold. I think there's a sort of equal yes and no. I have her, I don't have her. I want her, I don't want her. It's a craziness. That's not an excuse."

"I can't go on like this. I could get an apartment."

"You must despise me."

"No. It's more the opposite. I like you better than I did a week ago. I guess I like the truth. Even if the truth is that I'm not enough for you."

"That isn't true. I'm the one at fault. You shouldn't have to leave this house."

"It's okay. It isn't mine. It never was."

"I can't think what to do. Haigh, well, he's probably losing his mind, but he thinks he's going to find a way to keep me in the race."

"Do you want to be in it?"

He let himself think for a moment. "No."

"Act on that."

"Haigh is going to say if I get out, it may cause more speculation than if I stay in."

"I don't think you're going to beat the scandal. I think it's already here." Her voice caught. She was very tired.

"We . . . Say we take the boys. We go to Ireland. We live there for a couple of years. The schools are good."

"I have a job."

They sip at tea made just the way they like it. Elinor keeps greasing the wheels of their lives.

"I guess it was too good to be true, an idea like that."

"And the young women there are good-looking."

"Please don't."

"Is Ireland nice?"

"It's wonderful. People tell me even the food is good now. It's . . . beautiful there."

"Ireland."

COLLEEN DROVE HOME, up over river and dale—well, really the William Penn Parkway—to Squirrel Hill in the slow, slow slog of rush hour traffic. The river looked good today, and one little boat appeared not to be bothered by the pace and stress of the roads above. The city was alive with students—that was one of the problems; new ones didn't know their way around yet, so the traffic was even worse than usual.

The car radio bothered her; she turned it off. When she was alone, she often thought about her parents—the way they'd sagged when she told them they had been bad parents, they were in denial, and had been, letting themselves believe a kid could raise herself, figure it all out herself.

Maybe some did. She thought of children she'd seen on the job—the Philips kids who had lived on their own and were competent at everything and more mature than most adults.

She had needed to be safe—from herself, partly. She was born lively. Flirty, she supposed, but even when she didn't feel flirty, men thought she was flirting. Her uncle had thought so. It was just energy, curiosity, getting translated incorrectly.

Her parents had given her compliments from time to time, but mostly it was their way of avoiding responsibility, at the level of *Here, have a cookie.*

It was hard having spoken harshly to them for the first time in her life, but she wasn't sorry she had.

She still loved them.

Finally at her house, she lies on her bed, clothes on, deep breathing. Potocki has only been in her bedroom once. All their other times together have been in his bed. It's easier to land like a little bird and then fly away when you need to. Freedom. Freedom.

HE DRIVES HOME BUT can't make himself think about food yet. He has to *do* something.

Freddie has a good yard. He can at least get the hot coals out of his possession for a while and get himself some dinner and *then* think what to do next.

He drives to Freddie's place and manages to park on the street. Nobody appears to be inside—her truck is gone. No nosy neighbors poke their heads out. He walks calmly to her backyard and starts digging along the border with a piece of broken crockery. He listens carefully. Still no truck. And pretty soon the things are in the ground.

ELINOR HAD TRIED TO reason with Cal at the bond office to make his house arrest at her place in East Liberty. But he'd put a hand over hers, squeezed, and refused the offer.

Now she sat with him at his place—back in his neighborhood where the terrible thing had happened. He had let her make him dinner while the two of them cleaned up the place from when the police had tromped through looking for something to implicate him. They gathered up all the garbage and she put it out. It was lucky—this was a refuse pickup night.

Earlier she'd watched her son work. He was different, calmer.

Their dinner was just pasta with bottled sauce, not what she was used to, but she was glad to be with her son.

"Cal? Tell me about the jail."

"You saw some of it. The food wasn't good. The bed wasn't soft. The toilets smelled bad. It was . . . jail." He looked down at his wrist where he wore the watch again. "This watch got me some trouble. I refused to check it when they put me in, and then some guys wanted it."

"Oh. But you still have it."

He almost smiled.

"Did you make friends?"

"Not exactly." And though Cal hardly ever talked at length, he looked as if he wanted to say something, so she waited. "I watched people. It turned out I liked watching what they did, how they acted. There was some bizarre behavior. One guy hated me."

"Why?"

"I don't know. Most left me alone after the first day. One tried to be my friend."

"I can't believe you made it through all that."

"The funny thing is, I think I might miss it."

"Oh, please don't say that."

"No, not, not what you think. I don't want to go back as a prisoner. I get sick to think I might have to go back."

"I pray for it not to happen." She put her fork down carefully and sipped at water. "What do you miss—the people, the order, the schedule?" Had she sounded strident? She didn't want to.

"It's hard to explain."

"Try."

"One guy said he was going to kill me."

"Oh, my God."

"I kept wondering what he was going to do. And when. And then I went to court and they let me come home. I picture his face, how angry he is about not getting his chance to kill me . . ." He studied his ankle monitor. "I wish I could see his reaction. And, and then . . . say something to him."

"It isn't worth it," she said. "Dealing with hate."

"Sometimes it is."

THE FIRST THING TODD did when he got home from Freddie's place was go to his computer to look up the refuse pickup schedule for lower Oakland. Thursday, he hopes. Thursday would be good. He could arrange for a different car by then. When he saw what he saw, his spirits sank. *Tuesday.* Today was Tuesday. He wasn't ready. He didn't have an anonymous car. He would have to wait a whole week to plant the evidence. That's what he thought at first.

He was hungry, but he couldn't bring himself to cook or heat any of the things he'd just bought. His stomach roared. He ate a few crackers and then sat on his sofa, thinking.

He sat in front of his TV without turning it on. Ideas, ideas kept coming at him, bam, bam, bam.

He sifted through other times, other ways, he could plant the cell phone and wallet at Cal's place, but he couldn't come up with anything that felt as good as tonight. He was shaking. Again, uncharacteristically for him, he fetched a bottle of bourbon he kept in the cabinet in his dining room. He filled a bistro glass and drank it down in a matter of minutes. He didn't like feeling out of control—it was why he stayed away from booze, hardly ever succumbed—but sometimes, he tensed up so high, he needed it. Soon after he finished the glass of bourbon, he felt a little better.

His stomach roared again. He ate a few more crackers.

Seize the day. He couldn't wait a week. He'd get too nervous if he waited. His hallmark had always been swift action, immediate and sound decisions—he'd done the Cassie Price job with a few hours' preparation while Haigh thought about it and wanted to send in an old man to do it. As if Todd was likely to trust the fate of the campaign to some old loser named Frank Santini.

And now again he had to think fast and act fast. It would have to be tonight.

The first thing he had to do was put the pictures of Cassie someplace else, safe, to keep them in reserve for a second attack on Cal if necessary. Tonight he would go for broke: Plant the wallet and cell phone. The next trick was to get those things discovered. If tonight didn't work then he'd still have the photos to plant next week.

What a shame he'd bothered to bury the things at Freddie's place not two hours ago only to have to go back to fetch them. It was okay, he realized. Her car, he needed her car again. Or truck—even better.

He stared at the blank TV, popped it on, then back off.

All cylinders were cranking away. He had the phone situation figured out. He now owned not one but two prepaid phones.

So, he might as well do it—

It was only seventy-five degrees out, but he was sweating like a steelworker. He gathered several plastic Ziplocs from the kitchen and put them in his jacket pocket. He went out back and dug up his best dahlia.

Put on your thinking caps. His first-grade teacher always said that. He imagined it looked like the swimming cap his mother wore. If it was tight enough it could keep his brains in, working.

He walked to his car. This was it.

• • •

DOLAN, WHO WENT early to St. Regis while his boss went home for dinner, called Christie to report, "His mother just left. It's garbage night here, so she put out his garbage. That's the *only* activity. Nobody else is coming or going. Neighbor guy keeps sitting on his porch, looking curious. But that's it. Maybe you could use me better for something else. Or you could do something else if you need to." He stifled a yawn, but Christie heard it.

"It's okay. I'm about to come spell you. Hang on till I get there."

"Boss? What can the kid do? He's on house arrest."

"You're probably right. When I get there, you can go. I'll watch."

"You're spooky. When you get an idea, you're spooky. So, after you get here, I'll go get some caffeine in me and then come back."

"Up to you."

COLLEEN AND POTOCKI were in the plumbing van and just beginning to eat what he had bought for them when Todd Simon came out of his house with some kind of plant—they could see a flower and a stem and what looked like a bag of dirt—and he got into his car.

"Shoot. It looks innocent enough, but we ought to tag him."

"Good. I'm ready. I'll go." She handed him her takeout carton and quickly put on the glasses and hat.

"I don't like it."

"Sit tight. I've got it." She slipped to the front of the van, grabbed a clipboard, pretended to write something, then opened the door.

"Stay on the phone. If you need me, I'll start up the van," Potocki said.

"I'm fine."

She walked fast, clipboard in hand, to her own car and started it. She put her phone on speaker. She was keyed up—she could just see Simon's car ahead. She had to stay five cars behind at least, and the only thing she was thankful for was that the Saab was not totally ordinary. If she lost it, she might be able to pick it up again.

Her speakerphone told her Potocki was eating. "Save some for me," she quipped. He'd ordered them sweet potato ravioli with butter sage dressing and picked it up at Legume on the way to Todd Simon's place.

Funny. Most people on assignment ate junk.

For a while on Braddock Avenue she couldn't see Todd Simon's car, but she ran a light and muscled her way past a few other cars and caught sight of it again.

For a while, she didn't talk, but she felt she could sense Potocki listening. "Tell me where you are," he said after more time had passed.

"I truly doubt if this is anything. Don't worry. We're heading up Forbes and I think . . . slowing for that Dallas Avenue turnoff for Beacon."

"I talked to Dolan. He says nothing is happening at the Hathaway house."

"Yes. No surprise." That was surveillance 90 percent of the time: Nothing. "Todd Simon is, yes, turning to Beacon."

Ordinarily they would have put more men on, but Boss had his ways. And he was soft on Connolly. So far as she was concerned, it was a relief to hear Christie was more or less Democratic. "We're . . . yes, we're turning onto Bartlett. I have to stay way behind now. I think I saw him pull into this one driveway. It's too early to tell."

"Give me the address."

"I can only give you where I am now. He's about six houses farther up the street." She gave him a house number. "I'm hanging back for a bit. He might notice the car."

After a few minutes she drove up the street. Yes, the Saab was in the driveway of a house there. There was a black Sebring in the driveway, too. She couldn't see much past the battered white truck parked on the street, and she definitely could not see the man. "Think I maybe found the black car," she said.

TODD FIGURED FREDDIE was home since both her car and truck were parked at her place and inside a few lights were on. It wasn't certain. They could be out in Old Reliable's car, whatever it was. Todd knew one thing. He wanted the truck.

He walked to the backyard where he had buried the cell phone and wallet barely two hours before. He needed to get this next just right. He was breathing heavily. If she came outside in the few seconds in which he put the plastic bag with the wallet and phone into his coat pocket, if she saw, it would be impossible to explain himself, and so he shielded his work with his body, pulled on a pair of latex gloves, and removed the small trowel from the larger Ziploc that held it alongside the dahlia tuber. Sprouting from the tuber were three unready blooms and one slightly wilting elder bloom. If he'd known how brief the second burial of wallet and cell phone was going to be, he would have risked putting those things in his own yard, but it was too late to second-guess himself now.

He gasped to see the wallet and cell phone again through the writing on the plastic bag. He quickly fumbled the bag into his right jacket pocket. Then he summoned a jolly mood and began planting the dahlia.

Sure enough, just as he had hoped, the back door opened and Freddie stood there. This was good, though she looked none too pleased to see him. "You! I thought I heard someone. What is this?"

"A peace offering. I brought you a flower. My best one out of my garden. It's symbolic."

"Look. I told you I had plans tonight."

"I know. I'm an idiot. But—"

A man loomed in the doorway. Old Reliable was not at all old. He was a strapping fellow of the nonparanoid variety. "Anything I'm needed for?" he asked cheerfully.

"No, no, it's okay," Freddie said. "I'll be right in." There was a TV playing in the background. She gestured toward it. "My gardener works all hours. Just kidding. I'll explain when I get in."

"O-kay," said Old Reliable, and he left the doorway.

Todd said, "Speaking of working all hours . . . suppose your sweet gardener had to borrow your truck—not for a big tree, but there's a bureau I bought from some old folks who will sell it from under me if I don't get it. A couple of hours at most."

"I need my truck."

"You'll have it in the morning. That's a promise."

"Oh, Christ." She went into the house for a moment and came back to open the door and throw a key at him. "Put the key through the mail slot when you get back."

"I get it. I'll buy you dinner."

"The truck's out front. There are bungee cords in the back."

So. It was done. Phase one.

He got into the truck, adjusted the seat and mirror, and tucked the bag under the driver's seat. Then he pulled away only to turn the corner and park again. He went into Silky's for some food and drink. And to put in time until there was enough deep middle-of-the-night darkness to drop off some garbage at Cal's place.

"THIS IS WEIRD," Colleen was saying on the phone to Potocki. "He gets into the truck, messes around, then goes half a block, parks, goes to Silky's bar. I don't know who owns the truck, but he has a key to it. And, more importantly, whoever does also has a black car. I took the numbers."

"Let me have them. You keep him in sight."

She recited the plate numbers to him. "I can't go into Silky's. He knows me. The only one of us he hasn't seen is you. I can keep an eye on the truck, sort of."

"Do that. Be back to you in a minute."

What sense could she make of this? Was this the erratic behavior Christie was hoping for?

There was no place to park, so she had to keep circling. It was maddening. Finally she parked in the Giant Eagle lot and walked to the street. She had to hope the dusk helped to muffle her presence. She went as far up the street as she could while still keeping the truck in sight.

After what felt like a long time, her phone buzzed. "Yeah."

"Both the truck and the car belong to Fredericka Lorris. No priors. Anything on your end?"

"Nothing, nothing. I'm not up close."

"Lose him if you have to. Stay hidden."

"I'm pretending to shop." She dawdled for a time at the Rite Aid. She was forced to buy ice cream at the creamery and to eat it slowly, not that she ever minded dessert before dinner. She also killed a lot of time at the bank ATM and in the Giant Eagle lot before anything happened.

At a few minutes after ten, Todd Simon came out of the bar. She hurried to her car. Soon enough they were headed back the way they'd come, back to Simon's house.

Nothing. All this and nothing.

CAL STUDIES THE BAND on his leg. It's about an inch wide, metal covered in plastic, and it has a pager device on it. He's allowed to take a shower—that is interesting. For a bath—he never takes baths, so it's okay—he's supposed to hang his leg out of the tub. How amazing technology is, that this little thing knows how to connect to the box attached to his telephone, that this combination of devices knows how to call a guy who sits at a desk in a center and will raise hell if Cal leaves his house. He can't even go an inch past his front door, the man who set it up told him. Not an inch. The machine knows.

He starts the shower water running and strips his clothes off. He hasn't taken a long shower since he left home on August 13. He goes to the kitchen for a plastic grocery bag and nervously tries to tie it onto his leg. Then he worries that the plastic will somehow make it worse, trap water and set off the alarm—as if the band needs to breathe—and so he removes it. In the end the shower is briefer than he wants, and during most of it, he has stuck one leg out anyway.

Still, by the time the shower is turned off, he feels cleaner than he has for weeks.

His mother helped him change his sheets. Everything is fresh.

He is allowed to watch television. It seems strange—he clicks through the available channels, but can't get interested in anything— sitting around watching TV reminds him too much of jail. He's going to have to do something *inside* his house to keep from going nuts. Paint his own walls—they're not bad, but okay, he can do that. Learn to cook. Yes, he can get interested in that. Get a chess set and teach himself to play. What else?

He climbs into bed, fully expecting to lie there, eyes wide open, as he tries to figure out how his life ended up this way—what it all means, why anyone would believe he would have hurt that poor young woman. As he thinks about her, he realizes he never knew her well enough to know if she was simply friendly with everyone or if she liked him. She might have been faking it, he thinks now. She always followed some friendly chatter with an abrupt dismissal. He sees her more and more clearly. She wanted a job done well, not to mention quickly and cheaply, so she needed to keep the worker on her side. He doesn't hate her for it.

He's surprised to feel himself giving in to a deep, long sleep. Sleep gives him no choice; it tugs him downward. His leg could send out eight alarms right now and he wouldn't care.

IT'S JUST MIDNIGHT. Christie gingerly opens each of the two bags in Cal's yard to find, to his great relief, clean garbage—dried coffee grounds, food packaging, torn mail envelopes. Nothing much in bag one. In bag two, some clothing being thrown out. That's more suspicious. He takes the whole bag, walks across the street and into the church by the utility door he and Dolan are using. Dolan is perched on the second floor in an office area, looking out the window.

"You find something?"

"Nah. Clothes we should keep, in case we need them in future to test for DNA. Still, throwing clothes away is a bit strange."

"People do it, though."

"Okay. You ought to go home, get some rest."

"You staying a little longer?"

Christie shifted uncomfortably. "I might be a bit longer. If I can stay awake."

"Marina won't like it."

"She's good. Really good. She likes teaching, and she pretty much has a good role snagged in a production they're doing. She's happy."

"Excellent. I found a radio. Sit here. We can listen to music."

Christie laughed and settled as well as he could on an institutional metal chair. His phone rang. It was Colleen reporting.

He hung up. "Does she have anything?" Dolan asked.

"The black car. A black car. I'm thinking back. The man leaves his car, uses a black car, night of August 13. Tonight, leaves his car, uses a truck. Why? He doesn't want to be identified by vehicle. Something is going to happen."

"I'm with you."

Christie leaned forward, to the window. The radio behind him was playing jazz—something familiar, something Marina had in her collection. "What is this?" he asked.

"Miles. It's Miles."

He stared out at the black night. He was going to need an expert entomologist if Todd Simon's DNA matched the mosquito's meal.

Dolan looked at him. "Want to talk?"

"Just junk rolling around in my head right now. I want to get this guy. I want him."

"I get that."

The night wears on. He imagines a trial in which he presents evidence. He holds up a black dot. "This is my witness," he says. The black dot is a mosquito, plus the now dried blood that constituted its last dinner. Everybody laughs at him.

"How do we know the mosquito didn't just happen to fly in?" he's asked by the defense.

"From Regent Square? That's asking a lot of the little thing," he quips.

"But the suspect followed her home in the early evening. Can you prove he was not bitten in his car and that then the mosquito followed the young woman into her house and died?"

"It was smashed. Somebody hit it."

"Isn't it possible that she hit it? She saw it before it got to her."

"Then she would have had a blood spot."

"How's it going?" Dolan asks.

"Take a nap. Then I will."

AGAIN WEARING A pair of gloves, Simon removes the two photos that are tucked in the secondary bill compartment of the wallet.

He almost cries out. It's as if the photos have given off something electric. For a moment he feels she can see him, standing in his own living room, looking at her. In the one—it's Cassie alone, a glamour pose—she smiles, head over one shoulder, leaning forward. To think she carried this photo of herself with her. Liked to look at herself all right. The other—four girls hugging each other, all gorgeous, laughing—suggests she liked her sisters enough to carry them with her, too, every day. Or maybe, he thinks, with a welcome return of cynicism, she particularly liked the way she looked in that photo. He carries the photos gingerly to his bedroom and puts them down on the floor while he extracts from his closet a shoe box, way in the back, under other shoe boxes. In it is an old pair of dress shoes that have always hurt his feet. He peels off the innersole and fits the photos between the two soles. Breathing heavily, he puts the shoes back, the lid on, the box behind and under the other boxes.

He stands, a little dizzy, then collapses at the edge of his bed. Putting the photos away like that, he feels as if he buried her—again, the fourth time. He gets rid of her, but she has a way of springing back. She *was* . . . willful. And sure of herself. And uppity. How shallow life is, that because nature handed her physical beauty, she should have such power. Connolly fell for it. He, Todd, would have bedded her in a second, but she saw him as nothing more than a middle-aged party grunt. Did she and Mickey talk about him that way as they lay in bed?

He pulls himself to his feet. Work to do. He promised Haigh he would make this go away.

Still wearing gloves, he takes a supermarket bag to the basement, where he fills it with cleaning rags. He rehearses in his mind: Open the Ziploc, which now holds the phone and wallet, dump those things in among the rags. Then somehow wait until 4:00, 4:30 A.M. Phase two: Drop the bag at Cal's place. Phase three: Get to a pay phone and make a neighbor's complaint. Phase four: Wait until 5:30 when garbage pickup begins and use his throwaway phones to call Cassie's phone. The phone number is committed to memory, but he recites it like a mantra hundreds of times as he works. Through the bag he presses the ON button. A small melody and then . . . one bar, no, two. God bless Verizon. It's possible the battery will give out. It's possible nobody will hear it. But it's phase four of tonight's plan.

And if tonight doesn't work, he has the two photos for next week.

He climbs up from the basement and then up to his second floor, where he lies on his bed, fully clothed and shod. Who else? Nobody else could plan as he plans, fix it as he's fixing it. Haigh owes him, all right. What they always say, when somebody does the impossible, is "a million bucks and a trip to Hawaii," which is funny because he forgets to spend money—those dress shoes must be twenty years old—and he never takes vacations. For him a vacation from the panic and grind is a night with the likes of Rita or Freddie or Carola. Usually, the next morning he's ready to work again.

TWELVE

WEDNESDAY, AUGUST 26

EVERYBODY FELL asleep. Lights were out everywhere, the moon was a slender crescent, people were sleeping . . . Colleen was in the back of the van with Potocki. His arms went around her and they both nodded off.

Christie was lying on the floor of the church, having his turn at a nap. Dolan was at the window, his head hanging to the side in spite of the caffeine and his usual toughness.

Colleen was the first to come awake. "Oh, my God. The truck is gone. Let's go."

Potocki instantly began climbing to the driver's seat. "Where? When?"

"I think he just turned the corner. A sound woke me up. Get me to my car."

"There's no time. We're taking the van."

"It blows our cover."

"I know, I know. I'll stay way, way behind."

And he did.

They saw the truck go to the parkway, which was good news since at any hour of the night there would be other cars to help mask them. "It's up to us," she said, though she was sure Potocki was thinking the same thing. Boss told her he and Dolan were going home at midnight. They'd confiscated some garbage and felt they needed to conserve energy for watching tomorrow and tomorrow night.

Colleen couldn't help thinking that if Potocki hadn't been holding her, she might have stayed awake. And if he hadn't wanted to protect her, he might have taken her to her own car, which could have gotten closer to the truck. They'd screwed up. Oh, man, they needed to make this right. They needed to catch Todd red-handed at whatever he was up to. The white truck that belonged to Fredericka Lorris pulled off at the Oakland exit, and about twelve seconds later, they did, too.

They saw Simon, blocks ahead, turn onto Parkview. Potocki said, "It could be Cassie's place he's headed for. It could be Cal's place."

When they got to Parkview the white truck was no longer in sight. They rattled along, and when they passed an almost invisible alley, Colleen said, "He took that!" Potocki stopped, backed up, and navigated the narrow alley that led to the alley that ran behind Cassie's place and Iris Mender's place and that was totally bordered on the other side by Sestili's Nursery. The alley had a street name: Edgehill Street.

Colleen was right. Way up ahead on Child Street, the truck turned to the right, exiting that street. They could no longer see it. Simon had already passed both Cassie's place and Cal's place.

Potocki drove fast but slowed at Cal's place, where there were no lights on. The garbage was out—two bags. "Let me out," Colleen said. "Then follow him."

Earlier tonight, Boss had said he confiscated one of two bags of garbage. Did he? Because now there were two. She was opening the smaller of them when two figures ran out of the church toward her.

"Did you see him drop anything?" she asked.

They shook their heads. "We missed him. Was it Simon?"

"Yes. Using the truck."

She opened the bag, moving things around by manipulating the bag from the outside. "Rags," she reported. "And . . . oh, my God, Boss, oh my God. Phone. And . . . wallet."

She'd never seen Christie explode quite like this. He kicked at a tree. He cursed vehemently. "I should have pulled out all the stops. Used others. And—" He fell to cursing again.

"We didn't use a camera," Dolan explained. "Still. We have him, Boss. We have him."

Colleen called Potocki to find out if he'd found and stopped Simon, but she guessed the answer. He said, "Never caught him. I'm near the entrance to the parkway east. In case he goes for home. But I don't know where he is."

"He dropped the wallet and cell, John. Nobody actually saw him do it. But—just a sec. Something is happening."

Christie was on his phone. "What?" he exclaimed. And then, "What did they say, exactly?" And then he swore again.

She and Dolan looked at each other, too beat to guess.

Christie came to them. "Well, he's determined, all right. See, 911 just got a call from a neighbor, a concerned neighbor, supposedly, who wants to be anonymous. This neighbor says he saw Cal Hathaway open his door and fling out garbage. This neighbor thinks there's something funny going on with the garbage. Get this. The call came from a pay phone, but the funny thing is—this is choice, this is great." He laughed harshly. "Thing is there's an earlier call to Headquarters about a man messing with the garbage. From a neighbor. The first call was for real. The man messing was me."

"There's enough circumstantial evidence to hang him, right, Boss?"

"I have to talk to Hathaway."

Dolan and Colleen followed a bit behind Christie as he went to the door. He rang the bell and knocked several times before the door was opened by a very sleepy-looking Cal, who said, "I can't get too close to the door. This thing is set to ring the police station."

"I know," said Christie. "I know how it works. I need to ask you if you threw garbage out to the curb."

287

"No, my mother took it out for me."

"How about a couple of minutes ago?"

"No. A couple of minutes ago I was asleep."

"Okay, do you recognize this bag?"

"It's a grocery bag."

"Do you recognize what's in it?" Christie opened the bags.

"Looks like rags. Are they mine?"

"I don't know. How about the phone and wallet?"

"No," he said. And then he must have realized what was being asked of him. "Oh, no . . ."

"These things are not yours."

He shook his head. "How . . . how did they get there?"

"We're working on that. I'll send somebody in to talk to you."

The detectives walked to the curb. "Let's go find Simon," Dolan urged. "Make him give us some answers."

"We take him in and he'll get a good lawyer. A great lawyer. I don't want him getting away. I want . . . details. Dolan, you go into Cal's house and search the house and grounds to be sure, absolutely sure, he didn't throw the garbage."

Colleen's phone rang again, but it was only Potocki reporting again that he still had not found Simon.

"Just a minute." She handed her phone over to Christie. He listened and said, "Right. Not your fault. Go back to the house. Park the van as it was. I'll go to the place where the truck belongs. Let's get the whole pattern down." He grimaced. Colleen studied his fury. Yes, he must have fallen asleep, too.

By the time Colleen and her boss got to Fredericka Lorris's house the truck was back in place and the Saab was gone. Damn, damn, Christie said. Colleen called Potocki to tell him. He said the man and his Saab had not yet returned to Regent Square. It was five thirty.

Christie and Colleen sat in his car outside Fredericka's place, trying to decide whether to drive over to Regent Square or talk to Lorris first, when a sound from the back seat surprised them. "That's a phone," she said. "It's coming from—"

From the bag of rags, Cassie's cell phone gave off two rings, then nothing. Colleen reached for the back and removed the phone carefully, using the cloths to hold it. Christie wrote down the number of the caller. He dialed Headquarters to find somebody to trace the number, but the offices were virtually empty. "Maybe the same pay phone that made a 911 call," he explained to the desk sergeant. "See if you can find out for me. And trace it."

Not five minutes later, Cassie's phone rang again. This time it was a different caller number.

The desk sergeant called back saying no, it wasn't the same as the pay phone, which was located in Oakland.

The phone rang again, the first number.

"I get what he's doing," Colleen said.

"Yeah. He wants it to be found. Interesting fellow," he said.

Christie called Dolan to find out that Cal's place had yielded no evidence of packing or tampering with garbage. Since things were looking tame there, he told Dolan about the ringing phone and the location of the pay phone. "He isn't likely to be hanging at the pay phone, but drive by and watch for a while, just in case."

Dolan was saying something or other. Colleen could almost hear it. Christie answered him, "You're right, you're right. If there's nothing doing at the pay phone, you might as well get over here, join us." When he hung up he told Colleen, "Dolan is betting these new numbers calling and hanging up are prepaid cells and they won't be traceable. Still, we will run them."

Cassie's cell rang again. Christie grabbed through the plastic to answer it this time, but it had stopped by the time he got it.

"What were you going to say?"

"Something like"—he lowered his voice—" 'This phone ain't in service. Sorry!' But I'm a poor actor, so it's just as well I didn't have to play a happy garbage collector."

Colleen smiled. "I would have liked to see that performance."

"My wife auditioned for a play called *Dead Man's Cell Phone.* Something about the guy dies and his phone keeps ringing."

"Spooky."

"Come with me. We're going to wake up Fredericka."

"No need." Colleen pointed.

A woman in overalls and a T-shirt came out for the newspaper and went back in.

She and Christie hurried to the door. "Ms. Lorris. Police. May we come in and speak to you?"

"What is this about?"

"This is a homicide investigation." They showed their ID.

"Yes. Of course." She let them in. She still held the paper, folded. "Please. What can I do?"

"You can tell us about Todd Simon. You know him?"

"Yes. He's . . . he's a friend."

"A friend. He used your truck last night."

"To cart a bureau."

"Is that what he said?"

"Yes. He didn't?"

"He didn't. No bureau."

"Would you . . . like some coffee?"

"No, thank you," Christie said, which irritated Colleen. She really wanted a cup. Surely the smell emanating from Lorris's kitchen was killing him, too, but he was a stickler for not blurring lines. "Just a few questions. And would you jot down name, address, phones for our records. Do you work somewhere?"

"I'm an independent contractor. I have a card." She got up and went to her handbag sitting on a handsome side table. "I do renovations. Houses."

Colleen thought she looked okay, this woman, like a sensible hard worker. Fredericka seemed truly puzzled as she handed over a business card to Christie, who tilted it and read it.

"Ah. I see. What sorts of things do you do?"

"Everything."

"Can you rip out old plaster?"

"Oh, yes."

"That's a lousy job. Sure you're up for it?"

"I did it in a Highland Park house not long ago."

"Messy job, too. Tell me, do you ever wear those painter suits? What do they call them—coveralls?"

"My God . . . Is this about me? Are you asking about me?"

"I'm asking if you lent your car—the black Chrysler—to your friend, Todd."

"The car? No. Yes. One Saturday he wanted to try it on a trip. It was Saturday, yes, a week and a half ago."

"Did you ever lend him one of your coveralls?"

"No. Please. Tell me what this is about?"

"Yes. I'm getting to that. Just think back. Two nights before that. The night of August 13. It was a Thursday. Did you lend him your car?"

"I . . . remember that night. There was a Steelers game. I didn't get to see much of it because we were in Big Jim's and the TV was behind me. We had a sort of date. We took my car. He wanted me to drive. I did."

"What time was this?"

"Eight o'clock. Nine o'clock."

"He was with you that night?"

"Yes."

"All night?"

"Yes."

"Could he have taken your car out at, say, three in the morning?"

"It's funny you ask that. I thought it. I mean, I was asleep, but the next time I used my car, I thought he must have driven it, but I really don't know why I thought that."

"Try to think why."

"I couldn't identify it. I figured it was the seat position or something. Please tell me. I'm getting scared. I spent time with him. Two days. That was when . . . a woman he knew was killed. I can figure that much. Is that what you're asking about?"

"Yes. He's a suspect."

She clapped a hand over her mouth. "This is . . . this is horrible."

At that point, there was a knock at the door, and Colleen, seeing it was Dolan, went to let him in. Dolan introduced himself quickly. "Do I smell coffee?"

"Would you like some?"

"I need some."

"I do, too, actually," Colleen hurried to say.

Christie made a slight shake of his head, and even as Lorris went to pour the coffee, he kept questioning her. "So, to be clear, now, he *could* have gone out in the middle of the night without you knowing it?"

"Could have. Yes. It occurred to me maybe he went out for a new pack of cigarettes. He was up smoking when I woke. But I don't know. He could have had the new pack with him."

"And your coveralls? Were they missing?"

"I have several pairs. The one . . . was folded differently. I keep them in the garage." She put down two mugs on the table. "It might be kind of strong," she said.

"All the better," Dolan saluted her. But he was already wide-eyed with what he was hearing.

"The coveralls. Where are they?" Christie asked.

"I used them and then I tossed them. I'm sorry."

"We're going to need to have a team look at your car. And the truck. And the garage," Christie persisted.

"Of course." She sank down into the sofa. "I had a lot of work scheduled today."

"We can let you go to work. Do you have someone who can get you there?"

"Yes, I do. I have someone I can call. I'm stunned. I don't think Todd could do what you're saying. But you've put the idea in my head."

"I have a few more questions. He carried some sort of plant over here last night. Can you tell us about that?"

"Yes, well, I found him digging in my backyard. He said he'd brought something for me. A peace offering."

"Peace?"

"I think he just wanted my truck."

"Before we leave, can you show us what he brought?"

"Yes."

"Now if you had to appear in court, you would answer that you can't provide an absolute alibi for the night in question?"

"I was with him. We went to dinner. We went to bed. He could have gone out."

"And . . . he could have borrowed your car and a set of coveralls?"

"Yes."

"Right. Could we see the kind of coveralls you use?"

They went out the back door to her garage, where they saw that she had obviously ordered a boxful of the deluxe version of coveralls, with boots and a hood. Dolan, still sipping his coffee, murmured, "Amen," inclining his head toward a shelf that held a large box of ordinary latex gloves.

"Those gloves?" Christie pointed.

"Ancient. I've had that box for about five years. Maybe more. I started using different ones when I need light gloves. I keep the newer ones in the truck."

"We'll need to take a sample of these."

"Be my guest."

"I'd like to ask you to avoid him," he said. She nodded. "Would it surprise you to hear that he gave another alibi completely, another friend, a person who lives out of town?"

Fredericka drew herself up with dignity. "In personal terms, I knew he was completely unreliable. I made a mistake in thinking I could keep a light relationship going. It was unsatisfying. When he called me on that night . . . August 13 . . . I thought I'd give it a try with him. I think now I don't know who he was. If he did this thing, if he did, I hope you make him pay."

"What is it you liked about him?"

"He was entertaining. Upbeat."

"I see. We won't keep you much longer. Show us the plant he brought—which one it is. We'll have the lab look at it when they scrape your truck and car."

They walked around to her backyard. Christie and his detectives looked at the struggling dahlia she pointed to. He thanked her for being cooperative and forthright.

On the way back to the car, Colleen whispered, "You didn't ask about the mosquito—though I couldn't figure out how you could do that."

Christie slapped at his face as if to wake himself. "I'm tired. I'm too tired." He went back to the house, but there was no need to ring the bell. The woman was standing at the door, watching.

"We were wondering if you noticed, if you happened to notice, if your friend had a mosquito bite."

"Yes. Well, yes, he had one. It was nasty, too. He joked that it looked like a hickey. It was on his neck."

"And he got this bite when?" Christie asked.

"In the night, I guess." She stopped, thinking about what she had said. "I know he was bothered by it in the morning."

"This might seem very strange to you, but it is crucial that you don't talk about this visit or anything that we talked about, even a small detail like the mosquito bite, to anyone. It could seriously interfere with the investigation."

"I can hold my tongue."

"I thought so."

On the way to the car, he said to Colleen, "Thank you for that."

"When I talked to him, those two times, I thought he had a nervous tic, hand to his collar. He was scratching the bite. I had that all along and I didn't know."

At a bit before seven they sat in Christie's car regrouping. Christie called for the lab car to get the samples he needed. Dolan pressed all advantages with the phone companies.

The phone calls to Cassie's phone appeared to have stopped. Colleen studied the CALLS RECEIVED menu as well as she could through plastic. "There were two more," she said. "They stopped about fifteen minutes ago."

Five minutes after seven, Potocki called to say the Saab and its driver were now home.

"Let's go get him."

• • •

CONNOLLY AND HIS wife decided to have coffee in the yard at early breakfast. They had been talking but had reached an impasse. She had insisted she didn't want to give up her job, even for a term to go with him to Ireland. What if her chair didn't want to take her back? Finally Connolly suggested he take the children for a time. She had answered calmly that she refused to be away from her boys. They couldn't agree on anything much, and yet, as they tried to negotiate a plan, they spent more time together than they had in years.

"I'll go alone," he said finally. "It's not what I want, but I'll do it. Will you visit?"

"Long weekends in Ireland. What a wild idea."

"There are ways. If you got somebody to cover a class, you could start out on a Wednesday and be back Sunday night. I know it's a lot to ask, but . . . no, I can't live without the rest of you, so if you say no, then, then I probably won't go."

"How ugly is this going to be?"

"Very ugly. I can't imagine how Christie has managed to keep the . . . the thing with Cassie . . . quiet so far. It won't always be that way. And if Todd did what I think he did, there is no end to it. I could never come back to politics. Or . . . anything."

"Ted Kennedy did."

"I'm not Ted Kennedy."

"Meaning?"

"He had a hundred twenty percent vitality. A lust for life."

"You're a thinker. A brooder. You're a different personality, but it doesn't have to keep you from doing something good."

Cassie Price had told him he was like a saint, of all things, a saint. A thinking, brooding saint, afflicted by sexual hunger.

"I can't even think how to bounce back. I'm so . . . I'm undone. Defeated."

"It's going to take a lot of time. In Ireland or wherever you are, one day you'll wake up and you'll know how to be." She looked away, down at her coffee cup. He studied familiar things about her, the way her hair waved, the way she held the cup with two hands, the way she sat with her knees together, feet apart. He thought, She wants to come with me and doesn't know how. She loves me and doesn't know why. His eyes filled with tears. He'd let everyone down—his wife and sons, his father and brother, his party, the Price family. How did a man come back from all that?

AT WELL BEFORE EIGHT in the morning, Christie knocks on Todd Simon's door. He has Dolan behind him and the others backing him up at a small distance. It takes a while to rouse him.

Then Simon stands there rubbing his eyes and says, "Sorry. I'm half asleep. You'll see this is a mistake. But I'll come with you, of course." He smiles slightly, enough to press his dimples into service.

Neighbors poke their heads out of their front doors.

"It's okay," Simon tells them. "I promise."

By nine in the morning, they are sitting in one of the interview rooms at Headquarters and they have already asked Todd Simon multiple times about the truck, the black car, the trip in the middle of the night. He shakes his head and says with a kind of whimsy, "I'd love to talk, but I've been around attorneys all my life and I know I'm simply not supposed to. I'm sorry, but I'll wait until my attorney is here."

"Meanwhile, we need a swab. DNA."

"Not just fingerprints these days!" he says in pretend surprise.

As soon as Christie has the swab, he couriers it to the lab, and before it gets there, he is on the phone with Ann Cello, Colleen's contact over there, a jewel, a glorious jewel of a woman. He's leaned on Baitz as much as he can, and now he leans on Cello. "This is absolute priority. Think of it as . . . oh, I dunno, a whole institution coming down if we don't have our answer. Think of it as practically presidential. Please. Three days."

"Sir, I'm not . . . Everybody will tell me it can't be done."

"I've heard it can."

"I might get fired."

"I will turn somersaults for you."

"Three days. Okay. Okay, I will."

Christie meets his drooping detectives in his office. "Nothing we can do but wait. Simon sees his attorney at three this afternoon—some sort of hotshot from Harrisburg is coming in—I knew it, too, didn't I say? So let's all go home, sleep a little, and meet back here at five or even six. I know we're not much good now, none of us. We've been up all night—"

"Except when we fell asleep," Dolan mutters.

"Seriously. We need time to think."

"Six o'clock," Dolan begs. "I'm not as young as I used to be. As opposed to you."

Christie lets himself laugh. "Six o'clock, then. If we work it right, we get six hours of sleep. Good. Go home."

They get up to go to their cars, and Christie walks out with them.

Colleen walks alongside him. "Promised myself I'd talk to you," she says.

"Talk."

She feels a little like a criminal, confessing. "Potocki and I *are* an item, as you once observed. So I'm calling it what it is. We like working together, but we know we can't anymore. After this is over, I mean. It's hard to give up being partners, but the truth is, it does get in the way."

"What are you saying?"

"That we love our jobs. But he worries about me and I worry about him worrying."

"That part won't go away, but it's easier when you're not involved. I . . . like Potocki."

"He's a good guy."

"Yes." He can feel his own eyes soften. She looks as if she might cry. "Let me think how to scramble the pairings. I need some time to figure it out."

• • •

JUST LIKE THAT. IT'S done. Just like that. "I told him,"
Colleen announces.

"I'm sure it stung him some."

"He was fine. He's . . . Boss. He was fine."

"We need to get some sleep. Do you need to be alone?"

"No. You can come to my place if you want."

Potocki hesitates, surprised. "Okay. Yeah, let's."

TODD PUTS ON HIS thinking cap: If he names Haigh or
Benton, they will deny it. If he takes the fall, they will get him out.
They'll find a technicality. He keeps repeating this wisdom over and
over to himself as they put him in the scanning chair, fingerprint
him, do a preliminary arraignment by video.

"No bail," the magistrate says. He peers at the screen. This surprises him. He has some money; Haigh has lots of money. Earlier, as
he sat in Headquarters putting up with the detectives, he was working out what he thought would happen. He'd thought bail would be
set high, say a million, but he did the math and figured out how to
meet it—with Haigh's help. This is weird, all right—even Cal Hathaway got bail.

He doesn't yell or protest. He can work within the system. There
are bond hearings. He can get this no-bail ruling reversed.

Temporary, he says to himself. I will get out.

But what the hell do the police have on him? The phone and
wallet—have they been found at Cal's place? He can't ask; the police
are giving up almost no information. A good lawyer can get them
on that, right—false arrest, intimidation, blah, blah, blah. He drums
into his brain that he must insist he is innocent and otherwise shut
up, say *nothing* that could incriminate him. The problem with silence is it bores him.

They will try to provoke him.

His attorney has got to get information.

He squeezes his head. Thinking cap. The photos in his house were the *only* incriminating evidence, and when he saw the cars outside, when he heard the knock at the door, they went down the garbage disposal. He gave them a good long grinding. They're gone. Forever.

If it's something about the truck and what he was doing in the middle of the night, he must say he couldn't sleep, was out driving, hated the guy Cal for what he did to Cassie, drove by and saw Cal throwing out garbage. And if they get him on the phone call to the police, okay, he pretended to be a neighbor so Cal's garbage would be investigated.

And if they try to trace the phone calls made to Cassie's phone, they won't find anything but a prepaid number calling from the road. The phones that made the calls are gone. They're in the bushes along the parkway. Not a print on them.

Didn't he think of everything?

He sits in his cell for only a brief time, getting used to it. He is not going to be here long, but he examines the metal beds, the futon mattresses covered in turquoise plastic, the small bolted stool. Apparently, he has a cellmate, someone in the lower bunk who doesn't make his bed. After a full inspection of the place, he plunks his bedding on top of the upper bunk and goes down to the common area, where there are sounds of activity; he's a social creature, and this is where the people are, such as they are. So this is the Allegheny County Jail—basketball, chess, TV. Okay, not that he's surprised, exactly, but it's like a vacation in an ugly campground, hard earth, bad food. If you can exhaust yourself in play, you'll sleep anyway.

Haigh will send him someone good.

Is Connolly, probably having a nice lunch somewhere today, even the slightest bit grateful?

Todd takes a chair in front of the TV and watches a nature program with twenty or so other men. He's always liked nature—flowers that eat animals and such. He can tell that he is being watched, but he knows how to work a place like this. Already they're giving him space, as if he's somebody.

•   •   •

SIMON'S DEFENSE attorney, Morty Silber, is a long, wily, skinny man who pretends to slouch backward in his chair but who is reptilian, ready to strike. He arrives at Headquarters a bit before three, having demanded to see Christie, who has to rouse himself from the sofa in his office.

"I got into town early and went to the jail, where I stopped by long enough to introduce myself to my client. I intend to go back as soon as I've made a few things clear. I have advised him not to speak. He's quite worried about unfairness in these proceedings. He's wondered aloud to me if he is being framed—that you've got some wrong idea about him and you can't get it out of your head."

Christie shakes his head. For a moment that charge sounds almost true.

"He went for a drink with her. He liked her. A lot. And he's furious with despair about the fact that that kid, that worker, or some other jerk, brutally murdered her. Somehow because of the drink, you're after my client."

"The drink and the fact that he denied it and . . . other evidence, plenty," Christie says, baiting the guy.

Will Simon flinch when he hears it?

"And we're still gathering details," Christie adds.

Morty Silber smiles tightly at the sweet stupidity of the police, but he can't hold his composure. He slaps the table. "Just remember, there's such a thing as the discovery phase, and if you hold anything back, we're going to make a fuss you'll never recover from."

"Certainly. In time. In time you will have it all, counselor, and a good deal of it at the hearing." Christie, knowing that Silber would see the probable cause affidavit, wrote it in the most general terms. "Proximity to deceased on the day of the homicide, suspicious movement of vehicles, political motive, trip to original suspect's house in the middle of the night."

Silber makes a showy angry exit. "There may have to be reports filed on the handling of this case."

"I'm not worried."

Christie tries again for a nap on his sofa.

And succeeds, a little.

At six o'clock, he pulls his people together in his office. "Are we rested?"

"Yes, Boss," the whole group says. He doubts that it's true, though they look a bit more brushed up than he does.

"I've got a search warrant for Simon's house. We're on the proof phase now. I need for you to be supercareful not to contaminate anything. You all can start on the house; I plan to catch up with you in a bit. I want a complete search. The way I wrote the warrant was for trace evidence. That means you have a right to *everything*— the space under the cellophane in the cereal boxes, locked drawers, everything."

"What are we looking for, though?" Hurwitz asks.

"There was some dirt, soil, in the bag with the rags and the phone. More of that soil? Hairs, fibers? Written material. Her family and her officemates listed among the possessions in her wallet some photographs. They're not in the wallet now. And money, of course, was missing. Where are those things—right, I know, spent, destroyed, probably, but we have to look."

"Boss. It doesn't sound like you slept today."

"I did some, yes, a little. Just be totally thorough. You've pretty much got the whole evening ahead of you on this job. I'm sending the lab car—two techs—with you. Use them. It's going to be painstaking. To that end, I ordered a couple of pizzas up. I think they might be here."

"Yay, Boss," Dolan chanted. "I could have sworn I smelled pizza." So they went out to the hallway and there it was, yeasty dough and cheese to lift their spirits.

"I'LL GET YOU OUT," Morty said. "That's a promise. But here's the deal. You have to tell me everything. From before A to after Z. Everything. I'm good, but if I'm going to work with the facts, I need the facts. Leave out nothing. You understand. I need to know where and how you stood, everything you touched, everything."

"How do I know to trust you?"

"You have to. No choice."

"But what do they have? You haven't told me what they found out."

"Look. I've worked my sources. All they're coughing up at this point is the use of vehicles, the alibi, some tape that shows you leaving the parking garage behind the girl. It doesn't sound like much. They're biting down hard, determined. Tell me everything. Every breath you took."

Simon does this. As he talks, he is more and more amazed by his own planning, more and more interested in telling it.

It takes a long time. "I'm missing dinner," he tells Silber at one point.

Silber snorts, goes to the hall, summons an escort officer, and makes a request. He comes back saying, "They'll hold a tray for you."

And so Todd keeps talking. Then after what seems like hours, he finally goes to his lousy jailhouse dinner of sausages. The TV is on as usual, tuned to the local news.

At a quarter to seven, he hears about himself on the tube. They don't have a picture of him to show except a shot of him in the background when Connolly was making a speech. ". . . Connolly's campaign manager has been arrested in connection with the August 13 murder of Cassandra Price of Oakland. Police are not commenting on the connection between Simon and Hathaway, who is also in police custody for the killing. Michael Connolly was supposed to announce his candidacy for the gubernatorial race by the end of this week. He had no comment for media personnel today." Then there is a shot of the golden boy going into his office. That's all the hungry hounds were able to get today.

The money. The waste.

CHRISTIE DROVE UP to the mansion again and felt almost used to it—the beauty, the set-apartness. Connolly met him in the formal parlor this time. "I heard you arrested Todd Simon. I want you to know I'm planning—had been planning—to get out of the race before Todd made the news."

"Now is the time to tell me anything that will help prosecute him."

"Are you still looking at me?"

"Did you tell him to do it?"

"No."

"Did you order it?"

"No."

"You'd be willing to take a lie detector test?"

"Yes. Absolutely."

"Talk to me."

"I thought I was in love with her . . . Cassie. It wasn't real. She made me feel good. I haven't felt . . . good. I needed her for a way to keep going."

"Many a middle-aged man wishes for the adoration of a gorgeous young woman; some act on it."

"Some resist," Connolly said.

Christie said, "You are clearly feeling guilt."

"Cassie was not the first. I've messed up my marriage, that's for sure."

"But you're telling me you did not order a murder. And yet I can tell you're not surprised. Why did you not come to me about Todd?"

"At first I didn't believe it—wouldn't let myself believe it. It took a long time to come to terms with the idea. To tell you . . . ? Accusing another person, without proof, someone who has been loyal to you, is a serious business."

"Loyal?"

"Politically. He worked very hard for me." Connolly's face tightened.

"What did you just think of?"

"The day . . . the day it happened, and just before, Todd was at me, asking about women in my life, asking about what might come out in the campaign. I answered him truthfully that yes, Cassie was getting emotional, wanting more from me than I could give her. He, afterward, he said it was totally strange the way things happen, but that Cal Hathaway had killed her. For a while that made sense. She was so attractive. Many men wanted her. She knew it. I knew it."

"But she wanted to marry you."

"Yes. She did."

"And Simon wanted to protect you."

"Yes. My candidacy anyway."

"He had motive. Was anyone else involved?"

"I can't think it. These are not bad men."

"Maybe they are."

"When this is over—when you don't need me anymore—I'm going to go out of the country for a while. I'll be available. I'm not running. I need to be someplace where this is not the only thing people know about me."

"We'll do a polygraph before you go. I'll need all your contact information constantly updated. We'd have to keep in touch."

"My family is here. I'm not going to be so far that I can't get back in twelve hours total from your phone call to my arrival. I'll stay in contact. I may be flawed in many ways, but I love my family."

Christie left him, making arrangements for the polygraph the next morning at 7:00 A.M. when few people would be at the office.

THE DETECTIVES worked in Todd Simon's house well into the evening. Colleen, Denman, and Hurwitz used powerful flashlights, slanting them this way and that. Potocki sat working Simon's computer while Dolan went through his desk.

"I'm not seeing anything," Dolan said when Colleen poked her head in to check.

"I got one goodie," Potocki said. "Yesterday. He looked up the refuse schedule for the city. We can't convict him on that alone, but it helps."

Hurwitz and Denman studied the rugs and sofa in the living

room, looking for anything obvious in the way of hairs, fibers. They had the lab guys take samples even when they couldn't see anything, and then they opened the sofa cushions and searched inside. Colleen heard them say, "This place looks awfully clean."

At the time, she was in the kitchen pulling up cellophane from the cereal boxes and crackers. It was exhausting looking underneath and inside everything, but Christie thought the guy might have hidden some of the stuff he took from the wallet. It was a good thing Simon wasn't much of an eater—he didn't have a lot of boxes and containers around. She studied the floor for bits of the earth that might match what they saw in the bag with the phone and the wallet. She sat at Todd's kitchen table, thinking. Why would he plant the wallet with only some things out of it? And the supposed photographs? Either they were no longer in there when he took the wallet or he kept them out for a purpose—to look at them himself or to plant them at a future time. That meant they were still somewhere.

She went back to his home office. Dolan was gathering paper from the shredder for the labs to study. She asked him if she could have a look. With a magnifying glass, she did a first examination of the bits of paper. It was lucky for them that his shredder didn't work very well and thus they could see pretty much what kind of thing was in there. She did not see any photographic paper.

The others checked the garbage disposal as well and the kitchen traps and the garbage cans and the earth of the yard, looking for anything that signaled disruption.

Finally she and most of the others worked in the bedroom—only minus Potocki, who was still at the desk, hacking into Simon's files and reporting that there were tons of e-mails and letters, but nothing that mentioned Cassie Price.

The men from the mobile crime unit stood on the back porch at the moment, joking, until they were needed to take a delicate sample of anything. It all seemed hopeless.

Christie got there at ten o'clock. They all kept at what they were doing, and he, being a stickler, repeated much of what they had done once. He looked with favor on the garbage they had collected. There was one Ziploc bag he thought might be interesting because of the traces of dirt in it.

Colleen was going through clothing. It was amazing how many pockets there were in men's clothing. Simon was not even a clothes-horse, but still, he had a lot. The rest of the team was in the basement going over out-of-season clothes as well as every other inch of the place. She stooped down and felt along the wall of the closet but did not find anything. After that, she opened the shoe boxes, one after another.

Potocki came into the bedroom. "You look tired."

"I am still tired."

"Did he make his bed and we messed it?"

"No, it was like this, unmade."

"His life seems fairly ordinary on the surface. He did check the refuse schedule. We have that."

"I think this is soil in this shoe."

"I'll call the techs. I wonder when Boss is going to knock off. You know he didn't sleep today. He can't fool me."

Just then Christie came in and said, "Enough. We can do more tomorrow. We have to let some sanity prevail in our lives."

"Thanks, Boss."

"Squad meeting tomorrow morning. At eight."

MONICA TRIED TO explain herself to herself and couldn't. She was up late, at her computer. She was looking up flights to Ire-land. Then she was looking up ways to ship large containers of things to Europe. And then she was making a list of possible lecturers who could teach her classes. I'm a fool, she told herself. But insistently, she remembered the early days, the way Mike had worked at construc-tion one summer because he wanted to understand the workers and what their day-to-day stresses were. He had seemed so ready for a simple life. What happens to people? Is there a way to get back to basics? Ireland, like every other place, has a class system, and so there will be struggles to forget money and what it can accomplish. A song keeps running through her head—she can't think of what it is.

THIRTEEN

THURSDAY, AUGUST 27

THE DETECTIVES were gathered for the squad meeting and Christie was explaining the arrest of Todd Simon when Janet Littlefield came to the door to interrupt—she was holding the fort just outside the squad room and had taken a call from the desk.

"I'm sorry, Commander. It's important."

"Dolan. Take it over."

Artie hopped to the front of the room.

Christie got to the hallway. Littlefield came close to him, saying, "Man came to us. Wants to confess to the killing of Cassie Price."

"Huh?"

"That's what he said."

Christie eyed a small, very thin man seated near Littlefield's desk. The man immediately stood when Christie approached. It was impossible to gauge his age—anywhere from fifty-five to eighty years old. He was bald and bony. The cap he took off was an ordinary baseball stadium cap, which he traced around the rim as if he held a fedora.

"I'm Commander Christie. Your name?"

"Frank . . . Francis Santini."

"And you'd like to talk?"

"I want . . . I came to confess."

"You knew Cassie Price?"

"No. I was robbing her, then she found me."

"You didn't know her before that?"

"No."

"We should talk. Let's go find a room." He met Littlefield's eyes. "Tell Detective Dolan to cut it short and meet me in Room A." She turned to the squad room, where, Christie had not one doubt, she would handle it well.

"Can we get you something to drink, Mr. Santini?"

"Like what?"

"Coffee, water, a soda. That's what we have to offer."

"Coffee."

"Right." Christie guided him to Room A. "Have a seat."

He poured a cup of coffee, too curious to wait for Dolan, grabbed a legal pad, clicked on the camera from the panel in the hall, and entered Room A.

"Let's get some basics down first. Name. Address. Employment. Bank."

"All right," the man said. "Should I write down that I killed Cassie Price?"

"Not yet. Just jot down what I need. Employment, bank, doctor, all that."

The man wrote slowly. Christie studied him—bad skin color. He was ill. Liver problem kicking in. Drink?

Francis Santini. The legal pad held his address—he lived in Friendship. For doctor, he'd written a name Christie didn't recognize. Unemployed. His bank was PNC.

"Tell me about it."

"I was out of money. I was only planning to rob her. But she found me in her house and she was starting to scream. I ended up hurting her."

"You didn't know her?"

"No."

"Let's see. You live in Friendship. What made you decide to rob somebody in lower Oakland?"

Dolan entered the room at that moment. His eyes lifted slightly toward the camera. Christie took that to mean that the inner circle on the case was watching. "This is Detective Dolan. Just speak freely. Why did you go to lower Oakland to rob somebody?"

"I go down to Sestili's Nursery a lot. I always walk back and forth in that alley next to the nursery, just thinking, mostly about what I can't afford to buy. I saw the girl once, getting in her car. She looked rich, the way she was dressed. Her car was nice, too, all spiffed up. I figured she had something to steal."

"Why didn't you go in the daytime when she wasn't home?"

He appeared to think about this. "I thought someone would see me in the day. And I had a few drinks for courage that night and it seemed more possible to pull it off."

"Okay. Good. Very good. How did you get in?"

"I jimmied the lock to the back door. But she heard me and she came to the door. The door was open by then. I just kept working at it to show her her lock was bad and saying that somebody was worried about her and this somebody sent me to replace her lock with a better one. It was insane, but I just kept talking, trying to talk my way out of trouble."

"Why would she buy that spiel, in the middle of the night?"

"She didn't. But then she kind of thought about it some and she almost believed it. And I was thinking about how do I get to her money before she calls the police. But then she started to scream. I got scared. I was only going to knock her out and run, but she was getting wild so I ended up killing her."

"Hm. What did you use? Knife? The knife from the door?"

"No. I couldn't think of anything like that. I grabbed her around the neck. I didn't mean to kill her, but somehow I did."

"Then you ran?"

"Not . . . right away. I was freaked out to see her on the floor. I think I stood there for a long time to see if she would move. Then I looked for her purse and I found it. I took some stuff out of her purse and then I left."

"I see. Take it easy. We're listening." He looked at Dolan. "Detective Dolan might have some questions for you, too."

"Were you walking, you say? Not driving?"

"No, I drove down. I walked around on a different day, when I was parked at Sestili's."

"Right. Okay. Got it. What kind of car do you have? You have an owner's card?"

"It's on its last legs. I don't have any money."

"Can we see your card?"

The man removed a card from his wallet. It showed he owned a Garnet Red Oldsmobile, 1990.

"Is this a bright red?"

"No, it's more like a maroon color."

"Thanks," Dolan said. "Thanks for being so cooperative. Do you remember by any chance what you were wearing?"

"Just old clothes."

"Could we see them?"

"I threw them out the next morning."

"Why?"

"I don't know. They gave me the creeps."

"What were these clothes—do you remember them?"

"Gray pants. Gray sweatshirt with hood."

"Good, good. And what exactly did you take from her purse?"

"Her wallet. Oh, and her phone. I thought it might have minutes on it."

"What did you do with these things?"

"I spent the money. I kept the other things."

"Why would you keep them?"

"I was scared to throw them out. I thought what if somebody sees me or something."

"And you still have those things?"

"No."

"Where are they?"

"You had that guy accused. So I put them in his garbage."

"But what about the photographs?"

"I don't know anything about photographs."

"In the wallet?"

"I didn't see any. Maybe they dropped somewhere. I was pretty shaky."

"Mr. Santini, did you strangle the woman, Cassie Price, with your bare hands?"

"With my hands, yes."

"Were you wearing anything on your hands?"

"My wife, when she was alive, she used to dye her hair. I ended up wearing her plastic gloves. When I was doing the lock . . . I was worried they would tear so I put on these gloves I saw on the back porch."

Letter perfect, Christie thought. He raised his eyebrows to Dolan.

"We certainly appreciate you taking the time to come in and tell us," Christie said.

"Did you take down my confession? You weren't writing."

"It's on camera."

"Oh. Good, then."

"Mr. Santini? Why did you go to so much trouble to hide your tracks and then change your mind and come in here? Why did you plant evidence in someone else's property and then come in to confess?"

Santini nodded. "I know. I did, like you say, hide my tracks. It was all I could think at first—get away with it and go to church a lot. Then I felt bad that a young guy was going to die for me, but I still just kept quiet. Only . . . when I saw it on the news and a second guy was arrested, I don't know, something happened in my head. I couldn't stay quiet anymore. I couldn't stand myself, knowing what I did. Jail isn't so bad. Three squares a day."

"You've been in jail before?"

"Once. A long time ago I did a pretty good stint. And then like five years ago, but it was brief that time."

"What were you incarcerated for?'

"Robbery."

"And you're willing to do jail time again?"

"Yes."

"By the way, are you left- or right-handed?"

"Kind of both."

"I see. We're going to swab you for DNA, a couple of other things. Then you're free to go until we contact you."

Santini frowned. "You're not going to arrest me?"

"Probably not today."

"I thought you'd want to arrest me."

"There's time. You're looking pretty weak. Have you eaten?"

"No."

"Your wife died, you said. You have somebody to take care of you?"

"I live alone."

"A friend, a girlfriend?"

"I'm mostly alone."

"Well, I'm concerned. You don't look well. Could we get you to your doctor?"

"That's okay. What . . . what do I do next?"

"Just relax. We'll do a few things and get back to you. Can we get you something to eat?"

"I don't eat."

"Ever?"

"Just soft things."

"I saw some deadly doughnuts out in the office. They're soft. We'll cadge one of them."

While the inner core gathered in Christie's office, Christie, all politesse, served Frank Santini a doughnut and more coffee.

COLLEEN LOOKED AT the others and had to laugh to think she probably looked like they did—bug-eyed, waiting for Christie to return.

"It's too perfect," Dolan said. "He answered every point."

"Polygraph will tell us something," she said.

"It better," Dolan answered. "You noticed, he wants to be arrested."

"What do we *think* happened?"

"There's a virus going around—false confessions," Potocki said whimsically.

Hurwitz blurted, "What if he did it? What if we're missing the obvious?"

Christie strode in. "Three possibilities. One: He did it. Two: Todd Simon is paying off Santini to confess and has given him all the points. Three: Someone else, not Simon, is responsible for paying and instructing. So now"—he clapped his hands to his head and laughed—"we have to investigate Santini! I asked for his doctor. That is one sick man. If we have to bring a doctor in for an opinion, we will. We'll swab. We'll do the lie detector. We'll probably send Santini home and let him stew. Something will come of the stewing. Dolan, I want you to go to his doctor and his bank; Potocki, get me his priors, his acquaintances, and his family history; Hurwitz and Denman, cover the man's house—see if anybody comes to see him. Start the paperwork for his phone records. Greer, back to Simon's house."

"Okay, Boss. You're not letting Simon out, are you?"

"Not on your tintype." He paused. "I'm going to ask Connolly if Haigh ever knew Santini."

"Wasn't he something?" Potocki asked, admiringly. "Santini."

"Not a bad actor, my wife would say. A sad man, I thought. What's the sadness about—guilt or health or what?"

"He's dying," Potocki said. "I've seen it before. He's late stage. He either loves Todd Simon or he was desperate for money."

"You can't spend that much in the prison commissary," Dolan cracked.

"He's at the end," Potocki said. "The money is for someone else."

"IT'S A MATTER OF time," Morty Silber says to Simon in the interview room on Thursday morning. "You'll be free, as you rightly should be. By now there's been a confession. A full confession from the person who did this."

Todd thinks his elegant nervous lawyer has gone nuts. What is he talking about?

"You know that you didn't do it. You didn't do any of it. You didn't plant the evidence. All will be well by the end of today."

Okay. He gets it. "Who did it?" he asks. "You're not saying this is that kid confessing again?"

"You can't know who. You don't know who. But this fellow, let me say, he certainly is a consistent fellow, I hear by way of my contacts. He does not veer from his confession."

"It's not . . . Cal Hathaway? This person is going to go to prison."

"This person will not make it to prison. He'll die in jail."

He knows who it is, then. Brilliant. Isn't it? After all this, Haigh turns out to be brilliant. Simon gives a hoot of a laugh.

Silber stands and glowers at him. "Keep your mouth shut. Don't fuck it up, asshole. He doesn't want to clean up after you ever again."

Simon grabs at the collar of the tall long blade of a knife of a man, the Giacometti walking man, and he stops him in his tracks. "I don't want to be talked to like that ever again."

Silber shakes himself free and leaves the room, saying, "Some people don't know how to be grateful."

An escort takes Todd back to his cell, where he climbs to the upper bunk and lies down, thinking.

SANTINI IS HOOKED up to the polygraph.

Christie says, "I'm going to ask you a few questions. Only yes or no answers. Do you understand?"

"Yes."

"Are you ready?"

"Yes."

"Is this Thursday, August 27?"

Santini appears to calculate. "Yes."

"Is your name Francis Santini?"

"Yes."

"Do you sometimes go by the name Frank?"

"Yes."

"Did you once work for the United States Postal Service?"

"Yes."

"Did you ever work as a psychologist?"

He looks surprised, even confused. "No."

"Have you ever been incarcerated?"

"Yes."

"Did you come to our offices today to confess to a homicide?"

"Yes."

"Did anybody coach you as to what to tell us?"

"No."

"Are you receiving any payment for confessing?"

Slight pause. "No."

"Did you kill Cassie Price?"

He almost says no. "Yes."

"Thank you."

"That's it?"

"Yes."

"How did I do?"

"You did very well."

"What's next?"

"You go home until we contact you. We have some other work to do. Detective Dolan will be coming by your house in a bit."

Santini looks puzzled, but he leaves.

DOLAN REPORTED A few hours later that there was very little money in Frank Santini's account and so far no bumps in deposits. The man lived mainly on Social Security. After that, Dolan went to Santini's house, a sad little box in disrepair.

Santini was at home, even though he apparently wanted to be in jail. He was not much of a housekeeper. He sat on a littered sofa, staring at a TV. "Search warrant," Dolan said. "Sorry to bother."

"Go ahead. Search. I was expecting you."

Dolan looked hither and thither but saw nothing of use.

The polygraph machine didn't believe Santini did the crime, and neither did he.

"Where are your children?" Dolan asked. "Why aren't they here helping you?"

"They have problems."

"What kind?"

"Daughter is getting divorced and she's always hiding somewhere from the bastard. Son is an addict. He's been in and out of rehab. He can't pull it together."

"So you end up taking care of them," Dolan said easily.

"Yeah, I do."

"What I marvel at is . . . a caring man like you, how you could bring yourself to hurt that young woman? Why didn't you just let her call the police?"

"I don't know. Wasn't thinking clearly. Drink will do that."

"It certainly will."

He called in to Christie on the way to his car to puzzle over Santini, and he learned that according to Potocki all the priors *were* robbery charges. One was dropped. The victim in the case felt bad for Santini and said he knew Santini had money problems and family problems.

"We're getting a picture," Dolan said. "It's making a picture. Down-and-out family. What about Connolly? Did you get hold of him again on this?" Dolan got to his car and started it for the return trip to the office.

"Yeah. Connolly is seriously depressed. He says he doesn't know of any Frank Santini. Doesn't know if Haigh knows Santini. But he does say Haigh has tentacles to all parts of the state, people who do all kinds of work for him. You met Haigh. Would he pay off somebody to confess?"

"I don't doubt it for a moment. More's the point, would he pay off somebody to kill a girl if she got in his way? I wouldn't be surprised. He's a people pusher."

"Let's meet back at Headquarters. Whoever was involved, I want the whole lot of them. I don't stop until I have that."

"I'm on my way."

THE INMATES WERE all at the TV again, and Todd got down to the common area just in time to catch his golden boy saying, ". . . not be entering the race for governor this term. I have assessed that I need to spend time with my family. I'd like to thank the many people who urged me to run; I want to thank them for their efforts in my behalf. I will continue to oversee projects that I have begun."

Efforts? You'd better believe it.

It was all for nothing. It's so laughable.

Connolly did the announcement solo—no wife, no party officials at his side. He looked terrible. He was guilty, all right—he'd killed Cassie Price by making her love him.

"Who killed Cassie Price?"

"I did," said the cat.

"I did," said the rat.

"I did," said the pig.

FOURTEEN

SUNDAY, AUGUST 30

WHEN THEY CHARGED Santini with his false confession on Friday, when they explained that any payment that went to his son or daughter would be confiscated anyway, the little man gave up and admitted he'd been coached by Haigh and his secretary until he had every detail of the story memorized. It was just that, a story. That's what confessions were, after all, stories that attempted to make sense of something that didn't fit in the hum and drum of ordinary life.

It took the weekend to work with State Police to get the arrest warrants in order and to take Haigh and his secretary, Walter, and an associate named Benton into custody. Christie wanted Coleson and McGranahan to have a piece of the action, so he sent them to do the work on getting Rita Sandler arrested. They were happy to be included. They reported that Rita Sandler was surprised enough to try to talk them out of arresting her. She said her lie was a minor thing.

Christie kept chugging.

Even the mosquito cooperated and gave them Todd Simon's DNA. Christie was thrilled. He named the mosquito Bert and called it his littlest witness. The fact of Todd Simon's blood in the mosquito plus Freddie Lorris's testimony put Todd Simon at the scene of the crime.

All that accumulated information got Cal Hathaway a trip to Headquarters to check him out on the polygraph machine. He aced it. So the monitoring device came off his leg.

The kid stood there Sunday afternoon and shook Christie's hand.

Then Christie rethought the partnerships so he could announce them on Monday morning. He decided not to budge things too much. Here was the problem. Dolan liked working with Christie, and vice versa, but Dolan, always easy to get along with, when paired with Colleen a while back, showed terrible signs of jealousy. Hurwitz and Denman were terrific together, so Christie was reluctant to split them up. He decided that since Potocki and Dolan got along fine, he would try them together. Then once more he would be the one to work with Colleen. It was going to be okay. They worked well together.

Now, as Christie gets home late on Sunday night, the house is quiet. He doesn't hear Marina's voice. He stands at the kitchen counter, eats a few spoonfuls of leftover mashed potatoes, then a cookie, and thinks about poor Connolly, already on his way to Ireland. Well, he's done all he can do. It's over.

He climbs upstairs to find Marina has fallen asleep reading. He undresses and crawls into bed, exhausted, but careful as he is, the movement wakes her. Marina lies there, tumbled in bedclothes, trying to come awake. She reaches out for his arm. "Hey."

"This was a good one."

"You're glad you intervened?"

"Oh yeah." He drops his head onto the pillow. "Some cases—you end up knowing you did something big. This . . . this was one. Ugly in many ways, but calling those politicians on the kind of things they think they can do, freeing that kid, that felt good." But he's too exhausted to talk anymore and she's too tired to listen.

"I'm glad." She lets him come into her arms. They lie there like that for a long time, until he falls asleep.

• • •

TODD HAS BEEN THE recipient of jail wisdom. He nodded sagely as, one by one, they told him how to handle himself. One man warned him to watch his tongue, explaining that many of the men would want to know what he did, but if he told them, they would try to sell it, to use what they've got from him for their own freedom. He acted as if he'd never heard that before.

He played basketball a little, chess a little, watched television for most of the day, and when three, no, four of them asked why exactly he did in the pretty girl, he smiled and said, "Well, it's kind of complicated. Well, see, okay, I was seeing her. I'd been seeing her. We kept it kind of secret. I used a special prepaid phone when I called her because I was working on the political campaign and she was a worker in my boss's office—well, he wasn't my boss, I was more his boss, but never mind the details—and she said she didn't want anyone to know and definitely not her boss. I could see he had the hots for her. She was totally gorgeous. And I thought he was moving in on her, and of course I didn't like it, but I shut my mouth about it. Then one day, I go for drinks with her. She gets pretty drunk. She tells me she's in love with him and I get fucking furious but I'm not showing it, you know, just very cool, just being reasonable with her. I follow her home and I see this other guy, this housepainter or whatever, working on her porch. I'm thinking how I've been discreet like she asked and she's probably bonking everybody who wants her. You don't look surprised about all that—huh?"

"Tell it," said one pint-sized guy. "Sing it out. We all been with bitches."

"If we're lucky," Todd said. And they laughed.

"So I thought, Pin it on the guy. I did. I said, Pin it on that schlub. I went to her house in the middle of the night. She knew I was coming, I'd called her, but then I get there and she doesn't open the door. So I jimmy the door. Catch them red-handed is what I'm thinking. I get in. She finds me. She's alone, but she calls me every kind of name and tells me I'm not worthy to kiss the boots of the housepainter or whatever he was and that I'm a big zero in her eyes. Which I'm telling you is not how my other woman friends felt. This one bitch out of all of them doesn't appreciate me. So we got into it and I lost it and I strangled her. The truth is, I planned it out. I thought it might happen. I covered myself up—I mean totally, used a polypropylene suit. I even used her boyfriend's work gloves to implicate him. I thought of everything. I made it look like a robbery. Of course, we've all heard of that trick, but I pulled it off really well. I took her phone. I took her wallet. I buried them. They arrested the housepainter. Well and good. When they let the housepainter out of jail, I said to myself, Hell, I'm not done with this. It's his garbage night. I'm going to fix him once and for all. So I took the shit, the evidence from her handbag, and I put them in his yard. Good thinking, huh?"

Sounds good, they say. Sounds like you were thinking.

"One little mistake. Everything perfect and one little mistake."

"What was that? They saw you?"

"No."

"What was the mistake?"

"It happened earlier. Ha. Ha. Wouldn't you like to know?"

"Yeah."

"Tomorrow, my mates. Or the next day."

He'll tell them something else tomorrow. Something else the next day. They won't know A from Z.

One day he will tell them, Don't ever kill a mosquito and leave it around when you're busy doing somebody in. When his attorney first told him there might be trouble about a mosquito, Todd thought it was a joke. Then he realized maybe it wasn't. For one second that night, he had lost his temper. One split second. He slapped at the thing, dug it out of his collar, and that was that. What a joke. What a joke.

"I want to know," the small guy said.

"I know you do, bud. Later." It was amazing the way they flocked around him. "That's for another day."

I wanted her, she dissed me, I lost it. Funny. When he said it, it seemed utterly true. Stories go every which way, and where is the truth?

CAL THINKS ABOUT repairing his reputation in the neighborhood and of the other things he might do with his life—the new idea that keeps coming to him is counselor in the jail or in the prison system. Not that he wants to go back to school especially, but to be a minor Dr. Beni, going around talking to inmates, he thinks he could do that. Could be *good* at it, too. People have worked to rescue him, a possibility he never considered.

He imagines one day coming across a surprised Sidney who believes Cal has somehow, like a Houdini, unwrapped ropes and climbed out of a locked coffin. All by himself. Dead, supposed to be dead, and there he is again, alive.